The Baron
of
Magister Valley

BOOKS BY STEVEN BRUST

THE DRAGAERAN NOVELS

Brokedown Palace

THE PAARFI NOVELS
The Baron of Magister Valley

The Khaavren Romances
The Phoenix Guards
Five Hundred Years After
The Viscount of Adrilankha
(which comprises *The Paths of the Dead,*
The Lord of Castle Black, and *Sethra Lavode*)

THE VLAD TALTOS NOVELS

Jhereg	*Athyra*	*Jhegaala*
Yendi	*Orca*	*Iorich*
Teckla	*Dragon*	*Tiassa*
Taltos	*Issola*	*Hawk*
Phoenix	*Dzur*	*Vallista*

OTHER NOVELS

To Reign in Hell
The Sun, the Moon, and the Stars
Cowboy Feng's Space Bar and Grille
The Gypsy (with Megan Lindholm)
Agyar
Freedom and Necessity (with Emma Bull)
The Incrementalists (with Skyler White)
The Skill of Our Hands (with Skyler White)
Good Guys

The Baron
of
Magister Valley

STEVEN BRUST

TOR

A TOM DOHERTY ASSOCIATES BOOK
NEW YORK

THE BARON OF MAGISTER VALLEY

Copyright © 2020 by Steven Brust

Foreword © 2020 by Will Shetterly; Preface © 2020 by Adam Stemple; Afterword © 2020 by Jennifer Slaugh

Edited by Claire Eddy

A Tor Book
Published by Tom Doherty Associates
120 Broadway
New York, NY 10271

www.tor-forge.com

Tor® is a registered trademark of Macmillan Publishing Group, LLC.

The Library of Congress Cataloging-in-Publication Data is available upon request.

ISBN 978-1-250-31147-4 (hardcover)
ISBN 978-1-250-31146-7 (ebook)

Our books may be purchased in bulk for promotional, educational, or business use. Please contact your local bookseller or the Macmillan Corporate and Premium Sales Department at 1-800-221-7945, extension 5442, or by email at MacmillanSpecialMarkets@macmillan.com.

First Edition: 2020

Printed in Canada

0 9 8 7 6 5 4 3 2 1

For Rick and JoAnn

Acknowledgments

My thanks to Peter Cook, who told me Stuff about paper, and Scott Lynch who answered medical questions. Phillip Wiebe told me how to dissolve rocks. Alexx Kay (http://www.panix.com/~alexx/dragtime.html# PreTortaalik) was of considerable help keeping me from tripping over my own feet, as were all of those who have contributed to the Lyorn Records (http://dragaera.wikia.com/wiki/Main_Page). Brian Newell helped me keep track of who went where and how long it took. Emma Bull, Pamela Dean, Will Shetterly, and Adam Stemple gave much needed help on getting it into shape, as, of course, did my editor, Claire Eddy. A warm thank you to copy editor Sophia Dembling, to Irene Gallo, artist David Palumbo, and to the entire production staff at Tor, who make me look good. My humble respects are always due to Robert Charles Morgan, who started it all, and my agent, Kay McCauley, who helps keep it going.

Additional proofreading and copy editing by sQuirrelco Textbenders, Inc.

A BRIEF INQUIRY
INTO THE STRANGE HISTORY
OF THE PERSONAGE KNOWN AS

The Baron of Magister Valley

By Paarfi of Roundwood
{His arms, seal, lineage block}

Submitted to the Imperial Library
By Springsign Manor
House of the Hawk
On this 11th day of the Month of the Issola
Of the Year of the Dragon
Of the Turn of the Phoenix
Of the Phase of the Dragon
Of the Reign of the Dragon
In the Cycle of the Phoenix
In the Great Cycle of the Dragon;
(2:1/2:2/0/2)

Or, in the 290th Year
Of the Glorious Reign
Of Her Imperial Majesty Norathar the Second

Presented, with deepest Gratitude and Respect,
To my Esteemed Patron,
Her Highness, the Princess of Mermaid Cove
In Hopes it will Please Her

Foreword

1. One Word about the Work of Paarfi of Roundwood

Perfection.

— Shetwil of the House of Dzur, author of *The Purchaser of This Book
Is a Personage of the Finest Discernment*

2. If One Word Is Not Sufficient, Surely One Poem Is

paarfi of roundwood
in one word is just so good.
read him? yes, you should

— Shetwil, the acclaimed "Poet of the Dzur" and author of
*Should You Do Me the Insult of Refusing to Purchase My Book, Redeem
Your Honor with the Weapon of Your Choice at Dawn on the Morrow
by the Lightning-Struck Tree at Deep River Park*

3. Must the Poet Serve the Muse or the Patron?

That one word, "perfection," and no other, is all you, Dear Reader, need to be told before you begin the newest distraction from the pen of that most prolific teller of implausible yet impeccably accurate tales, the incomparable Paarfi of Roundwood. To give one word more, to say, for example, that what awaits you is an account of adventure and love and betrayal and revenge, is to limit your expectations of what you are to experience. Why would any honorable person cut short the moment when you hold a tome in your hands and only know that something delightful lies before you?

But that is my onerous duty. Glorious Mountain Press demands a thousand words when a contract has been signed, specifying that number of words as a foreword to Paarfi's latest work, and they will not pay if what's delivered is a word short, not even if the signer of the contract is as committed as Paarfi to choosing the one right word among the many that may be found in any dictionary (or one might say, any concordance) or thesaurus (or one might say, synonymy).

Nor will Glorious Mountain be content with a poem, though each syllable was chosen with the precision of a Dzur's blade flashing in battle.

A publisher who insists a contract for a thousand words can only be fulfilled with a thousand words does not grasp what Paarfi knows, that precision is the only trait of the true artist—along with concision and grace, of course—and let no one forget wit.

A publisher whose soul has more of the lawyer than the artist cannot comprehend that the right word in the right place is worth far more than a thousand wrong ones, just as the right Dzur before a narrow pass or bridge is worth far more than a thousand Teckla. Such a publisher fails to see the simplest truth: when a poet finds the one necessary word, the need for a thousand is no more and the contract should be paid in full. Such a publisher is like a landlord who cannot hear the truth that only a few days of grace are required before the last three months' rent will be paid in full, or perhaps another week at most, and surely not more than two, unless the payment has been misplaced by the post, in which case the poet is not to blame and a bit more than three weeks may be required, or at worst, a few months, though almost certainly not four more months. Such a publisher is like a lover who will not accept that art requires research for the sake of truth, and so to describe the moonlight playing on thrashing sheets, a poet might require a comely young person's assistance in recreating a scene from *The Shepherdess's Delight*, a thing done in absolute innocence and in no way affecting the vows of eternal devotion that poet has made to such a lover nor in any way justifying that poet's ejection unclad into the streets with insults and dinnerware hurled at his head.

But enough of the failings of others. A Dzur knows battles cannot be fought as they should be fought, but as they are fought. A publisher who demands a thousand words knows almost no one reads forewords. Such a publisher is buying a block of verbiage with a name above it that might help sell the book. Perhaps Glorious Mountain saw that Paarfi's audience likes thick books, so I was hired to attract those who like slim ones. Whatever the reason, there is a reason I am a poet and small-minded people are publishers. Did I get a word of praise when I delivered the only necessary word? No—I got a note saying I was 999 words short. When I offered my poem, was there any acknowledgment of its cleverness? No—there was only a note saying, "985 more."

So I conclude my efforts are not read by one who values quality over quantity. That such a person should publish Paarfi's work is an affront to all the gods of art, but so it is. Obviously, my pages are given to a clerk who serves as a computer, a word tallier, who ticks off the count.

Word Tallier, I offer you vengeance on those who treat you like a lowly Teckla—by which I mean no insult if you are a lowly Teckla, for it strikes me now that lowly Teckla may take umbrage at being called lowly Teckla. If so, know that I mean no insult in reminding you of your lowliness, nor, Word Tallier, did I mean to imply that you are a lowly Teckla if you are not a member of that base House. Tally the words in this piece. You shall find a full thousand. Assure your oppressor that the count is true and my money should be sent posthaste. A landlord will be content, an unhappy lover will be wooed at a fine tavern, and a poet who you may count as comrade whether you are a lowly Teckla or a child of a noble House will be grateful.

What, I am a word short?

Kumquat.

—Shetwil, author of *This Volume Will Adorn Any Bookshelf in the Most Becoming Way* and *If My Quill Is a Rapier, Have the Grace to Die*

Preface

I have always been a critic of Paarfi of Roundwood's works. Not his harshest critic, certainly, for there are those who hate his prose more than a Yendi hates a straight line. But if I never tore them apart sentence to syllable, neither did I ever say an overly kind word about them. With this in mind, I can assure you that I was greatly surprised to hear the Lord of Roundwood wished me to write the preface to his latest "masterpiece." So intrigued was I as to the reasoning behind this idea, I decided that before I took the contract, I had to meet the man himself and ask him directly why he would want me—an actual critic of the literary arts, not a barely-lettered Dzur willing to fawn for a thousand words if it gave him the smallest opportunity to advance the profile of his latest masterpiece, *How I Killed a Thousand Teckla with a Single Stroke of My Sword and Will Do the Same to You If You Do Not Purchase This Title,* or some such other drivel—to introduce his newest words to the public.

That is, if I could ever get a word in.

"Good afternoon, Lord Roundwood," I greeted him when he entered the small klava house he had chosen as our meeting place. He was taller than I thought he would be, as most writers of his years—especially those as irresponsibly verbose as Paarfi—are foreshortened by the time they have spent hunched over their drafting desks. He was also, I noted—again with some measure of surprise—a man of rather pleasing appearance: broad-shouldered, clear-eyed, with the chiseled good looks of his House and a countenance that spoke of measured insight and forthright honesty. I conjectured then and maintain now that it is only his abrasive personality that has kept him single all these years, as he is blessed in both fortune and feature, two traits that, we can all agree, weigh heavily on the female of the species' mind when selecting a potential mate.

"And to you, good Adain of Arylle. Let us get right to the point." His voice was a touch nasally, as if air had trouble making its way through the sharpness of his nose.

"I would like nothing more, sir."

"It pleases me to hear this."

"Uh . . . good?"

"It *is* good when two men such as us—not friends, but not enemies either—can meet congenially to discuss matters of such importance."

"As to that . . ."

"For surely men of the word, of the book, of *literature*, can put aside any worldly—and thereby, by their very nature, petty—differences to discuss matters of more scholarly import?"

"Surely," I agreed, though I was no longer sure what I was agreeing to or why.

"So let us discuss it!"

"I have come to do exactly that."

"You have a question then?"

"I do."

"An inquisitive mind is an active mind."

"Just so."

"And an active mind is ever young."

"If you say so."

"Which makes it life's deepest irony that children wish so deeply to grow up and the old wish nothing more than to be young again."

I surmised of a sudden that I had likely misjudged when I described the dialog he writes as "a ridiculous mélange of witlessness and repetitious retort made sensical only by the certain assumption that the author is paid by the word." Apparently, all this time Paarfi has just been recording his own, very real, conversational style.

He gave a sigh as he pondered life's ironies, and I saw my opening. "The introduction," I blurted. "Why me?"

He fixed me with his Hawk gaze then, finally concentrating on the matter at hand. "I am so confident in this book," he said solemnly, "that I wished my greatest critic to be forced to acknowledge the magnitude of its brilliance from the very first page."

As I mentioned earlier, there are certainly far greater critics of Paarfi's work than I. But perhaps Orthon the Eldest, who called Paarfi's seminal work, *The Phoenix Guards*, a "pile of hot steaming sludge, troweled into the reader's maw in great mounding mouthfuls, whereas a single bite of the perennially putrid prose would be easily enough to dissuade any trace of intellectual appetite" was unavailable. Or the Lady Monthrell, who attacked him personally, calling him "not very nice," (if one knows anything about Issola in general and Lady Monthrell in particular then one would understand how deeply in contempt she must hold Paarfi to utter such a statement publicly), could not be persuaded to put aside her personal feelings and associate with him for even a few hundred words.

I was certain dozens of other critics who had spent years heaping hatred on the work and personage of the Lord of Roundwood were much more qualified to be "his greatest critic" than I, but he did not ask them. He asked me. And he appears to have made a good choice, because after reading *The Baron of Magister Valley* I am forced to say—truthfully, reluctantly, and with the greatest amazement possible—that it is . . .

Good.

Not great. Good. But given Paarfi's previous work, we can consider "good" to be such a vaulting achievement that he is right in declaring this his masterwork, the pinnacle of his art.

It features characters of real depth, not the usual foppish caricatures who wander drunkenly through increasingly unrealistic adventures. Instead, *Baron*'s heroes' travails are torturous and dark and require inward journeys as well as outward.

Yes, self-reflection in a Paarfi book. What will his Dzur fans say?

Even his signature dialog is less of a chore to get through, as you actually care about the characters and feel you are slogging through it together.

So, as I approach the end of my assigned thousand words, I will, at the risk of my reputation, recommend to you, dear reader, this *good* book.

—Adain of Arylle, Critic of the Literary and Poetic Arts

In Order of Appearance

Eremit of Cryden, afterward Dust, afterward the first Baron of Magister

Livosha (Nedyrc): His lover

Coru: Livosha's servant.

Kefaan (Arin): Livosha's brother

Tiscara: Livosha's father

Cerwin: Livosha's mother

Nira: Livosha's sister

Horatha: A driver and servant of Cerwin

Waymin: A lackey

Nessit: Eremit's father

Sudora: Eremit's mother

Jerin: A groom

Dorin: Count of Westward, the local magistrate.

Director: Head of the jail on Burning Island

Suzil: Livosha's maid

Unnamed cutthroat: A mercenary

Unnamed mercenary: A cutthroat

Riffetra: The owner of the Wriggling Dolphin.

Emeris: A clerk

Gystralan: A money-lender and advocate

Traanzo the Younger, a nobleman, afterward Duke, afterward Prince: An Iorich

Traanzo the Elder: Father of Traanzo the Younger

Berwick: Orca, owner of a fishing fleet

Yanis: Berwick's son and heir

Magister: A prisoner

Biska: A servant

Ficora: An aristocrat, kinswoman of Emeris (not Eremit)

Tigra: A Jhereg

CAST OF CHARACTERS

Jailer: A guard
Guard: A jailer
Nyleth: An Issola, or perhaps not
Inmate: A prisoner
Wosca: A jailer
Kelsama: A prisoner
Fagre: A bandit
Doro: A bandit
Liniace: A bandit
Cho: A bandit
Alishka: A bandit chief
Nef: A bandit
Kitescu: A bandit
Jiscava: A bandit
S'rik'ki'ka: A demon
Hadrice: Berwick's henchman
Urastor: Traanzo's cloaklady
Sajen: An artist and forger
Keen: A Jhereg
Rennis: An Orca
Sheen: A pirate captain
Acilla: A pirate
Lan: Berwick's attendant
Nosaj: A pirate captain
Vokra: An Iorich
Daro: Countess of Whitecrest
Halvar: A Jhereg
Fidra: A cutthroat, afterward one of Berwick's guards
Istamar: One of Berwick's guards
Ironhead: One of Berwick's guards

Part I

BURNING ISLAND

Chapter the First

In Which Two Young People,
Unlike the Reader, Are Blissfully Unaware
of the Doom Hanging Over Them

On the fourth day of autumn in the two hundred and forty-first year of the reign of Cherova the Third, the Gods—if one believes, as many do, that the Gods are responsible for the weather—had granted an exceptionally fine day along that portion of the western coast, forming a part of the region known as Zerika's Point, that is called, for reasons of which we must confess our ignorance, the Sinking Hills.

The breeze from the Ocean-sea was mild and smelled clean, and even now, as dusk loomed, the air was warm and pleasant. The question of whether such a mild and delightful day is a fitting and appropriate way to begin a history in which the reader will bear witness to no small amount of violence, treachery, deceit, and sorrow (as well, to be sure, as proper proportions of laughter, honor, candor, and joy), is one we must answer in the affirmative, and for two reasons: One reason, the simplest, is that this is, in fact, the way the history began, and while mere statements of fact do not exhaust the study of history, even those desert-born mystics who are subject to the wildest flights of imagination agree that facts are where the study of history must take its departure. The other reason, however, is more complex, and we hope the reader will be patient while we explain our thinking in this matter.

It has been observed more than once that history, however broad or narrow its subject matter, and however sympathetic or detached the historian, and however momentous or trivial the final result, must inevitably contain elements of tragedy as well as comedy, for the simple reason that this is how all episodes, when thoroughly comprehended, eventually reduce themselves in the human heart. The author of these lines makes no claim of originality, but merely wishes to open this history by reminding the reader of this obvious truth.

This reminder, we believe, is especially necessary as we begin to set before the reader the history our duty has required us to relate, because of the sharp contrast between the events as they begin to unfold, and the expectation of the knowledgeable reader as to the direction in which they must inevitably move. That is to say, while our metaphorical curtain opens, perchance, on a setting that can only be described as happy, or even *idyllic*, we do not for a moment expect the reader to be lulled by this into thinking the events as they progress will continue in this fashion. Indeed, we flatter ourselves that the sophistication of our reader is such that a book which promised nothing more than soporific pleasantries would never have arrived in his hands to begin with.

Of course, the reader might justly ask why, then, we begin here instead of elsewhere? Above, we had the honor to assert in simple terms, *here is where our history begins*. Yet, wonders the student, could not this history begin fifteen years earlier, when a geologist named Veck found deposits of sealstone off the coast of Wetrock? Or five thousand years before that, when a sorcerer name Undira learned that sealstone often contains deposits of iron, lodestone, manganese, and occasionally even trellenstone, all protected by its marvelous properties from the ravages of the sea? Or yet before that, back to the First Cycle of the Empire, now all but lost in the mists of time, when bands of Orca came by sea, and Iorich by land, to tame the local savages and set up their dominions on this part of the coast?

Any of these might be reasonable choices, as each of these events plays an important role in the chain of causality that we have elected to set before the reader. But the exposition of history is more than science, it is also art—that is to say, in order to be successful, it must not only edify the intellective academic, but also stimulate the sensitive student, thus providing that unity of mind and spirit that is essential to true percipience. And it is here that we find the apparently arbitrary selection of the first element in our causal chain becomes determined by necessity: In a word, we are required to begin our history at that point which will not only provide the reader with an understanding of events in their unfolding, but will also excite all of the finer emotions—pity, catharsis, passion, elation—that are so necessary to the citizens of an enlightened society.

With this firmly in mind, then, as our reader finds his allotted seat (if we may be permitted to return to the theatrical metaphor upon which we found ourselves embarking), and as the last notes of the figurative overture fade in his ears, and his pulse, we permit ourselves to hope, slightly quickens in anticipation of the experience through which it is our humble duty to guide him, let the curtain rise on a particularly fine evening in the Seventeenth Athyra reign, in a place on the western edge of our Empire, some five hundred miles northwest of Zerika's Point, on the outskirts of a hamlet called Wetrock, where a pair of young people are engaged in an activity that, if tolerably rare in the Empire, is at least not uncommon in this small corner of it: to wit, they are watching the Furnace, briefly visible as it sinks below the Enclouding, turn from a bright, painful yellow to a soft, gentle red as it appears to fall into the Ocean-sea far away. The colors produced by this display, reds and purples and pinks, are of such a spectacular exuberance that the historian must pause in his narrative— unwilling as he is to interrupt the relation of events that are the heart of any chronicle, historical or otherwise—to advise the reader to make a pilgrimage to this region just to see it.

As the reader will no doubt have already deduced that the two young persons to which we have just had the honor to allude will become important as our history proceeds, we should waste no time in providing a cursory sketch of each of them.

The young man, for so we will call him (they were of an age whereby we might, with equal justice, call them a boy and a girl, or a man and a woman), was of between ninety and one hundred years of age. He was neither exceptionally tall nor unusually short, though more athletic in appearance than one would expect of an Iorich. His eyes were brown, mild, and deep set beneath a strong forehead that spoke of determination, and his lips, which were full and pouting, though much given to smiling, as was proved by the lines around them, nevertheless tended slightly down when at rest. His cheekbones were high, his nose straight with perhaps a hint of point, and his chin had that sort of dimple that is called a *cleft* among the nobility. In general, his features displayed an open and trusting expression, one more suited to sudden laughter than to anger. His hair was of a darker brown than his eyes, nearly black, and fell straight, if slightly disheveled, to his shoulders, revealing a noble's point that could only be said to exist by courtesy—should he ever wish to pass for a Teckla, he could do so without altering his hair. His chest was broad and strong, his fingers long and elegant. He wore a pure white shirt in the style of the time, which insisted that as much fabric as possible be present, and that it be bunched, gathered, and, if the reader will permit, *corralled* by means of cords and ribbons. Over this he wore a simple, thin, tan cloak which was, at present, thrown back over his shoulder, the better to enjoy the day. His leggings were the same tan as his cloak, and his boots were black and simple, if extraordinarily well made. He carried a sword and a dagger, though a close inspection would show that they appeared more decorative than practical.

The young woman next to him, her hand upon his arm in a gesture displaying mostly affection, though not devoid of an agreeable hint of possessiveness, was also easily seen to be an Iorich. Her eyes were bright with wit and intelligence, her gentle forehead spoke of kindness, and her chin displayed a firmness of character. Her hair, notwithstanding its pronounced curl, was of much the same length and shape as his, that being the style among Iorich at the time, though its color was a shade or two lighter, and her noble's point was far more pronounced. Her nose was small but well-proportioned, her cheekbones as high as his and even more strongly pronounced, providing her a face in which strength of character would seem to have the advantage over cheerful disposition, yet her lips tended naturally upward, and it could not be doubted that she was accustomed to smiling. If he appeared rather more athletic than is usual among Iorich, she seemed doubly so, with stout legs and wide, strong shoulders supporting a graceful neck. Her breasts were full and high, even under the loose tan doublet she wore over a simple white shirt, her hips strong without appearing large, and the carriage of her back, perhaps her most distinctive feature, was powerful yet relaxed, reminiscent of the Northern white wolf, with its confidence in its own power. She, too, wore sword and dagger, yet hers were simpler, more businesslike, and gave every appearance of having been used on more than one occasion, though whether in practice or in more serious conversation could not be determined.

These are two, then, with whom we have chosen to concern ourselves, and, now that the necessary introductory stage—of which we hope the reader will forgive the brevity—is past, it is time to discover something of the words being exchanged as they watched the glowing ball meet the horizon.

After a certain period of silence, during which, the reader may be sure, they took no small degree of pleasure in each other's company, the young man, whose name was Eremit, pronounced the single word, "Children."

"Well," said the young woman, who was known as Livosha, "what of them?"

"Do we wish them?"

"Ah, you say 'we.'"

"Well, and if I do?"

"You perceive, my friend, that I am unable to answer this question regarding we, for the simple reason that there are two of us, and I am only able to know the mind of one, that being myself."

"I confess your point is well taken, but then—"

"Yes?"

"Should you tell me your own opinion on this matter, and if I were to then tell you mine, it would be strange indeed if we were not able, by working together, to determine the answer to the question as it applies to both of us."

"I do not dispute you."

"And then?"

"Well, I will tell you."

"Good, for you perceive I am eager to hear."

"This is it, then."

"Yes?"

"I am most eager to have children with you."

"Ah!"

"And is this the answer you had hoped for?"

"To the very word!"

"Well, that is good then," said Livosha decisively. "The decision is made."

"And that decision is?"

"We shall have children. Perhaps several."

"I am the happiest of men," declared Eremit. "Although it should be added that my esteemed mother, she whose lands we are now occupying, and her husband, my father will, without doubt, be filled with joy as well."

"You think so?"

"Nearly. Am I not the last of my line? You must understand, my dear Livosha, that to such aristocrats as my mother and father, well, there is little that matters more than seeing their line continue."

"How, and does this not matter to you?"

"Oh, I am not indifferent," he said, reflecting. "And yet, that is not what concerns me most regarding the question of children."

"Ah, what does?"

"You wish me to tell you?"

"I do, and the proof is, I asked."

"That is true," said Eremit, struck by the extreme justice of this observation.

"Well?"

"Well, but it seems to me that any child who comes from your loin and from my seed must be someone with whom I should delight in spending time. Does it not seem so to you?"

"My dear Eremit—"

"Well?"

"Well now it is you who have expressed the very words I most wished to hear."

"Ah! In that case—"

"Yes, in that case?"

"It would seem to me that I ought to kiss you."

"Oh, I agree with this plan!"

"Then I shall carry it into action."

"And this very instant, I hope!"

"You see, I do not delay."

And with these words, he took her in his arms and kissed her soundly, she returning the caress with an enthusiasm that could not be mistaken, after which they both turned and continued watching the Furnace and the waves that crashed upon the rocks before them.

After some few minutes he sighed.

"You have sighed," she said, proving that she was not unaware of even the subtlest expressions of the man with whom she stood.

"That is true," he said. "I do sigh."

"But, what are you thinking that causes you to sigh in this way?"

"I am thinking of the three years that must elapse between now and when we are to be married."

"Ah, three years, well."

"Yes?"

"It *is* a long time."

"It seems like forever," he said.

"Still, we shall at any rate be busy during this time, which will help."

"Busy? Ah, you mean the preparations for the wedding."

"Well, that, yes. And other things."

He frowned. "Other things, my Levoshirasha?"

"Ah, ah! I love when you call me that!"

"Well, that is why I do."

"And you are right to."

"But, what other things, my beloved?"

"Why surely you recall that our families will be engaged in negotiation, both with each other, and with the local Orca, for mining rights, processing rights, and transportation of the newly discovered minerals?"

"Ah, yes! It is true, your presence is so overwhelming to my senses that, for the moment, I had quite forgotten."

"Well, we must not forget, my adored one," she said. "For it is this very discovery that will provide all of us with something of a fortune, and thus make life easier both for ourselves and our children, for we want them to have the best of everything, do we not?"

"Oh, I would never disagree with that. Indeed, I find that while money has never before had any hold on my attention, now that I contemplate a family, well, I should not mind in the least if there were sufficient to provide for our children. It is wonderful how such a thing can change one's attitudes, is it not?"

"Oh, I have noticed the same thing."

"Had these discoveries not been made, I think I should not miss them. But now, seeing the opportunity to make use of them, while at the same time helping our neighbors, I see nothing wrong with it."

"Those are my exact thoughts. Indeed, if this goes well, we could perhaps even improve the roads and the irrigation ditches, and so advance even the lives of the Teckla. Why should we not?"

Eremit nodded at this and said, "I am so far from disagreeing with this plan that I can think of no way to better it."

"And then?"

"Yes, my sweet Levosha, you are right. That will take up some considerable amount of time."

"Yes, we must find experts in extraction and learn how to extract from the sealstone the iron it contains and, more important, the lodestone and the *echtia*, and perhaps even trellenstone."

"That word you used, I do not know it."

"*Echtia*?"

"That is the one."

"It is the Serioli word for the metal that is sometimes called swordstone, or manganese. It can be combined with iron to create steel that is light, strong, and not stained or weakened by water."

"Ah! Yes, I have heard of swordstone. It is valuable indeed."

"It is, and thus our future rests upon it, and upon making arrangements to mine it, refine it, and transport it to Candletown, and thence along the Grand Canal to Dragaera City. Indeed, my mother has spoken of the possibility of extending the canal all the way to Threewillows."

"I must inform myself of these things."

"That is true," she said. "But I will help you, and thus the time will go faster. For while it is your family that owns the land—that is to say, the water—where the sealstone has been discovered, it is the Orca who are able to procure it, and it is my family that can refine it. Thus we will cooperate to the advantage of us all. And it may be that someday the Imperial armies, as far from here as one may be within the confines of our great Empire, will march east, and we will know that in their hands are weapons that have been made with material we have supplied."

"I cannot deny that I would feel pride in such an event."

"Who would not?"

"Then it is settled," he said.

"Then come, beloved. It is nearly time to dine, and you must remember that you have agreed to accompany me to my home to eat with my family, as we have so often done to our mutual pleasure."

"I have not forgotten, my dear Livosha, for not only is there the matter of your company, in which I take such delight, and that of your family, whose warmth and companionship never fails to please me, but there is also the question of your cook, Veska, who makes the most amazing fish soup, which soup, you recall, was promised me when you extended your kind invitation, and I warn you, I hold a word given as a pledge made, as any Iorich would."

"Oh, you need fear nothing on that score, good Eremit! I have said there would be fish soup, and fish soup there will be!"

"Then lead on, you see how eagerly I follow you."

They made their way through the small village of Wetrock, accepting the bows of those they passed with good-natured amenity, and so, after an easy and pleasant hour, passed up to Tebek Road, which led to the estate of the Baroness Tebek (in fact, this was the title held by Cerwin, Livosha's mother, but as it was never used, she being known simply as Cerwin, it will never come up again, and we include it here merely for the sake of completeness. That there are some supposed scholars who are willing to leave their students with incomplete information does not justify committing such a crime against knowledge ourselves). Upon entering, they were greeted first by Coru, the Teckla servant whom they had both known all of their lives. He took their cloaks and their weapon belts and remarked, "It is near dinner time. If my lady would care to change, we shall have to hurry."

"Now Coru," she said. "Do you not perceive I am with my friend Eremit? He cannot change for dinner, therefore I shall not."

"Of course, my lady. Your pardon. These old eyes are so used to seeing the young gentleman, that I nearly think of him as part of the family, and so did not consider him as a guest."

"So much the better," said Eremit, warmly pressing the old man's hand.

He followed Livosha into the dining room, where they were seated, and the promised fish soup—which, to be sure, was more of a stew, involving several kinds of seafood in a spicy-sweet cream broth—was delivered as promised. The soup was followed by a side of mutton, and then a baked pastry filled with the sweet local apple, just now coming into season. Eremit enjoyed the dinner, thanks in no small part to the gentle pressure of Livosha's leg against his, but also to the unending banter among Livosha, her younger brother, Kefaan, and her older sister, Nira. Her mother, Cerwin, the baroness, and her father, Tiscara, spoke little on these occasions, appearing to enjoy the company of their children, but they nevertheless made it plain, as they had on numerous previous occasions, that Eremit was welcome.

Eventually, Kefaan began teasing Livosha about her upcoming wedding night. Eremit noticed with some amusement the look that passed between the two sisters as the young man—he was, after all not more than sixty—assumed that neither Livosha nor Eremit had experience with the physical expressions of tenderness. This, however, was too ribald for Tiscara, who smoothly shifted the conversation to wedding plans and how long it would take to make the arrangements for the service, for the grand fête, the procession, and, of course, the two feasts. "At least," remarked Cerwin, "we shall not have to pay for an advocate to draw up the contract, nor worry about finding agreeable terms," which produced a general chuckle around the table because it was well known that everyone there except Kefaan and Livosha were, if not practicing advocates, at least licensed to be, as most Iorich were then, just as is still true at the time the historian has the honor of writing.

At length the repast had finished, and after bidding farewell to the family, Eremit bid a last, private farewell to Livosha.

"Will I see you to-morrow?" he asked.

"I can think of nothing that would give me greater pleasure," she said.

"Then I bid you good night, after one more of those kisses I treasure above all else. Ah, perhaps another after. And another."

"Ah, my friend," cried Livosha. "The two best parts of the day are when I first see you, and when we last bid each other good night. Come, have another kiss, and yet another."

"And now I must leave."

"You must."

"We cannot delay, the driver awaits."

"Yes, yes!"

"Until to-morrow, my adored one."

"Until to-morrow, my beloved."

And with that, he tore himself from her as if it required a physical effort, and at last made his way outside. As inevitably happened, he had denied needing a carriage, saying the walk was a mere ten miles, and, as inevitably happened, Cerwin had quietly decided and arranged for the carriage anyway.

It was a peaceful ride back; the driver, one Horatha, was not inclined to talk, and Eremit himself felt too at peace with the world to wish to disturb this feeling with unwarranted conversation: as is well known, it is those with the least to say who use the most words, which is why, as the reader has no doubt observed, this historian endeavors, without exception, to limit his use of words to the absolute minimum required to successfully convey the desired thought.

Upon arriving at his home—an impressive dwelling called Cryden House (or Quordon House as it appears in older histories, and was still sometimes called by the more elderly among the local Teckla), perched on an artificial hill facing Redsky Harbor—he bid farewell to Horatha and, it being by now past evening and into the night, entered his home by the side door. He carefully stepped over the prone figure of Waymin, his father's lackey, and went down the hall toward the stairs. He had not, however, gone more than a dozen paces before he was interrupted by Waymin, who coughed and said, "Your pardon, young sir."

Eremit turned around to see that Waymin was now standing. He nodded to the retainer and said, "Goodman Waymin, what would you?"

"Young sir, his lordship requests the honor of your company upon your return, and charged me to deliver the message, which I have now done."

"And it was well done, too," agreed Eremit. "Only—"

"Yes, young sir?"

"Where is my father?"

"Ah, yes. It would be useful for you to know that."

"Nearly."

"Then I will tell you: he awaits you in the study."

"Then I shall go to him directly."

"And you will do right to do so, young sir. And I, well, I will go directly to sleep."

This decision on the part of the lackey was no sooner announced than acted upon; indeed, Waymin's snores accompanied Eremit for some distance as he made his way to his father's study, located on the ground floor on the west side of the house, directly below his bedchamber and connected to it by a spiral staircase of iron that led up to a hole in the study's ceiling. This excellent arrangement, which permitted Lord Nessit, that is to say, Eremit's father, to easily visit his study whenever his sleep was disturbed, had the one disadvantage that, as Nessit shared a bedchamber with his wife, as was the custom of the lower nobility in those days, any conversation in this room that occurred after Sudora, the baroness, had retired must necessarily be carried out in whispers to avoid waking her, a grave discourtesy, and one of the few matters that had been known to upset the usual domestic harmony of Cryden House.

On this occasion, however, to his surprise, they were both in the study, awaiting him. His father had open before him several books of statutes and case law that Eremit recognized as pertaining to land disputes between Houses, at the top of which was Plofer's *Case Studies in Entitlement Conflicts Among the Great Houses Volume I*. His mother, at a small table, had before her the ledgers pertaining to the fishing boats and harvests.

As Eremit entered, his father looked up. "Ah," he said. "My dear son. I perceive you have arrived. And my soon-to-be daughter-in-law, Livosha, I trust she is well? And her family?"

"All very well, my lord papa," said Eremit.

"And the dinner," put in his mother. "It was pleasant?"

"It was delightful, my dear lady mama," said the young man. "But come, I perceive there is something of importance here."

"And you are not wrong in this," said Nessit. "Indeed, there is a matter about which, I give you my word, there is no question of joking."

"But come, my son," said Sudora. "Sit down in this chair, which we have caused to be brought in, and drink this glass of wine. And then—"

"Yes?" he said, a certain worry creeping over him. "And then?"

"Why, and then we will speak."

"Very well, my lady mama, I will of course do as you say, but I beg you to explain quickly, for I am eager to learn the reason for this unusual meeting."

Eremit sat down and, a glass of wine in his hand, leaned forward so as to be certain not to miss a single word of what was to be said.

His father turned around and looked at his mother, and then they both turned to him. "This is it, then," said the baron. "We have received word that there may be forces at work conspiring against us."

"How, conspiring?" said Eremit. "My lord, that is a strong word!"

"It is," agreed his mother. "And yet, if what we are told is true, well, it is the only word that applies. And you know that, as advocates, we are trained to use the precise word that best fits the meaning we intend to convey."

"Oh, with that, I am well acquainted. My own reading of the law has, if nothing else, convinced me of the absolute necessity for precision in language."

"So much the better," said the baron.

"But, who has formed this conspiracy, and in order to do what?"

"Ah, you wish to know that?" said his mother, with a glance at his father.

"I nearly think I do!"

"Then here it is," said the baron. "You know who Berwick is?"

"Why, that is the name of the owner of the fishing fleet."

"You are exactly right. He brings in the fish, we buy the fish, process them, and pass them off to Baroness Cerwin to transport and distribute them."

"Well, and?"

His mother coughed gently "It is Berwick who, we are told, is conspiring to take possession of our land, our interests, and even our home."

"But . . . are we certain?"

"Certain, my son?" said the baron. "No. It is possible we are deceived. Yet—"

"Well?"

"We have friends," said the baroness. "That is to say, some of Berwick's vassals are friends with some of ours, and his vassals, it seems, have little love for him, and so it was reported to us."

"It may be wrong," said Eremit, who was unwilling to believe in such treachery.

"It may," said his father. "And yet, what if it is not?"

"But, what can we do?"

"Ah, as to that . . ." said his mother, with a worried look at her husband.

"Yes, as to that?"

The baron cleared his throat. "My son, we must send you on a mission."

Chapter the Second

In Which Eremit Mingles with the Powerful

Ah!" exclaimed Eremit. "A mission!"

"Exactly," said his mother.

"Well, I am prepared to execute any mission that you, my esteemed father, and you, my adored mother, believe me capable of carrying out."

"So much the better," said his father.

"This is it, then," said his mother. "You must ride to Dorindom, the capital of Westward."

"Well, and—?"

"And there you must ask for an audience with His Benevolence, Dorin, the Right Honorable Count of Westward."

"Very well, mother. And then—?"

"Then you must present this—you see? It is the pendant that contains our Seal of Demesne, which proves you have come to him on official business."

"You see, I have taken the pendant, my lady. And then?"

"Then you must beg to speak to the High Justicer of Westward."

"But, my lady mother, is not Count Dorin himself the High Justicer?"

"He is, but as you should recall from your studies, the request for formal action in his role of justicer, rather than lord, must be explicit."

"Ah," said the young man, now beginning to understand the seriousness of the matter. "So it is official, then!"

"Precisely," said his father. "Do you understand?"

"I do," he said. "Only—"

"Well?"

"Can you not, mother, speak to his mind directly, and thus save both time and effort, as well as removing the need for an intermediary? For I know that you have studied sorcery for this very purpose, and that, moreover, you are well enough acquainted with him for this to work. The proof is, I remember you doing it."

At this question, his mother and father looked at each other, each countenance showing signs of worry. "That is it," said his father after a moment. "We are unable to."

"How, unable to?"

"We have been trying to touch his mind, and we cannot."

"But, how is that possible?"

"It may be," said his father, "that a spell has been cast to prevent such contact. Such things are possible, although finding a sorcerer able to perform such a feat is no easy matter."

"But then—"

"Yes?"

Eremit bit back the question he had been about to ask, for the answer occurred to him: this, in itself, was, if not proof of a conspiracy, then at least circumstantial evidence for it. "Very well then," he said. "I understand."

"It is good that you do," said his father.

"And, the instructions? I am to speak to His Lordship the Count and ask for the High Justicer."

"Exactly."

"And then?"

"And then," said his mother, "when you are speaking to the High Justicer—that is, to the Count as High Justicer—then you must explain to him what we have said about the conspiracy and beg him to investigate that matter."

"I understand."

"But there is more."

"Very well, I am listening."

"You must also beg him for assistance, in case it is true. You perceive, for men-at-arms, we have only Liban, the constable, and Aworu, the night watchman. Brave as they are, they are not sufficient to defend the estate from any sort of attack, and so we must ask for the aid of the Justicer's dragoons."

"My lady mama," said Eremit. "I understand this, but—"

"Yes? But?"

"Will I be able to convince him of the need? Will he not say it is nothing but rumor and suspicion? Even if I explain that something is preventing communication from your mind to his?"

"Ah!" said his father, putting his hand on one of the books he had been reading with a smile Eremit knew well.

"You have found case law?" he cried.

"Better than that," said his father. "I have found a statute! Attend me: 'Every body of troops shall be made available on request to subordinates upon testimony of cause except insofar as there is immediate and urgent need of this same body of troops elsewhere, in which case the matter will be adjudicated as per section four, above.'"

"Ah! Well, that is a point I can certainly make!"

"Here, I have written down the citation, as well as references to several cases in which this matter was addressed by justicers. You see, I wrap them, tie them with this ribbon, and place them in this pouch, which I hand to you."

Eremit took the pouch, added to it the pendant he'd been given, and said, "Very good, Father. I feel I am ready for this mission."

"So much the better!"

"I have given instructions," said Sudora, "for your horse, Stony, to be saddled, and for supplies for a ride of a day to be packed into her saddle-bags. This should be done by now."

"Now? Then, you wish me to leave at once?"

"Yes, this very instant. You are young, my son, and can withstand an all-night ride, which neither your father nor I are able to do. Should you arrive before to-morrow's noon, well, we hope that will be in sufficient time."

"And," added Nessit, "In order to accomplish this, I am now giving you, to add to the pouch, a note to the post stable at Hargon's Point, and another addressed to the one at Axelsbroke, so that you need not spare your horse."

"Apropos," said his mother. "Here, take this handful of money and add it to your purse. While you are unlikely to require it, still, there are events that can occur which are best handled by the use of a few coins."

Eremit took the money and added it to his purse.

His father said, "Now that you have what you need, you must be on your way, for you perceive this is not a matter in which delay is our friend."

"I understand," said Eremit. "Then I shall leave in an instant, stopping only to embrace you both."

"Ah!" said his father. "Yes, there is time for that!"

And, after having embraced them both affectionately, he at once left the study and made for the door by which he had arrived an hour before, only to be stopped by Waymin, who said, "Your pardon, young sir."

"Well? I hope what you wish is of some importance, for I give you my word, my errand will not wait."

"I am not unaware of this, young sir. But as for my wish, well, it is not my wish, but rather that of your father."

"Ah! Then I am all the more ready to listen. What is it my father wished?"

"To give you these, in place of those you wear."

As he spoke, Waymin handed over a belt, from which hung a sword and a knife. We would not be faithful to the truth if we did not observe that Eremit hesitated before accepting them. He could see, even though sheathed, that these were no marks of rank, but rather, useful, practical weapons, of the sort that might be used by an individual concerned with keeping his body whole and complete, while simultaneously hoping to disrupt the integrity of another's. It was this, even more than the mission, that made Eremit realize the full gravity of the circumstances under which he was to act. Now we should be clear that it was not fear that caused his hesitation—he had no trace of that. But rather the realization that along with the pouch and the sword belt came a responsibility such as he had never before faced, and he required time—only a moment, it is true—to remind himself of this, and to warn himself sternly that he must not for an instant take matters lightly. From this moment, everything he did carried a weight, and he must be prepared for it.

Eremit then nodded his agreement, and, as proof that he accepted both the gift and the responsibility with which it came, removed his old sword belt and handed it to the lackey, whereupon Waymin knelt and strapped on the other.

"Does it fit, young sir? Another hole can be quickly punched into the belt."

"No, Waymin. It fits as if it were made for me."

"So much the better, young sir. Then it remains for me only to wish you a safe and prosperous journey."

"May your wishes reach the ears of the gods," Eremit said. "And, if you would be so kind, see to it that a note is delivered to my Livosha explaining that I was called away on an urgent errand and so, alas, I cannot meet with her as I had intended to."

"It will see to it that a messenger is sent to-morrow."

"Thank you, Waymin. And with that, I must be away. Guard well my mother and father."

"Young sir, there is nothing to which I will dedicate myself more."

"Then I bid you good evening."

"And you, young sir."

Eremit stepped out into the night, which was cold enough to force him to wrap his cloak more tightly about him. He wished for a heavier one as he considered the leagues he would have to travel and the speed at which he would be riding, but begrudged the time it would take to fetch one. He proceeded at once to the stables where, as promised, Stony was waiting, dancing as if she were aware of the importance of the mission for which she had been chosen to play such an important part.

The groom, a young woman named Jerin, assisted him to mount, and, like the others, wished him a fast and safe journey and then shut the gate behind him as he set off at a good pace down the road.

Now Eremit, as we will see, had some experience as a horseman. Though the races and games by which the exceptional horsemen of the east perfect their skill were unknown in the west, still, it was expected that a nobleman would be given at least some instruction in riding, and no exception had been made for Eremit. He was, therefore, able to regulate his speed so that he took as little time to the first post as was possible without harm to his mount. After several hours of riding, then, he reached Hargon's Point. Having been here on numerous occasions while riding for pleasure, he had no trouble finding the stable.

He woke up the stablemaster who, upon learning who it was, apologized for the hasty words he'd uttered upon being suddenly awakened. Eremit delivered the first note into his hands, whereupon, with hardly a word being spoken, he was given another horse, this one of the sturdy breed that comes from the plains east of the Kanefthali Mountains and was renowned for endurance. After commending Stony into the hands of the groom, and, we should add, saying a fond farewell to the beast, who responded by nuzzling his neck, Eremit set off without another moment's delay.

While he knew the way to Axelsbroke, he had only been there once or twice, and so was worried about how long it would take to find the stable. Yet, in the event, it was already morning when he arrived, and so he saw, right off the road, the sign of a sleeping horse by which stables are identified. In this case, though he had never met the stablemaster, the letter provided Eremit proved sufficient, and he set off without ceremony or delay on the last stage of his journey.

It was late in the morning, then, when he arrived in sight of Dorindom Castle, having covered a distance of twenty leagues in less than half a day. Though cold, weary, and, indeed, exhausted, he felt, nevertheless, no trace of what we might call *sleepiness* as he put his final horse into the care of a groom and at once made his way to the castle gate itself, passing under it on foot along with Teckla and tradesmen who were busy buying and selling and dealing with the clerks and intendants of the castle.

Though anxious about finding himself in such a large and busy place for the first time, Eremit sternly reminded himself of the importance of his errand, and bravely strode up directly to the gate, where a pair of guards in Iorich livery and holding halberds kept a watch on the crowd. It was to one of these that he addressed himself in the following terms: "I am Eremit of Cryden, son of Nessit, and I have arrived with an urgent errand to His Benevolence the count. To whom ought I address myself for this purpose?"

"Usher next to the grand stairway," said the guard laconically.

Eremit gave him a friendly salute—though unsure, it must be said, just what sort of salute, and, indeed, what degree of friendliness was appropriate. Under any other circumstances, his alarm at being in such an unfamiliar environment would have, if not paralyzed him, at least made him hesitant. Yet, and we say it to his credit, the importance of his mission and the faith of those who trusted him drove his feet forward with a determination that utterly concealed any discomfort he may have felt.

His first challenge, as the reader may easily deduce, was to find the grand stairway. He concluded, first, that it must necessarily be a stairway, and, second, that if it were called "grand" then it ought not to be difficult of discovery. Therefore, it was with a certain optimism that he entered the interior of the castle to begin his search.

His first thought as he crossed the threshold was that, if the "grand stairway" was grand compared to the castle, well, it must quite grand indeed. He had now entered Dorindom Castle itself, the political, economic, and social center of Westward, one of the proudest counties in the Duchy of Handsfree, and for a provincial it had no less of an effect than someone from Dragaera City might have felt upon entering the Imperial Palace for the first time. The height of the ceiling was sufficient to generate awe: it was five stories tall, ending in a small dome surrounded by stained glass windows depicting scenes from the settlement of the region in the First Cycle by Queen Kolathnë, afterward Baroness Lowtower, from whom Count Dorin claimed descent.

The reader may observe that we have mentioned the height of the ceiling but not the overall size of the hall. The reason for this apparent omission on the part of the historian may be explained in two words: the hall (called the Hall of Greeting) was so large and, moreover, so full of humanity of all ranks and stations, that Eremit was unable to determine its size, beyond, in the most general terms, large; certainly larger than, in his experience, any single room had any excuse to be. And as Eremit cannot make this determination, and as we have chosen for this time to follow Eremit closely in his movements, it would seem to be a violation of the art of the writer as well as the science of the historian to provide the reader with information of which our friend was unaware.

This being clearly understood, we may now accompany Eremit as he pushes forward, on his countenance the inevitable smile of the lost provincial in his first encounter with what we might call civilization, which word we mean in its oldest sense of the culture of cities, in this case defined as an immense press of people, all of whom, unlike our brave Iorich, seemed to know exactly where they were and, moreover, where they wished to go. With shoulder and knee and occasionally elbow, and one hand, we must confess, upon his purse, Eremit made his way forward, looking around at all times, until at length he spotted what could only be the grand stairway: a wide, sweeping set of steps, all in white marble, that made their way up to a sort of garret marked by a black iron railing against which leaned several persons who gazed out at those below them with the attitudes of unconscious superiority that always accompanies viewing those who are, physically if not socially, beneath us.

In all of the press of Teckla, Iorich, Chreotha, and Jhegaala, as well as the occasional Tiassa or Dragon noble visiting from afar, one figure stood out to Eremit's ingenious eyes: a simply dressed man, standing utterly still amid the chaos, as a lone rock out in the Ocean-sea that is impervious to, and even bored by, the incessant and acerbating waves that insist on crashing over it. Though unaware of exactly how he knew, Eremit was instantly convinced that this personage, wearing the green and white of the House of the Issola, must be the very usher for whom he had been looking. Upon making this determination he immediately made his way before the individual in question, bowed and addressed him by naming himself and again repeating the nature of his errand, albeit in the most general terms.

The worthy Issola listened carefully, then said, "For this, you must climb this very stairway before which you stand."

"Very well, I will climb the stairway."

"And upon reaching the top—"

"Yes, upon reaching the top?"

"Proceed directly back until you see an arched doorway upon the side congruent with your right hand. You are aware of which hand is your right?"

"Nearly," said Eremit.

"So much the better. To ensure you have the correct archway, observe that there will be inscribed upon it the crow and staff beneath an iorich, this being the symbol of the house of Dorin."

"Yes, I will look for the arched doorway, with the house symbol engraved upon it."

"Pass beneath this arch and you will find his lordship the count's undersecretary, who will make the necessary arrangements. Apropos—"

"Yes?"

"While I do not know the precise nature of your mission, you have an honest face, and I perceive by certain signs that your errand is urgent. Moreover, my question as to your knowledge of your right hand might have been construed as discourteous. Therefore, in hopes of being helpful as well as making up for any slight you may have felt, I hand you this token, upon which is the symbol of the house, and which will indicate to the worthy undersecretary that he must see to your request at the earliest possible moment."

Eremit accepted the token, saying, "I thank you, and furthermore inform you that I consider you complaisance personified."

"Well, young man, let us see if you have understood."

"I have understood entirely, and this is the proof: I ascend this stairway and continue back until I see the archway with the symbol of the house of Dorin. I pass beneath the arch and hand this token to the undersecretary and explain my errand."

"You have comprehended my meaning in all particulars. It remains, therefore, only for me to wish you success."

"And you, my lord—may I say that the usefulness of your advice is only exceeded by the kindness with which it was delivered."

Then, with bows of mutual esteem, they parted, the one to resume his position, the other to follow the instructions he had been given. In the event, he followed these instructions so perfectly, that in a few short moments, he found himself before the very undersecretary of whom the Issola had spoken, and who proved to be an elderly gentleman of the House of the Chreotha who was seated behind a wide desk upon which a few papers were stacked in neat piles, and also upon which rested a large open folio.

For the third time, then, Eremit stated his mission. The old gentleman whom he addressed listened carefully and then, making no response save a slight nod, studied the folio before him, which appeared, from what the

Iorich could see, to be something in the nature of a ledger, ruled in each direction, with clear but small writing upon the lines.

"I'm afraid," said the undersecretary at length, in a low and wheezy voice that Eremit had to strain to hear, "that there are no appointments available with his lordship the count until next month."

"Well," said Eremit, "but, you perceive, it is a matter of some urgency. And to prove it, here is this," whereupon he handed him the token given him by the usher.

The undersecretary displayed no surprise as he accepted the token, but he did nod and say, "Well, if you will be so good as to wait here, I will attempt to ascertain if my lord the count can make time for you."

"And I will be most grateful to you for doing so."

"You may, if you wish, have a seat while you wait," said the gentleman before taking his departure. In the event, Eremit elected to remain standing for the simple reason that he was too anxious to sit—in fact, he was aware of a certain pounding of his heart, and it must be said that he did not so much *stand* as *pace without moving*, that is, he shifted his weight from one foot to the other and back, while his hands went from clasped behind his back, to a position where his right wrist was held in front of him by his left hand, only to return to their previous position, and so back. After these motions had continued for a quarter of an hour, the undersecretary returned.

"Well?" said Eremit.

The worthy gentleman seated himself behind his desk, coughed, arranged the ledger carefully, and, removing a quill from an inkstand, wrote something in it, after which he brushed it with sand. He then picked up the ledger, made a quarter turn, and blew gently. Turning back, he set the ledger down carefully, after which he looked up at Eremit who, as the reader may imagine, was barely able to conceal his impatience, and said, "Through that door, my lord, and all the way back."

Eremit exhaled loudly, then bowed to the undersecretary and, without wasting either a word or the time it would take to utter it, followed the directions he had been given. These directions, from which he did not deviate (a process made all the easier by how simple they were) brought him to a richly upholstered antechamber attended by a pair of guards in similar attire to those at the castle gate, save only for the addition of gold markings on the cuffs of their uniforms. As Eremit arrived, they crossed their halberds between him and the door and one of them said, "State your name."

"I am Eremit of Cryden," he said simply.

"Remove your sword belt," said the other.

Eremit bowed his head and did so, putting his weapons into the hand of the guard, who then, along with her companion, opened the way to let him pass, her companion even going so far as to open the door.

Eremit then entered a spacious, circular room, with one large chair against the far wall, which chair was occupied by none other than the count himself: a large man with broad shoulders, narrow eyes, and gray hair swept back to highlight his noble's point, which was especially pronounced. Standing behind him was another, an elderly Iorich woman marked by extreme pallor and a slightly stooped posture. She had her hand upon the arm of the chair in a gesture displaying mostly a need for support, though not devoid of a disagreeable hint of possessiveness. Some nine or ten others stood against sides of the room, speaking quietly with one another in pairs or simply waiting, watching the count. Of these, several were Iorich, dressed as justicers, but there were also Chreotha in the rich garb of merchants, and one young man of perhaps 120 or a 130, which is to say, not significantly older than Eremit, who wore the blue and green of the House of the Orca. This young man, unlike the others, did not watch the count, but instead his regard was fixed on Eremit with an intensity the young Iorich found as surprising as it was inexplicable.

Eremit, nevertheless, went forward to within several paces of the elderly gentleman, then suddenly stopped, as he realized two things of some significance: First, that all of the eyes in the room were now upon him, and second, that he was utterly unacquainted with the proper protocol for this circumstance. After a moment's hesitation, during which he cursed himself for failing to ask the friendly usher how to behave, it came to him that, whatever the protocol, he could not go far wrong by dropping to a knee and bowing his head, which thought was acted upon the instant it was conceived.

In the event, so far as he could tell, his gesture was well received. "Rise, Sir Eremit," said Dorin, giving the young man the title that, though rarely used, was formally his due as the oldest son of a baron within the House of the Iorich.

Eremit rose as he was bid and said, "Your Benevolence, I offer my thanks, and the thanks of my mother, the Baroness of Wetrock, for agreeing to see me, and I give you my word, the matter is of some urgency." As he spoke, he removed the pendant and extended it, saying, "It is my wish to come before the Lord High Justicer."

Something about these words appeared to upset, or, at any rate, startle the count, who, without taking the pendant, said, "Did you say Wetrock?"

"I did, Your Benevolence."

"And yet, this name was not pronounced to me by my secretary. He only gave your name as Eremit, son of Nessit."

"That is my name, Your Benevolence."

"Well, but I do not question that. But if you are of Wetrock, then your mother is—?"

"The Baroness Sudora, if it please Your Benevolence."

"Just so, just so." He frowned, and a stern look came over his countenance. "Why, then, did you conceal this fact when requesting an audience with me?"

"Your Benevolence?" said Eremit, who was by now confused, as well as worried; something was wrong, and he was unable to determine what it was, much less how to repair whatever breach he might have caused. "I do not understand what Your Benevolence does me the honor to say. I have concealed nothing. On the contrary, I have given my name at each stage. If I have not expressly mentioned my mission, it is only because it has been deemed a matter for your ears only, my lord."

"And yet, here you are, a messenger from Wetrock, and you stand before me, yet I had no knowledge that is what you were."

Eremit started to speak, but the count gestured him to silence and instead waved a finger to the woman who stood behind him. She bent over, the two of them had a whispered conversation that went on for some moments, during which time a feeling of dread began to rise within Eremit. Several times the count would speak into the woman's ear, and she would vigorously shake her head and then whisper back, at which time the count would look grim, or angry, or frustrated. At length, he whispered to her, and she appeared to consider it, then slowly nodded, at which point the count relaxed and turned to Eremit with a smile.

"Well, my friend," he said. "Let us set aside these mere matters of etiquette, shall we?"

"So much the better," said Eremit, who was still holding the pendant. "May then I speak of my mission? I wish to request an audience with—"

"No, no," said the count, with a wave of his hand. "I understand your mission to be one of exceptional importance and no small urgency, is it not?"

"That is exactly the case, if it please Your Benevolence."

"Then I wish to give the matter—whatever it is, for you perceive you have yet to tell me what it involves—my full attention. I am right, am I not, young man? You have not explained your mission to me, or mentioned it to anyone else?"

"I have not, Your Benevolence."

"So much the better! Then give me leave to conclude my morning's business and to eat a quick bite. After that, why, at the first hour after noon, I will see you in my study, which also functions as my private audience chamber, and, whatever this matter may be, I will give it my full attention and do everything in my power to see to it you are satisfied with whatever aid you may require. Come, what do you think of this plan?"

As it was just then halfway to the fourteenth hour, it did not seem to Eremit that waiting a mere ninety minutes would make a difference, and, even more, he did not see how he could refuse such a request without discourtesy bordering on insolence, which could do his cause no good. After making these calculations, he bowed low and said, "Then it remains only for me to thank Your Benevolence and promise that I will appear at the appointed time and in the appointed place."

"Then we are agreed," said the count. "Until then, my dear young friend."

"Until then, my lord," said Eremit. And, not knowing what else to do, he walked backward for several steps, bowed, and turned and left the chamber—which, we should add, if not the precise motions etiquette demanded, was, by chance, close enough to cause little remark and no offense.

Alas for Eremit! For, in the event, though he did not know it, a chance mistake in etiquette was the least of his worries. He left the chamber, recovered his sword belt from the guard, and returned, in all innocence, to the undersecretary, and there asked after the location of the count's private study, in order to be certain of arriving in a timely manner.

"It is simplicity itself," he was told in a voice so quiet he had to lean over to hear. "Simply proceed left until you come to a wide hallway on your right-hand side, marked, for reasons which I must confess I do not know, by a symbol of four vertical lines intersecting a single horizontal line. Take that hallway to the end, and there you will meet two guards, who will, if they have been given the necessary orders, permit you into the study."

"I thank you for your kindness," said Eremit uselessly, for the old man was paying no attention, but had already returned to his ledger and his notes.

Now Eremit considered the matter, and it seemed to him that, though the directions were clear enough, there was still a chance of him becoming lost in this strange, massive castle. If he might become lost, then, well, he would need time to be found. Under these circumstances, the sooner he attempted to find the room, the more chance, in case of mishap, that he would nevertheless arrive at his appointment on time. As he considered the matter much too serious to risk being late, he resolved to set out for his appointment at once, content to wait outside of the study as long as necessary.

The directions he had been given, as it happened, were both clear and accurate, wherefore in only a few minutes he came to exactly the place described, and there were, as promised, two guards in Iorich livery, though missing the marks on their sleeves, and even without the high boots affected by the guards he had seen before. He saluted them and said, "I greet you. I am called Eremit of Cryden, and I am here by appointment with His Benevolence the count, although I confess, I am here wonderfully early, wherefore I am quite willing to wait wherever you so direct me."

They looked him over, and one said, "You are, then, Eremit, of Wetrock?"

He bowed. "I have that honor."

"Son of the Baroness Sudora?"

"Yes, that is it."

"And you have a pendant to show His Benevolence?"

"This is it."

"In that case," said the guard, "you need not wait at all, but, on the contrary, may go in at once."

"How," said Eremit. "And yet it is over an hour before the time agreed upon."

"As to that," said the guard, "I do not say it isn't."

"And then?"

"Well, my orders are, first, to ascertain your identity, which I have done."

"Oh, as to that, well, you have carried out that order to the letter."

The guard bowed. "And after that, I was to desire you to enter the count's private study as soon as you wished."

"Well," said Eremit, "if those are your orders, I have nothing more to say about it. But do you wish for my sword belt?"

"Oh, as to that, certainly you must leave your sword belt with us, and, of course, it will be returned to you on your departure."

"I do not doubt you in the least. And the proof is, here, I remove my belt and place it willingly in your hand."

"So much the better," muttered the other guard. Meanwhile, the first one, after having taken Eremit's belt and set it against the wall, opened the door, then stepped to the side. Eremit, looking past him, saw a tidy, well-appointed room full of bookshelves and comfortable chairs. It seemed to be unoccupied, and yet, it would no doubt be a more diverting place to wait than standing in the hall; he told himself he must remember to thank the count for his kindness in this matter.

He then bowed to the two guards and stepped forward into the study, whereupon he was struck a blow in the back of the head and remembered no more.

Chapter the Third

In Which Eremit Takes a Journey in the Company of Unsympathetic Persons

The first thing Eremit experienced upon awakening was a feeling of illness in his stomach, followed by the realization that he was in motion; it was only then that he became aware that he was in pain—his back, neck, left arm, and right knee were all sore, attributable, perhaps, to nothing more than the movement of the conveyance. The pain in his head, however, was insistent, and so powerful it interfered with his ability to reason. He tried to think of where he was: in near darkness, shaking back and forth behind the *ca-clop ca-clop* of a pair of horses, but he couldn't remember, though it seemed, in his confused state, that he was on the verge of remembering, and then everything would make sense.

He looked around, in spite of the pain in his head that the light seemed to make worse, and realized that he was in the back of an iron carriage, the sort used to transport prisoners. There was a thin coating of straw at the bottom, and a barred window on each side.

His first thought, nearly instinctive, was to yell out of the window and ask why he was there, by what right, and whither bound. He did not do so for two reasons: first, because he remembered, from his reading of the law, that those who drove such conveyances were under orders to neither hear nor respond to anything said by a prisoner, and, second, because he was convinced that, should he yell, he would die from the pain in his head.

He felt around his head to see if there was a physical cause and found a good-sized lump in back, tender to the touch. How had it come to be there?

He shut his eyes and stretched out on the straw, grateful, at least, that there was room for him to straighten his legs. He tried to think, to remember how he had gotten there, but he could not. "Well," he said to himself, "but had I committed a crime, I should think I would remember. But then, what *do* I remember? The dusk, the ocean with Livosha. And then dinner, and then . . . ah, my head! There was something important I had to do. What was it? I cannot remember! What has happened to me? What caused to me to be in this place?"

It was only then he noticed that his hands and feet were free and tried to recall what the law said about when prisoners should, can, or must be secured, and when he was unable to remember, had the thought that if only he weren't in this carriage, he could find his law books and look it up, at which time he lost consciousness once more.

He was next awoken by a change in motion, to wit, the carriage stopped. His eyes opened, and, as one will do under such circumstances, took stock, as it were, of his condition. He no longer felt ill, which was all to the good, and the pain in his head was reduced, but he still could remember nothing after the dinner with Livosha, save that he had had something important to do. No doubt, he thought, he had somehow been mistaken for someone else, or in some other way an error had been made. But he was a practicing advocate, and, if not experienced, at least licensed and learned in the law. "Come," he thought to himself. "It will be strange indeed if this cannot be set right. Yet I wish I could remember—"

His thoughts were interrupted, then, by the sound of the locks being removed from the wagon door, which door was then opened. Eremit gasped, and the only reason his knees did not give way was because of the circumstance that he was already on his back.

He had seen those in the Kinship of the Mask before, of course— wherever there was a court, even in the most isolated district, there would be one or two Kinsmen in their pure, blank, gray masks, their gray robes with the markings of the Iorich, and their massive, scythe-like swords slung behind their backs making sure there was no violence during proceedings, and that prisoners were treated fairly, but never permitted to escape. He had seen them, but he now discovered, to his shock, how different it was when he, himself, was the object of their cold, impartial, detached attention. He had, it seemed, because of shock, and injury, and confusion, not realized, or perhaps had been unwilling to realize, the extreme gravity of his circumstances. But now, as the two Kinsmen opened the door and he looked at their masks, beneath which could be seen only distant, emotionless eyes, the full weight fell upon him.

One of the Kinsmen spoke, then, saying, "A quarter of an hour for exercise." He then nodded to the chamber pot that had been placed upon the ground and stepped back to exactly the proper distance that would permit him to draw his weapon and sever one of Eremit's limbs, or perhaps his head, if he were given cause. Far from giving them cause, however, the young Iorich found himself unable to move, unable to speak, but merely overcome with a poisonous mix of terror and despondency.

The Kinsmen said nothing: Eremit realized that they had seen this before, that prisoners sometimes were brought so low as to be unable to move, unable even to respond. But this, to the Kinsmen, was a matter of indifference. They had followed the rules and said what they were required to say, thus they had done their duty. And the knowledge of this bore Eremit down, and he could not help but cry out, "What have I done? What crime have I committed that this should befall me?"

It must be said that even in this state, he spoke not to the Kinsmen, whose perfect indifference he knew well, but to the gods, whose indifference he only suspected. Still, in the end, it made little difference to whom he spoke.

Years before he had had an undistinguished sword master who had managed to make of Eremit an undistinguished swordsman. But the sword master had taught him one thing that remained with him and came to his mind at this moment: "If you are scratched, make it seem as if you are injured; but if you are injured, act as if you were scratched. The knowledge of your condition is as valuable to your opponent as a low-line opening."

So then. Yes. He would not let them see his condition. He made himself rise and exited the wagon, doing his best to remain balanced on his none-too-secure legs, used the chamber pot, and walked within the prescribed area.

He looked around but could not identify the region; he had never been here before, and was unable to guess even what direction they had gone. The ground was flat for the most part, with some gentle hills, and no smell of the sea. He looked at the top of the iron carriage and saw that it was piled high with barrels and crates: crates for meals for himself and the Kinsmen, barrels of water and fodder for the horses. The quantity told him that there was a long journey ahead, and that his captors had no intention of stopping before its end.

One of the Kinsmen informed him it was time to resume the journey and placed a small basket into the wagon, announcing, "Your meal." Without a word, Eremit climbed back into the carriage and sat down as the door was locked and bolted, and the journey resumed.

Inside the basket was a loaf of bread, a cold leg of fowl, and a flask. He had a bite of the bread and one of fowl, then discovered he wasn't hungry. He drank some water from the flask and closed his eyes.

My son, we must send you on a mission.

Yes, yes. That was it. A conspiracy, a mission to . . . Dorin, the Count of Westward. And he had gone and been given a meeting. . . .

It gradually came back to his memory, but it took somewhat longer for him to fully realize the significance, and then he gasped, and suddenly, in spite of his resolve, he cried out. What had happened? Had the conspiracy been real, and, if so, had it been foiled? He clenched his teeth and his fists. It must have been real. At any rate, it had penetrated into Dorindom Castle, right under the nose of Dorin himself.

What would Livosha think? He must have been accused of a crime; would she believe it? When he came home, would she wish to see him? Home. Would he even have one? What had happened? And so he discovered the torment of ignorance. It came to him that, of all things, he most wished to speak to Livosha about his predicament. He had never been so alone.

He felt himself slipping into melancholy, or worse than melancholy, mania; it seemed as if he was only holding on to his reason as an inexperienced driver holds on to a maddened team: with no hope of controlling it, hoping only that by hanging on long enough it will become easier.

In order to distract himself, he stared out of the barred window, and so eventually deduced they were traveling north, although to what destination he could not imagine; he knew of nothing in the north that had the least to do with him. He then set about taking a careful inventory of his possessions. His sword belt was gone, of course; he had, himself, handed it over to the guards. He looked in his purse and found the "handful of money" he had been sent off with, and found that it totaled fourteen imperials, three orbs, and seven coppers: a goodly sum, and one he was pleased he had not been robbed of (for although robbing a prisoner was strictly forbidden by the Kinship, yet he also knew that this rule had sometimes been ignored).

Next he looked through his pouch and at once saw that the pendant he had been given was gone. In fact, everything had been removed except for a certain paper, tied up in ribbons. He held it near the window and saw that it was a reference to certain legal documents that he was to invoke while presenting his case to the Lord High Justicer. And it was seeing this that, if the reader will permit the expression, pushed young Eremit over the edge.

For a time, then, frustration and despair overcame his thinking, and he screamed and cried out and threw himself against the walls of the iron wagon over and over, calling out to the gods, demanding answers, demanding release, as a thousand thousand prisoners before him had done, and the knowledge that these cries and gestures were, to his guards, so much sand in the desert, could no more stop them than the knowledge of the hard ground beneath can stop a man from falling once he has begun.

At last, exhausted, he fell back onto the straw and, as the wagon made its relentless way forward, he welcomed the oblivion that claimed him.

He would never have a clear memory of the next month, as the iron wagon rolled steadily northward. It gradually became colder, both from the failing of the year and the steady northward motion; during one stop, of which there were four a day as well as a longer one at night, one of the Kinsman threw a heavy woolen blanket into the wagon. The young Iorich wrapped it around himself without a thought, and the journey continued. He and Livosha had spoken of working together to learn the spells that would permit them to speak to each other's minds, and, indeed, had spent pleasant hours discussing the pleasure in being able to have such conversations when one or the other was away. But alas, they had never gone beyond discussing it; reading the law rarely allowed one a great deal of leisure time. Nevertheless, he tried—imagining Livosha, or sometimes his mother or father, and attempting to form the spell out of sheer desire. We might say that, though disappointed, he was not surprised at his failure. And at least it provided a certain amount of distraction as the days and miles went by.

For a while, then, he gave himself over into imaginings, especially imagining that instead of devoting himself to the law, he had studied the magical arts, and thinking how he would cast spells to befuddle his captors and unlock the wagon and escape, as is so often done in romances (although, as he well knew, almost never in life, as the Kinship would always take precautions when transporting a sorcerer). These flights of imagination at first served to distract Eremit, but then they, themselves, became an additional source of torment.

After a full month had passed, Eremit became aware of new sounds. Though still taken by the lethargy of despair, he nevertheless looked out of the windows. Through the right-hand window he saw farm country, with rows of strong trees protecting plowed fields, though now, after the harvest, they were empty. Sometimes they would pass an oxcart going the other direction, full of supplies from the nearest town; sometimes a horseman would overtake them, a post rider at a gallop, or a nobleman riding for pleasure.

He realized suddenly that, once more, he was smelling the sea, only there were differences: there were more intense sulfur notes to it, and the seaweed seemed sweeter, and there was less of the odor of iodine than he was used to. Though he had not been keeping track of the days, nor had he made any effort to guess at their travel speed, he now calculated as best he could and concluded they had come north something like a thousand miles. If in addition to north their journey had taken them slightly west, then, from his memory of the maps he had once studied, they should be near the metropolis of Northport, the upper point of the Great Southwest Triangle, of which the other two were Candletown and Zerika's Point. Here, it could be said, truly, that the south ended and the north began.

But why would he be here?

He shook his head and once more lay down on the straw, an arm over his eyes.

When he was next let out for exercise and to rest the horses, he could see a long, sandy beach with gentle waves rolling in. He went as close to it as his captors permitted and watched. There are some who see the Ocean-sea as an enemy, some who see her as a very wet granary, some who see her as a challenge, and some to whom she represents freedom. It must be said that, of this latter group, few of them live near her; this is more the response of some who live far inland when coming to visit her for the first time, and they afterward dream of her as a means of escaping a life of hardship, or privation, or servitude, or ennui. Eremit, who had lived his life within a stone's throw of her shores, had never been one of these, though he had often admired her beauty as one might admire the beauty of a Dzur that has been taken in captivity and is being paraded through the streets: that is to say, a beauty, and yet one not to be embraced, but to be admired from a distance and treated with the highest respect.

And yet now, for the first time, something of that feeling came over him, and he longed to escape into her arms—not to take his own life; he had not yet fallen that low—but rather a more traditional escape—to sail away beyond the reach of his captors. The reader must understand, this longing never approached a plan, nor even an intention; he understood the Kinship of the Mask too well to even consider escape a possibility, nor would he have known what to do with such freedom as an escape would give him. Yet as he watched the endless roll of the waves, gentle as they were at that place and at that time, the longing came over him.

On hearing the command to re-enter the carriage, he took a last look at the shore, sighed, and climbed. The ride continued for several hours, until at last it pulled to a stop. Though scarcely interested, Eremit looked out, and saw that they were now in Northport itself, and, in fact, at the very port, which was proved by the oddly shaped harbor that is known so well, full of ships of all sorts, from heavy skybenders to powerful trimarans, to practical yawls, to yachts and sloops.

The door of the carriage opened, and Eremit saw the Kinsman was holding fetters and manacles connected by heavy chain. He felt a sudden thrill of fear at this sight, which was remarkable mostly because, until it happened, he had thought himself beyond feeling anything. Knowing there was no point in resistance, he held out his hands and stood quietly while he was thoroughly restrained, pleased—if the word *pleased* can be used under such circumstances—that the length of chain between his ankles permitted him to walk naturally.

One of the Kinsmen set out; the other gave Eremit a gentle push, then fell in behind him. In only a few steps, he could see where they were going, for directly before them was a ketch, fore-and-aft rigged, two masts, three sails, with the mizzenmast well forward from where it would be in a yawl. It had, no doubt, once been a fishing boat, perhaps a trawler, but now he could see the top of an iron cage sticking up from the hold to just beneath the height of the boom. *At least I will have room to stand,* he thought, noting the depth of the hold. The reader may observe that he didn't for an instant concern himself with where his destination might be; he was too stunned and melancholic to care. That he even gave a thought to such elementary matters as his future comfort was, in his own mind, worthy of note. He tried to rouse himself with the reminder that, sooner or later, there must be a trial, and, whatever had happened, whatever he might be accused of, he would no doubt need all of his wits to present his best case. Yet so overwhelmed was he by the frustration of not knowing what had become of his mother and father, nor Livosha, nor how this had all happened, that his spirit could only respond by assuming an apathy that, in its way, prevented his over-strained imagination from devouring his intellects.

They made their way onto the vessel. The captain, an Orca, bowed deeply to the Kinsmen and ignored Eremit entirely. One of the crew—there were four of them as well as the captain, all of them Orca—pulled open the grating, and Eremit climbed in without a word. The top clanged shut, and there came the click of a lock, then another.

As such cells go, Eremit knew, there were many worse. As he had surmised, he was able to stand up in it, and, like the wagon, it was large enough that he was able to lie down as well. Moreover, there was a bed of sorts: an iron cot built into the side, with a straw mattress and a thick blanket. There was also a slops pail that was permanently built in and opened to the water below. Many prisoners being transported had, as Eremit knew well from his study of lawsuits brought against the Empire for mistreatment, suffered in far worse accommodations.

He sat on the cot with his head in his hands, then lay down, staring up at the bars of his cage. In a short time, he felt the motion as the boat left the dock; this was followed by the sound of the sweeps being placed, after which he felt her begin to cut through the waves. The wind, which Eremit had not noticed, must have been kind, because presently there came the sounds of the sails being set, and the sweeps stopped. He felt it as she found her wind, and for an instant, all of his feelings were concentrated in the desire to be on deck, to watch as she rode the waves. As this was, of course, impossible, he bit his lips until the blood came and clenched his fists, until, at last, lulled by the gentle motion, he was able to relax.

He was given four meals a day, simple meals of fish and bread, but they helped relieve the tedium. More, he was permitted on deck twice a day to exercise, during which time the two Kinsmen watched him closely, for it was not unknown, under these circumstances, for a prisoner to take his own life by throwing himself into the water, the weight of the fetters, manacles, and chains making any thought of rescue impossible. The captain and crew, for their part, ignored him entirely, not even acknowledging his presence by so much as a nod of the head. In the event, Eremit had not the least intention of taking his own life, and this for two reasons: the first was that he harbored a fear of drowning beyond all other fears, and the second was that, though frightened and doleful and near despair, still, he had not yet given up hope. The very presence of the Kinsmen is why he had this hope, for they worked to see that the rule of the courts was obeyed, and before imprisonment, execution, branding, or flogging, by law there must come a trial. He was resolved, therefore, to attempt to keep his wits as sharp as he could, and, still more, to hold off the melancholy that threatened to overwhelm him, until he could be given a chance to defend himself against whatever charge, from whatever source, might be brought.

The journey lasted twenty-six days. Just after noon on the twenty-seventh, the young Iorich was on deck exercising when he saw they were headed into fog—indeed, the thickest cloud of fog Eremit had ever seen. The crew did not seem disturbed by it and entered without any change in course, nor even so much as ringing the ship's bell, as was usual under such circumstances. All that happened as they entered was that Eremit was at once directed into his cell, which he quickly realized was because the fog was so thick that his guards would be unable to see him even five paces distant.

The voyage continued, from this point, less than half an hour before there was activity above him, and the motion of the vessel changed. In the distance, he heard the ringing of a bell, but a far larger and deeper and more portentous bell than the one on the boat.

Then, at length, there came an odd sound, like the howl of the wind during a fierce storm, yet there was no corresponding effect on the vessel, and, only two minutes after that, there came a gentle *bump*, as if it were at a dock.

The hatch was raised on Eremit's cell, and one of the Kinsman looked down from out of the fog and gestured. Eremit climbed out of his cell and followed his guards to the gangplank, which he trod carefully, keeping his eyes fixed on the back of the head of the Kinsman in front of him. From what he could tell, he was on an island that was all mountain; that is, the slope was steep and seemed to run all the way to shore, save for a pathway that appeared to have been cut out of it and a wooden dock that jutted out from some thirty or forty feet. He was escorted along this dock onto the pathway, which proved to be made of flagstone.

Upon setting his feet on shore, accompanied as it always was by the odd sensation that the solid ground was moving, he having become so used to the motion of the boat, he found himself surrounded by six strangers, four of them in Iorich uniforms of the more traditional kind, another in the same uniform except wearing gold braid around his shoulder, and the sixth, surprisingly, appeared to be an Athyra, who wore simple dark colored robes and stood apart from the others. One of the Kinsmen produced a key and put it into the hand of the one with the braided uniform, whom Eremit concluded must be the leader of the guard company. This individual accepted the key and, as he did so, exchanged a deep, exact, formal bow with the two Kinsmen, whereupon one of the Kinsman turned to Eremit and said simply, "You have arrived."

The last thing the two Kinsmen did before returning to the ship, was to bow deeply to Eremit, as was the tradition, to signal that he was no longer merely a nameless object to be delivered, but was, to them, once more a person. The brutal irony of this traditional gesture, as if they had performed a service for him, struck Eremit almost as a blow, and he quickly turned away as he heard their heavy footsteps retreating up the gangplank.

He looked at the four guards and their commander, who now studied him with the same impersonal yet professional curiosity that a butcher might display when studying a kethna, and then the commander said, "Welcome to the Burning Island. You will follow me."

"Burning Island," remarked Eremit as he set in to follow his jailer while the others fell in around him. "How does it come to have such a name?"

The silence that followed this question was sufficient to convince Eremit that these guards, like the Kinsmen, had no intention of communicating with the prisoner. He sighed and contented himself with following the rocky path along which he was led, which at once began to rise and curve to the left. He could hear the crash of the waves on his right but was still unable to see anything through the intense fog.

The path continued for some small distance before turning abruptly into what appeared to be the side of a hill or a mountain, although Eremit had not been aware of anything on his left except the impenetrable fog. They entered through a sort of doorway that showed signs of having been carved out of the rock of the hillside and could be shut by means of a heavy, thick, wooden door, bound with iron bands, its hinges embedded in solid rock. Eremit's last view of the outside world was the fog, after which he followed his jailers into the hill.

He did not see the light of day again for more than six hundred years.

Chapter the Fourth

In Which the Author Is Embarrassed to have Nearly Forgotten about Livosha

We apologize to the reader if, in our desire to learn the fate of poor Eremit, we have accidentally neglected others toward whom the reader may feel some sympathy, or at least interest. At the top of any such list of persons must, it would seem, be Livosha, whom we have shamefully neglected, indeed, about whom we have nearly forgotten, since the first chapter of our history introduced her. That our attention has been taken up with other matters that seemed to us vital is no excuse for this neglect, with which the reader cannot help but be impatient, wherefore, as no apology is as acceptable as one that repairs the breach, we will, without further delay, return our attention to Livosha as well as to some of the other individuals whom our history has hitherto brushed past in a more or less perfunctory fashion.

In order to determine what has become of Livosha, we warn the reader, it is absolutely necessary to look into the past, to *back up*, as the teamsters say. We trust this requirement will not unduly disturb the reader, who, insofar as he has understood that this entire narrative is history, must have also understood that to turn our attention to events that have already occurred is not only a part of the study of history, but is, in fact, the very definition of it. Moreover, we will, in hopes of atonement, continue her history well past the point where we have left Eremit. If we must then look back again in order, in turn, to follow the events befalling the young gentleman, that, at least, we can leave to another time, another chapter, as we now turn our attention to the young lady.

Looking back, then: after the dinner, which, we must observe, Livosha found as pleasant as Eremit had, she went into the small but well-furnished library and busied herself for a few hours by reading Vestigan's *Commentaries On Procedure*, for, although she was not a licensed advocate, she had every intention of becoming one, and thus devoted herself to reading law

whenever not otherwise occupied—an idiom we hope the reader will forgive, as it is trivially obvious that anything one does, one does while not
otherwise occupied, that is to say, when not doing something else; nevertheless, the sense is that this was an activity to which, if we may be permitted, she *gravitated* and so engaged in more than nearly any other when the
opportunity presented itself. It should be obvious that by using the term,
while not otherwise occupied, we are able to convey this sense without the need
for a lengthy explanation, which could not fail to try the reader's patience.

After several hours, Livosha became aware that not only was she requiring herself to read the same passage two or even three times in order
to gather the sense of it, and not only did she feel her eyes drooping as if
they had minds of their own, and these minds had decided, each indepen-
dently and both together, that it was well past the time when they should
close, but she also realized that the hour had become quite late. These
factors, taken together, convinced her to put her book down and retire for
the night.

This decision was no sooner made than acted upon. She placed a
marker in the book—a thin gold cloth with her name and house emblem
cunningly embroidered upon it—and closed the book. Her thoughts, which
had until this moment been concerned with certain aspects of courtroom
etiquette and regulations, turned back to Eremit, and to their upcoming
nuptials, which thoughts resulted in her lips curving up into a contented
smile. She carried this smile with her—for it had occurred so naturally, it
could not be considered a burden—as she climbed the front stairway, with
its charming sculpted handrail, up to her bed chamber. She observed that,
in fact, it had become extremely late (indeed, it was just at this time that
Eremit, having received his mission, was mounting Stony to begin the ride
to Dorindom).

With the assistance of her handmaid, Suzil, she got into her nightclothes, climbed into bed, and at once fell into the deep, untroubled sleep
of those who are young, in love, and foresee only contentment, perhaps
mixed with a few happy surprises and a manageable number of minor ob-
stacles, the overcoming of which will only heighten, by contrast, the pleasure of the rest. This sleep, which was free of dreams, although not of that
pleasant, relaxed, even mildly euphoric sense that can come over the mind
of a sleeper whose natural disposition is cheerful, was interrupted in the
fifth hour after midnight, or at the time when Eremit was nearly midway
between Hargon's Point and Axelsbroke, by a loud sound best described
onomatopoeically as a "thud," which seemed to come from the floor below,

which is to say, the "first floor" as the Vallista and the Serioli call it, or the "ground floor" in the parlance of nearly everyone else.

She sat up in bed and reached for a robe, putting it on as she crossed the three paces between her bed and the door. The instant she touched the handle, however, she heard a scream that caused her first to stand frozen and unable to move, and after—be it understood this first reaction lasted only a part of a second—to open the door and run toward the sound. A few steps brought her to the top of the stairway, where she was greeted with a sight that nothing in her experience had prepared her for: there were some eight or ten individuals wearing dark clothes and masks and holding naked swords, standing over the body of her handmaid, Suzil, who lay in a pool of blood that was still growing—more blood, in fact, than Livosha had realized could be contained by a human body.

Her first thought, and we say it to her credit, was to try to remember where she had put her sword. That her sword was, in fact, in the same place it always was, and that only the extreme excitement of her senses drove this thought from her mind, must not be held against her, the more so as this location, that is, the place where her sword was kept, happened to be next to the very door that now stood open and which was blocked by several of the invaders, thereby making it, the reader must understand, impossible to reach without fighting through a press of hostile forces, which, however great her skill, she could not consider doing without the very sword that would be her object, thus creating a sort of "Kehat's Paradox," named for the popular character in folklore who remarked, "If I knew how to perform a listening spell, I could overhear Issyur's conversations in which he explains how to perform a listening spell."

To return to poor Livosha, standing at the top of the stairway, her heart pounding, unsure of what to do, she heard the voice of her father behind her calling her name. She turned and saw at once by the expression on his countenance that he was fully aware of the situation. In his hand was a sword, and next to him were standing her brother, Kefaan, and the servant, Coru, the latter holding a stout club. Her father said, "Here. Take your brother, and keep him safe."

"But, how am I to do that?" she asked as he pushed his way past her, even as four of the attackers began to climb the stairway while others began to run through the rest of the house.

Without wasting a word, as he took his guard position at the top of the stairs, her father said, "In the wardrobe in the west guest chamber is a passage; it is already open. Close it behind you. See to the boy. Now."

"Where is—"

"Your mother is looking after your sister. There is no time, my darling daughter. I cannot tell you where to go or what to do, only escape and protect your brother! Promise me you will, and then go!"

Livosha understood, both from her father's tone, and, even more, from the sight of the invaders coming up the stairs preceded by their swords, that there was no time to waste, that even the slightest delay could be deadly. "I promise I will keep him safe," she said.

"Then take this and go."

With this, he handed Livosha a device of some sort on a chain. She accepted it without looking, and, taking her brother by the wrist, she ran down the hall to the room set aside for visitors and where certain clothing was stored while it was out of season. As promised, the wardrobe was standing open, all of the clothing pushed to the side. There was a hole in the floor, and she could see the top rung of a ladder.

"Quickly," she told her brother. "You go first, and I will follow."

"But Papa!"

"Come, you heard him, did you not? We must follow his orders to the letter."

"Very well, I will do as you say."

"And you will be right to do so."

The young man then set his foot on the top rung of the ladder and began to climb down. The instant his head was beneath the level of the floor, Livosha closed the door of the wardrobe. Understanding that their only hope was to not be found, she pushed the clothing back behind her and then herself climbed down the ladder. She reached up and took hold of the door that covered the passage and, as she climbed down three more steps, pulled it shut behind her, at which time they were instantly plunged into darkness.

"I can't see!" said Kefaan.

Livosha nearly performed a light spell, but then, upon a sudden thought coming to her, instead said, "Well, but you have been studying the sorcerous sciences, have you not, dear brother?"

"And if I have, my sister?"

"Then let us see if you can use these skills to light our way, for I do not wish to stumble around in the dark along an unknown path to an unknown destination."

"Well, but sister, can you not perform this spell yourself?"

"Oh, I? Yes, I can, but I must guide us and watch for danger, and thus I do not wish to spare the concentration required for sorcerous activity.

Come, can you not attempt it? For you perceive, whatever is happening, we are in danger, you and I, and now is when you must step forward and do your part to bring us to safety."

"Ah, well. I will try my best. Only, let me continue down this ladder until I have solid ground under my feet once more."

"Very well, with this plan I agree."

They continued down for a considerable distance until Kefaan announced, "I am at the bottom."

"That is good, then. Make us a light."

"I am attempting to do so this very moment."

"I await you, then, with every confidence in your ability."

The reader, no doubt, has already come to understand that much of the reason Livosha asked her brother to do the spell was that she understood, with the acute sensitivity that comes naturally to some, that he would be less frightened if his mind were occupied with a task, and that, moreover, to permit him to feel useful under such trying circumstances could do the young man's spirits no harm.

After a lengthy pause—lengthy, that is, under the circumstances, by which we mean, long enough for Livosha to fear he would be unable to do it—a thin, pale-blue light occurred around them.

"I've done it!" he cried.

"So much the better," said Livosha, who, now that she was able to see, finished climbing down the remaining few rungs of the ladder and looked around. They were in a tunnel, it seemed, carefully and securely built from baked brick, tall enough to permit them to stand upright, and wide enough, although with little to spare, for them to walk side by side. The only direction it led off in was, if Livosha had not become confused, to the south. She remembered the object she was carrying, then, and looked at it: it was her mother's emblem in the form of a pendant made of platinum, set with a pair of rubies, with her lineage block cunningly inlaid in mother-of-pearl. Livosha put it around her neck, and, as she did so, she noticed a sort of peg on the wall. The peg, in and of itself, was scarcely worth observing, but the peg held a belt, and the belt held a scabbard, and the scabbard held a sword. She at once drew the sword and examined it with a skilled, though only somewhat experienced, eye. It seemed to be of good steel, with the markings indicating the famous Smithy of Hostra in Aussiar in Wirav. She tested the edge, and then the balance, and nodded her satisfaction. "Good," she said. "You perceive, we are armed."

We should explain that Livosha knew that whatever dangers they might encounter, it was unlikely that a single swordsman with a single sword would decide the issue—any meeting she was unable to avoid would likely involve more enemies than she could defeat. But merely having the weapon eased her mind; she no longer felt so helpless. She tried to put the belt around her waist, but it was too large, and she had no leather punch with which to shorten it, so she slung it over her shoulder and said, "Let us see what else has been left here, for it is clear this is an escape route planned for a long time."

They both looked and immediately found a sack with straps cunningly arranged so it could be carried over the shoulder, much as certain military units used for long journeys. Inside it were several sealed tins upon which had been engraved such things as, "dried fish," and "smoked sausage" and "jerked beef." In addition, there was a thick iron knife of the sort used to punch through cans. Livosha nodded her approval and picked up the pack, but Kafeen said, "No, my sister. You have the sword, you must do me the honor of permitting me to carry the pack, it is only fair."

"I will do so, then, since you insist upon it, but you must promise me that, should it become overly burdensome, you will let me know in good season."

"I give you my word."

She handed him the pack and helped him fix it over his shoulders until they were satisfied that it was as comfortable as it could be. He did not appear to mind the weight, at least not yet.

"Come," she said. "We must not delay a minute. Perhaps they will not find the passage, and at any rate they will not find it quickly; but it is best if we do not delay and are gone from here as quickly as possible."

"Gone from here," repeated the boy, his voice trembling and the light he had created flickering momentarily. "But gone to where?"

"As to that, I confess, I am as ignorant as an Easterner. Nevertheless, our lord papa said this is what we must do, and so we ought to follow his orders, do you not agree, my brother?"

"Yes, I agree," said Kefaan, though to judge from the hesitant tone, his agreement was neither absolute nor given with any great pleasure.

Before setting out, they took a moment to listen, but were unable to hear anything from above them. Without another word, they started down the tunnel. The light, of course, remained with them, permitting them to see either before or behind some twenty or twenty-five feet. Livosha attempted to keep a rough track of distance, both because she was aware this intelligence might be useful, and because, her mind working in much the same way as Eremit's would sometime later, she wished to avoid dwelling on what might be happening behind and above her.

After what seemed to her to be about the eighth part of a mile, they came across another ladder. Livosha hesitated, for the tunnel continued, and her father had said nothing about what to do under these circumstances. After giving the matter some thought, she said, "Good my brother Kefaan."

"Well," said the boy, obviously working to keep the fear out of his voice.

"Can you wait here, and keep the light-spell working, while I endeavor to discover whither this leads and if it is safe there?"

"But why must I wait? I should rather stay with you."

"Yes, I know. But you must be brave. It is my duty to explore, and we cannot risk both of our lives."

"Why can we not?"

"Because one of us must be able to speak, to say what has happened."

"But, what *has* happened?"

"As to that, I know no more than you, but—" she thought quickly, "—in the worst case, you must attempt to discover it and find a way to inform His Benevolence the count."

The boy was silent for a moment, then he said, "Well, I perceive it is my duty, so I will do as you say. Only, sister—"

"Yes?"

"You will be careful?"

"I give you my word, I will take no risks that can be avoided."

"Then I wait, hoping only you are not gone too long."

"I will return as soon as I can," she said, and climbed up the ladder awkwardly, for the sword belt made it difficult, slung as it was. It seemed a long way up, though in point of fact it was little different than the climb down had been before. At the top was a door similar to the first one. She listened and, upon hearing nothing, pushed the door open. Even before her eyes adjusted to the dimness, the smell told her she was in the stables. Her first thought was that they should get horses after being certain it was safe, but then she stopped—in fact, she more than stopped, she froze, hardly daring to breathe, because she suddenly heard voices, close enough to make out the words, though far enough away that they were probably on the other side of the wall against which the trap door had opened.

The first was a woman's voice, and she said, "What was that I just heard?"

The second voice belonged to a man, and the reply came, "I am convinced that it is rodents of some sort as often live in barns, for, you perceive, it came from the place we have only just inspected and found empty. In all probability, our presence excited them, and now that we are gone, they are attempting to reach what they consider safety."

"Well, the brats must be somewhere, and either we find them, or—"

"Yes, or?"

"Or it's no sleep, no wine, no completion-pay."

"They didn't come through here, at all events," said the man. "You perceive, the number of horses is right, none are missing."

"In my opinion, they're still in the house, in a hidey-hole of some kind."

"Well, I do not say you're wrong, but if they are, Fidra will find them, as he found the mother and the other girl."

"That is true, and if he does, well, he will cut their throats just as prettily."

"So much the better if he does, because in all truth—"

"Yes?" said the woman. "In all truth?"

"I do not relish cutting the throats of children, or of those who aren't able to fight."

"You killed the father quickly enough."

"He had a sword and was defending himself. And the proof is, he killed Cichani and gave Jir and Moriva wounds that won't heal quickly."

"I do not question that. And to answer you—"

"Yes, to answer me?"

"That sort of killing is no more to my taste than it is to yours. But it is, after all, what we agreed to do."

"Oh, I do not question that! We have been paid, from Berwick's hand to Fidra's, and from Fidra's to ours."

"And so?"

"And so we will do what we have agreed to do."

"Exactly."

"But come, wherever the two brats are, they must be somewhere, and now, having proven they are not in the stables, we must find somewhere else to look."

"Well, lead on then, I follow."

Livosha remained where she was, unable or unwilling to move, as she realized that she and her brother were now all that remained of the family. Her first thought was to draw her sword and find the two villains she'd heard talking and fight until they were dead, or she was, and then, should she be alive, go into the house and kill as many of the others as she could. And she nearly did so—that is, her hand was on her sword, and she had begun climbing the remaining rungs when she remembered that she had been given responsibility for her brother and had accepted that responsibility. *I promise I will keep him safe*, she had said.

Was there any condition? Could she somehow find a way to do what she wished without breaking her vow? After a moment, she realized she could not. The very simplicity of the contract precluded any special circumstances that could justify it being set aside. Moreover, she had promised her brother she would return, so it would require breaking two agreements. She must do as she had agreed. She stood there on the ladder, her head just above the door, and felt tears stream down her face, though she didn't make a sound. How long she stood there she was never certain, but after a time she heard a whisper from below: "Hsst, Livosha?"

She wiped her eyes with the back of her hand, took a deep breath, and climbed back down, closing the concealed door over her head. She made her way down the ladder and said, "Come, my dear brother. We must go on and see where the tunnel goes from here." And before he could ask any questions, she set off.

Livosha no longer attempted to keep track of the length of the tunnel; all of her efforts went toward continuing to walk, and keeping herself from revealing to her brother, by word or action, the extent of the tragedy that had befallen them, yet it must have been more than a mile before the tunnel ended in a heavy doorway.

"Where are we?" said Kefaan.

Livosha shook her head, though what went through her mind was, *The end. We are at the end. There is nothing after this.*

Livosha, we see, was as yet too young to have learned the most difficult lesson of life, the lesson that brings hope and despair together, and is how the one flows into the other, which lesson, although each individual (I include, to be sure, the reader) must learn for himself, which can be expressed in these terms: *There is always something after this.* Life continues, there is another step, another obstacle, another defeat, another victory. And when we have passed on from this life, whether to another or simply to a long, perhaps final, rest, still, life proceeds, and it takes our actions and uses them as it will in the endless, continuing progression of time.

While there is considerably more to say on this subject—indeed, entire volumes could be written on it, and the proof is, there have been—we are now in danger of straying from the strict matter of history into areas which are not only beyond our expertise, but we cannot even precisely name, for which reason we will at once return to Livosha, having now, we hope, given her time to consider the door in front of her, the brother next to her, and the horror behind her enough to have reached a decision.

The door—and we apologize if we ought to have sketched it sooner—was made of thick wood and bound with iron, with three heavy bars leading into iron brackets to hold it shut. A brief inspection told her that these were controlled by a lever next to the door at head height. After only a moment's hesitation, then, Livosha pulled the lever and the bars retracted. She gripped the two handles by which the door could be moved and pulled. At first, nothing happened, but then, at length, the door began to move. It opened, and she led Kefaan through it.

It was still dark, being either the late hours of the night or the early hours of the morning, as the reader prefers, and Eremit was still riding, having left Hargon's Point and being now on the way to Axelsbroke, but there was sufficient light from Kefaan's spell to see that she was in another stable, although, in point of fact, she would have had no need to see in order to make the determination that this was a stable, for, as the reader well knows, stables have an odor—beloved by those who love horses—that cannot be mistaken for anything else. This stable had six stalls, five of which were occupied.

There was a door to the stable. She listened but heard nothing, and, after opening it, looked out, and at once knew, from the position of the shore and of the few lights from the village, that this was Riffetra's House, formally known as the Wriggling Dolphin, but always called simply Riffetra's House, or sometimes simply "Riff's" by the locals. It had been built into the side of the same man-made hill upon which Livosha's home had been, and the door she had opened had emerged from inside this hill.

"Dim the light," she said, which order Kefaan followed instantly and without making an unnecessary reply.

It was quiet now, and what passed through Livosha's mind was theft. Could she steel herself to take two of good Riffetra's horses, or, worse, horses that might belong to a guest? And if she did, could she do so quietly enough? Because, as is well known, the discomfort one feels when engaging in an act of dubious probity is multiplied considerably when one is caught. As matters fell out, however, she was not required to make this decision. She heard the sound of a door closing, and, even as her heart raced and she was looking around for the fastest means of escape, she heard the sound of a low, raspy voice, which voice (or, rather, the individual to whom the voice belonged), said, "Who are you, and what are you doing?"

Livosha drew her sword and prepared to defend herself and her brother to the last when it came to her that the voice was familiar, from which she concluded that the individual to whom the voice belonged would, almost certainly, be familiar as well.

At that moment, Riffetra himself came into view, holding in his hands a staff that was taller than he was.

"Riff?" she said.

"Who is it? Identify yourself, girl!"

"It is I, Livosha, daughter of Cerwin."

"Ah, forgive me, good Livosha," said Riff. "In the dim light, I failed to recognize you. And is that your brother behind you?"

"It is," she said.

"But, why are you holding a sword?"

"Why? Well, for the same reason you are holding a staff."

"But, you perceive, you are in my stables."

"Well, that is true. Only I had not realized at first that is where I was."

"But how could you not know . . . ah! Did you, then, arrive from the underground passage?"

"You have guessed it," she said.

"And are you exploring on a lark, or were you sent there? You must understand, this question I ask you, well, it is of so much importance, that to answer with anything less than perfect candor could have disastrous results for you, and for me, and perhaps for others as well."

"In that case, since you insist upon it, I will tell you the truth."

"So much the better! And the truth is?"

"I was sent here, and by that route."

"Ah, ah! And who sent you?"

"My father, that being Lord Tiscara, husband of the baroness."

"So it has happened! Just as she said!"

"I do not know to what you refer as 'it' good Riff, no more than I know of whom you refer to as 'she.' Nevertheless, from my experience this very night, I am certain the answer is yes."

"Then there is no time to lose. You wish to escape, do you not?"

"My whole thought is bent that way."

"Then we must saddle two horses at once. You, young Kefaan, you ride, do you not?"

"I do," said the boy with a laconicity that belied his years.

"Then let us be about preparing them. Here, this is Bottle, who is small, but with an easy gait and good endurance, she will do for you, young man. And for you, Livosha, I would suggest Red, who can go all day without stopping and has such an easy gait that you might fall asleep while riding."

"I will accept your recommendations without question, good Riff."

"So much the better. Apropos, do you know where you are going?"

"First, to Cryden House, to speak with the baroness and the baron, and to Eremit. After that, to Dorindom Castle, where I will speak with His Benevolence. Come, what do you think of this plan?"

"I think," said Riffetra, and he hesitated. "I think perhaps you will do that, but perhaps you will not."

"I fail to understand you," said Livosha.

"Well, then you two begin saddling the horses. I will return briefly to the house, and then, well, then perhaps we will see!"

After these mysterious and even foreboding words, he left them. They had not yet finished saddling the horses when he returned holding a bundle, a purse, and a note. The purse contained some twelve imperials, which Riffetra pretended would be sufficient to get them to their next destination. The bundle contained three sets of clothing, simple garments of cotton and leather in brown and white, that is, with nothing to identify House or any other particulars. Riffetra turned his back while they dressed; Livosha made no mention of the third set, clearly intended for her sister.

When they were dressed, the innkeeper took their nightclothes and put them in a sack along with the third set, and put the sack into a stove that was kept there to heat the stable boy's bed (on those occasions when he employed a stable boy) on especially cold nights, and set it burning. When the fire was going well, he wordlessly handed Livosha the note, which was sealed with her father's stamp. She at once tore it open and read it by the light of the little fire.

The letter, which we will not withhold from the reader for an instant, and was dated a mere two years before, read as follows:

My dear children:

For some time now, we, that is to say, your mother and I, have come to suspect a conspiracy between Baron Berwick and His Benevolence, Count Dorin, in order to take for themselves the operations of the mining, refining, and transport of the sealstone deposit that has been discovered. While this conspiracy, we believe, is mostly directed at Wetrock, nevertheless there is reason to believe our family may also be in danger. We have on many occasions spoken to our good friends Sudora and Nessit, and, alas, they, generous-spirited as they are, remain unconvinced that Berwick would so conspire, and perfectly certain that Dorin could never have anything to do with such treachery.

We do not know when the attack will take place, nor in what manner, whether a direct, violent assault, or through the legal system, or in some way we have never considered, but we have made what arrangements we can to protect you, our children, whom we treasure more than anything else save honor. If you are reading this, then not only was there an attack on our home, but it came in such a way as to preclude any choice except the tunnel, which we have caused to be dug in secret, for exactly this reason.

Which of you are there, we cannot know; as of this writing, we can only hope it is all of you. Nor can we know all of the circumstances, save that it was necessary for at least one of you to escape this way. As for what to do next, all we know for certain is, you must escape! The worthy Riffetra, to whom we have entrusted your lives, has a small amount of money to give you to travel, and a map which will guide you to the town of Aussiar. In that town, you will find a moneylender and advocate named Gystralan, who will put into your hands the funds with which we have entrusted him and the legal documents that will prove your ownership of and entitlement to our property.

What direction this may take, my children, I do not know, and so I cannot give you more precise instructions. But your mother and I charge you with this, above all else: protect each other and preserve your lives. It is our fondest hope that you will never read this, but, if you do, know that you have remained, always, in the thoughts and hearts of your mother, as well as I,

Your Father,
Tiscara

Livosha put down the letter and, for a moment, stared off, as if into the distance, too overcome with emotion to speak. The silence was broken by Kefaan, who said, in the voice of someone twice his age, "They're dead, aren't they? Everyone is dead."

"Come," said Riffetra. "You must be on your way. The enemy is looking for you and must come here eventually. By the time they arrive, you must be gone, or all is lost."

Chapter the Fifth

In Which Livosha and Kefaan
Contrive to Escape

How long have you known?" said Livosha as they mounted their horses.

Kefaan guided his horse out of the stable door and said, "I thought so when you came down from the first ladder, but I knew it when I watched your countenance as you read the letter. May I read it?"

"Later," said Livosha.

"Come," said Riffetra. "There is no time. Here is the map you were promised. For now, simply go to the Farmer's Road to the south, and from there, begin riding east. Afterward you will follow the map."

Livosha took the map and tucked it carefully into her belt. She then guided her horse out of the door, but suddenly stopped and looked at the innkeeper. "What of you?" she said.

"Of me? Well, if you are gone before they arrive, perhaps they will never know I aided you."

"Well, but if they learn of it?"

He shook his head. "You must not concern yourself with that."

"And yet—"

"Please, I beg you. If not for yourself, then consider you are putting me in greater danger with each instant you delay."

"Well, I am convinced," said Livosha. "But I will not forget you." Without waiting for a reply, she guided her horse onto the road and at once broke into that peculiar but comfortable gait called a *rack* among horsemen.

After a quarter of an hour, Kefaan said, "Sister? If we were to find the Farmer's Road, ought we not to have taken the other fork?"

"We are not yet looking for the Farmer's Road."

"And yet, that is what we were instructed to seek."

"That is true, and soon enough we will."

"Then, if I may ask—"

"Cryden House," said Livosha laconically.

"But my sister, were we not told to go directly to the Farmer's Road, and so out of town?"

"Yes."

"Very well," said the boy.

As this was an area Livosha knew well, having ridden it a thousand times, they were able to reach Cryden House without appearing on any of the usual roads, which is to say, without risking detection. Yet even before they arrived, they knew what they would find, for the air seemed smoky, and a flickering red light occurred in front of them. They emerged from the orchard behind it, where as children Livosha and Eremit had stolen limes and where they had first kissed many years later. Concealed by the trees, Livosha saw that there was nothing left of the house—even the four chimneys were gone as if they had never been, and what remained glowed with heat, and occasional tongues of flame jumped up from the glow as some as-yet unconsumed piece of wood or cloth was discovered. No one, living or dead, could be seen. Livosha looked down, and beneath the feet of her horse she saw rubble that could only have come from the house, thrown a hundred yards by whatever force had destroyed the house.

No one could have lived through such a cataclysm.

To-day's reader, so used to the scientific wonders of modern sorcery, may wonder why she did not at least attempt to reach Eremit's mind. We must remind this reader that this spell—for spell it is, even if it has to-day become so perfunctory that we use it without thinking—was then difficult to perform, requiring dedicated study—study, we must observe, that Livosha, and nearly all Iorich, were devoting to the law when at the age at which an Athyra might study sorcery. We hope this will answer any questions as to why Livosha did not attempt to reach Eremit's mind, but, in any case, it remains true that she did not.

"Come," she said in a whisper. "We can take this way out of town." Kefaan followed without a word.

They were able to leave the village and, indeed, the barony of Wetrock without meeting anyone, and soon found themselves on the Farmer's Road, which carried them from lightly forested areas to cleared fields, back and forth, one to the other. As they traveled, dawn began to break, and, in the growing light, Livosha pulled out the map and studied it carefully. Her brother, who had been known all of his short life for loving the sound of his own voice above all other sounds, remained silent.

"Well," said Livosha after a moment. "It seems that thought has been given to our route with the idea that we may be hunted. It will be complicated, and it will be long, and we will have to sleep out of doors, but I do not believe our enemies will be able to find us so long as we follow the map."

"Our enemies," repeated the boy.

Livosha looked at him, and he returned her look with a calm, steady eye, and the expression on his countenance was one of determination; she did not have to ask to know that he had every intention of returning some-day and seeing to those who had done this, and she knew that any attempt to dissuade him from this course—even should she want to dissuade him, rather than, as was her inclination, joining him in this venture—would be futile. She only said, "My brother, I am so sorry this has happened. To us, but above all, to you."

"Come, sister," he said. "We have a long way to travel."

Following the map, they were soon in more of the lightly forested area, this time with no cleared fields or even signs of human life. The paths they followed were single wagon tracks at their best, and sometimes only horse trails, which they would have been unable to find, much less follow, if the map had not been detailed and full of notes on what to look for. These notes, we should say, were in Cerwin's tiny, square, neat handwriting, and each time she looked at the map, the sight of this well-known hand was a fresh wound to Livosha.

There were no inns along the way, and they did not wish to beg for ac-commodations from someone who might be questioned, and so they slept out of doors, which would have been worse except that they discovered that Riffetra had included in the saddlebags blankets and a cunning tent that could collapse into a wonderfully small bundle, and yet, when set up, be more than large enough to shelter them both.

They made fire from dead wood gathered in the forests, and, at Livo-sha's suggestion, took turns practicing the spells that dispersed the smoke so that no sign of their presence would be visible. They continued all that day, stopping only to rest their horses. That night they slept fitfully, afraid they would be caught. The next night was little better, and when Livosha went into a hamlet (unnamed, but clearly marked on the map) to buy fod-der for the horses, who had been set off with only enough fodder for two days, she was trembling the entire time. By the fourth day, they began to feel more relaxed, though they still often looked behind them. We should observe that it was taking them days to travel a distance that, were it in a straight line, was little more than what had taken Eremit only hours—let this be a reminder to those who pretend that the roads and post services of the Empire are of but little worth!

And it was then, on the fifth day of the journey, when they at last felt safe, that Livosha gave her brother the letter to read, and that one night, together, they at last gave in to their grief, spending the night in each other's arms and letting the tears flow freely. While this happened, making it the duty of the historian to report it, it is not our intention to dwell on it beyond the mere statement that it occurred; if we cannot exercise our right as the relater of incidents to, from time to time, draw a veil of decency over the heartbreak of those we are following, then, although we may still deserve to be called an historian, it is questionable if we deserve to be called human. The next day, exhausted as only a night of unquenchable grief can leave one, they continued their journey. After that, they spoke little while they rode, and even when they had stopped.

In all, the journey lasted eight days, at the end of which time—that is to say, in the middle of the morning of the eighth day—they arrived in the town of Aussiar.

Aussiar, located roughly half way between Wetrock and Candletown and nearly due north of Zerika's Point (by which we mean the geographical feature, not the city of that name which was south and west, nor the region itself, which is also referred to by that name), was in an area that had been settled later than most of those in the southwest, perhaps because of its distance from the sea—which is to say, it occupied a position with the Ocean-sea on three sides, but no closer than a hundred miles on any of them, and, though well supplied with streams, there was no river, and hence, no river traffic. And yet, during the Teckla Republic of the Sixth Cycle, an explorer of the House of the Tiassa named Wirev happened to be fishing in one of the streams and discovered a peculiar oyster which was not only quite palatable, but turned out to produce a freshwater pearl that can compete with and often surpass those from the sea in terms of lustre, surface quality, nacre quality, size, and especially color, with certain remarkably vibrant specimens found. This discovery—that is to say, the Wirev oyster—led, quite naturally, to the habitation of the region. When the agricultural qualities also became apparent (for the most part, the Duchy of Wirav produces excellent wheat and other corn, whereas most of the surrounding region tends to produce only grasses suitable for the pasturing of herd animals), it grew still more, along with highways connecting the main city of the region, Wirtown, with White Harbor (by which we mean, be it understood, the White Harbor in the southwest, not the one in the east or the one in the far north) on one side, and Zerika's Point (that is, the city) on the other.

The town of Aussiar was built not far from Wirton, where a small but significant surface iron deposit was found late in the Fourteenth Cycle. As it was the closest iron to anywhere within the Zerika's Point region, and as, moreover, it was on the White Harbor Pike, which meant that coal could easily be brought in from Candletown and its Grand Canal, it became a sort of hybrid city, to the right a mining town, to the left a center of smith-craft, and along with it, to some degree, a financial center, as a result of an influx of Orca who follow pearls the way a Dzurlord follows the sound of a brawl. At the time Livosha and Kefaan entered the city, it had grown to nearly forty thousands of people—the largest city they had ever seen by a considerable degree (if the reader wishes to compare, the capital city of Westward, where poor Eremit had been, held some eight thousands).

Livosha entered this metropolis with mixed feelings: while she was lost, confused, and certainly overwhelmed at the mass of people, as well as uncertain how to find a single moneylender in all of this, she also felt certain that, even if their enemies knew where they were, they could never find them in such a multitude.

As she stood there, lost, Kefaan said, "What is the name of the man we seek?"

"Gystralan," she said.

Kefaan nudged his horse up to the edge of the crowd moving along the widest street Livosha had ever seen and addressed a woman who was richly—or at least, cleanly—dressed for a Teckla, and said, "Where can I find Gystralan the moneylender?"

The woman stopped, made an obeisance, and said, "Imperial Street, my lord, on the east side, between the locksmith and the weaver."

He turned to Livosha and said, "Give her a coin."

"My lord!" said the woman. "I am not a beggar!"

"My apologies, good woman. I did not mean to give offense."

"No," said Livosha. "We only wished to give you this so you can drink our health." And she reached down, holding a silver orb.

The Teckla smiled, accepted the coin, and bowed. "Then that I will do, and the blessing of Barlen go with you on this day." She began to walk away, stopped, and turned around frowning and considering them. Then she said, "Imperial Street is this way, the direction I am walking, in a quarter of a mile. Turn there to the left." Then she bowed again and continued on her way.

"Well done, my brother," said Livosha.

Kefaan turned the head of his horse in the direction the woman had indicated and said, "Come, then."

They noticed that, of the other horses on the street, all of them were being led by dismounted riders, save a few old and tired nags that were pulling carts, and so they, too, dismounted and led their horses, in order to avoid standing out, both for reasons of safety, that is, because to stand out is necessarily to attract attention, which is undesirable for those being hunted, and in addition, out of respect for the customs of strangers, which is, or at any rate ought to be, instinctive in all persons of breeding.

So effective were they in this effort that no one appeared to so much as notice their appearance, which brought them, in due course, to the very street for which they had been searching, which street, if unmarked, was at least easily identified by the description which they had been given by the Teckla woman whose conversation, the reader may recall, we have just had the honor to describe, and who then, we may speculate, drank their health as promised and then went about her own business and continued a life which has not, alas, come down to us in detail, as it is so often the case, both in history and in our own lives, that individuals who have a greater or lesser effect on the course of our future may enter and leave with only an instant's worth of intercourse with us, which may lead us to believe (or, at any rate, to *act as if*, which is much the same in the result) that these people have no lives of their own, but are merely adjuncts to ours, an opinion or attitude that appears, we say with regret, to be more common as one climbs higher on what has been called *the social scale* (an idiom we make use of for the simple reason that we do not have a better one available), with the result that no small amount of sorrow and even misery can be attributed to nothing more than this simple perspective, although we must admit in all fairness that the reverse—that is to say, when those in the upper reaches of society display civility, decency, and an awareness of the humanity of others—they are deserving of praise in no small measure because their position in the community by its very nature runs counter to such a temperament, which praise, we hasten to affirm, is not required in the case of the historian, who is, after all, merely doing his duty by pointing out how easily such individuals as the Teckla woman are forgotten, and, moreover, attempting in some measure to remedy the defect by bringing this circumstance to the reader's attention.

Upon turning onto Imperial Street, they were able to identify, in short order, a sign with a lock and key on it in front of a small but permanent structure opening directly onto the street. Uncertain if this was the correct locksmith—for they had no notion, in a city this size, how many locksmiths there might be—they looked around for the weaver. It took them some few moments, because they had thought that, like the locksmith, they were looking for a permanent structure, but then Livosha pointed out a middle-aged Chreotha who sat with a small loom in one hand, a sort of long needle in the other, and three baskets placed about him. Near him, seated against a wall, were two girls and a boy, all of them Teckla, and all of them seemingly engaged in nothing at all except, as the saying is, "testing the perpendicularity of the building." Next to them was a door that opened into the same building that held the locksmith. Livosha at once opened the door to find a long, rickety-seeming wooden stairway leading up.

"Do you watch the horses," she said, to which her brother responded with a nod. Turning to the doorway, then, Livosha overcame her reluctance to set foot on the flimsy flight by pointing out to herself that it had, no doubt, been used many, many times, and the chances that it would pick this moment to collapse could not be so very great. She walked up slowly, but without any obvious hesitation, though the sinking of the steps and the squeaking sounds they made were not reassuring. Nevertheless, she reached the top in perfect health and found a door and clapped. Someone on the other side called for her to enter, and she did so, finding herself in a neat, two-room apartment, facing a young man, a Tsalmoth with a long, pleasant face, a friendly smile, and eyes that seemed to be permanently bloodshot, no doubt from time spent over tablets and papers.

Livosha bowed to this gentleman and said, "You are Gystralan?"

His eyes widened and he said, "I? Oh, not the least in the world, I assure you."

"How, you are not? And yet I was told I could find him here."

"As to that, well, you were not misinformed."

"So then, he is here?"

"Indeed. And the proof is, he is in the room behind me."

"Well, and you?"

"Oh, I am merely his clerk. I am called Emeris."

At this point, the historian must apologize to the reader for introducing the possibility of confusion between such two similar names as "Emeris" and "Eremit." We have done so because that is how the names have come down to us, and we do not feel it is our place to change them. But we assure the reader that not only will these two persons never meet, but they will never be near enough to each other for there to be any confusion. Had history worked out in such a way that this was not the case, we freely confess that we are uncertain how we might have avoided the circumstances, save by arbitrarily changing "Emeris" to something entirely different, such as "Manicamp," or perhaps "Malicorne," a decision we would be loath to make.

"In that case, Emeris," continued Livosha, "what must I do in order to have conversation with the worthy Gystralan?"

"As to that," he said, "it is the simplest matter in the world. First, I will go back and inform him that someone wishes to see him on a matter of business—apropos, it is a matter of business, is it not?"

"Entirely, I give you my word."

"So much the better. Then, after I have completed this task, he will, no doubt, tell me to send you into his office, after which you will be able to speak freely with him. He will, however, insist upon knowing a name; therefore, what name shall I give him?"

"Livosha, daughter of Cerwin," she said.

The clerk appeared to react to this name, as if he had not only heard it before, but heard it in some connection that he found disturbing. However, before Livosha could make up her mind about whether to ask Emeris about the peculiar expression she had witnessed upon his countenance, he had risen and bowed, after which he went back to the rear office and clapped outside of the door. There followed a conversation which Livosha was unable to hear, after which Emeris, his face now utterly devoid of expression, returned and said simply, "He will see you."

Livosha went into the back office, and Gystralan, an Iorich distinguished by broad shoulders, long arms, and a somber countenance, motioned her to a chair.

"Livosha, daughter of Cerwin," he said. "You are, no doubt, here to close out the account with which your kind mother and good father entrusted me?"

"You have understood my purpose exactly," she said.

"Then you will be pleased to know that there will be no difficulty in procuring what you are owed, and, moreover, the legal papers and documents I have been requested to surrender to you."

"That, my lord, is what I had hoped you would say to the very word. But how is this to work?"

"In the simplest way. I will go to that window and whistle, at which time a young Teckla will look up and will receive from me a message that I will write and then throw down to him, which will inform the individual who holds my funds to send over the exact amount needed to the very copper. This will arrive under a guard of two Dragonlords whom I have especially hired for this purpose. Then I will put the money into your hand in exchange for your signature on a receipt. At the same time as I hand you the money, I will sign over to you the various titles and documents, placing them in a pouch which I will also supply, and which is treated to be safe from the weather. Our business then being completed, you will be free to leave, except that, as a courtesy, you may, if you choose, accept my offer to have the two Dragonlords whom I have already mentioned escort you to anywhere you wish within the city, up to the very edge in any direction. Come, what do you think of this plan?"

"It seems to me to be a good one, only—"

"Yes?"

"How long will it take?"

"Well, I must write out the message, which must then be delivered. Moreover, the money must be counted and recounted so that there is no possibility of a mistake. The amount I am to deliver to you is such that it will require an hour for the counting. Then, with the return, I would say it will total—"

"Yes?"

"In not more than two hours from this moment you will have the money and the documents in your hands and be on your way. Apropos, the money will arrive in small sacks, suitable for hanging from the saddle of a horse, or from your shoulders, or on your back, as you wish. Have you someone to assist you?"

"Yes, my brother is with the horses on the street outside."

"That is good, for the money, I warn you, will be something of a burden."

"So much the better, for it will need to supply us with all we need for some time."

"Then, is my plan acceptable?"

"Entirely, good sir. May I wait here?"

"Not only may you, but I would encourage you to do so. You may wait in the outer office, and, if you wish, you may instruct Emeris to bring you and your brother some iced wine, so refreshing on such a warm day."

"Then I can ask for nothing else."

"You see, I am now writing the note. It is quickly done, and now I seal it, and wrap it around this weight with these three coppers as payment for the delivery—which, I am forced to say, will be deducted from your total—and bind them tightly. I go to the window and call—" at which point he cried out, "*Errand!*" loudly enough to be heard on the street, after which he continued—"you see, I drop the note to one of the waiting Teckla, who knows where to deliver it. There it is done!"

"I am grateful to you for your kindness and efficiency, and I will now retire to the other room and wait."

"And you will be right to do so," he said. "While you are waiting, I will prepare the documents and titles and call you when they are ready for you to sign. Emeris can be our witness, a task which he has completed on numerous occasions to my perfect satisfaction. Or if you wish, he will remain with your horses while your brother is the witness. At all events, I will call to you when it is time."

He accompanied her to the door of his office and closed it behind her. Livosha, for her part, seeing a pair of chairs against the wall, was about to sit in one when Emeris, his eyes wide and his face pale, said softly, "Hsst! You must leave! My master means to betray you!"

It is impossible to describe the effect these words had on Livosha. She turned and stared at him, her knees seemed weak, and she felt herself trembling. She walked over to his desk on feet that had instantly become numb, and whispered, "What is it you tell me?"

"My master," he whispered back, "wishes to keep the money entrusted to him, and, moreover, to collect a reward that is offered for you and your brother."

"But, how do you know of this?"

"I heard him discussing it with a certain young Orca named Yanis, son of Berwick, and—"

"Son of Berwick!" she said, only barely managing to continue whispering.

He nodded. "And moreover," he continued, "there was a note from Count Dorin asking my master to cooperate with Berwick in all matters."

"Shards! May I see this note?"

"Here it is. You may keep it. But hurry! They are coming for you now. The plan is to promise you the money and then send for certain forces he has hired to take you. You must leave at once."

Livosha was now trembling from head to foot. She tucked the note into her pouch and said, "But where can I go? I have no money, no one to turn to, no way to live."

Emeris was silent for a moment, then he said, "Go to White Harbor and from there take a ship to Candletown. I will give you a letter, which you will deliver to Ficora, a kinswoman of mine who is looking for a lady's maid. Could you accept such a position?"

Livosha didn't hesitate. "I must protect my little brother and live while I bide my time and seek a means to avenge myself. I can accept any position that will permit me to do so."

"Then here, I am writing. Let me sand it and roll it up, and I will use this, my own seal, so that she will know it is from me. I warn you, she is not a kind woman, being highborn within our House and used to having everything her own way."

"I will live," said Livosha simply.

"Have you money for passage? I have—"

"I have nine good imperials and a few orbs, and upon reaching White Harbor, we can sell our horses."

"That will be sufficient, then."

"I owe you a debt, sir."

"Not in the least."

"Yes, I insist upon it. And if ever I am able, I will repay you."

"You must go. They are coming for you now."

Livosha accepted the note and put it into her pouch and then realized that she was no longer shaking, her feet were no longer numb, and she felt strong and relaxed.

"I leave at once," she said, not whispering, but speaking in a low voice. "But I give you my word, should it happen that they find me before I have made my escape, well"—she touched the sword hanging over her shoulder—"some of them will never spend the money my capture has earned them."

With this, she sketched him a bow and went back down the stairs.

Her brother was there, still patiently holding on to the reins of the horses. He saw the expression upon her countenance and said, "We are betrayed."

She nodded.

"Shall we mount?"

Livosha considered for a moment. "No. It will attract attention and thus make us easier to find. We will walk our horses at a good pace, but we must not seem in a hurry."

"Very well, to this plan I agree. Only—"

"Yes?"

"Where are we going?"

"East," said Livosha. "We are going east."

Chapter the Sixth

In Which Eremit Learns of the Prison,
That Is to Say, the Jail on Burning Island

T he doorway led into a short hallway with a low, arched ceiling of brick and mortar, which ended in a long, long, stairway that curved down. To his right was nothing except a sheer drop, a pit, as it were, so wide Eremit couldn't see to the other side, although this may have been in part because of the lighting, of which there was little, save a few oil lamps hanging on the wall.

After a long way, he passed, on his left, a barred cell, but he was moving too quickly to have time to observe more than a figure lying prone on a sort of cot. After that, there were more cells, every fifteen or twenty steps, until at last the long stairway ended. From there, he was led down a corridor ending in a barred door with a guard seated next to it. On seeing them, the guard rose, unlocked the door, and let them through. Just past it, the hallway split into three, and they took the center path to yet another door with another guard. This pattern continued, until at length they came to a door behind which was an office with a desk, and behind the desk was a middle-aged Iorich, appearing well fed, with round cheeks like a Teckla's. He politely stood as Eremit entered.

"Welcome," he said with a smile that attempted to be friendly, "to the jail on Burning Island. I am the director, and you may address me as such. The Teckla call me Lord Director, but as for you, you may omit the 'Lord,' as it merely introduces ranking and hierarchy where none is needed, don't you agree? This will be your home for some period of time. You will soon learn the routine, and if you have questions, you may ask any of the jailers. You are number eighty-one, and that is how you will be known here for as long as you remain with us. If you have money, you may give it to me, and it will be used to secure more pleasing food for you. We have a full kitchen here and are able to procure certain delicacies. So long as your money holds out, you will receive the elevated meals, but it must be said, in all fairness, that even the meals served the commoners are of exceptional quality. So much so that I have on occasion eaten part of one myself, not only with no ill effects, but, on the contrary, even with a certain pleasure.

"As you are, it seems, the only son of"—here he glanced at a paper that was on his desk—"a baroness, you will have certain privileges, including a larger and more comfortable room, more candles, more paper, and a larger bed. You perceive, we find our guests are more contented if we use the words 'guest' and 'room' instead of 'prisoner' and 'cell,' for I have found that the happiness of our home—and understand that this is now your home—is improved by the happiness of all who live here. Of course, violating the rules of our home here will cause these privileges to be limited, suspended, or revoked, as, indeed, any good father will act in order to better instruct his children and maintain order in his house. Moreover, my dear number eighty-one, you needn't give any thought to escape, as worries the minds of those in less happy institutions than our own, for the simple reason that escape is impossible. In the first place, there is the phoenix stone, built into the walls from which our home is constructed, that makes sorcery impossible; you will notice when you approach your room that you will have no connection to the Orb. In the second place, we are located in the middle of the Ocean-sea, and no boats or ships are kept here at any time. And third, the entire island is an active volcano, which, through certain sorceries, we have arranged to be in a constant state of eruption, so that there is only one safe path out, and that one, of course, is easily guarded, as there are, by the very definition of 'only one,' no others.

"I pride myself on being an enlightened man, and it is my fondest hope that the benefits of this enlightenment work their way down to the meanest, lowest of my guests. For example, in the old days, it was the custom to separate men and women in such places, although why this was done has never been clear. But here we are all one family, and while any physical, written, or verbal contact is, naturally, forbidden, still you will see other guests on a regular basis, and making our home a true reflection of the rest of the world in all particulars has, we have found, had a beneficial effect on everyone's disposition.

"You will, no doubt, wish to know of the amenities and comforts we provide. Although no letters or other forms of communication with the outside world are permitted, nevertheless, we permit, and even encourage, our guests to write down their thoughts, as we find this helps ease their minds. To this end, you will be supplied with pen and ink and paper, and even given candles. Of course, all such writing will be turned over to us, which is done for your benefit, as it permits us to see any thoughts which might indicate our guests wish to do themselves injury, and this permits us to intervene in a timely fashion, for, you perceive, the safety and the health of our guests is our highest concern. Apropos, we retain a physicker who will see to any medical needs that may come up while we have the honor of your company.

"Moreover, we take pride in saying that, unlike any other similar institution—although, in truth, we believe there *are* no similar institutions— we not only permit our guests to walk freely about for an hour every other day, but even, as part of your privileges, every day, seeing and smiling to other guests, thus building, we believe, an agreeable sense of community among our guests and our staff. It is our contention that this intercourse promotes both health and happiness, and, with all modesty, it has seemed to me to have been fully successful in this matter.

"Beyond that, we have taken it upon ourselves to supply you with clean, fresh linen and blankets, as well as changes of clothing, four times a year, at which time you will also be permitted a bath, in your case, in hot water. You perceive how important your happiness is to us.

"I hope this will set your mind at rest so that you are the better able to enjoy the time you spend here. Therefore, unless you have any questions for me, you will now be escorted to your room."

Eremit, after this remarkable speech, was nearly unable to formulate any of the questions that were pressing on his attention. To cover his confusion, he bowed politely and said, "Thank you for your explanations, Director. I do, in fact, have questions, if you would condescend to answer them."

"Of course," he said. "That, after all, is why I am here."

"Well, then, my first question is this: If this is a prison, how is it that I have come to be here when I have never had a trial? And, if it is not, well, then, when is my trial to take place?"

"Ah, you wish to know that?"

"Certainly, Director. And the proof is, I have asked."

"That is undeniable," admitted the director. "I will, therefore, answer as well as I can."

"That is exactly what I was hoping you would say."

"This is not a prison, it is a jail, which distinction you, as an Iorich, understand perfectly well. That is, it is not a place of punishment for those who have committed crimes, but, rather, a place of holding those who are waiting for trial or judgment."

"Well, but, my trial?"

"Ah, as to that, I cannot say."

"You do not know when my trial might come up?"

"That information, you perceive, has not been given to me."

"Ah, well, I am not familiar with this institution, having never heard of it before, so I thought perhaps there was a custom, that is a usual time between when a prisoner—"

"Guest."

"—guest arrives, and the trial. That is to say, in general, how long are guests detained here?"

"That I cannot tell you."

"You cannot tell me? That is to say, this information is forbidden?"

"Oh, not the least in the world."

"But then—"

"I cannot say, dear sir, because I do not know."

"You do not know?"

"I give you my word, I am entirely uninformed regarding this."

"But, if you are in charge, how is it you do not know?"

"Why, because since I have been here, there is no one who has been called up for trial."

"What, no one?"

"Not as of yet."

"But, how long have you been director here?"

"Oh, not long. Only a hundred or a hundred and ten years."

"A hundred years!"

"Yes. Before that, I was merely one of the guards, but then you perceive, I was promoted."

"But, how long were you a guard here?"

"Nine hundred years."

"So then, you have been here more than a thousand years?"

"I have. I think of it as my home."

"And in all of that time—"

"Yes, in all of that time?"

"In all of that time, no one has been released for trial?"

"No, but, you perceive, it could happen."

Eremit felt his head become light. He said, "And the prisoners—that is to say, the guests—how long have they been here?"

"Ah, as to that, there is number thirty-five, who has been here for nearly three thousand years. I believe he is the oldest."

"So, then, no one has ever been released that you know of?"

"Not for trial, nor for any other reason, except—"

"Yes, except?"

"Our guests are invariably released when they die."

The implications of these statistics sank in so hard that Eremit was unable to find words and merely stood, speechless, until the two jailers came to escort him to a cell—which we will refer to it as, in spite of the preference of the "director," as he is pleased to call himself. We do this because, as an historian, we find it our duty, above all else, to name things by their right names, whereas the director, of course, being in some measure a statesman, must use terms that will better advance his interests. It is for this reason, that is to say, precision, rather than any sort of judgment upon the individual who uses words to conceal rather than reveal, that we have elected to use the terms we do. This being understood, we will say that Eremit was brought to a cell entirely unaware of how he'd gotten there, at which time his fetters and manacles were removed using the key that had been turned over by the Kinsmen, and the door was shut, after which came the sound of the bolt being shot.

Though still too stunned to give it conscious thought, he was nevertheless aware, as the director had said, that the instant he had crossed the threshold of the cell he lost his connection to the Orb, to the Emperor, to the Empire. It is hard for the reader, who no doubt was born with the connection, as we all are, and has had it for his entire life, and, we suspect, has never given it a thought, to understand what it means to lose it. The shock of sudden isolation, of loneliness, is all the greater because its presence, its distant comfort and reassurance of the existence of a wider world, and a world, moreover, that is regulated by the power, knowledge, and compassion with which we are all familiar, has never been questioned, or even been present in one's awareness.

The state of Eremit's mind was, however, so disturbed, that this fresh wound, this new burden, merely added to what we can only call his trauma. Indeed, it may be the case that his, if we may so call it, spiritual concussion actually shielded him from the full effects. Though he felt a sudden weakening of his knees, he recovered long enough to take himself to the cot and stretch out, turning his face to the wall, and he remained that way for several hours—awake, perhaps, yet not fully conscious.

After some considerable time, he stirred, sat up, and for the first time, looked around his cell. The walls were of granite mixed with a mortar that seemed especially hard. The door was wood bound in iron and contained a single window with bars placed so that a hand could barely fit through it. He stood up and measured the cell, which proved to be seven paces by four, which he was able to determine by the simple expedient of testing it, having found, as have so many others, that practical experimentation is the best method for determining facts. His furnishings included a cot, a washbasin, a slops bucket, four candles with sulfurs, and a writing table and chair on which sat a water pitcher and a small cup. There was no window. He pressed himself against the door and looked. The cells had been cleverly put into an arrangement whereby they were staggered, so that it was impossible to see the face of anyone else.

Upon reaching this conclusion, he sat down at the writing desk, observing that it contained drawers, which he quite naturally opened. One contained all that was needed for writing except the paper—that is to say, it contained a quill of moderate quality, though nothing with which to sharpen it, along with ink and a box of sand. The other drawer, naturally enough, contained paper of a quality that, as Eremit was able to determine instantly, was far from the best, yet sufficient to take ink without the need of finishing. There were, in all, some twenty sheets of paper. Having no interest in writing—especially, we may add, writing that would be read by guards—and no skill in drawing, Eremit closed the drawer with a shrug.

He returned to his cot, lying on his back staring at the featureless ceiling for some time, until he heard the door opening. Though he was only scarcely interested, he did turn his head to look. Two jailers and another, no doubt a servant, or perhaps an inmate given special privileges in exchange for his labor, were standing there, the servant holding a tray. He set it on the writing table, which, it would seem, also functioned as a dining table, and said, "Here is your meal, eighty-one." After this, without ceremony, the jailers closed the door, locking it behind them.

Eremit continued to lie on the cot for some time. He was aware that he was hungry, yet also that this did not seem to be a matter of concern. *No doubt,* he told himself, *sooner or later my hunger will be great enough to give me reason to move. I doubt that, whatever my fate is, it will be to starve to death with food an arm's length away. I will eat. But not just now.*

An hour later the door opened again, and the same two guards and servant appeared. The servant removed his tray of uneaten food, glanced at the chamber pot, and left. Before closing the door, one of the jailers said, "Two hours until all candles must be out," and left. Sometime later, the hallway light—such as it was—was extinguished. At this, Eremit shrugged, got to his feet, and blew out the single candle that was burning. The cell was at once plunged into darkness so absolute he had to feel his way to the bed. He lay on his back for some time, drifting gradually to sleep.

What woke him was the delivery of another meal—breakfast, he assumed, as he could smell coffee on the tray, and, moreover, as he was informed he could now light the candles. He wished to continue lying where he was, but he realized that, once the door had closed, it would be hard to find the sulfurs, and so if he were to have light, now would be the time to act. Therefore, though with no great will, he rose and lit two of his four candles. He then drank some of the coffee, which proved to be strong and bitter, yet he could feel the effect on his spirits almost at once as he developed a half-hearted, or, if the reader prefers, *lukewarm* interest in the food before him, which he then set out to investigate.

The tray was of thin wood from the neeora tree, useful for certain sorts of crafts because of how easily the layers separated by the rings, how pliable it was, and how well it took a polish. It was, however, neither strong nor heavy, and it would tend to fall into pieces before it splintered. In short: it was a difficult wood to make a weapon out of, but useful for creating inexpensive disposable objects of various sorts. On the tray was a single utensil, a spoon, also crafted from the same wood, and obviously pressed into shape rather than carved. Beneath the spoon was what could charitably be called a "napkin"—that is, a piece of paper, rather than cloth, and one, moreover, that was treated in such a way as to fall apart upon the least contact with ink, or, indeed, with any liquid whatsoever. Should any writing take place, Eremit realized, it would only take place on the prescribed paper, which was no doubt counted carefully by the jailers.

The food itself was simple enough: there was a small piece of beef, one of the cheaper cuts, that the cook had managed to stop short of burning, though Eremit wondered how he was expected to eat it with a spoon and no knife. In addition there was a legume pudding (thus proving that this was, indeed, breakfast, as certain culinary traditions that we know in our own day date from far, far in the past), fresh carrots, and a stunted-looking pear. Eremit ate a bite of the pudding and found it palatable. He had another, then pushed the tray away. He remained there at the desk until they cleared away the tray. An hour later, a servant came and brought him new clothing and asked for his. Eremit complied, and was soon dressed all in garments of thin, white cotton, except that he was permitted to keep his boots. "I am directed," said the servant, "to inform you that your clothing will be cleaned and will be returned to you when you are called for trial."

Eremit studied the face of man who said this, clearly an old Teckla, but could find no trace of irony in his countenance. Eremit then shrugged and let the old man go on his way.

He remained in the chair, staring at the wall in front of him, for another hour, until the door was opened once more. This time, the jailers informed him that he was to exercise with the other "guests," as they were called. Without a word, Eremit rose and went into the corridor, where he learned the exercise consisted of nothing more than walking back and forth along the corridor along with some twenty or twenty-five other prisoners, all wearing white. He did as instructed, not so much as looking at any of the others, although he was somewhat aware that a few of them were looking at him, no doubt because his was a new face.

There were only two things of interest during this time. The first was that, at one point, a jailer called out loudly, "Number ninety-two! No talking to other guests!" to which Eremit's only thought was, *I wonder how many prisoners there are?* The second was Eremit's observation that the jailers took this time to methodically visit each cell, no doubt to look for contraband and count up the amount of paper that had been used.

At the expiration of an hour, a whistle blew, and they all returned to their cells.

Some time later came what Eremit assumed was the noon meal: fruits and vegetables and a small glass of watered wine, brightened by the addition of sourdough bread; Eremit was certain this bread was the "extra" his money had purchased him. By now he was aware of being hungry, though he still had no appetite, but he forced himself to eat at least some of it. He refused to think about, to consider, what had befallen him, but his mind wouldn't stay away from it, like a swimmer caught in an undertow—the more he tried not to think about it, the more it seemed to pull him in. Yet when he did think about it, it felt as if he were drowning.

It seemed to him, on reflection, that the period of walking had been better than sitting still, and so he rose and began pacing. He continued this for nearly an hour before lying down on the cot once more. There were two more meals that day; he ate little of either one.

The next day he was given new candles to replace the ones that had burned down, and he thought to try to make conversation with the jailers. "Sir," he began.

"Yes?" said one of them, proving that, at least, they were not forbidden to speak to the prisoners.

"I have a question about the rules."

"Ah, well, it is good that you concern yourself with the rules, for, you perceive, you are then less likely to break them by mistake, which would make life less pleasant for all of us. So then, ask your question, and if I can answer it, I will, and if I cannot, I will find someone who can."

"Come, you are most complaisant."

"Well, we are under orders to see to our guests' happiness as well as we can."

"So much the better."

"As to your question?"

"It is this: are we permitted visitors?"

The two jailers looked at each other, and the one who had not spoken before said, after clearing his throat in a sort of long, low rumble, "That is a difficult question to answer, young man."

"How, difficult?"

"Well, you perceive, there are rules, and then there are circumstances."

"Sir, I confess freely that I do not understand the answer you have done me the honor to give."

"Then I will try to explain."

"I would be grateful if you did."

"There are no *rules* to prevent it."

"Well, I am glad of that. And yet, you place a peculiar emphasis on the word *rules*."

"Ah, you noticed that?"

"Nearly."

"And how did you interpret it?"

"It sounds as if—"

"Yes?"

"That, while there are no rules to prevent it, other things might."

"That is good. You have grasped my meaning entirely."

"I am happy to have done so. Only—"

"Yes?"

"What are these circumstances?"

"Ah, you wish to know that?"

"I have been wishing for nothing else for an hour!"

"Then I shall tell you. First, there is the mist."

"The mist?"

"Why, yes. Surely you noticed it when you arrived?"

"Ah, ah. Yes, there was fog."

"Yes. That is the result of the hot steam produced by the volcano, and of the ash striking the cold water. There is nearly always a blanket of mist surrounding the island, such that it is nearly impossible to approach."

"Well, I understand that. What else?"

"Second, it is dangerous, because of the hot ash itself. Indeed, there is a sorcerer here who is trained to control these things, otherwise no boat would ever land with supplies, and soon we should all become tolerably hungry. Ha ha ha!"

Eremit did not find this as amusing as did the jailer, but he only said, "I understand, then."

"And third," said the jailer.

"There is a third reason?"

"Why yes, the most important of all."

"If it is the most important of all, then I want to hear of it."

"And you shall, for I am about to tell you."

"You perceive I am listening."

"The third reason is, no one knows you are here. Now, young man, you must excuse us, as we have other calls to make." The jailers shut and locked the door, leaving Eremit sitting on his cot, staring straight ahead, unable to speak, and, in fact, nearly unable to breathe.

This last blow, which crushed the final hope out of Eremit's spirit as a blow to the stomach will drive out all of one's breath, left him in a state that can only be called utter despair. He fell into the routine of the jail easily, and naturally, and without concern—eating, sleeping, exercising—as he was expected to, all of it, however, in what might be considered a daze, as if his existence were merely a dream from which it would be possible to wake up. One day, while walking the halls with the other prisoners, one of them overtook him, and, while passing, whispered in the special way prisoners have of speaking without appearing to do so, "I am Fezor. What is your name?"

"Eighty-one," said Eremit, and continued walking.

Chapter the Seventh

In Which We Meet Several Unsavory or Unpleasant Persons

At this time, the author must, though not without regret, turn the reader's consideration to several persons who are, in one way or another, less agreeable than those whose actions have, hitherto, absorbed our attention. For this action we must plead strict necessity and deliver with it the assurance that we would not subject the reader to such unpleasantness if it could be avoided. We hope, however, that by now the reader knows us well enough to feel a certain confidence that such a sojourn will be made as brief as can be contrived while remaining consistent with the task we have set ourselves.

This circumstance, we might add, is not unusual in the study of history. The natural motion of historical events in all of their complexity must inevitably bring us face-to-face, as it were, with the cruel, the nefarious, the depraved elements of humanity. The fact that, without such individuals, the kind, the honorable, the decent would have no opportunity to display these characteristics does not, alas, make any more pleasant the necessity to explore such moral degradation.

And yet we must insist that such necessity is not justification for, as some of our brother historians favor, immersion in such abasement, indeed to the point where they appear to actually *wallow* (if we may be permitted the word) in all of the worst aspects of humanity, taking a sort of grim, and, we insist, unhealthy pleasure in bathing themselves and the reader in such aberrant corruption. We make no apologies for expressing our strong opinion on this subject. The reader, indeed, is invited and even expected to draw from this the conclusion of how important it is. The existence of evil must be acknowledged and even understood if one is to comprehend the development of history, and, still more, to recognize and value the good, but we maintain that it is possible to understand the most loathsome examples of human behavior in such a way as to not glorify them, an opinion, alas, not shared by some who take up the pen and foist their vision upon an unsuspecting public. We must state, in fact, by way of confirmation, that even certain historians with whom we most vehemently disagree on nearly every aspect of how to approach historical studies, and what conclusions may be drawn, and how to approach the selection of facts, are firmly in concert with us on this vital matter.

With this clearly understood, we trust the reader will permit us to move forward to the details of those individuals whose activity our history now absolutely requires we depict.

First, it is our duty to bring the reader to a new location, that being Adrilankha. The reader must keep in mind that this is not the Adrilankha of our own happy day—that is to say, the capital city of the Empire—but, rather, a simple port city, a center of commerce and trade and even some degree of manufacturing. Situated at the mouth of the Adrilankha River, built on and around the hills and cliffs overlooking the Ocean-sea as well as the harbor level itself, it grew up in a region where the mix of farmland, jungle, and pasture permitted some degree of self-sufficiency, which, when combined with the rich produce from the north sent down the river, and the bountiful fish and seafood available both in the Shallow Sea to the east and the Ocean-sea itself, it is no wonder that it had grown into a considerable metropolis, rivaling Dragaera City herself in most ways, excepting the arts and sciences, in which Adrilankha was poorly supplied until later years.

We have come here to make the acquaintance of someone who has hitherto not been mentioned in our history, in spite of having a vital part in it, that being an Iorich with the uneuphonious name of Traanzo. This name, we should make clear, was not his name as it had been given to him at birth (that was Ciadric, which name was never used); rather he was always and exclusively addressed by the name of his duchy—or, to be more precise, he was so referred to after the events we are about to describe, wherefore, to avoid needless proliferation of names, we will begin by using that name at once. Traanzo, then, was a man of some twelve or thirteen hundred years of age, with a keen eye, a sharp noble's point, and a lineage within his House that included some number of High Justicers going back as far as the Eighth Cycle.

Of his ducal palace we have nothing to say, as it was far away and, indeed, he had never seen it, it being run by his seneschal while his steward saw to the estate, merely sending him money on a regular basis. Instead, Traanzo lived in what had been his summer home, what he described as, "a small property" in a hilly area of Adrilankha somewhat to the west of what would become the imperial palace, and somewhat south, though not quite in sight of the Ocean-sea. It was a mixed area, most of the houses showing signs of wealth, some extreme wealth, and yet in places they were crowded together more than the estates of the wealthy usually are. Traanzo's house had a more significant estate than many, surrounded by a tall iron fence.

At the time in which we are choosing to look in on Traanzo, while Kefaan and Livosha flee Aussiar and Eremit settles into life in jail, he—that is to say, Traanzo—has just received word that his father is asking for him. He at once stood up from where he was consulting with his Master of the Hunt about plans for a hunting party in the forest to the northwest, and climbed the stairs to his father's bedchamber, where this personage, wasted, frail-looking, with hollow eyes and bony fingers, lay upon the bed, surrounded by his physicker and his secretary. The physicker caught the younger man's eye, and, with a gentle shake of the head, indicated that he had done all that was in his power, and the time was at hand.

The old man, his voice pale, if we can be permitted such an expression, by which we mean lacking in color and vibrancy, said, "My son, it is my time."

"I am sorry to hear that, father."

"Well, but there are things I must say to you before I move on to my next life."

"I am listening."

The dying man gestured for the others to leave the room, which they did after bowing respectfully. Then he said, "Lean closer, my son. That is right. Soon, to-day, you will have the Traanzo name. Alas, my ambition was not fulfilled, but I flatter myself that I brought us closer."

"Closer, father?"

"There have been secret negotiations, and I believe that all is in place for you to become the Iorich Heir. I die happy knowing that you will be Prince Traanzo. You will accept?"

"Of course, father!"

"Good. There are a few matters to which you must attend. In my secretary is a secret drawer." Here we must interrupt to make it clear that this usage of "secretary" referred to a sort of desk, not the individual who had just left the room and whose drawers, secret or otherwise, form no part of this history.

"Very well, father. A secret drawer."

"It is opened by pulling a catch inside the top of the lowest drawer on the left."

"I understand."

"Within it are various papers detailing a place called the Burning Island."

"But what is this place?"

"It is a jail, my son. A secret jail, where we, and where our friends, place those who inconvenience us."

"My father, there is a secret jail? People are held there without trial, merely for being inconvenient to us or our friends?"

"You have understood exactly. Does this shock you?"

"Why yes, I confess that it does. Why not kill them?"

"Oh, you ask that?"

"I do."

"You have studied to be a justicer."

"And if I have?"

"Do you recall the case, *The Empire's Challenge of Tikara*?"

"Ah, ah! Now I understand perfectly."

"So much the better. For from now on, you must take this responsibility. Upon it rests our hopes. If word were to get out, well, we—that is to say you—would be ruined."

"And do these papers contain all the information I need?"

"All of the names of those incarcerated, codes for those who requested they disappear, and of the location of the jail, the secret means of reaching it, the names of those in charge and the means of reaching them, for which you must use sorcery, and therefore, must learn the mind of the individual to be reached. For this purpose, when I am gone, you will summon him to you, and thus work with him until your mind can touch his."

"Then this paper must be protected at all costs and destroyed if necessary."

"You understand exactly. It was through this means that we have established the friendships that will, in short order, make you the Iorich Heir, and chief justicer, and chief advocate for the House. Once you have this position, you perceive, you will be under the protection of the House and of the Empire and no one may touch you."

"You have left me a great legacy, father. I will see that it is preserved."

"So much the better. Ah! Ah! There is pain in my chest! I am fading! Take my hand!"

"Here it is."

"I cannot feel anything. The light is going. Farewell, my son, it is all in your hands now!"

The old man gave a rattling last breath, and his eyes closed. Traanzo (who now, we should add, was the proper possessor of the name we have been giving him all along), let go of his father's hand and walked out.

Before going on we must, for the benefit of those of our readers who may not be legal scholars, explain the old man's words when he referred to *The Empire's Challenge of Tikara*. This was a prosecution for murder that had taken place during the most recent Chreotha reign, in which a spirit had been summoned to testify against the woman, that is to say, Tikara, who had been accused of murdering him. Such events—that is to say, the summoning of the dead for purposes of legal testimony—were, of course, an infrequent but not unheard-of event. What made this case of interest was the argument by Tikara's advocate, Lady Wyndra, that so much time had elapsed between the murder and the testimony, it being over a thousand years, that the memory of the spirit could no longer be relied upon. The dispute had gone up to the High Justicer who had, in the end, ruled in favor of Tikara, who was then released, a free woman, until she was killed in a duel with her alleged victim's grand-nephew a month later.

We hope the reader will understand why a mention of this matter was sufficient to explain why under certain circumstances, it might be better to keep particular individuals alive but out of the way rather than killing them. By "better," of course, we are speaking only in terms of practicality; the ethical and moral questions involved, though forming what Lord Yog-syp would refer to as the subtext of the discourse, does not enter into this discussion for the simple reason that neither the old man nor the younger one gave it a thought. The reader is invited to draw from this whatever conclusions seem appropriate.

Traanzo, then, upon emerging from the room, nodded to the physicker and the secretary and said, "He is gone."

"My condolences," said the secretary.

"My sympathies," said the physicker.

Traanzo shrugged, summoned his steward, and ordered him to make the funeral arrangements, and to see that his father's body was removed, and that the room be thoroughly cleaned, and that his own possessions be brought in by the nightfall.

It was some ten or fifteen years after the events that we have just had the honor to relate that Duke Traanzo at last became Prince Traanzo. It came in the form of a letter requiring his presence in the capital for the ceremony of his promotion. Though not, in fact, overly fond of ceremonies, this is one he proposed to enjoy.

Moreover, and we must say this to his credit, he had not forgotten the obligations he had made, and thus made a point of reassuring his supporters of his continued fidelity, displaying the virtues of memory and loyalty. We make this observation to stress the point, sometimes forgotten by our brother historians, and even more often forgotten by literary artists, that we are all of us complex beings made up of innumerable facets, some of which reflect the world around us in a way that may please the sensibilities of our fellows, and yet others that will displease our sense of justice and honor. That Traanzo had compromised the principles of his House in trading justice for position is not something we can, or, indeed, have any desire to deny. But to conclude from this that he personified unmitigated evil would be a travesty to historical truth, and, more, to the understanding of human character that must underlie historical truth.

To take as an example the career of Sourwood, one of the most barbaric of the Elde Island pirates (a group that, we are happy to say, vanished with the Interregnum, being unable to compete with those that sprang up from our own shores); one might justly lay all manner of crimes at his feet, and yet if one were to make even a cursory examination of him, one would find a deeply troubled man, and one with an agreeable romanticism about him, who would bring wreaths of flowers and jewels to Ewisha, his beloved, and who was known to engage in considerable exertions to rescue drowning sailors—those he had himself attacked, and those who had experienced other misfortunes. We bring this up not to excuse his undeniable crimes—we do not consider it our place to justify or condemn—but rather to point out the multiplicity of characteristics that define each of us. That a supposedly reputable historian could publish a work on Elde Island culture that includes passages about such a person that create such a false, indeed, impossible impression of his character is astonishing. And to find such poor craftsmanship—for historical disquisition is, after all, as much of a craft as masonry, sorcery, or wine-making—makes us question not only the qualifications of such an individual, but of those who approved his elevation to such a prestigious and responsible position. We will not, however, dwell on this matter longer than is strictly necessary to make what we consider an important observation, for fear that certain persons will consider such a criticism, not on its merits, but rather as a sort of petty and vindictive response to extraneous events. That the very accusation of pettiness can only prove the very pettiness of those who make it is, while nearly too obvious to require proof, nevertheless not a matter we are willing to take time from our history to demonstrate.

Traanzo, then, after sending various missives to his various confederates, prepared for the journey to Dragaera City, which, as it was completed without incident, culminated in a ceremony unmarred by anything untoward, and was followed by a safe return to Adrilankha, we need not spend any of the readers' valuable time discussing.

In Dorindom Castle, some weeks after the death of the elder Duke of Traanzo, His Benevolence Count Dorin received a message via the post. As it had the seal of His Highness Prince Traanzo, and as Dorin had been waiting for many months (or, in fact, years, if we include all of his correspondence with the old duke) for a response to a request he had made to the duke's son (that is to say, the one now known as Traanzo), he retired at once to his library for some privacy to open it. As this letter cannot fail to interest our reader, owing to its vital connection to the matters we are discussing, we do not hesitate to reproduce it in full:

Your Benevolence, *it read,* I thank you for your letter of the 9th inst. congratulating me on my new position. Though you are too delicate to mention it, I have no doubt it has occurred to your mind to wonder if this change will do anything to expedite the matter on which you corresponded, first with my late and revered father, and afterward with me. My news on this is better than it could be, although not as good as you might desire. While I now have the power, as Iorich Heir, to execute your request, nevertheless, the creation of a dukedom requires Imperial consent, and with the recent ascension of the House of the Phoenix, all Imperial matters remain in a state of confusion. So while I can promise to carry out your request, I fear it will not be as soon as you or I would wish. I hope this delay, which I promise will be as short as possible, does not diminish your affection for,

Your friend,
Prince Traanzo

Dorin sighed as he read this, but then shrugged. He stood up and crossed the library to where the portrait of his mother hung. "Not yet, I fear," he told it. "Alliances with Orca and princes work, but they take time. I should like to marry and have children, though, alas, you will not be able to meet them. But I have vowed never to marry beneath me, and what sort of marriage would I have were I to wed as a count, with a count's bride, and then become a duke? I will wait, mother, because you always told me that patience is rewarded. Your wishes for a dynasty will be carried out, mother, but not quite yet. Meanwhile, excuse me, I must respond to this letter the prince has done me the honor to send, and then, well, I have a county to manage, and clients to advise. Marriage plans must wait."

Marriage was also, as it happened, on the mind of Berwick as we look in on him for the first time. In particular, the marriage of his son, which subject, we observe, was of significantly less interest to Yanis, the son to whom we have just had the honor to refer. The two of them, that is to say, Berwick and Yanis, sat in Berwick's vault room engaged in a conversation upon this matter. Now, the reader must understand that the vault room contained no vault, and, moreover, was the very room that in days past the Baroness Cerwin had called her alcove; but the tradition among the nobility of the House of the Orca was that one would entertain business associates in a well-appointed room that also contained the Orca's supply of bullion, and thus it was the term Berwick used for the place in which, at this moment, over mediocre white wine, he was discussing Yanis's future.

"But Father," protested the younger man when Berwick had completed his disquisition, "I am following tradition. Surely you cannot question tradition."

"Well, let us see. To what sort of tradition do you refer?"

"We are Orcas, and, therefore, above all, sailors."

"Well, and then?"

"Surely it is the tradition for sailors, when ashore, to carouse? To, as they say, 'let loose?' To celebrate?"

"My son, you have been on shore for over a hundred years; might it be time, at last, to end the carousing? We have made great strides in this last century. The mining operations are running, as is the smelting and the transport. All that is missing is that we establish ourselves permanently, which requires there be an heir. Alas, if your mother had lived, perhaps you would have siblings to whom I could turn."

"Father, you are not that old. It is not too late—"

"Oh, no! You will not turn this conversation to me! I have done my duty, the proof is, well, you are here, and we are rich. Moreover, if we include the investments I have made with the Imperial treasury, with the funds of His

Benevolence, our wealth stands to grow. But I wish to see it secure in my family, and for that, there must be a good match."

"Well, but didn't we have a good match? The Lady Askaani would have been a most suitable bride."

"You are aware, are you not, that the Lady Askaani, and, I may add, her fortune, are unavailable to us until and unless Wetrock should be raised to a county? And, as of yet, the House has not yet even confirmed me as baron, although I am given the title by courtesy."

"Well, but is that my fault?"

"In a word, my son: Yes."

"But, in what way was it my fault? You had a task, I had a task. I completed my task, you did not complete yours, though I say it with all respect."

"Your completion of the task, as you call it, resulted in the explosive destruction of Cryden House, which, in turn, resulted in an Imperial investigation that has delayed the appointment of the barony, and thus the elevation to county, and thus the marriage."

"I beg to submit I was merely thorough."

"What you call thoroughness, my son, I must insist was ill-conceived and without finesse; in a word, clumsy."

"You say clumsy, I say thorough. You say rainstorm, I say rainstorm, we both get wet.[1]"

Berwick did not reply to this observation, but merely continued. "Moreover, one of the family, that is to say Eremit, survived."

"You say survived, and I—"

"Well, you?"

"I say was disposed of."

"Very well, I concede the point. Nevertheless, you must, in your turn, concede that the reason for the delay is the Imperial investigation into the destruction of Cryden House."

Yanis shrugged. "Very well. But then, if that is delayed—"

"Well?"

"So must be any marriage plans."

Berwick sighed. "Very well, I will no longer insist upon a good match. Now, I merely wish for a match."

[1] Neskita neskitae, presumably regional variations in pronounciation.—SB

"Then I will offer you this bargain, Father: if you continue your efforts to become baron, I will look for a match, and, in addition—"

"Well?"

"Upon the day you become baron, I will become betrothed, and on the day you become a count, I will marry."

Berwick considered, and at length decided it was the most he was going to get. "Very well," he said. "I accept."

Yanis bowed.

Chapter the Eighth

In Which Eremit Makes the Acquaintance of
an Interesting Person

As for Eremit, on the Burning Island, it must be said that he settled easily and naturally into the routine of the jail: he ate his meals, he took his exercise, he slept. In this way the days went by, and the months, and even the years. Inside the Burning Island, there was no day, no night, no summer, no winter. Each day was the same as the last. Sometimes a prisoner would die, usually in the dark, while sleeping, and the body would be taken away; or once in a while a prisoner would go mad from confinement and ennui and be taken away to some unknown part of the island, and perhaps years later the cell and number of the deceased or the madman would be given to another, at whom the prisoners would stare at exercise for few days, and then the excitement, such as it was, would end. It must be noted that some prisoners, lost in their own private torment, or beaten down into a state of hopelessness, didn't even share in this activity. Such was Eremit, or rather, number eighty-one.

As such institutions go, it must be said, in all fairness, that Burning Island was among the kindest to its prisoners, particularly for that unenlightened time before the happy reign of Zerika IV, followed by the veritable renaissance in all aspects of life introduced by the glorious reign of Her Imperial Majesty Norathar. That is to say, privileges were only removed with cause, and punishments such as beatings and floggings were few, only delivered after warnings had been given, and, even then, were delivered with nowhere near the crippling severity that was, alas, not uncommon in those days. And as kindness as well as cruelty will inevitably flow down from above, so it was that the natural indifference to suffering tinged with malice and the casual abuse of authority that either draws one into such work as being a jailer or is the natural result of years of engaging in this activity was, in large measure, mitigated, to the benefit of the institution in general and the prisoners in particular. Eremit, for his part, had never suffered the slightest punishment, for the simple reason that his very apathy tended to ensure that he would not draw the attention of those jailers who took particular pleasure in barbarity or the exercise of power. He went through the motions of life, uncaring, unfeeling, propelled by inertia. He had been on the Burning Island for one hundred and nine years before he was singled out for punishment.

It came about in this way:

It was during the hour of exercise, and Eremit (for so we will continue to call him, except for occasional references to his number in order to underscore his melancholia, and, we freely admit, in hopes of generating an emotional response in the reader commensurate with the circumstances) was going through the routine as he always did when a certain prisoner suddenly cried out, clutched his chest, and fell to the ground. Now this circumstance, though rare, was not new to Eremit's experience; nevertheless, in spite of his apathy, the sound and the sudden motion caught his eye, as he happened to be facing the individual.

The prisoner was an old man, certainly well past his three thousandth year, with the high forehead, pale eyes, and elongated face of the Athyra. As he clutched his chest, his head came up, and by chance he looked directly at Eremit. The expression on his countenance was one of pleading, one that said, as clearly as words could have, *Though I am in jail and beyond hope of rescue or salvation, I do not want to die.* This expression was so eloquent and so powerful that it penetrated the layers and walls of apathy, that it penetrated, we may say, to the very core of Eremit's being and moreover struck our poor Iorich as a blow. It was the first emotion he had experienced in more than a century, and, without being aware of what he was doing, he moved toward the man.

"Number eighty-one," called a jailer. "Return to your place!"

Eremit reached the prisoner, who by now was supine and staring upward, having somehow contrived to fall on his back. As Eremit watched, he gasped, his eyes wide and staring, and then his breathing stopped.

"Number eighty-one! Stay away from number eighty-two and get back into your position at once!"

Eremit knelt by the side of the man known as number eighty-two.

"This is your last warning, eighty-one!" said the jailer, in a tone in which no trace of joking could be found.

When Eremit had been reading law, in particular, personal damages law, there had been an especially memorable case from the most recent Tsalmoth reign in which a man was being sued for having broken another man's clavicle by a blow. The defense contended that the blow had saved his life, as the individual's heart had stopped, and the blow, it seemed, had started it going again. In the end, the case was settled privately, but it had been discussed in Hurv's *Personal Injury, Public Good* because of various legal points raised by the victim's inability to either permit or refuse the treatment. It had remained with Eremit for entirely different reasons: at the age of ninety, when he had come across it, it had seemed to him a fine thing to save someone's life by simply striking the person in the chest.

While this did not consciously go through Eremit's mind, the effect is the same as if it had: kneeling by number eighty-two, he made a fist and brought it down hard directly above the man's heart. This having been done, he was uncertain as to what to do next—whether a second blow would be helpful or more likely to inflict damage without the possibility of rendering additional aid. As he was considering this question, his arms were grabbed from behind and he was pulled away, yet, at that very moment, number eighty-two gasped and began breathing again.

This was all Eremit was able to see, as he was then dragged away. He attempted to walk, but as is well known by those with experience in these matters, once the authority figures have decided a prisoner, criminal, or disturber of the peace is resisting, any effort to cooperate is treated as further resistance, the result being, when he attempted to walk, he was struck on the back, in the legs, and on the side of the head by the clubs with which the jailers enforced their authority—for even a simple club becomes a powerful weapon that gives the wielder a significant advantage when no one else is armed.

After being dragged a considerable distance, he was brought to a room filled with devices used for the chastisement of malefactors, a category into which, for the first time in his life, Eremit now found himself. His shirt was torn off him, and he was secured to a square post by means of rope around his wrists being attached to iron rings somewhat above head high, at which time was he left there.

His thoughts at this time were difficult to describe; the awareness that he was to be beaten was present, but, as it were, *distant*. More pressing upon his mind were two different ideas: above all, there was a strange exhilaration that was, we may say, beating down over a hundred years of carefully built up inner walls, if we may use such an expression to describe the way his injured spirit generated distance between his consciousness and what we may poetically call his soul in an effort to protect the latter from complete destruction. The exhilaration could perhaps be expressed in the single phrase *I have saved someone's life,* which thought reverberated through his mind, accompanied by an emotion that was less elation than astonishment, even wonder, that he could have done such a thing, and, moreover, that he could feel himself responding to having done so—from a distance, it seemed, and almost as if responding to a stranger, but nevertheless responding.

In addition to this thought was a second. Less urgent, less profound, but still present, it was a thought that took the form, *I wish I could scratch my wrists*, for the ropes that had been used to bind him were neither soft nor smooth, and thus caused a certain irritation that continually impinged itself on his consciousness.

After some time, perhaps an hour, perhaps more, he heard the door open, and he heard, in a voice he recognized as belonging to the director, "Have you anything to say?"

Now Eremit, by this time, was so lost in the struggle of conflicting emotions taking place within him, that, although he heard these words spoken, they did not, in his confused state, seem to have anything to do with him, wherefore he didn't answer. His silence, after a moment, was taken as a negative; the director said, "Begin."

Need we describe the following moments? Is it not sufficient to say that the poor Iorich was beaten with a severe leather flogger constructed so as to deliver the most pain with the least effort, and that, nevertheless, the effort wasn't spared, but was, on the contrary, delivered with a cruel yet impersonal enthusiasm and skill? May we only say that he cried out, his body becoming rigid, sweat pouring from him? What words could we find for this? Could we speak of strokes burning, of the torment? Does the reader wish to know how high went his voice with each laceration, as the blood began to flow? Enough! In our own day, we have come to recognize as barbarism such activities, whatever the motives with which they are carried out, and so in our present day all such have been forbidden except when carried out upon Teckla, who do not feel pain as gentlemen do. Indeed, it is so much the case that we now view these activities with horror, that certain of our fellow historians have taken to using such descriptions as an easy method of losing the reader's sympathy for anyone who inflicts such an ordeal on another. While we do our best to avoid passing judgment on those in the past who had not the advantage of our own wisdom, still, we do not feel it necessary to dwell on the event itself in order to convey what is, for our purposes, and we hope for the reader's, most important: that when it was over, Eremit was unable to move without assistance and could only sag helplessly in the arms of the jailers who returned him to his cell and pitched him onto the floor therein. Later, much later, he was able to rouse himself sufficiently to make his way to his cot and lie face down, still moaning softly.

By the time of the next exercise session, he was able to move, albeit slowly. His shirt had not been given back to him; to have a prisoner's welts and scars show after a beating was a means used to remind others to avoid falling into similar errors. Eremit, of course, cared nothing for this, being fully taken up with not falling over. This he managed, and it was only as he returned to his cell that he wondered if number eighty-two had been there; between the concentration required not to fall over from weakness, and the habit of not looking at anyone, it hadn't occurred to him.

The next morning he awoke feeling a little better—so much so that he felt able to sit at the desk again when breakfast arrived. He accordingly rose from his cot and made his way to the desk chair and sat down in front of the tray, at which time he frowned, uncertain of what he was seeing. He leaned closer, and, yes, there appeared to be the corner of a piece of paper sticking out from a crack in his wall that he hadn't even been aware existed. He stared at it, afraid to move, wondering what it could be. It must have come from one of the jailers; no one else was able to get into the cell. But what could a jailer wish to tell him? Might one of them be apologizing for having given him the beating? It seemed impossible. And yet—there it was, a small piece of paper that had not been there before.

He felt his heart palpitating as he stared at it, as if his heart, if not he himself, understood that this was to be a key moment, a turning point in a life that he had thought past any turnings at all. He hesitated, not so much afraid as feeling that he was about to cross a threshold, that once he picked up that paper, nothing would be the same again. That nearly any change would be an improvement was undeniable, and yet he waited. He had some coffee, and a bite or two of the legume pudding, and then more coffee. Then he lit a second candle, pushed the tray to the side, and took the paper.

It was a single sheet, folded once, of a type of paper he had never seen before: rough, oddly green, with just enough finish to hold ink. He unfolded it. The paper, it seemed, must have been of higher quality than he had thought, for the writing was neat and precise, far more so than is possible on bad paper. The words were few and simple. It read: *Thank you. You saved my life. You have made a friend, and I promise you will not regret the suffering you have endured for me. I will soon write to you again. Burn this and mix the ash in with your sand.* It was signed with the single initial, "M."

If his heart had been palpitating before, now it veritably pounded.

He read it again, and a third time, and yet a fourth. He found that his hands were shaking. How was it possible? How could the message have come to him? In fact, how could the message have been written? It wasn't the paper the jail had issued, yet what else could be used? He leaned forward holding a candle and tried to see into the crack in the wall from which he'd pulled the paper, but it appeared as nothing more than a tiny fault, hardly noticeable.

At last, suddenly realizing he did not know how much time had passed and afraid of the return of the jailer for the tray, he put the paper into the candle flame. When it was burning, he took out the sand and held it over it, let the ash fall in, and mixed them together. Then he blew out the second candle and sat back in the chair, attempting to still the beating of his heart.

That day at exercise, for the first time since he had arrived on the Burning Island, he looked at his fellow prisoners. He was surprised to realize that all of the faces were familiar—it seemed as if, though unaware of it and certainly without intending to, he had absorbed the features of those with whom he shared exercise time. Looking at them now, he formed the conclusion that each of them had come from the nobility. This conclusion was based on the visible presence of a noble's point on each (save one or two who had such unruly hair that the noble's point was hidden), and, moreover, on his memory, that it was his position as a noble that permitted him exercise every day instead of alternate days, and he recalled that there were the same number of prisoners here on each occasion.

Having noticed this, he looked for number eighty-two and saw him at once, shuffling slowly, a hand on his chest, his breathing heavy. Eremit attempted to make eye contact, but eighty-two (for so we must call him until we have another name, which, the reader may be assured, we will before too much time has passed, whichever interpretation one puts on "time," that is, the passing of time as Eremit experiences it, marked by episodes in his life, or the passing of time as the reader experiences it, marked by the turning of the pages), but eighty-two appeared entirely unaware of Eremit's existence. The Iorich considered this and concluded that the Athyra was unwilling to take the chance of a jailer suspecting any sort of connection or contact between them. This theory received a certain confirmation at the end of the exercise period when, for the merest instant, number eight-two caught Eremit's eye and gave him the briefest yet the most significant look, a look which was over before Eremit was even aware of it, yet which he was certain was not his imagination.

When he returned to his cell he found he was trembling with excitement. He stared at the crack in the wall, and even after he had blown out the candle for the night, continued straining to see it, impossible though it was. He woke up early, even before breakfast had arrived, and lit a candle. When he found there was nothing there he was utterly crestfallen. That day during exercise, he once again tried to catch the eye of number eighty-two, but this time there was not the least hint of recognition. He frowned; had he imagined the look yester-day? Or, gods, had he imagined the note? Had his mind finally gone so far into despair as to be unable to tell reality from imagination?

That night he tossed and turned for some time, feeling feverish and disturbed and wondering if he would wake the next morning a full-blown madman, to scream and be taken away like the others. The next morning he awoke with the arrival of breakfast, and looked, and caught his breath as, indeed, there was, once again, the edge of a piece of paper sticking out of the crack.

He rushed to the desk and pushed the tray aside and eagerly took the note, unfolded it, and read.

My dear young friend. I was unable to write to you yester-day because of a sudden attack of weakness. Thanks to my own phys-icking, I am now recovered, so much so that I was able to exercise yester-day, although I did not dare acknowledge your glance. And now my friend, I have no doubt you wish to know how I am able to write to you, and, moreover, if you will be able to write to me. Soon you will know! For now, here is what you must do: write something, anything, so long as it gives the jailers no cause for suspicion. But before writing, you must trim the paper, as if you required to have neat, fine edges, as many do. You can do this using your spoon, which has a sufficient edge for the purpose. You must collect all of the scrap you have trimmed and place it on your breakfast tray to be taken away. You must do this again to-morrow. Soon, there will be more. For now, that is sufficient to start. Burn this note as be-fore, and I look forward to the day when you will be able to freely exchange thoughts with

Your friend,

M

Once again trembling with excitement, Eremit quickly ate his break-fast, then removed a paper from the drawer. He scrupulously followed the directions he had been given, trimming the paper down to neat edges and setting the scrap onto the tray. Then he dipped his pen into the ink and began writing:

> In order to not forget my legal training, in case it should someday be useful again when I am called upon to defend myself against whatever charges have brought me here, I intend to set down the history of various cases I have studied as well as I remember them. I shall begin with the matter of Nothrim, a criminal proceeding, in which Lady Nothrim, Countess of the House of the Hawk, was accused of stealing certain funds from her employer, a Lyorn named Hunandis. The accusation . . .

In this way, Eremit filled up the entire sheet so quickly that he had finished by time the jailer arrived to remove his tray. "Ah," said the jailer. "You have begun writing, I perceive."

"It passes the time," said Eremit laconically, though, once more, his heart was palpitating furiously because, although he knew he had broken no rules, he felt that he had embarked upon a course that was forbidden, and he imagined the jailer could know this merely by looking at him, for, as Eremit had never gone so far as to embark on his law career, he had, as yet, no practice in dissembling.

"So much the better," said the jailer. "Leave what you have written out, and we will collect it when it is time for you to take your daily exercise."

"I will follow your instructions exactly," said Eremit.

The jailer appeared to see nothing unusual in the prisoner having trimmed the paper; the servant picked up the tray and they left him alone with his thoughts, thoughts which, we daresay, the reader can well imagine. Why must he write? And why the insistence on trimming the edges? How could this turn into the ability to write to the mysterious "M"?

The next day, although another note came, it brought him little closer to understanding.

> My friend, *it read*, you must write again to-day, and again trim the edges. This time, however, of the paper you have trimmed, you must hold back the tiniest part—that is, an amount that might cover the fingernails of one hand, no more. Carefully take these scraps and, lifting the mattress off of your cot, remove one of the screw bolts that holds the leg to the frame, which you should be able to do

if you are determined. Once this is done, you will find a hollow spot at the top of the leg that is suitable for concealing those scraps of paper you have removed. This, my friend, you must do every day, only you may gradually increase the amount of paper you secret away. Never, however, take more than that on one long side of the page, or the jailers may notice, and all would be ruined. I will not write you again for some time, indeed, not until we are ready for the next step, after you have gathered sufficient scraps. This note, as the others, must be burned, and the ashes mixed in with your sand. Until the next time, my friend, I remain—

M

Eremit did as he was instructed, concealing the scraps in the palm of his hand until the jailers had left, after which, with no small amount of labor, he succeeded in removing the leg of his cot and finding the hollow area in the top of it. He replaced the leg and returned the screw bolt loosely to its place.

As instructed, he continued every day to write out from memory the history of a case he had studied, and trim the edges of the page, and set aside a little more each day. Needless to say, Eremit was curious about how these scraps might be turned into paper, and moreover, how once he had paper he would manage to get a message to his correspondent. He forced himself to remain patient, however, as, day after day, he continued writing and trimming and hoarding the tiny scraps of paper in the hollow pocket of the leg. His supply of paper diminished but was replaced by the guards, as were the ink and the sand. If the guards were in any way suspicious, they did not indicate it by word or expression. Eremit finally noticed, one day, that the hollow place in the leg seemed to be getting full, and wondered if he should begin filling another leg, but the next day, there was another message.

To-day, my dear friend, *it read*, you must take the next step. Drink your coffee until only the last dregs remain. Then heat up the pudding by holding it over the candle, though not too close as you must not burn the bowl. Just before the pudding would begin to boil, a thin liquid will appear on top, the oil of the particular legumes. Put this into the cup that held your coffee, and to this, add the paper shavings you have been collecting. Stir these well, then, removing your mattress, spread the resulting mixture on one of the slats of the cot. Put the mattress on top and lie down in the cot for an hour. After this time has elapsed, raise up the mattress, and you will find a sheet of paper, such as I am now using, sticking to it. Peel it off and hold it over a candle, though not too close, for a quarter or half an hour, until it is dry. To store the paper, make a narrow slit in the side of the mattress near the wall, for when they look under the mattress during the exercise period, they will not notice it. You can make the slit simply enough by undoing some of the threads that hold it together, which threads you can put into your slops bucket. Push the paper deep into the middle of the mattress, and here you can store twenty or thirty sheets without them being detected. Also, I caution you to carefully wipe down the bottom of the bowl to remove the inevitable marks that will be left by the candle's heat. Do not attempt to write anything yet. As this paper is, you perceive, now full I will explain how to write and how to get a message to me to-morrow, when you hear once more from your friend,

M

Though so filled with nervous excitement he could scarcely make his hands behave, he nevertheless followed M's instructions so well that, by the time the jailers returned to collect his tray, he was lying on his back, apparently taking his ease, his fingers laced together behind his neck, watching a spider working industriously in a corner of the cell. He was nervous while exercising, for, although he trusted his mysterious correspondent, he feared he had made some error in carrying out the instructions. All went well, however, and that night he fell asleep lying on a small sheet of greenish paper that he had produced, it almost seemed, from nothing.

The message the next day, which Eremit pulled from the wall with an eagerness the reader may understand without additional emphasis from the historian, read as follows:

My good young friend, I can only hope that you have been following my instructions. While I see that the notes I have been sending have disappeared, I cannot know if you have been able to carry out the necessary operations successfully, thus permitting us to exchange thoughts. You can, I am sure, imagine the eagerness with which I now write to give you the last details. First, in order to write, you must dip your quill into the inkpot, and then hold it still, and wait for a moment before writing, as the ink must be somewhat dry before it is applied to this paper we have created. When you have completed writing—and oh, with what desperation I long to read your words!—and given the ink some five or ten minutes to finish drying, you must fold the note in half, as thinly as possible, even as you see my notes come to you. Remove again the screw that holds the leg onto your cot, which screw you have, no doubt (or so I hope!) already left loose, and, scraping it upon the wall, create a sharp edge. This will, no doubt, take a full hour or more, during which time you must hide the note in the place you have hidden the sheets, for it will be nearly time for exercise before you are done. You must then wait until the noon meal, at which time you must slide this sharpened screw into the crack in the wall which I have created, and by which means I have been passing you my notes. This will cause the crack to widen temporarily, and permit you to insert the note, which you must then, using the handle of the spoon, push as deeply into the crack as you can manage. This will push it past the thickness of the wall and permit me to take it. That is all there is space on this paper for, so I close by saying that I am as eager as a bride to hear what it is you will say to,

Your Friend,

M.

Once again, Eremit followed the instructions to the letter, if the reader will forgive a small play on words. So successful was he in this, that, shortly after the noon meal had arrived, he was able to push a note through the wall, a note which, in a trembling, eager hand, read as follows:

My dear friend and teacher, for so I will call you, it is with unmitigated joy that I have received each of your notes, and if this reply from me should only give you a fraction of the pleasure I have felt, then you must be happy indeed to see it. But come, my friend, who are you? Why are you here? What is your history, and how is it you know how to create paper from scraps, and how to open cracks in walls? Please reply. For my part, I am continuing to entertain our hosts with case histories recalled from my study of the law (for you perceive, I am an advocate) so that I can produce more of your marvelous paper, which I will use to write you once again, telling you, should you wish it, the history of your dear, good friend,

Eremit

The reply the eager young (for the reader will recall, he was still scarcely two hundred years of age) Iorich read the next day, in addition to expressions of joy in receiving the note, and, moreover, begging Eremit to tell his history, began to tell the mysterious correspondent's own story. This exchange of histories continued for some time. The reader, of course, has no need to hear Eremit's tale, as he has, we hope, been following it with us as it has been revealed on these very pages. As for the mysterious Athyra, it is our belief that his history is of such a nature that the reader will wish to learn of it as Eremit did. It is our contention that to continue in the form of notes would likely become tedious, wherefore we will exercise our right as the author to pull into one piece the remarks that Eremit was only able to read in sections. This description by the Athyra, then, of his own story is how, without preamble or delay, we will begin the next chapter of our own history.

Chapter the Ninth

In Which Eremit and the Reader Together Learn
Something of the Mysterious "M"

I was born, my friend, on an estate not too distant from Dragaera City. So close, in fact, that we thought nothing of visiting it every five or six years. Once I was old enough to begin my sorcerous studies, therefore, I spent time in the House itself, and its library, which, as you can imagine, is unparalleled in matters of sorcery and philosophy. My studies at first were undisciplined, as a young man's will be; I read whatever came my way, absorbed as much as I could without serious work, and went on to the next.

This all changed when I happened to come across an old volume in quarto, dating back to the Ninth Cycle and written by a certain Lady Braidre, called *An Inquiry Into the Nature of Learning*. In this work, she brilliantly laid out the different means by which we determine what is truth, and the various means whereby we use these methods to guide our lives. This small book—for it was not, you perceive, a large volume—opened up for me a new world, a world where the mind of the individual became merely another factor of nature, which then led me to a study of the various methods by which we poor human beings acquire knowledge and, even more, skill, and how they—that is to say, *skill* and *knowledge*—compare, and under what circumstances each may be used. Now this, by itself, was well enough, yet I went further, and, by my third century, I had developed the hypothesis that, in short, it was possible for anyone to become not merely skilled, but an expert at anything—that is, that the lowliest Teckla might, by the application of certain methods, become an engineer, a sorcerer, a poet, a musician, regardless of natural talent.

In order to test and refine this theory, I did two things: first, I acquired a position as an instructor at Pamlar University, from which I had been graduated not long before. And, second, I set about acquiring and mastering every skill I could, thus permitting me to examine the efficacy of my ideas both on my students and, above all, on myself. I studied sculpture, and statesmanship, and sorcery, and agriculture, and the culinary arts, and swordsmanship, and natural history, and the making of paper and ink, and other things besides, looking always for ways in which the mastery of one discipline would feed into learning of the next. Thus, by the time of my two thousandth year, I had acquired a certain success, gained a certain reputation among academics, and mastered a number of skills no one would have expected of an Athyra—who are expected to understand natural and sorcerous philosophy, but hardly expected to be craftsmen, engineers, or fighters. I had even published a few small works, which had been received with interest, if not without the skepticism that is a natural and, I might add, healthy aspect of the academic world. In fact, I achieved such a success that not only did my students begin calling me "magister," the highest term of respect that can be bestowed upon a teacher, indicating one has gone beyond mastery of a skill, and even of many arts and sciences, and achieved proficiency in communicating this mastery to others, but my colleagues even began referring to me as *the* magister, and soon I was simply called Magister, as if that had been my name. I accepted this term, not as my due, but nevertheless as the honor it was, and, moreover, as a goal to which I committed my life, and so no longer used the name I had been given. I was Magister, and I was determined to earn the title so thoroughly no one could question it.

Had I been satisfied with this, my good friend, then I should not be here to-day. But alas, I was determined to carry my work further and to prove—above all to myself—that my ideas were sound. And so it was that I accepted a position with a nobleman, a duke, in point of fact, who had a child he wished to make into what I had been striving for—that is, to help a young person master as nearly all of the arts, crafts, and sciences as was possible for one individual to know. How could I refuse? I had a free hand as to method, a liberal account for books and such other tutors as I might require, and a large study of my own; in short, all I could wish for. And so I said farewell to the academy that had been my home for so long and began my work.

I quickly learned of my error: the child was a monster. Undisciplined, self-willed, with no interest in anything save easy amusements. I had never met such a child before, and, frankly, did not know what to make of him or how best to proceed. Here, my methods failed, for not only was I unable to teach an unwilling mind, but, moreover, I could find no book or tutor to instruct me in how to make the mind willing. After thirty years, by which time the child was a young adult, I had to confess my failure to my employer. And it was then, in that conversation, that I made the error from which all else has followed: a small error, a minor mistake, and yet, as the fable of the norska and the teapot tells us, catastrophe begins with the most minute miscalculations. It came about this way: as I was tendering my resignation, with great regret and many apologies, he asked me, "But, after all of this, what will you say to those who suggest your methods are inherently flawed?" I had thought it a simple question, with no ulterior motive, and so I answered in as simple terms: "Your Grace," I said, bowing, "I will merely say that I cannot teach one who refuses instruction."

"That is what I wished to know," he said.

Of course, my dear friend, now that I have had time for reflection, I know what transpired: he feared for his child's reputation and so would not permit any ill word to escape. Though unwilling to commit murder, for reasons that I do not understand yet hope to deduce someday, he found another way to ensure my silence. He bribed some corrupt Iorich or another of his acquaintance, for it seems as if corrupt individuals have a way of finding each other, to have me charged with having committed a detestable crime with this child, and so I was taken away by the justicers. In my foolishness—for one small error, as we have said, so often leads to greater errors—I was convinced that I should receive a trial, and as my rank entitled me to testify under the Orb, which cannot fail to tell truth from falsehood, that would without doubt have caused an acquittal and repaired my reputation. Thus I waited patiently and did not attempt to reach my family or my friends, until at last I was brought here, to this island, where I have been ever since.

That, then, is my history. Though broken and betrayed and nearly without hope, still, in my own heart, I call myself Magister, to retain some faint spark of who I once was and what I hoped to be.

Eremit heard—or, to be more precise, read—this story with the deepest emotion. Only one who has been betrayed can truly understand the terrible mix of emotions—anger, sorrow, and helplessness—that follows from such an experience. He wrote back, full of sympathy, and expressed hope that Magister—for so Eremit now thought of him—would take some solace in having found another to whom he could give hope, or, if not hope, at least an interest in continuing the battle or, rather, campaign, that we call "life."

The reply to this was remarkable. It was the shortest note Eremit had yet received, and it said simply: *Do you wish to learn?*

His reply was equally laconic: *Yes.*

The next message, though Eremit didn't understand it, caused a thrill to shoot through him: *Use the sharpened screw to inscribe a circle on the wall behind your bunk. Let its radius be the length from your wrist to your elbow. If you use your sand to fill in this circle, you will discover that it becomes nearly invisible.*

This puzzled Eremit for some time, as he was uncertain which was the *radius* of a circle, and which the *diameter*. He solved this problem by picking up his coffee cup and rolling it along his desk, noting the distance it covered. As this distance was clearly less than six times the distance from the one edge of the cup to a point across from it, he concluded that the shorter distance, that is, half of the distance alluded to above, must be the radius, and using this calculation, which would have made Perista, his teacher, proud to know he had remembered it (notwithstanding the old woman's thinly pressed lips and furrowed brows upon learning of his inability to remember which was diameter and which was radius), he measured out the circle and, after moving the bunk, carefully inscribed it in the wall, after which he replaced the screw, rubbed sand into the circle, and pushed the cot back, wondering where this was leading.

His instructions the next day were to remove a second screw from another leg, as Magister (for now, the reader perceives, that is what we are calling the worthy Athyra) pretended that using only one would cause it to wear away and thus be useless for helping to deliver notes. This he sharpened as he had the first.

The following message required him to make a sort of paste using a few grains of the rice that was an inevitable part of dinner, ground flat with his spoon, the acidic wine that also came with dinner, half of the piece of bread he was given, and the sand that was used for writing. Magister cautioned him to be careful with this sand, as should it run out too quickly, it might make the jailers suspicious. He nevertheless made the mixture as directed. This mixture, then, went into the groove he had drawn the day before and only filled in with sand. The glue-like substance, Magister explained, had the property of gelling into a solid yet pliable form and would disguise the work he was doing, and had the additional property of being able to be removed and replaced repeatedly without losing its shape or its color.

After that, he worked diligently with the screw, slowly deepening the groove. The dust that collected from this work he laboriously gathered up, adding some to the sand, and disposing of the rest in his slop bucket. This continued for days and months, for it was slow work, and he had to be certain that he appeared innocent any time a jailer appeared, which necessarily interrupted his progress. But at last there came the day when he wrote to Magister to tell him that the groove in his wall had now reached the depth of the screw he was using as a tool, and he wondered what it was he should do next.

The answer came the next day: he was to repeat the process, only this time, instead of a circle with the radius of his forearm, he was to make a rectangle, against the floor, the height of his hand, half of that in width. Moreover, this time, instead of pushing his awl—for such, in fact, it nearly was—straight in, he was to attempt to find a sharp angle, with the intention of being able to fully remove a section of wall, which he was then to slowly, over the course of days, hollow out, in order to create a hiding place, although what was to be hidden there, Eremit could not guess. Nevertheless, he carried out the instructions, depositing the rock he slowly scraped from the wall in various places: some in his slops bucket, some in his sand, some on the floor of the hallway while exercising. He was pleased the hole was he creating was no bigger, or disposing of the rubble would have been impossible.

At length it was completed: a small, shallow hole in the wall, covered by a strip of the gel that could be easily removed yet acted to conceal the telltale signs of its presence. He had thick callouses on his fingers now from the scraping, and both screws had been worn down significantly, yet, for whatever reason Magister had ordered it, the work was done.

The instructions the next day were the most difficult yet and including a warning that this was the most perilous part of the plan, as it was the most likely to be noticed by a jailer. *Yet,* said Magister, *the stakes are worth the throw, and betimes a risk cannot be avoided.* Following his instructions, then, at supper that night Eremit squeezed the juice from the lemon that accompanied the flatfish and rubbed it around the edges of the tray. Then he heated up a corner of the tray over the candle, rubbing more of the lemon juice in as he did, until, at last, one corner of one layer of the neeora wood began to curl and peel back. After that he had to work quickly so as to be done before the jailer returned. He had no more lemon juice and so he used wine, carefully spreading it on the opening, heating it then pulling it back.

He was nearly done when he heard the key in the lock.

He had nowhere to conceal his work, and it was impossible to deny his activity. Was there something he could say? Could he somehow put an innocent face on it?

He still had come up with nothing to say when there was a loud, anguished cry from nearby, that is to say, from the cell next to him—in other words, from Magister. *Ah, the clever Athyra!* he thought. The door did not open. Eremit finished separating the top layer and, not wasting an instant or a motion, hid the piece of wood under his mattress. He returned to the desk, wiped the bottom of the tray, and quickly put his food on it, finishing by taking a large bite of the fish so that it would not seem odd that his lemon had been used but the fish was still whole. Even as he swallowed, the door opened.

"My good sir," he said. "What was that sound? It sounded as if someone had died."

"Only an old man screaming at a dream. He'll go mad soon, if he doesn't die first."

The servant took his tray and appeared to find nothing odd about it, and the jailer left Eremit alone and shaking.

The next morning after breakfast, but before the tray had been removed, he took the thin sheet of wood and, using oil extracted from the legumes, the same as he had in making the paper, he carefully shaped it into a crude bowl, which he then hid in the wall of his cell in the compartment he had made. He did not know what was to be stored in the bowl, but his success in having come this far gave him a certain measure of confidence— indeed, a sort of confidence he had never known.

The oil from the legumes (as the reader has no doubt deduced, these were the longpods, the properties of which are well known) was also used then, over several days, to apply coat after coat on the bowl until it had built up a thick sheen, as though to protect it, although from what Eremit was unable to guess.

The answer was not long in coming. Now the reader must understand that the meals served to the prisoners, including such variations as the extra allowances for those with money (Eremit's, of course, had run out many years before, though he hadn't particularly noticed), were on a regular monthly schedule. Thus, had he taken an interest in the matter, he could have predicted precisely what sort of food he would receive at any particular meal on any particular day. While breakfast was always the same, lunch on the first day of the month would involve a turtle soup, dinner on the second of the month inevitably featured prawns in what could charitably be called a cream sauce, supper on the third day must include battleton cheese, and so on. It was therefore not surprising that Magister, in writing to Eremit, could predict what would be on his desk that day.

The instructions, then, though somewhat complicated, were not impossible. Eremit first memorized them, then carried them out exactly as they had been given.

From breakfast, he took the meat and held it over the flame so the tip was burned, and beyond burned, even blackened, until the end was really nothing more than carbon. This he placed into the hole he had made against the floor. From lunch that day—it being the fourth—he took the apple cider, poured it into his bowl, set that next to what once had been the meat, and waited. Magister pretended the carbon would absorb odors, although he told Eremit that, with all of the smells that were naturally in the prison, there was little enough reason to worry.

It took four months before the cider had turned into vinegar, but by then he was able to add more, as Magister said that once the process began, it would work on any new cider that was added more quickly. When this happened, he went on to the next step, which involved mashing the apple he received at lunch on day nine and then stirring it furiously until, after laboriously removing the pulp, he had sugar water. He removed the concealing strip from the wall and used his finger to apply the sugar water. After waiting for it to soak in, he then put the vinegar on top of it and waited.

In less time than he had thought—that is to say, only a few minutes—a fine dusting of powder emerged from where the rock had dissolved. To be sure, there was no visible sign of progress, yet the dust itself convinced him of the efficacy of Magister's ideas. Still following the directions, he gathered up the dust as well as he could and put it in the hidey hole until the eleventh day, when supper included winterfish.

Now as winterfish is, we believe, unknown to many if not most of our readers, we must say two words about it. It is not, as some in the south believe, a kind of fish; rather, it is a preparation for fish. It is used in the region around Finger Cove, east of the Twisted Forest—that is to say, too far north for any but the most hardy of folk, and too close to the Great Sea of Amorphia for any but the most foolhardy. These people, in order to survive in the winter when the fish had all gone so far west (or, perhaps, simply down; there is some disagreement on this subject), had taken to preserving fish using a complex processing method involving lye, which thus preserves it from the heat (as well as any animal with the least discrimination) so that it may be eaten in the winter. A similar method, with a similar name, was used on the Burning Island, although it was presented to the prisoners once a month regardless of season, perhaps as a punishment.

On the eleventh day, then, Eremit removed the dust he had extracted from the wall and mixed it in his water cup with lye squeezed from that evening's winterfish. After mixing this carefully, he then applied it to the cell wall opposite the desk, as if he were painting. This disposed of the dust, which otherwise may have caused the jailers to notice that something was wrong, and, the dust of one wall naturally being the same color as the other, the change was not noticeable even to most exacting eye—so much the less, then, to the jailers, who were scarcely glancing at it.

The reader may well understand that this process was lengthy. And yet Eremit did not become impatient. Quite the contrary, he found the gradual, slow progress to be calming. He needed not think of what had befallen him in the past, or what might be his future; he merely continued making gradual progress on his wall. He continued writing his notes—both the ones for the benefit of the jailers and the secret ones to Magister, who responded with reassurance about how far he was getting, and promising that it would all be worthwhile.

As well as he could, following as always Magister's directions, he attempted to make this progress downward from the top and toward the center from the sides, and last there came a day when the entire section of the wall came off in his hands. He held it, amazed; and although there no depth whatever to the hole behind it, still, for the first time, he could see that it would become a tunnel. He put the section of wall back and attached it with the long strip of gel (or, rather, the third such he had made, as the others had lost their effectiveness after repeated use).

He eagerly told Magister about it. The latter complimented him upon his progress, and so he continued. Days and months and years went by as he worked, deepening the tunnel, until it was so deep that Eremit could stretch out in it without even his feet appearing in the room. At this point, he was instructed to make a right-angle turn to the left, and he carried out these instructions, continuing his slow and steady progress through what he now realized was nothing less than the side of the mountain.

How often can we speak of the passing of years? The reader must understand that this progress Eremit made was slow, and that, as a natural consequence of this circumstance, a great deal of time must necessarily elapse; yet it is an undeniable fact that when writing history, one must write of *incidents,* that is to say, of actual events that have taken place, and to merely repeat identical occurrences cannot advance the reader's understanding of how matters came to the conclusion they did, nor, which is more important, advance the reader's understanding of the general laws that regulate the unfolding of human events in all their complexity. For, indeed, if the reader is unable to draw any inferences that may relate to that reader's own life, then is the study of history even worthwhile?

Therefore, we will not speak of the burning of meat, of the creation of the vinegar from the apple cider, of the squeezing of the lye into the dust-and-water, of the wearing away of rock, of the adding of this rock to the wall of Eremit's cell. The reader must simply accept that considerable time passed until one morning after breakfast—we cannot specifically say when it happened in more detail than that, nor make any reference to the outside world, for Eremit had no notion of what might be happening in the outside world, nor, indeed, any conscious awareness that it still existed—a section of rock turned to dust and, in the light of candle he was holding, he found himself face-to-face with Magister.

"Well, my friend," said the old man with a warm smile. "We have done it and can now visit each other freely."

Eremit, almost beside himself with joy, embraced the other as well as he could in the confined space of the tunnel and said, "You perceive, I am so overcome with happiness that I am trembling. Is it the case that this tunnel now runs from your cell to mine?"

"It is indeed; thus, so long as we are careful and are each in our own cell when the jailers come, well, there is no limit to the time we can spend in each other's company."

"To have a friend," said Eremit, "to be able to speak with another person, well, it has been so long, I am astonished I still recall how to do it."

"In truth, I am not so far from having forgotten myself, for you perceive, I have been here for a long time."

"That is true! Apropos, when we meet—"

"Well, when we meet?"

"It must be in your cell, not mine."

"Well, but why does it matter?"

"Ah, my friend," said Eremit, "I must not ask you to spend time bent over in this gloomy tunnel!"

"Oh, as to that—"

"Well?"

"We shall see. But for now—"

"Yes, for now?"

"We must each return to our cell and close up our wall, as it is nearly time for our daily exercise, and it would not do for the jailer to find our cells empty."

"With this I agree," said Eremit. "Or for us to be found in the wrong cell, wherefore I must return that way, while you go that way."

"That is exactly right," said Magister.

"Only, will I see you to-morrow?"

"Of a certainty. For to-morrow, at last you begin."

"Why, begin what?"

"Learning."

"How, learning?"

"Yes, for I intend to teach you if you are willing."

"I am more than willing; I am even eager. And yet—"

"Well?"

"What is it I am to learn?"

"Everything," said Magister.

In Which We Discuss Learning, Escape Plans, and Learning Escape Plans

The next day, Eremit didn't even wait until he had eaten his breakfast; he went through the tunnel and emerged in Magister's cell—a cell which we need not describe as it was identical in all respects to Eremit's save that the desk was on the other side, so that, had there been no wall between them, they would have been facing each other. Magister had removed the cover of his wall and was seated at this desk, his own tray still full. When Eremit emerged, Magister greeted him with the following words, "Well, what of your breakfast?"

"How, my breakfast?"

"Yes, you have hardly had time to eat it."

"Well, no. So great was my eagerness to begin learning whatever it is you have to teach me, I simply left the instant the jailer had closed the door."

"I understand that, my young friend. Only—"

"Yes?"

"You must now retrieve it, for we shall have need of it. Now hurry and waste no time, we have scarcely an hour before the jailor will return, and you must then be back in your cell, although we may then resume after the jailor has left."

This answer, which Eremit had not expected in the least, nearly caused him to ask questions, but then he realized that these questions would do nothing except to take up time better spent in whatever lessons Magister had in his mind to deliver, so he merely said, "I will return with it in a moment."

"And you will be right to do so."

He went back through the tunnel and, an instant later, had returned with his tray. "Well, here it is. What shall I do with it?"

"Set it down next to mine. I shall sit here, on the bed, while you sit at the desk and attend to my words."

"I promise you, I am attending to nothing else."

"That is right," said Magister.

"And so, what will you teach me?"

"Look there. What do you see?"

"Here? I see my breakfast."

"Well, and what of it?"

"What of it, Magister? It is the same as every other day's breakfast. You perceive, it is the one meal of the day which does not change."

"But how does it taste?"

Eremit frowned, trying to understand what he was being asked. "Taste, Magister? Why no doubt as it always tastes. The pudding can be eaten, and on some days, well, the meat is not badly burned."

"But have you attended to this taste?"

"In fact, I must confess I have not."

"Well, but have a bite now. Taste the meat. Come, chew it, attend to it. What are your thoughts?"

Eremit picked up the meat and bit into it. "It is plain. There is little to say of it."

"Why is that?"

"Magister? Why, because that is how it tastes. Or, to be more precise, doesn't."

"Is it not because it has been cooked so long that the flavor has been driven out of it?"

"I do not deny this."

"Well then, what can be done?"

"Magister, unless there is a way to reverse cooking, there is nothing to be done."

"Ah, but you see, that is where you are wrong."

"Then I hope you will correct me."

"Your hope will be fulfilled, for I am about to do so, and this very instant at that."

"Then I am attending you."

"What do you think of the pear?"

"It is small and, to judge from most of the others that I have eaten in the past, not so crisp as one would like, yet not utterly devoid of flavor."

"And what would happen if you were to tear it open and rub it on the meat?"

"Why, I should have meat flavored with pear."

"And would this be a bad thing?"

"I had not considered the matter."

"You may consider it now. Or, if you wish—"

"Yes, if I wish?"

"You may try it."

"I will do so."

He did as Magister had suggested and then had another bite of the meat.

"Well?" said his teacher.

"It is unusual."

"And?"

"It is certainly an improvement over the meat by itself, or the pear by itself."

"Ah!"

"So, then, I have learned something."

"What have you learned, my young friend?"

"That the juice of the pear improves the flavor of the meat."

"Well, but there is more, is there not?"

"Oh, I do not doubt there is more, my dear teacher."

"And then?"

"But what is it?"

"It is the first lesson. No, I tell a lie. It is the first *two* lessons."

"Well, then I hope you will explain them to me plainly."

"I will, and this very instant."

"Then I am listening."

"The first is, you are able to change the flavor of your food to make it more to your liking."

"Very well, I accept that. And then?"

"Whatever your circumstances, there are choices to make, and things you can change, and ways to make them better."

"Whatever my circumstances?"

"So long as there is life."

"I understand."

"And will you remember?"

"I nearly think I will remember every word that falls from your lips."

"Ah! Then I will endeavor to make each word count."

"So then, what is next?"

"Next, let us see about the pudding."

"Well, but, are all the lessons to be about food, Magister?"

"No, my friend. Rather, the reverse is true."

"How, the reverse?"

"Yes."

"My teacher, I fail to understand the answer you have done me the honor to make."

"Then I shall explain."

"I am listening."

"All the lessons will not be about food; rather, the food will be the key to unlock all of the other lessons. Come, attend me. By understanding the way to approach the food we eat, especially under such circumstances, and what can be done with it, you will have the key to understanding everything else you may wish to learn."

"But, how can that be?"

"That is what you must learn. Come now, what do you think of the pudding?"

Over the next days and months, Eremit learned that a few drops of coffee could improve the flavor of the pudding, whereas the coffee could be improved by the addition of sugars carefully extracted from certain fruits. He learned that crumbling bread over the winterfish and then using the heat from the candle to melt cheese over it made it far more palatable. He learned that the sweetreeds, ground and heated and with a drop of wine, made an excellent relish for the kethna spits. Soon he began experimenting on his own, testing the apples with the boiled fowl, adding nuts and raisins to the barley soup. Sometimes the results were good, sometimes not. He discussed the results with Magister, and slowly came to understand flavor combinations and how to use them.

One day, in the midst of one of these conversations, Magister said, "And so, my young friend, how do you decide which combinations will work?"

"I have tried them and noticed patterns."

Magister nodded. "That is so. To notice patterns, and to see how they might be extended, that is one of the things that is at the heart of learning. Apropos, should you ever come to a place where you have a kitchen and a full selection of food, limited only by the region and the season of the year, think what sort of creations you could make!"

"Why, Magister, I fear that, under such circumstances, I should be lost, unable to make a decision."

"Not in the least. The techniques you have learned will prove useful there, too, for in preparing a meal, you always start with one simple thing. Perhaps you have, because of a certain longing within you, or the tastes of a guest, selected kethna. You will then find yourself considering how best to prepare it: roasted, stewed, perhaps even broiled. This will naturally bring to your mind roots, herbs, and seasoning that will bring out its flavor best when prepared in this way and, having considered that, you will discover that other matters—the fruit, the wines, the accompaniments—will all come together as if there had never been any question of it."

Eremit sighed. "I should have loved to have you prepare me a meal, Magister."

"Ah, but, you perceive, that is what I am doing. I am serving you a feast of the mind, my young friend. You have been consuming it well, for you must be aware that nothing gratifies a chef as much as observing the pleasure of those who partake in his creation."

"It is true, I have been feasting. And yet—"

"Well?"

"It seems the more I consume, the hungrier I am."

"Then you are exactly the sort of student for whom I wish to prepare these delicacies of thought, the latest of which, you said, is to see patterns, which is important. But it must be said that, in the natural way of things, as you have learned this, you have also, unknowingly, received another lesson."

"Ah, have I? Well, so much the better. What lesson have I learned? For, you perceive, if I have learned it, well, I ought to know."

"To answer, I will ask another question."

"I recognize you so well in that! Ask then, for you perceive you have my attention, my dear teacher."

"Once you have found a combination that enhances the flavor of foods, what determines how successful it is?"

As Eremit opened his mouth to reply, the scholar held up a finger. "Think before you answer, my dear Iorich. Think carefully. And also consider this: in your studies of the law, what made one advocate great, while another was merely good? And yet a third: how were you so successful in exchanging notes with me, and even creating this tunnel through which you now visit me? Can you distill these matters, that appear so different, down to a single one?"

Eremit thought for a long time, then at last he nodded. "Yes, Magister. What they have in common is attention to the smallest, most minute detail, neglecting nothing."

Magister smiled. "Very good. That is the lesson of lessons, that will guide you in all of your future learning, beginning with the next lesson, which is something every gentleman ought to be proficient in, and that is fencing."

"How, fencing? And yet, you perceive, we have no weapons with which to practice, nor space in which to move. And moreover, I fear that you, my dear teacher, would not survive such exertion as it would take."

"All of those things are true," he said. "And none of them matter. I shall instruct you in the art and science of defense so well that no enemy, no pair of enemies, will dare approach you, and you will master this skill without ever leaving your chair."

"Is this possible?"

"Do you doubt me?"

"No, Magister. I could never doubt you."

"So much the better. We will begin this training to-morrow."

In spite of these words, it must be admitted that Eremit could not understand how he could be made an expert swordsman without so much as stirring—it seemed impossible. And yet his faith in his teacher had grown with every passing day.

When he arrived the next day, Magister wasted no time. "You have two attributes in a fight," he said. "One is your senses, the other your muscle."

"And my sword, my teacher?"

"An extension of your muscle, of course."

"Very well, I accept that."

"The senses now, the senses are how you know what your enemy will do, for you observe your enemy with sight, and sound, and, on occasion, touch. Even smell, at times, because you can smell when your enemy is afraid. And there is also everything around you, which you may use, or which perhaps your opponent will use. Your senses inform you, and your muscles react to this information. What this means, my dear friend, is that you must focus all of your attention on observing, which means your muscles must know what to do without giving them a thought."

"Well, I understand that. But will this actually give the skills of defense?"

"My friend, should you ever find yourself free again—"

"Well, if that should happen?"

"Then two day's practice with a weapon, and two hour's practice with a teacher or an opponent, and you will find that you know all you need in order to defend yourself."

"Then let us begin, for though I doubt I shall ever be out of here, well, it is good to learn skills even if they may never be useful."

"Ah, you perceive, there is another lesson you have learned!"

"So much the better. I am ready to begin."

"Good, then. Now, make a fist and squeeze it as hard as you can, so your muscles are like a stone. There, you see? Now release the fist and feel how the muscles feel like water. The stone and the water. Each muscle can be like the stone, or like the water, and to learn to wield the sword is to learn which muscles must be in which state when. Do you understand?"

"I think so, Magister."

"Then that is what we will do. We will work with each muscle until it responds to your will. You must be able to make the least toe on your left foot be like a rock, while the others flow like water. Once you can do this, any physical action you wish to take becomes possible; you will be able to fence, to dance, to engage in acrobatics, to play an instrument of music, for all physical skills are merely the ability to control which muscles are like rock and which like water, and to make these muscles serve your will. Let us begin, then. We will start with your right hand."

For years, then, Eremit studied. He learned each muscle and how to control it, and later he learned that there were even gradations between the rock and the water, and how to make his body follow the will of his mind so that even as he took his mandatory walk each day, he would let his stomach tense, or shift his weight, or control the movements of his arms. And as he did, he observed more and more of the movements of others, especially the jailers, seeing where they were strong and where they were weak, where they were graceful and where they were clumsy. He could see weakness in another, and he became aware that, had he a weapon, he would know how to defeat them.

"So then," said Magister. "What have you learned?"

"Magister," said Eremit. "You told me that there was muscle, and there were senses. Now I have learned that each contributes to the other. That is, the more I can control the workings of my own muscles, the more I can see how another uses his, and the more I observe the movements of another, the more my muscles will know how to respond without the need to think of them."

"And so, if you are not thinking of your muscles, and if you are in a fight, of what then are you thinking?"

"I am not, Magister. I am watching and listening and using all of my senses."

"And will you look for advantages?"

"No, Magister. I will be aware, and my arm will find the advantage, as well as the dangers, without a need for me to look."

"You are," said Magister, "an excellent student. The best I have ever had. Had the child I tried to teach been as willing to learn as you are, well, there is no need to think of such things."

"You are too kind, Magister."

"Not in the least."

"And will I now learn something new?"

"Yes, there is another lesson I am preparing."

"Well, and what is that lesson?"

"Language."

"Well, I should be able to manage that, because I speak in language already."

"Do you speak the ancient language of your own House?"

Eremit shifted his weight and said, "Well, a little. You perceive, it is not an easy language. There are ninety-six verb forms, most of them having to do with when the action took place, how the speaker knows of it, the intention of the subject, and degrees of confidence of the speaker in the intention of the subject."

"These will come naturally."

"Very well, I accept that. What else?"

"The language of the Yendi."

"The Yendi have a language?"

"Certainly, and, moreover, a very useful one, for it involves humming or whistling and rarely sounds like speech. Indeed, once you have learned it, you and I could speak openly during exercise with the jailers being unaware, not only of what we spoke, but that we were speaking at all."

"I should like that."

"Then, also, you must learn Serioli. Because if you are fluent in Serioli, the ancient tongue of the Iorich, the whistle-speech of the Yendi, and our own Northwestern tongue, there is no language that you cannot learn with a little application. Moreover—"

"Yes, moreover?"

"Each language involves thinking differently, and so each helps you understand something of the culture that produced it, and, by contrast, even something of our own, because there are things we have never questioned that learning another language causes us to evaluate."

"Well, but can you give me an example of such a thing?"

"I will do so."

"I am listening."

"In certain Eastern languages, as well as at least two of the languages of the Cat-Centaurs, there is no way to refer to an individual whose sex is unknown."

"I do not understand."

"Consider a sentence such as, 'Some unknown person is at the door, please tell *gya*[2] to come in.'"

"Well, what of it?"

"These languages do not permit such a formulation."

"But then, how . . . ?"

"In different ways. Some of them use a plural form, but others—"

"Yes, others?"

"Other use the masculine form to mean the sex is unknown, others use the feminine."

"And yet—"

"Consider two things: what it tells us about a culture that does so, and what it tells us about our own culture that we had never before considered this matter."

Eremit frowned. "I am uncertain."

"And you should be. Yet this is something to consider and, moreover, it is an example of the sorts of discoveries you will make while studying languages. You perceive how valuable it can be."

"Well, that is true. I am convinced."

"So much the better. Then let us begin. State the forms in ancient Iorich that you remember for the verb 'met,' as in, 'I met a stranger to-day.'"

And thus they were off on a study of languages, leading naturally and, perhaps inevitably, to a study of linguistics, which in turn often involved excursions into comparative culture. While skill with language did not come naturally to poor Eremit, by diligent work and patience, he eventually came to both comprehend the most tangled sentence structures and pronounce the most difficult phonemes in some twenty languages, some of which he did not even know the source of, after which Magister pretended he would have such a foundation that he could build from these to as many others as he wished. Indeed, from then on (although we will continue to represent the speech in the Northwestern tongue for simplicity's sake and will not bring up the matter again), they moved about freely from language to language in their conversation, until Eremit scarcely noticed when they

[2] For obvious reasons, I've used the untranslated word here in order to convey the sense of the lesson. —SB

changed from the whistle-speech of the Yendi to the guttural harshness of the ancient tongue of the Dragon, or the barbarous yet melodic agglutinative tongue of the Easterners of Fenario.

"And so," said Magister on a certain day (using, in point of fact, one of the inflected languages of the Cat-Centaurs), "it is time for your next area of study, and one that will continue the process of making your mind more flexible, subtle, and powerful."

"So much the better! But what study is this?"

"Sorcery."

"How, sorcery?"

"Exactly."

"But here we cannot reach the Orb, from which sorcery comes."

"Well, and so? Neither had we a sword."

"That is true, Magister. But how can you teach sorcery in the same way?"

"You remember how muscles can be water, or stone, or somewhere between them?"

"I nearly think I do."

"Well, but this also applies to the mind."

"How, it does?" said Eremit, astounded.

"I give you my word."

"But, what muscles are there in the mind?"

"Consciousness, the exact matter upon which your awareness is focused, and how strongly you concentrate on it, and how much you maintain awareness of those things upon which you are not concentrating, these are muscles. Moreover—"

"Yes, moreover?"

"You have learned of patterns. You must know, from the sorcery you have already studied, that to grasp the power that flows to you from the Orb is above all a matter of finding the pattern in which to shape this power so that it corresponds to your desire."

"Well, that is true, Magister."

"We talk of spells, but a spell is only a means of directing our minds into the proper patterns, and a way to help our concentration and direct our focus. It is said that the ancients, before the creation of the Orb, could use the power of the Great Sea of Amorphia in this way, and indeed, that was how the Orb was created, by Zerika the First, and the Athyra Sholandir, and the Vallista Caerdwin, and the Chreotha Mar, who worked together to contain the power, trap it, direct it, and so put it under the will of the Empress. Do you understand what I am telling you?"

"I think I do, Magister. And yet—"

"Well?"

"To feel as if one is pulling the power with no power, how can this be?"

"You will not feel it, you will imagine it. You were taught how to create light in a dark place?"

"Certainly."

"And how to ignite a fire on tinder?"

"You perceive that was the first spell I was taught."

"And how to make a sudden, sharp noise by collapsing air?"

"Of course."

"And how to chill your wine?"

"To be sure, and the proof is, I have even used it for that purpose."

"Then that is all you need. Those four spells, the first ones we all learn, contain the building blocks of all others: motion within the ethereal, motion within solids, motion within air, motion within liquids. If you can recall those spells, that is all we need to learn. Do you comprehend?"

"Entirely."

"Good. Then let us begin. Close your eyes, my friend."

"Very well, they are closed."

"There is a tray of food on my desk."

"Yes, Magister. I know because I saw it."

"Also upon this tray is a spoon."

"Well, I agree that there is a spoon."

"At what angle does it lie relative to the tray?"

"I do not remember, Magister."

"Then attempt to see it."

"But, how?"

"Your eyes saw it, thus your mind made a note of it, even as an artist would do with pen and ink. It is still there, you have only to bring it to the forefront of your mind."

"I see it, only I do not know if I am seeing a memory or only imagining."

"Ah, ah! Open your eyes, my student! You have now found the greatest challenge. We have imagination, and it is a blessing and a curse. At times it permits us to create in our minds what doesn't exist so that we may bring it to be, and at other times it fools us into thinking the unreal is real already. To harness this power, and to make it work for us, is the greatest challenge of sorcery, and philosophy, and will enhance every other skill you possess. It is this, above all, that is required to master the science of learning. It is why training in sorcery is so important, though you may never cast another spell in your life."

"And Magister, will I be able to learn this?"

"I have no doubt that you will."

"Then I am eager to begin."

"You have already begun. Close your eyes once more."

We would be remiss in our duty if we gave the reader the false impression that these lessons—and these latest lessons above all—happened quickly. On the contrary, years went by, and, almost unnoticed by Eremit, Magister became weaker, moving more slowly during exercise and taking longer to recover afterward, for he was old, and there is neither knowledge nor sorcery that can defeat Time and its handmaiden Age; even Sethra Lavode, it is said, is not immune, though the power of Dzur Mountain, of the Great Sea of Amorphia, and the magics of the Halls of Judgment have conspired to make it seem so. But even here, to understand that the mere appearance of agelessness has required the combination of the three most powerful forces in the world is to have some idea of the unstoppable power of Time.

And yet, if Eremit was not aware of it, we may be assured that Magister was, and the proof is, he spoke of it. "My dear young friend," he said one day, for so he called him, in spite of the fact that Eremit had, he believed, now passed his four hundredth year. "I am growing old and slow, and though my mind is still sharp to a nail, well, this old body is beginning to tell me that its time is nearly up. Ah, ah," he said, holding up his hand as Eremit began to speak. "I beg you, no words of false reassurance; have we not learned to see what is before us and to look at truth, however unpleasant we may find it? Is this not so, my friend?"

"It is, Magister. And yet—"

"Then look and observe, dear boy. Is what I say not true? Do you not see the signs? The spots on my hands, the pronounced veins, the trembling that I cannot control; observe the hollows of my cheeks, and my sunken eyes beginning to dim. No, it is nearly time for me to begin the next adventure, or, at any rate, to end this one. I am sad that I will be denied Deathgate, for the journey through the Paths is, I am told, an adventure of the greatest kind. But I have not begun this conversation to descend into self-pity, still less to ask you to pity me. No, this is merely an event like others, but one that has a valuable feature that few events have."

"Well, but what is this valuable feature? For you perceive, my teacher, that I see nothing of value in it."

"It is this: unlike so many things that happen, we know that this is coming, and this permits us to plan for it, not as a possibility, but as a certainty. So then, let us plan!"

"But, Magister, what sort of plan can there be, save for a private service of remembrance that, I give you my word, I will carry out with great emotion."

"As to that, I am uncertain. Yet I will think upon the matter, and you do the same, and we will see what sort of ideas come to mind."

"Very well, my teacher. To this I agree."

"Good. Then let us return to our studies."

"I should like nothing better."

"Then do you recall the Bellows of Cromlow?"

"Certainly."

"Describe it."

"First, the power must be formed into—"

"No, no. My error. I meant describe its effect and use."

"Ah. It is a combat spell, to be cast on one's self in the midst of a long and fatiguing battle, or else in the midst of any other difficult and extended physical activity, to restore energy to the body, which it accomplishes by improving, for a short time, the efficiency of the transference of air into the blood."

"Very good. And, do you remember the Lochar's Spin?"

"I do, and the proof is, it is a means to protect one's self from dust storms, by enclosing one in a pocket of swirling air."

"Yes. And again, Jajin's Hat?"

"To keep rain off of one's head by forming a shield of the rain itself."

"And the Cold Steam of Arbo?"

"To turn water into fog to provide concealment."

"Good. Now, what would happen if they were combined?"

"Combined, Magister?"

"Attend me."

"Very well, I am attending."

"The control of water from Jajin's Hat, the swirling bubble from Lochar's Spin, manipulation of air from the Bellows of Cromlow, the separation of the parts of water from the Cold Steam of Arbo."

Eremit considered this for some time, then he looked up. "What is your plan?" he said.

"Ah, you see the pattern, then?"

"You speak of your death and hint at plans, though you deny having one, and then you speak of a combination of spells that could permit one to breathe in the Ocean-sea."

Magister smiled. "The spell to breathe in the Ocean-sea is difficult."

"I should think maintaining the concentration for long enough to reach land would be impossible."

"Very difficult, certainly. Impossible? Perhaps not."

"Has anyone succeeded in breathing in water in this way?"

"Yes, it has been done."

"And for how long?"

"Ah, you ask that?"

"It would seem important, Magister."

"Well, Hrivan, during the most recent Vallista reign, managed to maintain it for—"

"Well?"

"Nine minutes."

"Nine minutes?"

"Yes."

"But, you perceive, to reach the shore by walking on the floor of the Ocean-sea would mean—"

"Days, perhaps weeks."

"Which I nearly think is more than nine minutes!"

"As to that, you are not wrong."

"And yet?"

"Perhaps you can better his efforts."

"But then, what of the volcano?"

"That, you see, is why I must be dead."

Eremit frowned. "Your body will be removed, put in a sack, and thrown into the sea."

"But, you perceive, those do not all happen at once. The jailers who discover the body will at once put it into a bag, lock the cell, and inform the director. An hour later servants—or, to be more precise, prisoners who have agreed to work in exchange for one of the cells with a window, which cells you may remember passing when you first entered—will fetch the body in its bag, and under the supervision of the jailers, throw it into the Ocean-sea. The sorcerer of the island will be there while they are doing this in order to cause there to be a place where it safe for them to stand, for otherwise they would be burned alive."

"So then, your plan is for me to replace you in the bag."

"You have understood exactly."

"So that I am then thrown into the sea."

"Where you will at once be able to use sorcery. You will sink to the bottom, for the bags are weighted. You will then cut your way out of the bag with the sharpened screw you have been using, and you will walk to the mainland on the floor of the Ocean-sea."

"And yet," said Eremit. "Holding the spell for days!"

"To be sure, that is a consideration."

"And there is another consideration, my teacher."

"And that is?"

"Well, it requires you to be dead, therefore, if I escape, it follows you will not be able to escape as well."

"That is true."

"If there is to be an escape, I should prefer a plan which permits us both to escape."

"I am too old, my friend, for any escape to be possible. I have given this matter thought. I have contrived handles on the inside of the piece of wall that closes it, made of the same material as is used to seal it. Also, I have attached that seal to that piece, so that, should you be here when I die—which I hope you are, as your presence could only ease my passage—the tunnel will not then be discovered. You perceive how much consideration I have given the matter. Come, you must agree."

He said this with such a tone of finality that Eremit could only lower his head in acceptance.

"So then," said Magister. "We must solve the problem of the length of time you can concentrate on breathing beneath the waves. But if we solve this problem, will you agree with my plan?"

Eremit remained still, his head bowed.

"Please, my dear friend. I must pass from this life soon. All that I now wish is to know that I have given my student a chance for freedom."

After a moment, Eremit said, "Very well, dearest of teachers. I agree."

Chapter the Eleventh

In Which Livosha and, Presumably, the Reader, Are Astonished at Kefaan

The reader, no doubt, is impatient to discover what has become of Livosha in the hundreds of years that have elapsed since we last saw her. Her intention, the reader may recall, was to travel to Candletown along with her brother, and, submitting to the need once more to cast our eye on an earlier time than that which we have lately been discussing, we may say that in this she was entirely successful. She had no trouble finding a hostel not far from the pier and, still having some money left, selected one that was clean and well-appointed and had the name, "Fishwives" after a sign showing several fish in the traditional gold winglets of the bride. She left Kefaan there to rest while she procured clothing more appropriate to a lady's maid than what she had been traveling in, after which she returned to the inn herself.

The next morning she caused a bath to be delivered, cleaned the dust of travel from herself, and dressed herself in the outfit she had selected: a simple but elegant ankle-length tan dress with a thin white belt, a hint of white flounces, and only slightly raised shoulders. She then inquired at the inn after transportation, whereupon the hostess caused a carriage to be summoned. She paid for the carriage for the day and instructed the coachman to drive her to the estate of Lady Ficora, which proved to be in a hilly part of town distinguished by graceful trees, wide avenues, and large manors, all of which were enclosed, as if by rigid custom, in tall, black iron fences set in stone.

Having at last arrived, the carriage stood in front of the gate for some few moments, until Livosha noticed a rope hanging next to the gate and traced it back to the house by means of certain tall poles driven into the rock-covered ground next to the path. She left the carriage, gave the rope a good pull, and waited.

Presently a man came out, riding toward them on the long, gently curving road from the manor to the gate in a small, elegant chaise pulled by a single white horse. He seemed to be a Teckla of middle years, his clothing well cut in the red and silver of the Tsalmoth. He stepped out of the carriage and, looking at Livosha, gave her an exact bow.

"My good lady, I am Biska, servant to her ladyship the Countess of Ficora. How may I serve you on this day?"

Livosha bowed her head and, speaking through the gate, said, "I have a message for her ladyship from her cousin in Aussiar."

"A message from her cousin," said the Teckla somberly, "will no doubt be well received."

"So much the better. Then be so good as to deliver this to her ladyship."

"Of course, my lady. I will carry out at once this commission you do me the honor to give me. Would you care to come into our home while awaiting a reply?"

"Nothing would please me more," she said. She turned to the coachman, handed him a few more coins, and bid him wait, which he promptly agreed to, the more readily as he had, the reader may recall, already been hired for the entire day. The Teckla assisted Livosha into the chaise and drove back to the front door of the estate. Once there, he helped her down, then led the way into the manor, and so into a waiting room.

In due course, she was summoned to see Ficora, who appeared to be a woman just beyond middle years, with a pinched face and an expression on her countenance in which annoyance warred with self-righteousness. Livosha gave her a courtesy to which Ficora responded with a nod, and did not offer Livosha a chair.

"So, then, you have a letter from my worthless nephew."

Livosha was uncertain how to respond to this, both because it would be rude to disagree while simultaneously being rude to aver the worthlessness of a nephew to an aunt; but, even more, because the phrasing left Livosha uncertain whether Ficora had made a statement or asked a question. The Iorich therefore contented herself with bowing, which, to judge by the sniff the Tslalmoth made, appeared to answer.

"Do you know," Ficora continued, "that this insolent boy writes to me once a year begging for assistance? He pretends to be unhappy working for a man he calls a 'tyrant' and tells of fourteen hour work days, of being forced to leave his flat when his wages were reduced, and similar nonsense, as if I had nothing better to do with my time than worry about him. If his mother, my sister, were still alive, I'd give her a basket of words, I assure you. Discontentment with one's place has never led to happiness, nor has begging. I despise beggars. Don't you?"

"My lady," said Livosha, bowing again and hoping it would do as a reply.

We trust the reader need not hear of the interview in all of its details; it was drawn out and thorough, and Livosha was required to swallow her pride and refrain from observing that the Iorich was, in fact, higher on the Cycle than the Tsalmoth—meaning, of course, that Livosha's status ought to be higher than Ficora's, a circumstance that appeared not to matter in the least to the countess. In the end, Livosha was able to secure employment sufficient to provide for herself and her brother at the cost of some hours—and then years—of humiliation. Should the reader have never faced circumstances where one must swallow one's pride, the historian congratulates the reader on having such fortune, for it is well known that no one is exempt from facing these circumstances. Indeed, even in the fair halls of the academy, it is not impossible to find one's self in a position where one must watch an inferior colleague—indeed, a colleague who treats the entire study of history with no more respect than an illiterate peasant treats books, who invents theories to suit his fancies and then gathers half-researched facts to support them, who, rather than seeking to understand historical law, sees history as only the working out of the dream of a preposterously personified "fate," who treats the incidents of history as a traveler treats the grains of sand in a desert, as if each one were as important or unimportant as any other—where one must watch such a colleague, we say, receive positions and honors (and, of course, the associated lecture tours) properly the due of serious historians, merely because of gossip and rumor concerning one's personal life that, even if true, could have no effect on the quality of one's work.

We mention such circumstances, the reader may be assured, only to show that we understand how trying it must have been to Livosha and, moreover, to warn the reader (for a study of the past that provides no material to guide the future is necessarily without merit, whatever the opinions to the contrary certain supposed scholars may propound from the high positions they accidentally occupy) that such humiliations as these are an inevitable part of life, and when faced with this sort of experience, one ought to carry on bravely, doing one's work, and never permit one's self to become bitter or resentful.

Certainly this is how Livosha carried herself. It may be that the reader wishes to hear the details of the trials the poor Iorich endured from the countess; if so, we must, with regret, deny the reader that pleasure. It can make no difference to history how often and in what manner Livosha was told what a poor maid she was, nor the tasks she was required to repeat, nor the hours of bitter discourse directed, when not at her, at the other servants, at the local aristocrats (those in the lower orders of society, of course, were rarely discussed, and then only in terms of contempt and dismissal), at her House, at the other Houses, and at society at large. It is sufficient, in the opinion of the historian, that these things occurred, and that Livosha endured them.

She and Kefaan found lodgings in the Meethra district, not far from the market area and an easy walk from the Hillside (the name, as she learned, of the area where Ficora lived) and she at once went to work. The countess for whom she worked, as the reader may perceive, was no more agreeable than the one who had interviewed her, a natural circumstance as they were the same person; yet Livosha accepted the harsh and unreasonable demands placed upon her with a graceful calm, like a scholar who is only devoted to his studies and cares little for accolades. In the morning and in the evening she continued to train in swordsmanship, convinced that, sooner or later, there would be an accounting, and she wished to be ready. At first she hired tutors for Kefaan, but she quickly discovered that he had no interest in learning, and with her duties, she hadn't sufficient attention to spare him to even attempt to correct this deficiency. Far from attempting to discover how he was spending his days, she, it must be admitted, made an effort not to speculate. The reader may judge her harshly for this, but the reader ought to remember that she was scarcely older than he was, that as a sister she had no parental authority, and that with the effort it took her to, first, please the countess, second, continue her training in arms, and, third, resist a constant desire to test the second upon the first, she would have been unable to attend to him save by surrendering the notion of sleeping, a solution which is, as no doubt the reader knows, impossible to carry out over any significant length of time. That he returned in the evening and was still there when she left in the morning was all that she wanted to know.

Livosha continued in this way, then, and, as with Eremit on the other side of the world, the days turned into months, and the months into years. Livosha had learned so much that her sword master could no longer effectively teach her, and so she hired another. At around this same time, Kefaan began showing up with small amounts of money, which he would silently hand to Livosha as if challenging her to ask where it came from, a challenge she declined.

Over the next few years, however, as he began supplying even more money, her curiosity began to war with her fear of hearing an answer she wouldn't like. Their relationship had changed, of course: the difference between the age of one hundred and the age of sixty is far greater than the difference between the age of two hundred and the age of one hundred and forty, and yet another hundred years brings them even closer together. They were on a more equal footing now, and any notions either of them had once had of Livosha taking care of her brother had long vanished. And so it was that she returned home from a day on which she had been brushing the countess's hair now too hard, now too soft; on which the tea was too hot and took too long to arrive; on which her clothing was laid out in such a way as to surely wrinkle; on which any girl plucked off the street in Dripping Alley would do better.

She came home, made herself tea into which she poured a small quantity of oishka. She removed her shoes and had just had a sip when Kefaan came in, bowed to her, and handed her a purse.

"This is tolerably heavy," she said.

He shrugged. "Well."

"Where did it come from?"

"You are asking me that?"

"I am."

"You truly wish to know?"

"Yes. And the proof is, I have asked."

"That is true, and yet—"

"Well?"

"I had thought this was something you would have preferred not to know."

"And so it has been, my dear brother. But now I wish to. You perceive, things change."

"Very well, I accept that things change."

"And so?"

"I will tell you. But—"

"Yes, but?"

"But not to-day. I will tell you to-morrow."

"Why to-morrow?"

"Because you are tired, and you wish to drink tea which, if my nose does not deceive me, has been flavored with oishka."

"You are not wrong about that."

"Whereas to-morrow is Endweek, when you are permitted to leave early, and when we habitually visit the market."

"That is true. And then?"

"While we visit the market, I will answer your questions in full."

"But why wait until we visit the market?"

"That, also, you will learn to-morrow."

"Very well, it seems I must accept it."

"That would be best, believe me."

The next day, as agreed, they went to the market together, each with a basket. The market at Meethra was one of the largest in Candletown, being located between the pier and Farmer's Gate (which would have been an excellent name, as it was the road by which most farmers entered Candletown, if there had, in fact, been a gate there). The market, we should say, though most busy on Marketday, had custom all five days, only closing down for a few hours late at night and on certain Imperial holidays.

On this occasion, they walked past the stores, wagons, tents, carts, and tables where they were most accustomed to shop. Livosha, content to let Kefaan take the lead, matched her pace to his, which was in the nature of a stroll or even an amble. In this fashion, they went most of the way around the large circle that made up the bulk of the market and was where the most prosperous merchants had, by one means or another, secured a spot. A few "streets" (they were known by this term, though they were, in fact, mere pathways or aisles, some of them not even fully paved) went off to the side, making the market in some measure resemble a wheel that had been designed with a peculiar number of spokes of different lengths and placed at odd intervals. It was one of these they took. The reader must understand we cannot give the name of this street for the simplest of reasons: it had none. When some traveler would ask after a merchant known to be along this street, the directions involved pointing and saying, "that one," or, perhaps, "the street by the man selling brightly colored yarn." However, as Kefaan knew where he was going, proved by the lack of hesitation in his stride, this problem did not arise in this case.

After some few moments, they came to a peculiar sort of merchant— peculiar in that he appeared to have nothing to sell. There was a thin metal table, cunningly crafted so that it could be folded up and moved, and behind it was a wooden stool on which sat a broad-shouldered, large-headed man with short, neat hair, wearing the black and gray of the House of the Jhereg. Seeing him and, moreover, seeing Kefaan approach him, Livosha's heart sank as she prepared to have all of her worst fears realized.

The Jhereg nodded to Kefaan, looked at Livosha, and permitted (or, perhaps, caused, it is unclear precisely how deliberate such an action is in certain cases) his eyebrows to climb, indicating either surprise or curiosity, presumably at Kefaan appearing in the company of someone he didn't know.

"Tigra," he said. "This is my sister, Livosha. Livosha, meet Tigra, a friend."

"Friend," echoed Livosha doubtfully.

"Ah," said the Jhereg, rising and bowing. "Your sister. Well, it is an honor, my lady."

Livosha, shocked into courtesy, returned the salute.

"Have you anything for me?" asked Kefaan coolly, as if the question were the most natural in the world.

"There is nothing now, for you perceive we are not accustomed to seeing you until Marketday."

"Yes, I understand that."

"Perhaps, however, as the evening comes on. There have been rumors."

"Ah, rumors!"

The Jhereg nodded. "There might be a dispute between Fith and Nirin."

"I beg your pardon, but I think you mean, *another* dispute."

"I accept this correction. Should this be the case, of course, it is in everyone's interest for it to be settled quickly and without any unpleasantness."

"I understand that."

"And so?"

"And so, my friend, I will return at a later time."

"Until then, my friend. Lady Livosha, it was a pleasure." He bowed once more as Kefaan led his sister away.

"And so," remarked the young man. "That is where the money is coming from."

"A Jhereg!"

"Ah, you noticed that?"

"Nearly."

"And then?"

"But, my brother, what are you doing for him?"

As they returned to the main part of the market, Kefaan gestured around them. "All of these wagons, tables, tents, and permanent structures, do you see them?"

"What of them?"

"They are not given free of charge."

"Well, I had not thought they were."

"The city, you perceive, demands compensation based on an ingenious formula involving the amount of space taken up on the road, for which they have a marvelous term, that being *frontage*. Is it not clever? A special word that means only 'amount of street, measured in feet, that is used for a temporary business.'"

"Very well, I accept that there is such a word. And then?"

"Well, but that is not the only charge."

"How, it is not?"

"No. My friend Tigra also collects from them, using his own system, which is not nearly so complex."

"This makes me curious about many things: the system he uses, why is he paid, how he collects, and what your role is in all of this."

"Those are astute questions, my sister, and I will not hesitate to answer them."

"Then I am listening."

"To go in the proper order—for sequence is always a vital aspect in any disquisition—"

"Oh, I entirely agree!"

"—I will begin with the matter of the service for which Tigra accepts payment."

"That is not the sequence you did me the honor to list above, nevertheless, I am listening. The service. And that is?"

"To prevent such unfortunate incidents as fires, beatings, robberies."

"But, cannot the City Guard protect against such things?"

"Not from Tigra."

"You mean he would do them himself?"

"Certainly, if not paid."

"But that is illegal!"

"Nearly."

"And the City Guard?"

"He pays them."

"That is bribery!"

"Without doubt, 'bribery' is a word that can be used for such an activity."

"But, what is another?"

"Custom."

"Well, but—"

"Come, my sister. Let us not dispute over words. You wished to know the system he uses?"

STEVEN BRUST

"I do."

"He has determined, by his own methods, which locations are the best, and charges more for those."

"I agree that it is simple."

"So much the better. And the way he collects is the easiest matter of them all: he has certain persons who work for him, some of the House of the Jhereg, others of the House of the Orca, who, once a week, pass from one to the other and accept such contributions as have been agreed upon." We must remark here, in passing, that while the prejudice against the House of the Jhereg—that is, the assumption that they are a House of criminals—is false, as most Jhereg are merely landlords, was as false then as it is to-day. Still it cannot be denied that nearly all of this sort of crime involving organized groups was, then as now, carried out by those who were Jhereg.

Livosha, then, after listening to her brother, said, "And should one refuse to pay?"

"Ah, that has never happened. For, you perceive, it is believed to be bad luck."

"Bad luck?"

"Of the worst kind. And last, you asked after my role in the entire matter."

"I did ask that, and yet—"

"Well, and yet?"

"I am no longer certain I wish to know."

"As to that, well, I will not attempt to convince you either way. You must choose, and I will accept your choice."

"You are very complaisant, my brother."

"I try to be, my sister."

"Very well, then. Tell me."

"Since you ask, I will."

"Then I am listening."

"Here it is: At certain times, arguments and disputes will occur among the various merchants. One might pretend that the angle of another's table interferes with traffic that would be going to him, or that a certain individual is 'hawking,' that is, calling out to bring in business, in such a tone as to drive another's customers away, or that the smell of the droppings from one's horse interfere with the aromatic qualities of nearby flowers, or that a single man on a chair making certain items has permitted his tools and supplies to overflow his allotted area."

"Very well, I understand there can be disputes. And then?"

"It used to be that such matters were brought to Tigra to be settled. It happened, however, that Tigra had little skill, and took less pleasure, in finding equitable ways to settle these matters, with the result that it often cost him in both silver and in less tangible coin, that is to say, in annoyance. Upon observing this phenomenon, I one day offered my services as adjudicator, saying that I would, without charge, speak to those involved, and if I were able to settle the matter peacefully, well, I would then ask him to pay me whatever he might think it worth. As it would cost him nothing if I failed, he readily agreed, and was so pleased with the result that he gave me a silver orb. After that, I began doing so on a regular basis as matters came up, for I discovered I have a talent for helping individuals come to see the justice in another's position, which, as you are aware, is the first step in finding a compromise."

Livosha was quiet for a moment after hearing this. Then she said, "But, you perceive, you have allied yourself with a criminal organization."

"Certainly," said Kefaan.

"And you have done this for money?"

"Not the least in the world."

"How, it was not for money?"

"Oh, I do not mind money. On the contrary, it is easier to get along with it than without it. Yet, I should not have associated myself with criminals merely to be paid."

"I am glad of that. Only—"

"Yes?"

"It brings up a question."

"Oh, I do not doubt that. In fact, my dear sister, I believe I can guess the very question you wish to ask."

"I am certain you can and do not doubt you, my brother."

"You wish to know: if it was not for money, then why have I done so?"

"You have guessed exactly."

"And you wish me to answer?"

"I should like it of all things."

"This is it, then. For friendship."

Nothing he could have said would have astounded her more. "How, for friendship?"

"Exactly."

"But then, you have done this because that Jhereg, whom you had never met, was a friend?"

"Oh, no. Not in the least. You misunderstand me entirely. It was not because he was a friend."

"Well, and then?"

"It was because I wished him to become a friend."

"But why could the friendship of this Jhereg matter to you?"

"Because I have gained certain benefits from it, and I expect to gain yet more."

"But to what benefits can you be referring?"

"Ah, you wish to know that?"

"I nearly think I do!"

"Well, in the first place, I now know people, or, to be more precise, know people who know people who are able to discover things."

"You say 'things.'"

"And if I do?"

"The word is not precise, and you know I believe in precision."

"Then you wish to know what sort of things?"

"That is exactly what I wish."

"Then I will tell you."

"I am listening."

"For the most part, whatever I wish to know."

"But, what do you wish to know? And about whom?"

"About whom, my dear sister, I think you can guess."

"Ah! You mean Berwick!"

"Yes, Berwick. And—"

"Dorin."

"Exactly."

"But what have you discovered?"

"I have only begun my researches, but I can tell you that they are living well on our lands and have become wealthy. They managed, somehow, to forge your signature on documents, making it look as if we had sold them our lands, and so had Baroness Sudora, poor Eremit's mother. So much so that Berwick is attempting to have his barony raised to a county, and Dorin wants nothing less than a dukedom."

"And will they get these things?"

"Such matters take time, but it seems likely."

Livosha looked down to hide the rage she felt building up inside of her and that she was certain would be apparent on her countenance.

"My sister, you are trembling," said Kefaan.

"Well."

"You perceive, my goal has not changed."

"I understand that it has not."

"And?"

"I agree with your goal. While there are aspects to your methods I dislike, still, I recognize the utility. Moreover," she added, lifting her head and managing a small smile, "the additional money is, in all honesty, not unwelcome."

Kefaan embraced her warmly and said, "Lest you worry, I will also tell you this: in order to bring any sort of charge against me, the Empire would be required to dig far into the laws on abetting criminal enterprises, which are notoriously poorly written and thus easily defeated by a clever advocate and, moreover, not as a rule worth the expense to prosecute, even if, by some unlikely chance, Tigra should come under investigation."

"Well, that does make me feel better."

"I am glad that it does. And there is more I have learned."

"Well?"

"Your Countess, Lady Ficora."

"What of her?"

"Has it not seemed odd to you that she, a Tsalmoth, has managed to retain her wealth and position while her House is so low on the Cycle?"

"In fact, I had remarked upon this very phenomenon."

"And to what did you attribute it?"

"Great good fortune."

"Well, but some believe that it is exactly the Cycle that determines our fortune, good and bad. If so, then the answer has not only failed to answer the question but, on the contrary, has only asked it again using other words."

"Well, but then, what is your answer?"

"What do you know of Elde Island?"

"What everyone knows, my brother: that it lies a few scant miles to the south of Ridgly, and there is trade between its king and the Empire."

"And has it ever seemed odd that it has never been conquered?"

"I had not considered it."

"Consider it, I beg."

"Well, I am considering it."

"And?"

"I do not know."

"Most do not, it is not something widely spoken of."

"Well, but you know?"

"It is something I have learned."

"And that is?"

"That Elde is home to a large tribe of Serioli."

"Well, and then?"

"And this tribe has preserved the art of crafting weapons able to destroy the soul of those they pierce."

"I know of these weapons, of course, though had not where that they were still being crafted. What do you tell me?"

"It is true. The process takes years for each weapon, but they have accumulated enough of them over the Millennia that the Empire is not anxious to attack."

"Well, but what has this to do with Lady Ficora?"

"Attend me. These weapons, called Morganti, are illegal."

"I think so! Mere possession carries a death sentence!"

"And yet, they are highly prized among the Jhereg."

"And then?"

"And so, as when anything is highly prized but illegal, a secret trade occurs."

"Ah, you have learned this from your Jhereg associates."

"Well."

"Go on, there is a secret trade in Morganti weapons." Livosha could not repress a shudder as she spoke these words but continued listening.

"Such a trade cannot occur in Ridgly, because the fifty miles between it and Elde are too rigorously patrolled."

"And so?"

"And so it remained for someone with sufficient determination to find a new route for them, something the Empire would not have expected. A long, circuitous sea route from the far side of Elde all the way past the Imperial navy to—"

"Candletown!"

"Exactly."

"Then Lady Ficora—"

"Facilitates these trades, from various innocent merchants, to Elde, and then back to the Jhereg."

"And yet I have never seen her engage in business."

"She does not. After having set the trades, she lets others carry them out, and keeps a large portion of the profits."

Livosha considered this remarkable news for some time, then said, "That is astonishing, without doubt, and yet, how does it help us?"

"Oh, as to that, it does not. But I thought you would wish to know, first, because it tells you something of your employer, and next, because it tells you something of how efficiently my friends can gather information."

Livosha nodded. "And so, my brother. You have sources of information that have brought us a step closer to our vengeance. And yet, what next?"

"Ah, as to that, well, I don't know. Information is all very well, and even vital, and yet—"

"And yet," she finished, "our enemies are powerful, we are not. We have no documents with which to dispute their claims, and no power to attack them."

"Attack them!" said Kefaan. "So far are we from attacking them, that, well, we must be on our guard at all times, for I have also learned—"

"Yes, you have learned?"

"That they have never stopped seeking us."

"Shades of the Paths!" cried Livosha. "Then we are in danger?"

"I will not lie, my sister. We are. Between your work for that . . . that countess, and my spending my time here in the market, it will be hard for them to find us. Nevertheless, they are attempting to."

"Then we must do something," said Livosha. "I'll not wait by as helpless as a Teckla while being hunted by murderous dogs."

"I agree, only, well, what can we do?"

"As to that," said Livosha, "I do not know. That is to say," she amended, "I do not know *yet*. But I will consider the matter. Apropos—"

"Yes?"

"You have means of gathering certain information."

"Well, and if I do?"

"Might you be able to discover who it was who forged the signatures on the papers that gave them the claim to our lands?"

"Ah, ah! I had not considered this!"

"Then consider now, I beg you to."

"I am considering it even as we speak."

"Well, and?"

"It may be that I can discover this. In any case, I am resolved to try."

"Good then."

"And while I do that, what will you do?"

"I? I will be doing two things."

"Let us see, then. What is the first?"

"The first is, I will be considering all that we know and attempting to discover a plan by which we can overcome our disadvantages and strike those who have so injured us."

"Very good. And the second?"

"I will re-double the energy with which I practice on the lessons given me by my sword master, in hopes that I will soon have reason to use them."

"With these plans, I cannot but agree," said Kefaan. "But as to our immediate goals, permit me, my sister, to suggest something else we might do."

"Of course, my brother. I will listen with attention to anything you may suggest."

"This is it, then. It is Endweek, we are at the market, and we have baskets."

"Well?"

"For now, let us be about our weekly shopping."

Seeing nothing wrong with this plan as stated, they at once put it into practice.

Chapter the Twelfth

In Which Magister Reveals His Final Secrets

The study of sorcery led naturally and, one might say, inevitably, into the study of philosophy, which is to say, the study of truth in all its meanings and the methods by which one might determine it. Philosophy of the mind led to natural philosophy, and from there to what Magister considered the highest and most important study of all, that of uncovering the secrets that lie within the heart and thus drive the actions of the human being, that strangest, most complex, and most nuanced of all the animals, with the possible exception of the Serioli, whom many, including this historian, believe to have intelligence and subtlety of mind at least as great as our own. Many believe, and have even said in so many words, that this is the only study suitable to the true scholar. That this opinion is sheer nonsense—for it leaves out all of the myriad interconnections between ourselves and the world around us that play such an important role in who we are and in how we interact with each other, and indeed we might justly add that anyone able to express such an opinion is proven, by this very fact, to be an individual who is by nature, training, and inclination, even if he calls himself an historian, unsuited to grace the halls of an institution that pretends to serious study, except, perhaps, as one who cleans the floors after the actual scholars have left for the day—that this opinion is nonsense, we say, does not prevent us from agreeing that it is, indeed, a matter of importance. Certainly this was the opinion of Magister, and as he is one of the individuals with whom we are, at present, concerning ourselves, his opinion must, perforce, be considered of more value than our own. It is, we are forced to add, an indicator of the sort of mind that deserves to be in a position of some authority within our fine institutions of learning and knowledge to be able to subdue one's own beliefs and perspectives in the service of historical truth. That such matters as unimportant, minor indiscretions should—even if such calumnies were true—be permitted to interfere with the burning need of the young for education, as well as the great requirements for the expansion of knowledge and understanding that are of benefit to an entire society, in other words, are permitted to have an effect on the appointment of important academic positions, is nothing less than a sign of an institution, and even a society, in decline.

With this clear, then, we return to our observation of Eremit and Magister, who have begun the very study to which we were just referring before our important, yet admittedly periphrastic, discussion of some of the broader issues.

"To look at a man," said Magister, "and to see where he will shy away from a decision, and where he will move without thought, and what he will sacrifice for, and what he will not, is to know that man, how to defeat him, or, what can be more powerful, how to save him from defeat."

"More powerful, Magister? That is to say, saving someone can be more powerful than defeating him?"

"Certainly."

"But, how is that?"

"In the simplest way. I will explain if you like."

"I should be very happy if you did."

"Then I shall explain at once. If you defeat someone, that person is gone, and can be of no benefit. If you come near defeating him, near enough that he comes to fear you, honor may compel him to overcome this fear. Whereas if he feels in your debt because you have saved him, honor will compel him to aid you."

"Well, but—"

"Yes?"

"You assume honor."

"And if I do?"

"You must concede that there are those without honor."

Magister shrugged. "But, you see, everyone is honorable in his own mind; even those who claim to be rascals and scoundrels nevertheless, to themselves, privately believe there are actions from which they would refrain. So much is this true that when they violate this conviction, they require themselves to invent a justification which they pretend excuses it, and then instantly create in their minds a new set of standards from which they tell themselves they will not deviate. We all feel that we live by a certain code and believe that principles are important to us."

Eremit frowned. "You think those who put me here, for whatever reason, were acting on principle?"

"I am convinced that they managed to convince themselves that, in some way, for some reason, they had the right to do so."

"And yet—"

Magister held up his finger. "Let me explain."

"I am listening, then."

"There are some—and as you appear to realize, not many—who truly guide their lives by principle and will accept suffering, privation, even death, to avoid deviating from those principles. However, even those who do not live by principle will find ways to convince themselves that they do."

"And then you say there is no difference?"

Magister shook his head. "On the contrary, there is all the difference, and if you only take one lesson from me, let it be that one. To truly live according to right and wrong, and to have thought out right and wrong and know you consider them so, and to hold to this conviction in word and deed no matter the circumstances is the foundation for true greatness, and, more important, goodness."

"But then?"

"The caution that goes with this is to remember that those who have no honor do not think of themselves as without honor. This is important if you are to make either an enemy or friend of such a person."

"Well, I understand."

"Good then. Apropos, we have never talked about your history."

"I wrote it out to you, my dear teacher."

"Oh, and I read it. Yet, there are matters that, perhaps, you have not considered. You perceive, you, yourself, have just shown us that there is a connection between the events of your past, and the study upon which we are, at present, engaged."

Eremit, though he did not like to dwell on that dark time, nevertheless nodded and said, "Very well, then let us speak of these things."

"To begin, tell me again what happened from the moment you arrived at Dorindom. Saying it again will make it clear in your memory, as well as mine, so that we can together search for a nuance that might strike us as important."

"Very well, Magister."

With this, Eremit repeated what had happened from the time he had arrived at Dorin's castle, a repetition we do not need to make, both because we have hopes the reader will remember it, and, moreover, because the reader who does not can simply turn back a certain number of pages (the exact number, of course, depending on whether this present work is destined to appear in *quarto* or *octavo*, a question that is beyond the influence of the historian, though certainly of great concern to him) and reread the passage in question.

Magister listened to the story without a word until, at length, Eremit spoke of awakening in the coach on the way to Burning Island. Then he frowned and fell silent, thinking, an activity in which he frequently engaged before speaking, making him in some measure unusual amongst his fellows. Having reached that point and given the matter a certain amount of reflection, he said, "What, then, is your opinion of the count's involvement?"

"The count? That is to say, His Benevolence Count Dorin?"

"Exactly."

"Why, I had never considered that he might be involved."

"Then consider it now. Come, what do you think?"

"Well, what reason have I to think he had something to do with what became of me? You perceive, as an Iorich, I require evidence to support any supposition."

"And you are right to. But consider this: did you not observe a young man, near to your own age, who was singled out by the attention he gave you when you came in?"

"Why, I did. A certain young Orca."

"Recall him to your mind."

"I am doing so."

"Have you any explanation for why he, unlike the others, would have been giving you his consideration as you entered the room?"

"I have not thought of the matter."

"Pray think of it now."

"Very well, I am thinking of it."

"Would you say, from the way he stared, that he knew who you were?"

"Oh, certainly."

"And do you know who he was?"

"Not in the least."

"Then you had never met him before?"

"Never."

"So, then, how could he have known you?"

"Perhaps I was described to him."

"Ah! Yes, that would explain it. But—"

"Yes, but?"

"It only brings up another question: *Why* were you described to him?"

"Well, so he should be able to recognize me."

"But think, my friend. Who could wish him to recognize you? Who might have described you in such a way that, upon recognizing you, he would have gazed as intently as you have said he did?"

"I don't—"

"Come, of what House did you say he was?"

"He was an Orca."

"And what Orca is concerned in this matter?"

"Berwick."

"Has Berwick a son?"

"I have heard so."

"Of what age?"

"A little older than myself."

"You have seen Berwick?"

"I have, on the occasion of his visiting my home to discuss business."

"And is there a resemblance between Berwick and this young man we have been discussing?"

Eremit nodded.

"Well, then," said Magister, "now you know who was the stranger so intent on you."

"That is true."

"Now you must ask, why was he there?"

"Well, no doubt to represent his father."

"Ah, but in what matter? That is to say, what was occupying all of his father's attention at the time?"

"Ah, ah!"

"So you see?"

"But still, for His Benevolence the count to have been involved—"

"Let us consider, then. The conversation he had with his adviser—for as you describe it, she seemed like an adviser."

"I agree with that."

"But upon what was he seeking advice? What had just happened?"

"Well, I had given him my name."

"And this name, had he expected it?"

"Expected it? So far from expecting it, I feared I had committed a breach merely by pronouncing it!"

"So then, once he knew who you were, he required advice."

"That is true."

"At the end of which, having agreed, he gave you certain directions."

"Yes, he did."

"Which you followed."

"To the letter."

"And what happened when you followed them?"

"What happened? Why, I was struck upon the head!"

"And who was it who struck you?"

"Why, it was the count's men. But they could have been paid by another."

"That is true. And then, what would have happened?"

"Happened?"

"Yes, when you failed to appear at the appointment the count had done you the honor to make."

"Why, he would have sent someone to investigate."

"And was it known where you were?"

"Oh, certainly."

"So then those who struck you—"

"Would have been searched for."

"And would they have been found?"

"Perhaps they would have changed their garb."

"And then? While carrying you?"

Eremit frowned. "I was brought here."

"By whom were you brought?"

"The Kinship of the Mask."

"But who has the right to command the Kinsmen?"

"An officer of the court."

"And who is the highest officer of the court in Westward?"

"Well, it is the count."

"So you see."

"I understand what you are saying. And yet the count—"

"No, my friend," said Magister, shaking his head. "It is not certain, for nothing is, but you must consider that it is likely that the count was involved in the matter from the beginning."

Eremit sighed. "What a fool I was."

"No, merely young."

"Well."

"So, then, you must consider what to do."

"Do, Magister? I am in here. What can I do?"

"You are here, yes. But you will not be forever."

"I admit that is possible."

"And I say it is certain."

"You believe this, Magister?"

"So much so that I wish you to consider the question of what you will do when you are free."

"I confess I had not thought of it. In fact, Magister, even now, it doesn't seem as if it were something that could happen. It seems I am here, I have always been here, I will always be here."

"Oh, I have nothing against that. Let it seem unreal to you. But consider it all the same."

"If you will have it so, I will agree to consider it."

"And so, what will you do?"

"If I am free, well, the first thing I will do is discover the truth."

"Well, but what will you do when you have found it?"

"Ah, well, you perceive that depends on what the truth turns out to be."

"You reason like an Athyra. But there is something else to consider."

"I am always glad to be considering other things."

"So much the better. What you must consider is, while you are searching for the truth, what will your enemies be doing?"

"But how can I know that?"

"In the simplest way: I will tell you."

"Ah, well, then certainly I will know. So, what is it they will be doing?"

"Attempting to kill you."

After considering this, Eremit nodded. "I cannot question their wisdom in pursuing such a course."

"I do not dispute you, my dear young friend. Nevertheless, we must consider how to respond, for, you perceive, it is possible to admire a decision made by one's enemy and nevertheless consider the best way to defeat it."

"That is true," said Eremit, struck by the extreme justice of the remark.

"So then, how are you to defend yourself?"

"I have some skills now. Should I be free, well, I would have a sword and, moreover, certain sorcerous abilities."

Magister nodded. "I should teach you how to fight with both at once, as the Dzur do, for this will give you no small advantage against those who must choose one or the other, and your ability to control where you focus your attention gives you the key to managing to do both with no small skill. And yet—"

"Well?"

"Even with that, you have powerful enemies."

"I do not question their power," said Eremit, who, we must remind the reader, was able to have this conversation on such a subject only because, while in his head he accepted Magister's words, in his heart, he did not truly believe he would ever escape, and thus it was to him a matter of conjecture and supposition, rather than any sort of planning for events that might come to pass.

"You are right not to," said Magister. "Consider that they have high political position, and, as you know, political position is merely an expression of potential force, just as a spell that is already prepared, as in a flashstone, is an expression of potential sorcerous energy. Thus, the greater the political heights upon which your enemy stands, the more violence he is able to summon against you."

"I understand that completely. But what then must I do?"

"You must have your own power, of which I have given you a certain amount and will continue giving you more."

"That is good, then."

"But more, there is yet one more secret I have to impart to you."

"Ah, ah! A secret!"

"Exactly."

"Then you perceive I am eager to learn it."

"In that case, I must tell you certain aspects of my history that I have, hitherto, made no mention of."

"Very well. I am glad to listen to more of your history."

"And you shall."

"Then I am ready."

"When I left Pamlar University to begin tutoring the child whom I have already had the honor to mention—"

"Yes, I recall that."

"—I did not at once report for that duty. Instead, I took a short time, only five years, to pursue certain studies of my own."

"What was the nature of these studies?"

"At first, I became fascinated with death—that path which we all must tread sooner or later. I became curious about where it ultimately led."

"Did you learn the answer?"

"I did not, because, after learning a part of the answer, my interest changed direction and, as I was at this time free to follow my whims, well, I went off on, as the sailors say, a new course."

"Very well. But what was this new course?"

"It involved the study of pathways to—"

"Yes? Pathways to?"

"Other worlds!"

"Are there such?"

"Oh, certainly. You perceive, we have all traveled one many times when we were sent over Deathgate Falls to the Paths of the Dead."

"How, that is another world?"

"Exactly. That is precisely what I discovered."

"And so?"

"Well, I wished to pursue this matter, to see what I could learn of other worlds, how to see them, hear them, perhaps reach them, maybe even communicate with those who live there."

"Yes, I perceive that would be exciting. But—"

"Well?"

"Did you succeed?"

"Ah, that is not an easy question to answer."

"I trust, however, that you will do your best."

"Oh, certainly."

"Then I will be content with that."

"Very good. In the course of these studies, I learned that certain parts of the world were, if you will, more subject than other parts to reaching other worlds."

"Deathgate Falls?"

"Exactly."

"So then, you went there?"

"Not the least in the world."

"So then, what did you do?"

"Why, I did what scholars always do: I read."

"Yes, it is true, scholars are known to read."

"I studied all such accounts as I could find and discovered a few places where, perhaps, pursuits might be useful. And then, when I was ready, I set out."

"You set out?"

"Yes, for, having by this time acquired a theory—"

"Oh, oh! You had a theory!"

"Well, at least a hypothesis."

"Very well, Magister, you had a hypothesis."

"And, having this hypothesis, I thought to test it."

"That was well thought, too. Only, having had this thought, did you then put it into practice?"

"I did. Or, that is to say, I set out to. I went to a place about which I had read. It was winter when I arrived and, as it was far to the north, you perceive, it was very cold. I had on coats and cloaks and woolen garments and still had to call upon my sorcerous abilities to keep me from freezing to death on several occasions. At last, however, I reached my destination. I had completed the preparations for my experiment—indeed, I was about to take the last step—when I was struck a blow to the front of my head. I admit, my friend, that my eyes were closed and I was concentrating so fully on my work that none of my senses warned me that anyone was nearby until it was too late.

"Ah, my friend, the irony! Had I only had ten more seconds, nay, five, then, if the experiment had worked, it would have been of such a nature to have solved the very problem which prevented its completion!"

"But who struck you? And what was the nature of the experiment?"

"I will reveal all to you. I was struck, it seems, by bandits, for there were many in those regions in that day, long ago, after the depredations of the Copper Wars that consumed so much of the Seventeenth Jhegaala reign. The blow knocked me senseless, and when I awoke, I was many miles away, bound tightly, as my captors attempted to determine whether I could be ransomed or whether I ought to be killed outright.

"They were careful with me, I will say that, my friend! They recognized that I was a sorcerer, and so they hung Phoenix Stone about my neck—apparently they had a acquired a small amount which they kept on hand for just such occurrences. They watched me day and night and kept me bound so that I had no chance to escape. My only hope was to convince them I could be ransomed. And yet, who had money for a poor itinerant scholar? My family were all long gone by this time, save certain distant relatives with whom I had no contact, and of course, even if the university would have been willing and able, I had resigned, and so they had no responsibility to me. My new employer, well, I was not yet even in his employ, why should he rescue me?

"All I could think to do was convince them I had a wealthy patron who would be willing to ransom me. I made up someone and wrote out a message that would go nowhere, but at least would give me some time. While we waited, I laid myself out to be agreeable in the hopes that, perhaps, once the deception was revealed, they would have come to love me a little. I made suggestions for improving their meals with what few resources they had, and soon they began to release me and permit me to cook for them, although I was watched closer than ever at such times.

"There was a young lady there among the bandits, a fierce fighter, as I could see by how she moved. She gave her name as Alishka, though that, of course, was not her real name; as you know, Ali'vashika is Serioli for "one who has been betrayed." That is all I ever learned of her story, though I could see, though she wore the clothing of no House, she had once been a Lyorn. But she was interested in cooking, and so I taught her, and in a short time, we became friends. One night, as it was her turn to guard me, we spoke at length, and I told her my story, and she said, 'You have no ransom coming, have you?' I confessed I had not. 'Well,' she said, 'then you must be gone before the morning. I don't know if we will chase you, but if we do, we will be fast. Go west, and do not stop until you reach Landing Point, where you can find a ship. You must hurry and stop for nothing.'

"'But what of you?' I asked her.

"'Ah, you must not worry. Either they will not touch me or—'

"'Or what?' I asked, for I was not keen to see another suffer for helping me.

"She gave me a wicked smile and said, 'Or they will wish they had not.'

"With that, she cut my bonds, removed the Phoenix Stone, and sent me on my way. You must understand that I did not dare return to my experiment for two reasons: First, because I no longer knew where I was; they camped in the hollow between two hills I had never seen before, using blankets for makeshift tents, and I was afraid that they would catch me while I searched for a familiar landmark. Second, because I was not certain my experiment would work, and if it did not, well, I would have no defense if they caught me again.

"And so I followed her directions, and they brought me in time to a small harbor town where I was able to beg passage in exchange for work, and so I returned to the task I had agreed on, for my five years were now up."

"That," said Eremit when he had concluded, "is a remarkable story, Magister. And yet you have not explained what it was you were attempting to do."

"Yes, I have not. But that is my final secret, and I will now tell you."

"You perceive I am listening."

"Very well then. Here it is. But what is that feeling?"

"Feeling, Magister?"

"Yes! The blood is pounding in my ears, and I cannot feel the fingers of my left hand, and—Ah! Ah!"

These sudden cries from Magister were accompanied by a clutching of his chest and a widening of his eyes.

"My friend, my teacher," cried Eremit. "Are you well? You must tell me that you are well!"

"My poor friend, I cannot tell you that. On the contrary, I now feel myself falling from this life, and soon I will be gone."

"It cannot be!"

"But it is. An hour from now, this body will be lifeless. Do you remember the plan?"

"Ah, ah! How can you speak of this plan? You are my teacher, my mentor, and even my second father. I cannot permit you to die!"

"You cannot prevent it, my son, for so I will call you. You must listen."

"But—"

"No, you must. Attend me, I beg of you by any affection you have for me."

"Very well," said Eremit, his voice trembling. "I listen."

"Teaching you has given my life meaning. So much so that you must carry out the plan of escape, and so doing, my life will continue in your actions. It is my last wish. Will you deny it?"

Eremit, though he felt tears on his cheek—tears he had not felt since his first days on the Burning Island—took Magister's hand tenderly and said, "Very well. I will carry out your wish."

"Then here, take this," As he spoke, he removed a thin silver chain from around his neck, at the end of which was a tiny, multi-faceted jewel of a peculiar purple color. "Put it around your neck and do not remove it."

Eremit put it around his neck and said, "There, it is done."

"Good, then. But there is more."

"More?"

"I have one last secret I have to impart to you, my son. So listen well, for I have only a small amount of time."

"I am listening," said Eremit, though he only managed a whisper.

Magister closed his eyes tightly for a moment, then opened them. It seemed as if perhaps he could no longer see, for he reached out with his hand and found Eremit's arm, which he gripped with a surprising strength, as if to communicate by touch the urgency he was unable to fully convey by voice. He was silent for what seemed to Eremit a long time, until the Iorich was afraid he would breathe his last before saying another word, but then he began speaking.

"There is a place due east of Mount Kâna, in the Kanefthali Mountains," he said. "It is called the Narrows, though it is in truth more than fifty miles wide. Beyond it the Cold Sea opens up, extending north for more than seven hundred miles. There are fishing villages all along the southern coast of the Cold Sea, and one of them is called Dinshouse, and it is marked by a tall structure on the very edge of the sea that is built of a peculiar material found only in that region that is called white shale. From this village, if you go due north for fifty miles, you will discover that you are climbing and soon will be among the Everchill Bluffs. One of these hills is covered with coldweed, a bright green and yellow plant that grows through the snow. From the top of this hill, travel east, and you will soon find yourself in a place that is called the Valley of Dust. That is your destination. Do you understand?"

"I do, Magister. And here is the proof. East of Kâna, the Narrows, the Cold Sea, Dinshouse, north to the Everchill Bluffs, coldweed, the Valley of Dust."

"Good. You must remember this."

"I will, only, when I am there, what must I do?"

"The valley extends some seven miles, and at the end is a cave that is, from time to time, occupied by mountain bear, or darr, or bandits, who seem to take turns with it by some system of their own. Should it be bear, they must be driven out; if darr, of course, they can be ignored; if bandits, you must wait until they are gone or negotiate with them in some way. The cave is not deep, and at the back of it you will find a design traced into the ground in gold paint. You will no doubt have to clear rubble, bones, and still less savory substances, but when you have done so, you will see a circle in the midst of the design. You must sit in this circle facing to the south, that is, toward the mouth of the cave and, holding a knife, you must complete the pattern by drawing a single line. It will be clear which line to draw, and where to draw it, when you are there."

"Very well, I understand these instructions you have done me the honor to give me. But what am I then to do?"

"Once you have completed the pattern, then—ah! Ah! I cannot see, my friend. Where are you?"

"Here, here, dear Magister. Can you not feel me touching you?"

"I am dying, my dear son. Do not forget to carry out the plan, it is all I wish."

"I will not fail you, I promise."

Upon hearing these words, the old man smiled, and his eyes cleared, so that for a moment, he looked upon Eremit, and then he drew a deep breath, and, as he exhaled, his eyes rolled up.

Eremit bowed his head, took the old man's hand in his, and wept.

Chapter the Thirteenth

In Which It Is Demonstrated that Circumstances Alter Cases

So long did Eremit spend weeping over Magister's body that he was very nearly caught by the jailers. He ducked into the tunnel and managed to close it behind him just as the door opened. Because he had pulled it shut, he had been unable to return the bed to its position, yet he hoped this would be attributed to the death throes of poor Magister.

He returned to his own cell and threw himself onto his cot. When the jailers came with his dinner (for it was shortly before dinner that Magister had breathed his last) he didn't move or stir. He heard the commotion in the next cell and recognized the sounds as the servants putting Magister's body into the bag, and wept more.

The thud and clank of Magister's cell door slamming shut made him suddenly remember the plan he had promised to carry out. It took, in fact, considerable effort to raise himself up from the cot, as if sorrow had a tangible weight that was now pressing down upon his back. Nevertheless, he managed it, and was sitting up when they returned for his tray.

"Ah, you haven't eaten," remarked the servant.

"Well."

"You heard that number eighty-two died?"

Eremit managed to nod, and yet hearing his friend called only "number eighty-two" filled him with such a sense of outrage that it was all he could do not to express his anger to the poor servant in terms that would have left the man bleeding on the floor. Eremit sternly reminded himself that Magister would have strongly disapproved of any such action and, moreover, that the servant was hardly to blame for the rules of the jail. When Eremit did not reply, the servant merely took the tray away, and the jailers locked the door.

From this moment, Eremit knew he had to hurry if he was to carry out the plan, and, moreover, the jail had suddenly become for him that hateful, abhorrent place that, in truth, such institutions usually are for most of the unfortunate souls who are locked inside of them. Eremit had first been too numb to feel this, and, after, too busy, and then too involved in his lessons. But now, suddenly, in addition to the grief for his friend, he felt that he couldn't remain there for another night. Thus he at once opened the tunnel and, he hoped for the last time, made his way to Magister's cell.

He was just on the point of pushing open the portion of the wall used as a doorway when he heard sounds, in fact, voices, coming from just beyond it. He pressed his ear against the wall, careful not to press too hard, for it would certainly not help his plans should he sprawl into the cell. He listened closely and was able to make out the voices he recognized as those of two of his jailers, who were, it seemed, engaged in some sort of conversation.

"But in all my years," said one, "such a thing has never happened before."

"So you have said, my friend," said the other. "And you have said it three times now, and each time I have replied, nor in mine."

"Well, but then, it is unprecedented," said the first.

"With this I agree," said the second. "Indeed, it may safely be said that any event that has never happened before is, the first time it happens, unprecedented."

"Have you no curiosity as to why?"

"Oh, as to why, I have no need of curiosity."

"Curiosity is not something one needs; it is something one either has or doesn't have. And for my part, I have some. Why is it that, for the first time, instead of throwing a body into the Ocean-sea, we are to preserve it in the cold room, wait for the next boat, and send it to Northport? I have curiosity and wish to know the answer. You have no curiosity—"

"I have no curiosity," the second interrupted, evidently growing impatient, "because I know."

"How, you know?"

"Certainly."

"But how could you know?"

"In the simplest way: I was in the outer hall when the director explained it to the night commander, and I happened to be placed such that I could hear every word."

"So you understand the reason for this strange order?"

"In every detail."

"And will you tell me?"

"Ah, you wish me to tell you?"

"Obstinate fellow, it is an hour since I wished for anything else."

"Then I will explain. It is according to the wishes of a certain individual known as Traanzo."

"Traanzo? I have never before heard this name pronounced."

"Neither had I, and yet, that is the explanation."

"But who is this Traanzo? Were you able to glean anything from the conversation?"

"Only that he is highly placed in the House of the Iorich, perhaps a High Justicer, perhaps the heir, and that—"

"Yes, and that?"

"He gave certain orders at the time of number eighty-two's incarceration."

"Well, but that must have been nearly four thousand years ago."

"Perhaps it is a son or a daughter."

"Well, that is possible. But then?"

"The orders were that when number eighty-two died, his body was to be returned to Traanzo, in order—"

"Yes, in order?"

"In order to permit certainty of death."

"How, death is uncertain?"

"It seems this number eighty-two had certain information that could be damaging to Traanzo, and so nervous was he concerning it, that he would be unable to rest until he had, himself, seen his face."

"There will be little enough to see after waiting for the boat, the trip to Northport, and then to wherever is his final destination."

"He is to be packed in ice, and, once he has arrived in Northport, spells to preserve his body from decay will be applied."

"Ah, well, I perceive that, in this matter, there is no question of joking."

"That is right. So then, we must see that this body is brought to the cold room, where it will be stored. Someone will be along presently with the shutter, and we will go along."

"Very good then. Those are our orders, and so—"

"Yes, and so?"

"So, I will carry them out. And yet—"

"Well?"

"I have sometimes wondered."

"Oh, as to that, well, in spite of your opinion about my curiosity, I have sometimes wondered too. But on what subject have you wondered? For I perceive you were less speaking in general than of a specific subject."

"You are perspicacious. This is it, then: A powerful Iorich causes this body to brought to him to ensure himself that he is truly dead."

"Well, and?"

"And there are no names here, but rather each prisoner—that is to say, guest—is known by the number of his cell."

"This is true."

"And, moreover, although we are licensed as a jail under the auspices of the House of the Iorich, yet, no one has ever left here for trial."

"You are right once more. But then?"

"Have you never wondered if, perhaps, all here is not entirely within the law?"

"Ah, ah!"

"Well?"

"Come, my friend. You do yourself no favor by speaking of such things, nor do you do me a favor by causing me to listen."

"Then you do not wish to discuss it."

"Never in life."

"Very well, then, it shall be as you wish."

Eremit pulled his ear back, trembling. His plan was gone! Not only were they not to throw Magister into the Ocean-sea but, moreover, they were not going to leave his body unattended. He made his way back to his own cell and once more threw himself onto the bed.

And yet as despair threatened to close over him, he nearly imagined he could hear Magister's voice in one of their conversations. *A plan has failed*, he would say. *What then?*

Then, Eremit must reply, *find another.*

That is correct.

But how? What other plan can there be?

Though he didn't have an answer yet, as this imaginary conversation played itself out in his mind, he felt himself becoming more steady; he felt, as the Dragons say, his soul firmly planted in his feet, by which they mean that this person is calm, alert, and ready for what may come, which effectively describes our good Iorich at this moment.

He considered all that he knew of the jail, of the guards, of the circumstances. He began by admitting to himself that it might not be entirely bad that the plan had failed because he was, in all honesty, far from certain he could have walked along the ocean floor while continuing to breathe for the miles and miles it would have taken. So, then, what other plan could he find?

He cast his memory back to his arrival and slowly recalled every step he had taken, each turn. He recalled the way his footsteps had echoed while descending the pit, and the feel of the stairway. In his mind, he reconstructed the passageways to the director's office and then, hardest of all, he brought back to mind the walk to his cell, when he had been in such a state of shock that he had not even noticed whither he was bound.

This done, he went back still further, to the voyage he made from Northport. He recalled every day, and when he could look up and see the sails, and which way they were set, and when he could not, and what this meant for the wind direction, and, moreover, how much leeway a ship such as that must make.

He sat back on his cot then, leaning against the very wall behind which was the tunnel he had so laboriously constructed, year after year. Hours and days passed. Trays were delivered and taken away, and still he sat, only rising once a day to go through the daily exercise as a sleep-walker will, still remembering, forcing himself to recall how the boat had cut through the waves when he was on deck, and the few times he had felt the furnace, and where it had been.

At last, after four days, he rose and saw a tray of food. He moved over to the desk, sat down, and ate every bite, drinking the watered wine. Then he said aloud to the empty room, "Well, as I sit here, I am facing south by west. The mainland is ninety miles southeast of me, which would put me at very nearly the northwest corner of the Empire. And, though he didn't know, the cave of which poor Magister spoke is four hundred miles in that same direction overland, whereas by ship it would require a voyage of a thousand miles south just to reach the Narrows, and then hundreds of miles north again just to reach Dinshouse.

"So I know where I am and what direction I am facing.

"What is to prevent me from continuing the tunnel straight out? Nothing, except that there is the matter of the volcano, which has been enchanted to destroy anyone appearing outside except on the one path that is constantly watched.

"Well, I have no solution, but I will consider the matter. And, as I consider the matter, well, it is back to making vinegar from apple cider. At least I need not concern myself with where to put the dust anymore—there is no need to paint it onto my walls, I will simply fill in the tunnel Magister and I worked so hard to build. If my calculations are correct about the height of my cell and the thickness of the mountain, it is not more than eighty feet of tunnel that is needed. So then, to work, and as I work, I will consider the matter of this inconvenient volcano."

This decision was no sooner made than acted upon.

So, then, for some considerable time—the reader must understand that each foot worn away was more than a year of effort—he devoted himself to his work while letting "the bottom of his mind," as the saying is, consider the matter of the volcano and the distance to the mainland. His progress, we must say, was significantly faster than it had been when carving out the first tunnel, as he saved significant time by not needing to worry about the debris. We must also add that, while he failed to arrive at any answers about the two vital questions that concerned him, the discipline of mind that he had learned held him in good stead, and he continued to consider these matters without becoming in the least frustrated.

While he continued to miss his friend, he was able to, in some measure, ease the pain by recalling conversations they had had, and sometimes even imagining new ones, in which his agile mind would provide both sides of the conversation on some subject that had taken his interest. These subjects, we should add, covered a wide range, but the subjects themselves are of no importance; what matters for now is that he was thus able to fully occupy his mind and, in some measure, set aside his sorrow at losing what was, in fact, the longest friendship of his life. The bitter irony of this being the case, that is, it being his incarceration that provided him with a rewarding companionship lasting far, far longer than any other in his life until then, is not new to those with the misfortune to have been imprisoned for lengthy periods of time.

These thoughts, of course, did not occur to him as he continued his patient work, inch by inch, wearing away at the stone between himself and the outside world, until at last there came a day when, by his calculations, he believed that one good, hard push would get him through. Here he stopped, because he considered that opening the tunnel to the air would cause a change in his cell, perhaps in temperature, certainly in smell, and if this change were noticed, it could cause an investigation that would ruin everything. So then, having stopped, he turned all of his attention toward solving the two questions that still perplexed him. He told himself that if he could solve the first—that is, find a way to leave without being subjected to intolerable heat from the steam and ash of the mountain—he would take his chances with the other. He did not, it must be said, feel any confidence in this plan, but as he had as yet not solved the first problem, he need not worry too much about the second. "Because," he told himself, "if I am burned alive before reaching the water, well, I will hardly need to concern myself with breathing; and if, on the contrary, I remain here, then I am able to breathe perfectly well. Thus, the question is how to achieve the answer to the first problem."

It happened, however, that he was able to solve both of his problems at once, and it was thanks to the attention he paid to food that he was able to do so. It came about this way: He picked up an apple that regularly came with dinner on the eleventh day (as well, we should add, as supper on the fourteenth, and lunch on the third), and bit into it, observing that it was pleasantly crisp, as so often it was not.

He frowned as he considered this. In the outside world, as the reader is aware, the fruits and vegetables we eat are determined by the season: We will eat oranges and green onions in the spring, lemons in the winter, and so on, contenting ourselves with dried fruits when they are out of season. Yet the jail on Burning Island had no such policy; if the fruit was out of season, well, it would be delivered just the same, preserved as well as could be, which often meant not very well at all; he had discarded as inedible countless pears and no small number of artichokes. It was as if a rigid diet had been determined and such matters as the practicality of supplying it were considered unimportant. This, however, combined with the knowledge of natural philosophy he had acquired from Magister, gave him clues that were as useful as if the fruits had only arrived in season.

He considered the apples.

There were, he was certain, no apple trees on the island. Thus, why was this apple crisp, in distinction to others that were not? What, he asked himself, determined the crispness of an apple? There were three factors, he decided: First, the exact variety of apple, of which there were more than a thousand in the Empire at the time (a number that has since tripled, or perhaps quadrupled, depending on the outcome of a dispute among natural philosophers on what constitutes a distinct variety of apple), next the length of time since it was picked, and third, its temperature at the time it was eaten. This last he dismissed at once as having the least to do with the matter, and, moreover, all of the apples he had eaten were at the same temperature.

As for the first, he dismissed that as well, for the simple reason he could tell by flavor that all of the apples he had eaten were of the same variety and that, moreover, the apple cider he was turning into vinegar was also of that same variety.

So, then, that left only one factor, or *variable* as the arithmetists called it (we did not mention Eremit's studies of the arithmetics as they play little role in our history, yet they happened) remaining: the length of time from when the apple was taken from the tree to the moment when Eremit consumed it. This, however, had itself three factors: the season of the year, when the apples arrived on the island, and how they were stored.

If he accepted that they were stored identically (probably in the "cold room" to which poor Magister's body had been consigned, which would account for the tastelessness of the red nightshades), then that left two. So then, eating an apple as crisp as the one he had just had required two things: it must be between late summer and mid-autumn in the outside world, for that was when apples became ripe (excepting the late-apple, which the one he had eaten certainly was not), and it must have been delivered to the island recently.

How recently?

He took another bite and carefully considered. He remembered the other apples he'd eaten, trying to recall exactly when they had been crisp, when soggy, and when very soggy, and concluded that, during apple season, fresh apples arrived every month.

Then he set about remembering the other foods, especially fruits and vegetables, and considered what he could determine about their arrival dates and frequency. Alas, though his memory had been well trained, it was insufficient to this task; he simply could not recall the pattern of variation in the taste and texture of the different foods.

Nevertheless, from that time on he set out to do so, and so it was that, in less than a year, he had made an important conclusion: Boats arrived with supplies exactly three times every month: on the second, the fourth, and the fifteenth as he was counting days (which he knew was not the same as the seventeen-day month of the outside world). His next conclusion was more difficult, in that it required estimates on matters he knew little about, yet he had spent his youth (now, alas, gone forever!) by the Ocean-sea watching ships come in and go out, and so he concluded that, once having arrived, the ship or boat might remain at the island for an hour.

Should he escape in that hour, well, there were two possibilities: If it were a ship, he could stow away in it; if it were a boat, he could steal it. In either case, he would be off the island.

Of course, it was impossible to say exactly when the boat would arrive, as this would depend on the wind, which no one could predict, and even the best sorcerers of the House of the Orca had never managed to do more than influence in small ways, changing the direction by a point, moderating a gale slightly, generating just enough of breeze for steerage way during a calm.

He frowned then.

But if there was no way to predict the exact arrival time of a supply ship or a prisoner boat, then how is it they were able to control the deadly ash and steam produced by the volcano; that is, how were they to know when to use the sorcerous skills in order to provide a safe landing?

There were only three possibilities: The first was that there was a means of communication, that somehow the captain was able to let those on the island know the arrival time. The second was that there was what might be called a pre-determined gap, that is, some number of hours on certain days when it was safe to arrive. The third was that, in fact, there was never any volcano at all, but only a spell to generate mist that was used to convince the inmates that escape was impossible.

This last idea so excited Eremit that he at once jumped up to test it. He made his way down the tunnel to its very end and placed his hands against the remaining layer of rock. Alas, it took only a short time for him to be aware of the extreme warmth that had penetrated this thin layer. So the volcano, at least, was real.

He returned to his room, sat on his cot with his back to the wall and his legs drawn up, and considered the matter. There were, then, two more possibilities. If it was the second, then how long would the opening be? This could make all the difference. Or, to the left, if it was done by some sort of communication, then what form of communication? Was it mind to mind? If so, there must needs be few captains, and, moreover, they must never switch, even if one of them became ill or injured.

"Then let us assume," he told the empty room, "that there is a certain amount of time left open for the ship or boat to arrive. How long would it be, and when would it be? Well, if it is to be the same time every day, then it must naturally be near the middle of the day, so that even in winter, when the days are short, the captain is able to direct his vessel. So, if that is the case, then, obviously it will be with noon as the middle point. How much time on either side? My journey from Northport took twenty-six days. But a twenty-six-day journey, well, with variations in wind, could be as little as five days, or as many as seventy. How, then, to determine when the arrival will be? Moreover, each arrival of fruit has been consistent, as I have proven during this last year.

"Let us consider that twenty-six-day journey. Might the captain have deliberately gone slower in order to arrive on the correct day? Yes, it is possible. I remember, toward the end of the journey, the sails seemed less taut on some occasions. And then—Gods! The bell! As we arrived I heard a bell from the island! That was the signal that it was safe to enter!

"But can these same boats that transport prisoners on a journey of unknown length be supplying food? Of course not, the transports are irregular, as needed, whereas the supplies come three times every month.

"Well, then, the boats that supply us are not coming from Northport, but from somewhere considerably closer. I have established, I think, that the mainland is ninety miles away. What is there? Could there be some convenient port? Well, why would there not be? I know little of the northwest corner of the Empire, but if there is a coast, well, there are coastal villages. If there are coastal villages, there must be fishing boats. If there are fishing boats, there are piers, or wharfs, or quays, or at least jetties, any of which might be used to launch some sort of boat or ship to cross the ninety miles to this island, and it would be a strange wind indeed that would not prevent a boat or a ship from making a ninety-mile journey that could be determined to end within, let us say, between four hours before noon to four hours after noon."

And so, while not a completed plan in all particulars, he now knew how he would escape: An hour after noon on what he called the second day, or the fourth, or the fifteenth, he would break open the final barrier to freedom, climb down into the water, use the spell he had perfected to walk on the bottom to the boat or ship, climb in and, in the first case, steal it while the crew was unloading, and in the second case, hide himself. By the time he was found to be missing, he would be on the Ocean-sea, beyond the reach of the jailers.

Well, but, what if he opened the way and found no ship or boat because he was too early or too late? "Well," he said, "in that case, I will wait until the time of the evening meal, which will give me several hours, and, if no ship has arrived, I will return to my cell and await the next one. Then, of course, the seal will have been broken, and I will risk discovery because of changes in the odor of the cell. So then I will choose the second, and if my luck is bad, then I can try again only two days later, which will, if I am fortunate, be before the jailers have noticed the oddness."

To-day was the twelfth of his own particular counting. So then he must wait seven more days, and then: Escape!

For the first time, the idea of being free seemed like something that could actually happen, and he felt his heart racing at the thought. He went over the plan in his mind, considering how he would steal the boat, if boat it was, or considering the best place in a ship to hide and, in either case, how to enter it without being seen.

And he waited. Seven days.

Then six.

He felt an eagerness, an impatience, that was entirely new to his experience. He worked to keep this feeling off his countenance when he exercised, and when the jailers came to his room, he made certain he was lying on his cot, his face to the wall.

Five days.

At breakfast, he calculated that after finishing it, he would have twenty-one more meals before the moment he executed his plan, and he counted them down.

Four days.

He recalled a breathing exercise he had been given: slowly, in through the nose, out through the mouth, which Magister had pretended would relax him. He used it now and found it somewhat successful, although still, the hours and even minutes dragged as they never had before.

Three days.

He reviewed the plan again, looking both for defects and for ways in which it could be improved. He ate his meals slowly, drawing them out, lingering over them, and then, when nothing else worked, he returned to pacing in his cell, as he had hundreds of years before: seven paces, turn, seven paces.

Two days.

He ate, he paced, he went over the plan, he sat and breathed. He recalled songs from his childhood and sang them in a low tone.

One day.

He awoke before breakfast. Soon breakfast would arrive, then lunch, then dinner, then supper, and then he would sleep. Then to-morrow's breakfast, and to-morrow's lunch, and then an agonizing wait for the jailer to collect his tray, and then—

He sang again for a while after exercise. He ate, not even tasting the food in spite of Magister's lesson on the subject. Dinner came and he lay on his cot, beneath the wool blanket. The jailer, seeing him tremble, inquired if he were ill, but he assured the jailer that it was only a passing chill and he would be well to-morrow.

To-morrow!

That night, he sat down at the desk to eat his supper, that is to say, the antepenultimate meal he hoped to eat in that place, after which he retired and, though full of nervous energy, he at length managed to sleep. The next morning he arose and paced his cell until his breakfast arrived, whereupon he set into it as a welcome distraction. As he was eating, something entirely unexpected happened, but in order for the reader to understand what it was, we must now turn our attention back to Livosha and Kefaan, which we will do at once, now having concluded this chapter of our history and being prepared to move on to the next.

Chapter the Fourteenth

In Which Livosha Meets an Old Acquaintance and Kills a New One

After their conversation in the market, life for Livosha returned, in a certain sense, to normal. Though concerned to know she was being pursued, she nevertheless carried on with her work, and, as she had promised, practiced harder than ever to perfect her skills as a swordsman. One day—in fact, it was another Endweek several years after the events we have had the honor to describe in our previous examination of Livosha's history—she happened to be taking her ease with a cup of white wine when her brother returned.

"Ah," he said as removed his cloak. "Is that a Farinori? And, if it is, may I trouble you for a cup?"

"Oh, certainly," she said. "And I pour it the more readily because I have purchased an entire case, and that thanks to the money you have been supplying to our little enterprise."

"We have, then, an enterprise?" said Kefaan, removing his boots and accepting the cup.

"Well, such is what I would call it."

"In that case," he said, drinking, "I can report that our enterprise, as you call it, has to-day made certain progress."

"Oh," said Livosha. "Progress! Well, I do not object to progress. On the contrary, I welcome it."

"Then I have little doubt you will welcome this news I bring you."

"Then here, drink your wine and sit in that chair, that is right. Now, tell me what you have learned."

Kefaan sat in the chair, stretched his legs out, and drank some more. "I will tell you, then."

"You perceive, I am eagerly listening."

"This is it: I have learned the name of the forger."

"Ah, ah! You have!"

"Without question. You perceive, my friend Tigra was able to discover certain things."

"Well, but then, who was it?"

"A certain Chreotha named Sajen. He pretends to be an artist, though he's had little success. He lived right here in Candletown."

She frowned. "Candletown. Yes, certainly, that is where they'd have found someone. And yet, you say 'lived.' Is he dead?"

"No, but he has left the city. I do not yet know where."

"Do we have evidence of who hired him?"

"Evidence, my sister? Do you mean, evidence that could be used to bring a prosecution?"

"Exactly."

"There is no such evidence. Those who are behind this have been too careful to permit any such mistakes."

"Then we must find a way to cause him to be forced to testify under the Orb."

Kefaan frowned. "That will not be easy."

"With this, I agree."

"Moreover, if anyone knows we are attempting this—"

"Well?"

"Come, my sister. We have seen these people work. What will they do if this is discovered?"

Livosha thought it over, then shuddered. "They will have him killed, won't they, in order to prevent their crimes from being discovered."

"That is right."

"Then what must we do?"

"We must stay far away from this Sajen until we are ready to move."

"Move, my brother? Move in what way?"

"As to that, well, I don't know. You perceive, we do not yet have a plan."

"Yes, I had been aware of this circumstance."

"Can we come up with one, sister?"

"Not yet, I think. There is too much we don't know."

"Then I shall continue learning what I can."

"And you will be right to do so. But for now—"

"Yes, for now?"

"It is time to visit the market."

"So much am I in agreement with this plan that I am prepared to leave at once."

"So much the better."

They at once put this plan into action, and soon found themselves again in the market, once more each with a basket, testing fruits, examining vegetables, and exchanging gossip with merchants. Livosha held and caressed a Cordiri Longsword made of Hudalo steel with a reinforced tang and a hilt that could have been made for her hand. She sighed and returned it to the merchant. Kefaan, for his part, gazed longingly at yellow- and red- and blue-colored large-cut silks imported from Elde and dyed locally, but didn't touch them.

They moved on, passing by a distillery supplier full of copper tubes, vats and buckets, and past a sweet old man who had been selling his home-grown cut roses, loveyous, and carnations as long as anyone remembered, at which point Livosha suddenly stopped, gasped, and grabbed Kefaan's arm with the greatest possible emotion, such that he instantly looked at her, then followed the direction of her gaze.

We can well imagine the reader's reaction to this development. No doubt, thinks the reader, Livosha has either seen someone she recognizes and didn't expect to see, or perhaps someone who, for various reasons based on dress, attitude, and other subtleties, she has deduced is a threat, or perhaps something entirely different, but, in any case, the reader must necessarily conclude that Livosha has been startled, and therefore the reader is liable to be as well. Perhaps, the reader speculates, we are about to see a threat, even violence directed at the pair we have followed for so long. Might they be in danger? Is it possible, the reader wonders, that, as the result of such violence, we may, in fact, lose one or both of these persons with whom (at least in the hopes of the author) the reader has developed a certain sympathy? Is there to be tragedy? Then perhaps the reader frowns, thinking, *would the historian so cruelly deprive us of the company of those we have come to cherish?* Even if the facts require it, thinks the reader (or so we speculate), what sort of brute, with no sympathy for the finer sensitivity of the reader, would so callously separate us from those we love? Or, wonders the reader, will there be excitement? Or will there be significant information suddenly revealed both to Livosha and, necessarily, to the reader?

The reader may rest assured that we have no intention of artificially generating suspense that does not flow naturally from the events of history, wherefore, we will answer these questions without delay.

"That Teckla!" said Livosha. "I know her!"

"Which Teckla?"

"Do you see? Where I am looking. Of around five or six hundred years, in the green pantaloons and pale headband, with the drooping eye."

"Well, my sister, you know her. And yet you must know many Teckla."

"That is true," said Livosha.

"So then why is this one remarkable? I conclude that she is remarkable because, well, you have remarked upon her."

"That is true, I did," agreed Livosha, who could not deny the validity of the observation.

"So then?"

"Well, in the first place, I know her from Wetrock."

"Ah."

"In the second place, she once served Eremit and his family."

"Well, to be sure, that is worthy of some notice."

"And third—"

"Yes, and third?"

"I had thought she was dead."

"Ah, now I understand entirely."

"I am glad that you do. Come, we must speak with her."

"Very well."

Still holding her brother's arm, she led the way to the Teckla whom we have just had the honor, through Livosha's voice, to describe. Livosha stood beside the Teckla, who was examining the contents of a table filled with exotic and aromatic cheese. The Teckla glanced at her, politely moving out of the way and lowering her eyes, then looked at her again, more slowly, and an amazed and delighted grin broke out on her countenance.

"My lady Livosha!" she cried.

So effluent was her unconstrained joy that Livosha could not help smiling in return. "Yes, it is I, good Jerin. And this is my brother Kefaan."

"My lord Kefaan!" she cried. "Why, he was but a child when I saw him last, upon the occasion of the Migrant's Feast in the fall of eighty-one, that is to say, four eighty-one, when he was brought for his first salt tasting."

"You perceive," said Kefaan, "As considerable time has passed, well, I have grown."

"That is true," said Jerin, struck by the extreme justice of this observation.

"But," said Livosha, "how is it you are not dead? I saw what became of the manor."

"Ah, you wish to know that?"

"I do, good Jerin, and the proof is, I have asked."

"That is true!" cried the Teckla. "Well, then I shall tell you."

"Come," said Kefaan. "Let us move away from the crowd, to an area where we can speak without being overheard."

"I agree," said Livosha, somewhat abashed that she had not thought of this herself, yet pleased that it had been thought of for her.

Kefaan led them to an out-of-the-way and empty corner of the market, where they could not fail to see anyone who approached. Upon reaching it, Jerin said, "So, shall I now answer your question?"

"Yes, yes," said Livosha breathlessly. "How did you survive the explosion?"

"In the simplest way: I was not in the house."

"How, not in the house?"

"I was in the stables, tending to the horses."

"Ah, the horses!"

"Yes. The blast killed poor Spark outright, and left Rose, Hopper, and Sapphire so injured that I was forced to cut their throats with the mercy-knife. Of all the horses, only Ginger was unharmed, for she was in the back stall, and so when the stable fell down, as a result of the explosion, a slanting beam happened to land in such a way as to protect her and, moreover, me, for I was at that instant brushing her."

"Well, but what did you do?" asked Kefaan, who had now become interested in the events the Teckla was relaying.

"Why, I ran! I had thought to take Ginger to help me escape, but, in the first place, I did not know how I would feed her, as I had no money to buy fodder."

"Well, I understand that," said Kefaan. "And in the second place?"

"I feared that anyone seeing a Teckla riding such a beast might conclude I had stolen her, which, after all, would be not far from the truth, and that, upon this conclusion, I might have my head separated from my body, as is done with those who steal horses when they cannot afford an advocate or a trial."

"Well, I understand that," said Kefaan, who, being an Iorich, was perfectly aware of the veracity of the Teckla's words. Indeed, we must observe that Jerin's comment was entirely true at the time of which we have the honor to write, and if to-day such injustices as execution without trial for the peasant have been alleviated, it is only thanks to the beneficence of Her Majesty Norathar, carrying forward the work of Zerika the Generous, and it behooves us to express our gratitude to these enlightened rulers, for it is a simple truth that the only way the poor and unfortunate of the would come to have better lives is when those above them kindly grant these boons, as no such improvements can occur as the result of the actions of the afflicted themselves.

"So then," continued the Teckla, who of course had continued speaking without reference to the historian's disquisition, "I ran to the shore and hid myself in Mistress Potter's boat."

"And it was well done, too," said Livosha.

Jerin bowed to acknowledge the compliment Livosha had done her the honor to pay her and continued. "After that—for I perceive you wish to hear my history—"

"Certainly," said Livosha.

"We are most curious," said Kefaan.

"After that," continued the Teckla, "Mistress Potter permitted me to remain in the boat and was so complaisant as to carry me along the coast as far as Lowfang Rock."

"Well, and then?" said Livosha.

"Since that time I have been making my way along the coast, looking for work as a groom and managing to find work on fishing boats."

"And so you came here."

"Yes, my lady. I have recently secured a position as stable boy for a certain Dzurlord named Baroness Frith. I am promised promotion if I serve faithfully and well."

"And would you like to be stable master yourself some day?" asked Kefaan.

"Well, my lord, you perceive I have never lost my love of horses. Such would be my highest ambition."

"I understand. I hope you achieve this goal, and I thank you for telling us your history, engaging as it was both for myself and my sis—but Livosha, you are frowning."

"Well, and if I am?"

"I should like to know what causes you to frown."

"Well, the horses."

"What of them?"

"I will address my question to Jerin, for, you perceive, I have a question that she can answer."

"That is wise, then," agreed Kefaan.

"And so," said Livosha, now speaking to the Teckla, "you have explained what became of Rose, Hopper, Sapphire, and Ginger."

"I am glad that I did, my lady, for it was my intention to do so."

"And you succeeded admirably."

"That is gratifying."

"And yet—"

"Well, and yet?"

"If my arithmetic is not wrong, and I may say without false modesty that it rarely is, then that is four horses."

Jerin frowned, concentrated, and ticked off the names on her fingers, after which she looked up from her fingers and said, "My lady, if you are wrong, well, so am I, for my number agrees with yours."

"So much the better."

"Oh, indeed!" said the Teckla. "For, you perceive, I am not an arithmetist, and have never studied ciphering, and so I feel no small pride at thus arriving at a number so close to—that is to say, identical with—the one you deduced."

"You pride is justified, good Jerin. And yet—"

"Well?"

"It seems to me that there should be *five* horses."

"How, five?"

"Yes. Attend me. Sudora had a horse."

"That is true, and the proof is, it was Ginger."

"Nessit, for his part, had two horses."

"They were Sapphire and Rose."

"And then there was the horse they kept in case a guest should wish to ride."

"That was Hopper, who was always restive and fiery until he was mounted, at which time he became the most gentle beast who ever trotted."

"Very good. But then—"

"Well?"

"Eremit had a horse as well."

"Oh, certainly. Stony. She had markings upon her nose that looked like two rocks, and she could gallop all day without a rest."

"But then—"

"Well?"

"What became of her? For you perceive, she was not among the horses you listed."

"Oh, what became of her?"

"Yes, exactly."

"I should imagine she was left at the post stable in Hargon's Point."

"Hargon's Point?"

"Yes, it is a village—"

"I know where it is, good Jerin, for I have been there many times. And yet—"

"Well?"

"Why would Stony be there?"

"Well, no doubt young Eremit left her there, for, you perceive, he would have exchanged her for a fresh mount."

"But when would he have done that?"

"Why, on the night of the explosion, my lady."

"What is it you tell me?"

"Perhaps you did not know? On that very night, young Eremit was sent on a mission."

"A mission? To where?"

"Dorindom."

"Dorindom?"

"Exactly."

"But, what was the nature of the mission?"

"Oh, as to that, I give you my word, I have not the least idea. And yet—"

"Yes, and yet?"

"To judge by the expression upon his countenance that night—for it was the last time I ever saw the poor young man, and so I remember it well—to judge by his expression, I say, it was a matter about which there was no question of joking."

"To Dorindom," repeated Livosha.

"And so," put in Kefaan, "he was not in the explosion."

"Oh, not at all."

"But then," said Livosha, "if he was not killed, perhaps he is alive!"

"Well," said Kefaan, "if you are saying that he is alive if he is not dead, I cannot dispute this reasoning, and yet I can think of no reason for believing he is not dead."

"But, why would he be dead?"

"In the first place, if he is not dead, where is he?"

"As to that, I cannot say, except that perhaps he is doing as we are, that is to say, hiding."

"Well, that is true. But, but in the second place—"

"Yes? In the second place?"

"If he arrived at Dorindom, would not the count have, well, I loathe to put it into words, hate to say it my dear sister, but might he not have had him killed, as he had all of the others killed, with the exception of us, and that not for lack of trying?"

"That is true," said Livosha. "And yet—"

"Well?"

"We do not *know* that he is dead."

"I do not dispute you on this point."

"And so, I would wish to discover it, to be certain."

"My sister, I fear what will happen to you if you permit yourself to hope."

Livosha was silent after he said this, then looked up and met his eye. "I understand," she said, "what you do me the honor—and the kindness—to tell me. Nevertheless, I must know."

"Very well," said Kefaan. "If that is your choice, I accept it. But how are we to find out?"

"Ah, well, as Vithraw said to Drusk about the broken bottle, you have touched the exact spot."

"And then?"

"Do we know anyone who knows anyone who might have been at the castle, and perhaps seen him enter, or leave, or while he was within?"

Kefaan gave this question a moment's consideration, then said, "No one I can think of."

This entire time, Jerin, whom the reader may recall, had remained silent, as if she had no part to play in this exchange of thoughts among those of such a higher station than herself. At this point, however, she cleared her throat, thus attracting the attention of the two Iorich, which, having secured this attention, she bowed and said, "Is there a way in which I can help?"

Kefaan frowned. "You wish to help?"

Livosha tilted her head and said, "Are you aware of what you would be helping with?"

"Why," said Jerin, "you wish for vengeance against those who have injured the Baroness of Wetrock and her family, and, if I may be permitted to make a deduction based on your presence here—"

"Oh, by all means, do so," said Livosha.

"—also your own family."

"You are not wrong," said Kefaan.

"And then?"

"But, how could you help?" said Livosha.

Jerin considered this question, then said, "I am good with horses."

"I do not doubt that," said Livosha. "And yet—"

"Also, I can cook."

"I have nothing to say against cooking," said Kefaan. "But—"

"In addition, I can fish."

"Fishing," said Livosha, "is a good thing, no doubt. And yet—"

"I know my letters," said Jerin.

Kefaan nodded. "Well, but—"

"Also, I can hear things."

Kefaan stopped. "You hear things?"

The Teckla nodded. "Certainly I hear things."

"But," said Livosha, "what sort of things do you hear?"

"Why, the sort of things people will say in front of a Teckla that they would never say in front of a person. And moreover—"

"Yes, moreover?"

"Servants talk to each other."

"How, they do?" said Livosha, who had been unaware of this circumstance.

"I give you my word, it is so."

"And then?"

"I can speak to servants, who will gladly tell me things that their masters have said in front of them, not being aware of their presence."

Livosha looked at Jerin as she went over certain episodes in her past and considered them in, as it were, a new light. As she did this, the Teckla looked down as if embarrassed. At length Livosha looked at her brother with an expression of inquiry, to which the latter responded with a shrug like a Lyorn.

"Very well, then," said Livosha. "I agree that this is valuable. But do you know anyone who was in Castle Dorindom at the time Eremit arrived?"

"I have a friend I see nearly every day who has a sister who works in the kitchen of Dorindom Castle, and the proof is, they both learned their letters in secret in order to write to each other, which they do every month, sometimes more."

We should add, for the sake of those of our readers who are unfamiliar with history, that laws forbidding Teckla to read have changed a thousand times within the Empire, and were at times different among the various Houses, and at times varied by duchy. At the time of which we have the honor to write, the Empire had forbidden it, but the law was roundly ignored by those who had a reason for wishing a servant to be lettered, or by those who, such as Livosha's mother, simply did not care—thus we learn that, even among the Iorich, some laws were considered of more importance than others, a circumstance which, we dare to suggest, has been true as long as laws have existed.

"Well," said Livosha as she considered the remarkable intelligence she had just received from the Teckla, "and so you might learn something?"

"It is possible."

"And you are willing to try?"

"If your ladyship wishes."

"Oh, I wish very much."

"Then I will do so."

"You are a treasure, I tell you so."

"And if I learn something, what then?"

"I will," said Kefaan, jumping in suddenly, "give you a way to reach me." Livosha looked at him, and he said, "If there is a rumor or a hint, I beg you will let me look into it. I will tell you what I learn, but at least you need not be tormented by an endless series of false trails."

She nodded. "Very well, then. I agree with your plan, although it seems to me that you do not truly think it possible that he lived."

"Perhaps I do not."

"And yet, it is possible."

"How? You perceive, we know that Count Dorin was part of the conspiracy, and we know that poor Eremit walked innocently into his very keep. How could he have been permitted to escape?"

"It is true that, if he arrived at the castle and gave his name, the count would have had him killed."

"Well, but, why would he have not given his name?"

"Either because he suspected there was danger, or—"

"Well, or?"

"He habitually called himself Eremit, son of Nessit, because of how often he was told he took after his father."

"Yes, and so?"

"But his mother was the baroness, and it would have been her name that the count would have alerted his retainers to listen for."

"That may be true. But, what then?"

"Then if he had been admitted to see the count, in front of witnesses, well, the count would be unable to kill him without it being known, an action that would ruin everything."

"I understand, dear sister. And yet, if this is true, and the count feared to kill him, well, where is he?"

"I admit I do not know. But still, it is possible."

To this, Kefaan could make no answer, although, in fact, he did not, to judge by the expression on his countenance, appear convinced.

"You do not appear convinced," said Livosha, who was, in the natural course of things, able to come to this conclusion sooner than the historian, who must wait until after events have occurred in order to discover them to the reader.

"That is true, my dear sister," said Kefaan. "And yet—"

"Yes, and yet?"

"This uncertainty will not prevent me from investigating the matter as thoroughly as I am able. And so, as we have agreed, good Jerin here will speak to those she knows, and convey to me what she learns, and from there I will discover what I can."

"Do you think your, that is to say, your *friend* will be of any assistance?"

"It is not impossible that he will. In any case, should Jerin learn anything, that is how I will begin."

"Very good, I agree with this plan. Apropos, Jerin, how are we to reach you?"

"In care of the stable master of Baroness Frith, Frith Estates, Hillside."

"Does the stable master know his letters?"

"As well as I," she said. "But how am I to reach you should I be so fortunate as to learn something?"

"You see," said Jerin, "using this stub of pencil, and this scrap of paper, I write out where Livosha and I are lodged. A note sent to this address will not fail to reach us."

"Very good," said Jerin, accepting the paper as if it were a five-imperial gold piece. "I will write when I learn something."

"Very well, then," said Kefaan. "It is agreed."

Jerin bowed very low. "Thank you, my lord, my lady. I will endeavor not to disappoint you."

"We will see you soon," said Livosha.

"It cannot be too soon for me," said the Teckla.

"With this," said Kefaan grimly, "I cannot disagree."

They went their separate ways, then, Livosha and Kefaan to continue their business in the market, Jerin to return to her own home and resume her duties.

It was, in fact, only ten days later—a testament not only to the industry of Jerin and Kefaan, but, we are forced to add, to the efficiency of the post—that Livosha, upon returning home, was greeted by the sight of her brother anxiously pacing the floor. As she walked in the door, he cried, "Ah, you are home!"

Without even waiting to sit, she said, "You have made a discovery."

"I have been uncertain," he said, "whether I should even tell you what I have learned, for nothing is certain, indeed, what I have discovered is so far from certain that I can only barely call it possible. And yet—"

"Well, and yet? Speak! You see I am dying!"

"Six days ago, I received a letter from Jerin—whose hand, I must say, is remarkably good for a Teckla—"

"You are killing me, Kefaan!"

"—and I have been looking into the information she supplied, with the help of my friend, who has been extraordinarily helpful, and—"

"Kefaan!"

"He was arrested."

"How, arrested?"

"The count swore out a writ of felony, which, as you know, he may do on his own without the need to present evidence, as he is the person to whom the evidence would need to be presented."

"But, arrested for what?"

"That I was unable to learn."

"And taken where?"

"My sister, it is my opinion, I am sorry to tell you this, that he must have been taken off to be murdered."

"But then, why arrest him?"

"For appearances. He was seen, unconscious, being carried from the castle by the Kinship."

"The Kinship!"

"So then, he is taken away to somewhere private, and—"

"Kefaan!"

"Well?"

"The Kinship would never lend itself to such doings."

Kefaan frowned. "You are right. I had not considered that. And yet, if not, where is he? There is no record of him in any prison, nor has there been a trial. If he lives, well, where?"

Livosha was silent for a long time, then. "The Kinship brought him somewhere, somewhere they thought it was right to bring him, because they would not have done anything else, and because they keep records, and thus, even if we cannot see the records, they would put themselves at risk by doing anything else."

"And then?"

"Where could they have brought him where you could not find him, but that seemed to the Kinship to be proper?"

"What are you thinking?"

"That there is, somewhere, a secret prison, known to the powerful in the Iorich, and maybe others, and to the Kinship, but to no one else."

"Why would such a prison exist?"

"*The Empire's Challenge of Tikara.*"

"I don't understand—ah, ah! Yes, I see what you mean."

Livosha nodded and said, "So it is possible."

"But if such a place existed," said Kefaan, "how would we find it?"

"There is the law," said Livosha. "And, as has been discussed in the legal philosophies, the very existence of the law implies the potential for it to be broken."

"Well, and?"

"So then, if those who work with the law cannot find us the answers—"

"Those who break it might!" cried Kefaan. "Yes, my sister, you reason like an Athyra, as I have had more than one occasion to observe."

"And then?"

"I will use all of my influence, all of the friendship I have accumulated, and seek to discover if such a place exists, and, if so, where it is."

"My affection for you, my brother, has never wavered, but now it is beyond my power to express."

"So, then, you are not sorry you saved me?" he said with a smile. Then, without waiting for an answer, he picked up his cloak and said, "I will not waste a minute, but, on the contrary, will begin my investigations at once. I give you my word, if there is anything to be learned, well, I will learn it."

For some few weeks, then, nothing out of the ordinary happened, although Livosha struggled with an impatience that was difficult to contain and even more difficult to conceal. Was Eremit alive? If so, what had been done to him? Had he been starved? Tortured? The thought filled her with such anger that, distracted, one day she put Lady Ficora's wine glass on the incorrect side of the lady's chair.

"What is wrong with you," snapped the countess. "If you cannot even pay attention to the simplest tasks, then—"

She broke off because Livosha, still thinking of what might have been done to Eremit, had turned and looked at her with such an expression on her countenance that Ficora only coughed, muttered, "Well," and condescended to adjust her own wine glass. Moreover, her ladyship had, remarkably, nothing to complain of in the service she received for the rest of the day.

It was two or three months after that, which is to say, the middle of summer, which in Candletown meant time spent on the beaches or finding high places where the breeze could reach, that Livosha was walking home from work. The heat of the day had mediated as evening came on, and, in fact, the light was failing when a gentleman in the dress of the House of the Issola, and moreover, extremely well cut, featuring a white doublet open at the chest, green hose, green boots, with a few emeralds and rubies tastefully pinned here and there, caught her eye. As they approached each other, he held up his hand, bowed, and said, "Might I trouble you for a moment, my lady? I am a stranger here, and have become lost."

"I will be glad to help you in any way I can," she said.

"You are very kind."

"Well, then? What is it you wish?"

"Are you familiar with a certain Lady Ficora?"

"Nearly. I have just come from her estate."

"Ah, so much the better! Then you can direct me there?"

"It is the easiest thing in the world, for we are at this moment, on the very street."

"Then it will be easy. Apropos, I am called Nyleth."

"A pleasure, Nyleth."

"And you?"

"My name is K'hidith," said Livosha.

"Ah, well, that is an unusual name to be sure."

"Indeed," said Livosha. "I am told that it comes from a peculiar game played by the Serioli, and is the cry the winner makes to end the game."

"Oh, indeed?"

"Yes. Would you like to know the exact translation?"

"Why, I would like nothing better."

"It means," she said, "'You lose.'" As she pronounced these words, she drew her sword and instantly passed it through the body of the man before her, who gasped and sank to his knees.

"You have killed me!" he said.

"This may be true. Although it is possible that you could still be saved. You perceive, I am not a physicker, and am therefore uncertain as to your prospects or prognosis."

"But why—"

"Why I did run my sword through your body?"

"Yes, that is the exact question to which I desire an answer."

"Then I will explain my thoughts that led up to my decision to act."

"I would be grateful if you did."

"This is it, then. With the Issola at the very bottom of the Cycle, seeing one so richly appointed is bound to incite suspicion."

"Well, I accept that. I am used to clothing of good cut."

"And then," she continued, "you demanded my name when, being suspicious, I chose not to give it. No Issola would be so rude."

"Ah, I understand that."

"And finally, when I gave my name, I perceived a certain astonishment, as if I were not who you had expected me to be. Thus I became certain that you were not only not an Issola, but, to judge from your complexion and countenance, almost certainly an Orca, and one, moreover, sent to do me harm. This I confirmed just now, when a concealed dagger fell from your hand."

"Well, but—"

"Come, my friend. Answer my questions like a good fellow, and I will see if I can find treatment for you."

"I have no reason not to tell you the truth, the more-so as I am nearly dead. Therefore, I accept your terms."

"So much the better. Who sent you?"

"Berwick," he said.

"Then he knows where I am?"

"He has traced you to Candletown. There are many of us now looking in each area."

"And yet, you asked for the home of the Countess Ficora."

"I thought that, perhaps, you would find work in service, and inquired as to who had servants of the House of the Iorich."

"That was well thought."

"Thank you."

"Have you told anyone else?"

"No, and now it seems I will not be able to."

"That remains to be seen. If I am able to save you, will you keep this matter to yourself?"

"As for the idea of searching among servants, I give you my word I will. And as to the fight—"

"Well?"

"It is hardly something I would boast of."

"Very well. Those are all my questions, then, and, as I have promised, I will attempt to find assistance to save your life."

"You are gracious."

"Well. Wait here."

As she said this, she withdrew her sword from his body, at which time he gasped, and his eyes grew wide, and he pitched forward onto his face, stone dead.

"Ah," she told the corpse. "I had not realized that would happen. You have my apology. And, moreover, I apologize for cleaning my weapon on your fine clothing. But now, unless I wish to draw attention to myself, which I give you my word I do not, I must away to home, where I will tell my brother what I have learned, and we will together consider how this new development affects our plans, such as they are."

Having politely explained this to the dead man, she sheathed her weapon and returned home, noting, "Well, I find that I am trembling. And yet, I do not feel afraid. Perhaps this is a natural reaction to killing one's first enemy? Perhaps I ought to feel sorrow, and yet, he had every intention of killing me, and I do not believe he would have been sad if he had done so."

With these thoughts running through her mind, she returned at once to her home, fortunately being some distance from the body before she saw anyone.

Chapter the Fifteenth

In Which the Author Discusses the Problem of
Travel in Historical Narrative

U pon Livosha reaching her home, she found Kefaan was already there, and he perceived at once by the expression on her countenance that something of significance had happened. She quickly related the entire history.

When she finished, he frowned and said, "So then, we are near to being discovered."

"We are."

"If we are discovered, we will be killed."

"It seems likely."

"If we leave before we have learned what we need to know, our work will be delayed by years."

"That is also true."

"How are we to decide then, sister? You have always been the one with the longest head. What must we do?"

Livosha considered.

"When will we know for certain, one way or another, about the existence of this mysterious jail?"

"There is no way to know. To-morrow? A year? Ten years?"

"And how soon until we are discovered?"

"An hour? A day? A month?"

"You perceive," said Livosha, "you are giving me little enough help with your answers."

Kefaan spread his hands as if to say, *those are the answers there are.*

"I will," said Livosha after a moment's consideration, "go to work to-morrow, but I will take a different path, one that does not leave me on the street. And I will find useful activities that permit me to keep a watch and see if the estate is being observed, or if anyone arrives asking questions."

"Very well. And I?"

"You will continue as you have been: attempting to gather our answers. If there is a way to do so more quickly, then do so; otherwise, well, we will continue as we have been."

"For how long?"

Livosha thought a long time, then said, "I will risk ten days. We are well concealed, the person most likely to have found me did so, and is dead. They cannot know that it was by my hand. So then, after ten days, we will admit defeat, and will flee, and start over elsewhere."

"Where?"

"The Capital is big, and easy to get lost in, but I hate being so far from the sea; you perceive, I am not used to it."

"So then?"

"We will take a ship down the coast to Hartre or Adrilankha. They are large and busy and we can find ways to hide in either place."

"Very good, my sister. I accept this plan."

"Apropos, you will be on your guard at all times, will you not?"

"Certainly. And I do not need to ask, for I am certain you will, as you demonstrated so aptly to-day."

"And you are right. And now I retire. Good night, dear brother."

"Good night, my sister."

The plan was put into action at once—Livosha continued her work, but used different, cunning paths to and from her employer every day, and hoped that they would make a discovery before they were, themselves, discovered. But now Livosha was not hopeful; ten days pass quickly!

It was, in fact, four days later that Kefaan, returning home, said, "There is something I must tell you."

"Are we found out?"

"No, not in the least."

"Well then, my brother," said Livosha, relaxing, "remove your boots, sit down, permit me to bring you a cup of wine, and tell me."

"I agree with most of this plan."

"How, most? But, with what do you disagree?"

"With you bringing me the wine. You perceive, you are sitting, I am standing; moreover, your activities are more strenuous than mine. Therefore, I will fetch the wine."

"Very well, with this plan I agree."

Kefaan got a cup, came to the table at Livosha's side, and said, "Ah, but not that wine."

"Well, but is it not a perfectly acceptable wine?"

"Oh, it is acceptable, and yet not what we should be drinking. Come, let me dispose of that."

"Why, you have just thrown a nearly full bottle out of the window!"

"And if I did?"

"But, can we waste wine?"

"We can to-day. To-day we will drink this."

"Is that the Musara?"

"That is exactly what it is. Where are the tongs?"

"They are next to the brazier, on the side-board."

"I have found them. The coals are still hot. So much the better."

"You are, then, determined to open our only bottle of Musara?"

"So determined, in fact, that I am doing it. You see? The tongs are hot. I circumscribe the neck. I dip the feather, and there, the neck is off."

"Well, so you have opened it. We must then drink it."

"You see, I get you a new cup. And here, I bring it to you, and set my own next to my chair. I remove my boots, and now we drink. Ah. It is delightful."

"Oh, to be sure, it is a splendid wine. Only—"

"Well?"

"It seems that such a wine should be used for celebration."

"That is my thought as well, my sister."

"So, then, we are celebrating?"

"That is what we are doing."

"And what are we celebrating? I give you my word, the only thing I can imagine we have to celebrate is this excellent wine, and, you perceive, to use a bottle of wine in celebration of itself seems odd."

"Odd, perhaps, yet perfectly reasonable nevertheless. However—"

"Yes, however?"

"That is not what we are celebrating."

"Ah, it is not?"

"Not the least in the world."

"So then, we are celebrating something else?"

"You have understood me exactly."

"I often do. But then, do you intend to tell me what it is we are celebrating? For you perceive, it is less of a celebration if two are drinking wine, but only one knows why."

"Very nearly an epigram, my dear sister. Yes, I will tell you."

"And I hope you will do so at once."

"In fact, I am about to."

"Then I am listening."

"Then you want me to begin my explanation?"

"Shades of the Paths, obstinate man! It is an hour since I've wanted anything else!"

"This is it, then. It is called Burning Island."

"But, you perceive, this tells me nothing. *What* is called Burning Island?"

"The secret jail run by the Iorich, where they put those they do not wish to bring to trial, but cannot permit to run free."

Livosha sat back. "Then it is real!"

"It is."

"And . . . and Eremit?"

"There is only one way to know if he is there."

"And that is?"

"Why, to go and look for him, of course."

"Then you know where the island is?"

"Ninety-two miles northwest of a village called Ivaacim, in Longview County, far in the northwest, indeed, at the very most northwestern point of the Empire."

"If we are going that far north, well, I am glad it is no later in the year. Come, we must prepare for our journey."

"And you must give notice."

"Notice? I shall perhaps give notice to her skin by puncturing it a few times, I have not yet made up my mind."

"Well."

"Apropos, how are we supplied with money?"

"Let us see. I have forty imperials."

"And I have nineteen. Good. With that, we can easily use the posts in order to arrive the sooner, and stay in the best inns to arrive the more rested."

"So then, what must we do?"

"I must write a note to my sword master, for it would be rude to have her arrive and expect to find me."

"Very well, a note to your sword master. What else?"

"Arrange for the posts."

"I can do that. What else?"

"What of your friend?"

Kefaan smiled. "Upon receiving the news, I told him I would be gone for some time."

"Well, then. I think the next thing to do is—"

"Why, to pour some more of this excellent wine."

"Sethra Lavode herself could not improve on this plan."

In a single day, all of their preparations were complete. Livosha did, in fact, return to the countess, but only to say farewell to the other servants, and to collect her last pay, which the countess pretended she had forfeited by leaving without proper notice. Livosha, who had only spoken to her so that no ill thoughts would be directed at Emeris, who, the reader may recall, was the Tsalmoth who worked for Gystralan, and who had secured her the employment, in the end settled on half of her wages and the promise that Livosha would not seek legal remedy for the rest, and, with pleasant words to her fellow servants, even the Teckla (she and Biska had formed something of a friendship in spite of their differences in rank), she left Ficora's estate, making sure to take a particularly circuitous route back, as being caught at the very last minute would have been too bitter to bear. She was not, however, and moreover, a thorough inspection told her no one was watching their home.

The next day, having thrown out or given away (on the street where they lived, there was little difference between the two) everything that they had accumulated over the centuries but no longer needed, they took a carriage to the first post station. Livosha had only a small valise, suitable for the back of a horse; Kefaan had one similar, but also a long, thin cloth bag at which Livosha looked with some curiosity.

"And, what is in the bag, my brother?"

"How, you don't know?"

"But, how could I know?"

"I had thought you would guess. Well, but here."

He handed it over, and (as we have no doubt the reader has guessed, and, indeed, been waiting for with more or less anxiety since it was first mentioned), opened the cloth to reveal the longsword Livosha had been admiring at the market. She stared at it, drew it partially out of its sheath—which itself was a work of art, wood bound with steel inlaid with mother-of-pearl in the form of an iorich, a hawk, and a tiassa connected with gold wire. She looked at her brother, and before she could speak, he shrugged and said, "Well," and smiled.

"Cracks and shards!" cried Livosha. "It is . . . it is beautiful!"

"So, will you give it a name?"

"No," she said laconically, continuing to caress the sword with her eyes.

In the confines of the carriage, she managed to remove her old sword and hook the new one onto her belt, then she held her brother's hand until they arrived at the post station. They paid the driver and got out, and there was Jerin, who bowed deeply, a gleam of excitement in her eye.

"My lord, my lady," she said. "Are we ready?"

"Nearly," said Livosha. "But, have you a weapon?"

"I? Not the least in the world."

"Then take this," she said, offering her old sword.

"My lady! I am a Teckla! Even if I knew how to use such a weapon, well, it is not permitted for me to wield a sword."

"That's true," said Livosha, and shrugged. She drew the sword, discarded the sheath, and, with a quick motion, broke the blade over her knee, leaving about eighteen inches still attached to the hilt. This she held out and said, "There. Now it is a knife."

"A knife I can take, my lady," she said.

"Then let us be on our way."

They paid the post service, chose their first set of horses, mounted, and set out for the northwest, leaving behind Candletown, the most immediate threat, and the ability of the author to describe events on a daily basis without wearying the reader beyond all bounds of reason. It is well known among all who concern themselves with narrative that to follow the figures in whom we are interested on a long journey presents an interesting and important challenge, not quite like any other except in the most general sense, which is, what are the details that will best convey the sense of the event? Some historians have taken to inventing incidents that never actually occurred, merely to preserve the reader from ennui. Others have evaded the entire matter by making such assertions as, "They arrived." The latter, in our opinion, fails to provide the necessary sense of the experience, which is in its own way inevitably transformative; the former, of course, except in the case of those authors of pure fiction who may arrange incidents to suit their fancy, is simply, in our opinion, impermissible.

So how, then, to solve this dilemma? Often the historian attempts to simply summarize the salient points, for example by mentioning the speed of their travel, or observing that, though the travelers wished to arrive soon, still, they didn't know what would await them on the island, and so agreed that it was better not to arrive exhausted. For this reason, they stopped every evening.

Alternately, one might pick a more-or-less typical day and discuss that they switched horses four times at post stations, stopping for quick meals on each occasion, their own nerves, which insisted upon arriving soon, warring with their bodies, none of which had been riding on horses, and therefore all of which required a certain amount of time for the muscles to become used to this activity. We must add, in all fairness, that though all three travelers experienced various amount of discomfort as a result of this, none of them, at any point, went so far as to even mention it.

Another method frequently used in such circumstances involves providing small yet telling incidents on the journey, such as when Kefaan discovered he had failed to repack his favorite shirt, and they had to backtrack a mile because he refused to leave it behind. Or the occasion when Livosha secretly filled Jerin's water-bag with oishka, to the hilarity (and sharing) of all. Or we could mention the time when Livosha's cinch broke, causing only a short delay while the clever Jerin repaired it, but threatening a much longer one until Livosha was dissuaded from her desire to return fifteen miles in order to have strong words with the post master.

Which of these shall the author choose in this instance? One, or a combination? We mention this because we see our role as, not only to discuss history in its sense of a revelation of events and explication of their interconnectedness, as well as deduction of the general laws that determine the unfolding of history as physical laws determine the properties of objects, but more, to reveal to the astute reader the inner nature of history in its sense of the narration, that is to say, the recounting of these events and laws. The reader must understand that, to the serious historian (a category to which the humble author of these lines aspires to belong), the value in understanding events of the past is inseparable from the value in communicating this understanding to others. It is this, in fact, that requires such care, such *conscientiousness* in determining how to present the incidents to the reader, a fact which appeared in this author's most recent letter to the head of the Department of Historical Studies at Pamlar, in the course of making certain suggestions for personnel changes, in which the disinterestedness of the author is proved by his refusal to suggest himself for the position whose present occupant he decries.

However, to return to the history which the reader, with every right, expects us to make the focus of our attention, we may say that, after a ride of some days, during which summer ended and autumn began, Livosha, Kefaan, and Jerin arrived safely at the small port of Ivaacim.

This village—for so we must call it, as it is of roughly the size of Wetrock, to which we have already given that appellation—was named for the first baron (if the reader will permit a liberty, as the term "baron" was not then in use, hierarchies being less rigid) in the First Cycle, wherein which, in the ancient tongue of the House (or, rather, the tribe) of the Dragon it signified "landing place." That there are at least twelve other villages within the same region with names also meaning "landing place" need not concern us, as they are, each of them, translations from different, although still extinct, languages. The only significant contribution of Ivaacim to history is that it provided a real setting for T. Waterford's fanciful tale *The Chowder Wars*, based on the conflict among the different villages of the region as to the proper way to prepare seafood—a conflict that is real enough, although, so far as the historian has been able to determine, has never actually produced more violence than an occasional insignificant brawl, although this is a subject upon which the author will gladly submit to correction should any evidence to the contrary emerge. This willingness to change one's opinion in the light of new information, we might add, is another means whereby an historian with integrity may be identified and separated from a pretender who, for example, continues to maintain that Markingham Castle was built for defense against Easterners in spite of *over fifty letters of the period* that conclusively demonstrate that its first use was as a storage area for grain which was required to be protected from local brigands.

Upon arriving (on foot, as they had left the horses at the nearest post station, some eight miles distant), they at once discovered that there were no inns within the confines of the village. As it was late in the day (and, we may add, this far north the nights tended to become uncomfortably cold even in high summer, and it was already into autumn), they found themselves in something of a quandary. That is to say, the plan had been a good night's sleep and an early departure. While considering what to do about this unforeseen circumstance, they walked down to the water itself, which featured a curiously shaped, narrow jetty, which, after two hundred feet, curved sharply to the right, then to left, and then out at an angle. The reader may speculate as to the reason for this object to have been constructed in this fashion, perhaps having to do with natural formations of this part of the shore, different times and purposes of construction, or alcoholic consumption by the designer; the author, having no definite knowledge on this question, will content himself with the simple description we have had the honor to provide. Along this jetty were tied up six or seven small fishing boats, which is to say, four trawlers and two or three spearingboats. In addition, there were several smaller vessels that had been pulled onto the shore, fishing boats with removable keels so they could be used in shallow water or, indeed, pulled up onto the beach. A cargo ship of the square and bulky type known as the Rivermouth Schooner stood low at double anchor, unprotected from the sea by any harbor or bay. Last, at the very end of the jetty, was a yawl of the type known as the Three-Ton Tara (named for the clever Teckla from folklore), securely fixed fore and aft and with all masts struck.

"My brother," said Livosha.

"Well?"

"I would like you to make a supposition."

"That is, you propose, and I suppose?"

"Ah, that is cleverly put; now it is you who flirt with epigrams."

"Not in the least. But then, begin with your proposal for supposition, for I am eager to hear it."

"This is it, then: Suppose you had a commission to supply a prison island with fresh food."

"Very well, suppose I did."

"And suppose, moreover, you were to base yourself in a region with good agriculture, fruit, and some herding animals, as well as seafood."

"An area such as this in which we are now standing?"

"Precisely."

"Very well, I am supposing it even now."

"And suppose further—"

"What, there is more?"

"Of a certainty."

"Very well, then. I am complaisant, and will suppose as much as you like."

"So much the better. Suppose, then, that some number of times every month, you were required to deliver these supplies to a prison island some ninety or one hundred miles away, through seas that were rarely if ever monstrous, with winds that were inclined to blow from between two and twenty knots directly perpendicular to a line from you to the island."

"I am supposing all of this even now."

"Well then, under these conditions, what sort of craft would you require?"

"My sister, that would depend entirely on a question to which I have not been given the supposition."

"Let us see, then. What is the question?"

"How many prisoners am I supplying?"

"As to that, well, let us say between fifty and three hundred."

"That is a large range."

"Well."

"If I were to assume a number somewhere in the middle—"

"Yes? If you were?"

"Then the ideal boat would be something like a Three-Ton Tara."

"Such as, in fact, the one we see before us."

"Exactly like it."

"That, my dear brother, was my thought, and I am pleased to hear it confirmed."

"I, in my turn, am pleased that you are."

"And you, Jerin?" said Livosha.

"How, you ask me?"

"Certainly."

"Well, in my opinion—"

"Yes, in your opinion?"

"I have become proficient in jumping from a small boat onto a dock or a pier while holding a rope, and then fixing the rope to an appropriate portion of the dock with the use of a clever knot taught to me by fishermen. That is my opinion."

"That is good, then," said Livosha.

"This skill," said Kefaan, "may well prove useful."

"I hope it does."

"But then," said Livosha, "there still remains the problem of where we are to spend the night, as the inn here does not let rooms."

"As to that," said Jerin. "If you would permit me to make inquires, it may be that I can find a solution."

"And for my part," said Kefaan, "I believe no solution is needed."

"How, not needed?" said Livosha.

"Not in the least."

"But then—"

"I propose," said Kefaan, "not to remain here at all, but rather, to see about the use of a boat, to go out to the island this very night, and attempt to discover Eremit, and, if possible, free him."

Livosha, for her part, felt her heart suddenly beating. "Then you believe—"

"I believe we should find a boat, and that we should not waste a moment. Come, you perceive the wind is strong, and is perfectly placed from the north by northwest to bring us to our destination. Why wait even a minute?"

"To this plan," said Livosha, her voice trembling, "I subscribe with my whole heart."

"Then let us see who will rent us a boat."

After some degree of searching among those who were, at that moment, removing the day's hauls from their various boats, they found a fisherman who seemed willing in principle to sacrifice a day's catch in exchange for sufficient money to account for two days' worth of such work, the more readily because he was an Orca, and thus understood that, while it is possible that fish in the Ocean-sea will turn into coins in the purse, nevertheless there is risk that on a certain day they will; whereas coins in the purse are, in fact, under all conditions, coins in the purse and not subject to vagaries of wind, wave, or any sea god who may or may not exist.

After sufficient conversation to ensure this worthy that he was not turning over his vessel—that is to say, his livelihood—to persons with no understanding of its workings, they quickly came to an agreement. All three of them having grown up on the coast, there was no question of needing a pilot, and, moreover, no question of them being cheated on the cost of renting a boat for a night. Thus they acquired the use of a fine little sloop with a low profile, that could be sailed by any one of them, and easily by two, and would be ready, the owner promised, as soon as he had finished unloading, which would be within that very hour. They left him alone to work, and indeed, in an hour he was standing next to the craft, just cleaning the residue off her deck. He showed them how he had everything rigged to the cockpit so he could sail her by himself, and mentioned that he had removed the trawl, as they had said they wouldn't be fishing; they signified that they understood these things. They paid him, and he informed them that she was called the *Carilia*.

"A pretty name," said Kefaan.

"I am glad you think so," said the fisherman, who was younger than middle years, with broad shoulders, a pronounced jut to his chin, and hair that he kept long enough to stream in the wind. "I named it in honor of my fourth wife, in hopes of impressing and delighting her, and because the craft reminds me of her, a pretty little thing, yet requiring to be coaxed rather than managed."

"Your fourth wife?" said Livosha. "Well, but how many times have you been married?"

"Three," said the Orca.

"Well," said Kefaan, "we shall endeavor to take good care of the *Carilia* and return her to you unscathed."

"So much the better," said the Orca. "Then I wish you fair winds and clear sight. Apropos, do not go into the mist."

"Mist?" said Livosha, looking out at the Ocean-sea and noting, though the light was fading, and soon the Furnace would be briefly visible above the horizon, there was no trace of mist.

"There is an island some ninety miles to the west by northwest," he said, "that is always surrounded by mist, because there is a volcano on it that, by some marvelous property, is always in eruption, yet never emits lava. The ash flows into the sea, creating a mist around it. If you go into the mist, then you will, without question, be burned to death, and I will not see my boat again."

With this the Orca took his leave, holding the money he'd been given and making his way to the local tavern where he presumably proposed to spend it.

The three of them looked at each other. Livosha spoke first. "A volcano."

"In mist," said Kefaan.

"How distressing," said Jerin.

"What should we do?" said Kefaan.

"We should set out," said Livosha.

"And," said Kefaan, "when we find the mist, and discover this volcano is in fact exactly the island for which we are looking, which we will? What then?"

"Then," said Livosha, "we will reflect."

To this Kefaan agreed, and they pushed the boat into the surf and climbed in. The Furnace appeared somewhat to the left, and Livosha was reminded of the day when she and Eremit had watched it descending from their home in Wetrock. Long disused skills came back to them quickly, and they were soon running at, as near as they could guess without using the log, three knots.

A few hours later the breeze freshened, and they began moving faster through the water, heeling a little, and sending spray off to the leeward.

Dark fell and they continued on, guiding themselves as well as they could with compass spells. The light of dawn slowly grew, and, even as it did, they saw, directly in their path, what seemed to be an oddly contained fog bank. They looked at each other and, by mutual unspoken consent, spilled the wind and studied it. The light grew, and the fog did not seem to dissipate. They waited without speaking, worried, yet determined.

"Well?" said Kefaan at length, when it was clear that, even in full daylight, the fog would not blow away.

Livosha shrugged, took hold of the mainsail line and the tiller, and continued toward the island.

"To turn around," she remarked, "well, it is impossible."

"And so?"

"And so we will go closer, but slowly. You see how I only capture a fraction of this breeze?"

"Very well, then. Let us go closer."

Jerin said nothing, but looked at the two of them and shrugged. The *Carilia* drew near the fog bank.

At that moment, on the western edge of the Empire, it was still early in the morning. But in the capital city, more than two thousands of miles to the southeast, it was just past the eleventh hour after midnight on the 17th day of the month of the Vallista in the 532nd year of the reign of his Imperial Majesty, Tortaalik the Third.

Chapter the Sixteenth

In Which Something Unexpected Has Happened

As Eremit sat at his desk consuming, as he thought, his penultimate meal, he heard the sound of a very loud bell, or rather gong, emitting a single peal, as if it were an alarm. In all of his centuries in the jail, he had never before heard this sound, and one must have experience in living in such a contained, rigid environment for this long to truly understand how remarkable, how thrilling, and at once how terrifying is the thought, *something new is happening*.

This thought, that something was happening, was more true than he could have imagined, indeed, than anyone could have imagined, on the island, or anywhere in the Empire, saving only one or two souls who were directly involved. Some two thousand miles to the southeast, right in the heart of the Empire, amid battle, rebellion, treason, and assassination, there came such a moment as, forever after, would be the defining instant for every citizen in the Empire; that is to say, it was the moment from which everything was dated *before* or *after*, the moment after which nothing could ever be the same. It was the destruction of the capital, the vanishing of the Orb, the fall of the Empire, all in a single cataclysmic juncture.

The narrowness of the subject matter of this volume prevents us from describing in detail the effect of the Disaster, but surely, unless the present generation have utterly abandoned all pretense of scholarship, and even responsibility, no such description could be necessary. In any case, it is hardly our duty to remedy any such lack; we have taken it upon ourselves to tell the history of Eremit and Livosha, and it is to this and this only that we must devote ourselves. We therefore leave to other historians, as well as, to be sure, painters, poets, novelists, musicians, story-tellers, playwrights, and others, to speak of the terrible devastation and loss of life of the initial explosion, of the even more extreme suffering caused by the disappearance of the Orb as well as of the security and protection provided by the Empire, and of the invasion by various barbarians from the south and savages from the east, each bringing their particular depredations, physical and moral. We are only concerned, at this moment, with a tiny spot that is only barely visible on most maps of the Empire (and even missing entirely from some) in the far northwest corner, a mere speck, where, would it be magnified as by the marvelous sorceries of Lady Ponfir, we would be concerned with a mere speck within *that*. That of all the tragedy and horror (and, we admit, occasional heroism) of that moment, we should focus on only one person is, to the right, ironic; yet, to the left, also fitting, as catastrophe on a grand scale inevitably plays itself out through each individual; that we, as historians, must necessarily bring the actions of millions of individuals together in order to understand the processes that we are investigating does not change the entirely personal nature of any major event.

With this firmly in mind, we return to Eremit, who, upon hearing the bell, stood up, and with an instinct common to all prisoners, rushed to the door of his cell and looked out to see if there was anything unusual to be observed. In fact there was, and though clearly important, its meaning could not be determined except in the most general sense. It was, the reader must understand, at the time when two jailers and a servant were accustomed to come by and collect the breakfast trays. What Eremit saw, however, were several trays being tossed carelessly to the floor as the jailers ran at breakneck speed back toward the center of the jail. The servant, in this case an elderly Jhegaala woman (for the servants selected were nearly always very old prisoners) stood in the middle, looking around, uncertain what to do. Eremit thought to call her over, hoping to ask questions to which she might know the answers. He was forestalled, however, by all of the other prisoners along that stretch of corridor, who were clamoring to her with similar questions, with the result that, as we have stated, she stood where she was, looking around wildly.

The next stage was inevitable: Various prisoners began shouting explanations for the bell and the strange behavior of the jailers. As is usual when there is urgency but no information, imagination took the place of knowledge, and hopes and fears took the place of facts. Thus cries began to go up, "The volcano has gone out of control and we are to be burned alive!" "A dragon-wave has come and we shall be washed away and drowned!" "The Empire has arrived to arrest the jailers and release us all!" "The prisoners in the next corridor have all broken free!" and so on. Eremit, we say to his credit, did not participate in this upheaval of irrationality, either in contributing to it, or in giving any of it credence.

And yet, he told himself, it was clear that *something* was going on. Something big. Something important. When life is confined, for centuries, to a single isolated place, like a village in a valley amid impassible mountains, the outside world seems to be an unreal place: anything that alters the routine from an unknown cause—the illness of the director, a change in cooks, a new jailer—might be attributed to the world outside, yet, truly, in their bones, as it were, the inhabitants—by which we mean both prisoners and guards—cannot imagine an event outside that could have any effect on activities inside. They were separate worlds: the seen and the unseen, the real and the imaginary, the living and the dead.

So Eremit watched, and listened, and attempted to consider what could be the happening. In fact, any of the things mentioned by other prisoners were possible, but there was no reason to believe any of them. He waited, and the clamor died down, and the servant-prisoner walked down the hall, hesitantly, until she was out of sight. Prisoners shouted to each other for a while, and then became silent.

The time for lunch came and went. As did dinner. And supper. Still, nothing and no one; it seemed as if they had been deserted, left alone in their cells to starve. Now, no one spoke or cried out, each prisoner silent with uncertainty and fear. And then suddenly, Eremit frowned, taken with the uncomfortable feeling that something was missing and that, simultaneously, he was missing something.

One of the most difficult things for the human mind to bring to a conscious awareness is when something that has been a constant yet subtle sensation is suddenly gone. The reader may recall times when, for example, an itinerant scissor-sharpener is on the street nearby, and the grinding noise, at first such an irritation, soon blends into the background sounds of the city until, when it stops, one frowns and tries for some moments to understand what has changed.

Eremit stood in the cell concentrating, until suddenly he realized what it was. He had been in a state of distress when arriving on the island, and this had increased through the time of his meeting with the director, and was worse after, and so he had never been aware of—

—The rumble.

The unending sensation that was half sound and half feeling but, now that it was suddenly, for the first time, gone, unmistakable: The volcano was no longer erupting.

Eremit tried to control his fevered imagination and think clearly. The eruption had stopped, yes, but he was still on an island, and there was no boat. And yet—

And yet—

He took a deep breath, a look around the room, and the screw from the bed. He kicked the bed to the side so that the leg fell off, and, using the screw, scratched certain symbols on the wall above where it had been. He removed the cover of the tunnel and flung it aside, then climbed through the tunnel. The tunnel that he had worn away inch by painstaking inch flashed by him almost as if he were at a run. When he reached the end he stopped long enough to place his hands on that portion of the wall beyond which, he believed, would be freedom. Yes, there was still warmth, but not as much as there had been. He took a deep breath, and struck it with his left shoulder. When it failed to move he struck it again. On the third blow, it gave way with a crack, and fresh air blew into his face.

Fresh air!

Never in his life had anything tasted so exquisite to our Iorich as that first breeze, crisp with the autumn, full of the sea-smell that brought his childhood back so clearly along with memories of Livosha, and the beaches and orchards of Wetrock. For a moment he was unable to move, so fully had the scent and the feel taken him, but then he came to himself. This was not the time to enjoy freedom: He was still on the island. He must steel himself to, somehow, use the water breathing spell in spite of the risks.

At this, he realized that he should now be able to reach the Orb, and use sorcery again for the first time in—how long? How long had it been? It didn't matter. He reached out.

Nothing. He must, he decided, still be too close to the cell, or perhaps the Phoenix Stone permeated deeper than he had thought. Well, then, he would move away. He stepped out of the tunnel onto on a hard, rocky slope. It had been so long since he had needed to walk anywhere or seen anything but perfectly flat ground, that for a moment vertigo took him, and that peculiar feeling that is like dizziness but raised several octaves, combined with a kind of nausea and accompanied by near panic, as the world seems to make no sense to the body, suffused him.

He waited, hoping it would go away, and it gradually did. He stood on the slope for a moment longer, and recalled the direction he was facing. Southwest, then, he decided, ought to be *that* way, to the left, and so that way he moved, and gradually down the slope as well. Even as he watched, the mist cleared, blown away by the sea-breeze, and as he neared the bottom of the sloping side, he beheld the restless Ocean-sea that whispered to him of freedom. It was dark, but the Enclouding reflected back some sort of beacon that was lit above him, and his eyes, so used to seeing by the light of one or two candles, easily picked out where his feet should step.

He continued down and to his left, the crashing waves getting closer all the time, until he could hear them clearly like a childhood song one has all but forgotten. He tried once more to touch the Orb, but failed. Could it be that, as an unused limb will atrophy, his ability to sense his connection to the Empire had failed? What then? Could he swim ninety miles? He felt himself to be, if not in good condition, then at least not unhealthy. If his choices were to remain on the island or attempt to swim ninety miles through the Ocean-sea, well, then he would do it. If he were to drown, or be eaten by a sea-serpent or an orca, or bitten by a sea-snake, well that would be better than remaining here!

He arrived at the level of the surf, staying just above it, continuing around until, by his calculations, he should be facing the mainland. And there he stopped, staring.

There was a boat!

He stared, uncertain if it were real, or a product of his fevered imagination. It seemed to be a sloop, with a mainsail and a jib, and one that he ought to be able to manage by himself, and there it was, with no one near it! He crept closer, looking all around, and still there was no one. No one!

He hid himself behind a ledge and carried out a more careful inspection of the area, and when he still saw no one, began to do so again, and until he suddenly thought, *Fool! Suppose you spend so much time looking for someone that you wait until someone returns! What then? Now! Take it now!*

And with this thought he jumped, and in ten steps had reached the dock. In the drawing of a breath he had cast loose the two ropes that secured her, and stepped aboard.

"Well," he told the boat. "As there is no one of whom I can ask permission to come aboard, I must ask myself. And, having asked myself, I shall certainly grant myself permission! Come now, this cannot be hard. Drop the jib and fix it in place so. Then the mainsail, and I perceive all the lines come together; this has been rigged by a sailor who wanted to sail without help from anyone. Now we push off from the dock with our foot. Still no one? So much the better! Now to pull until we catch the wind, rope in one hand, tiller in the other, ah, there my beauty! That is our breeze! Yes, you should like it just a bit more abaft the beam, would you not? Well, it will serve nevertheless, and you must take it as it is. There, my sweet boat! How bravely you swim. Look, do you see? So quickly, and the cursed island is already behind us!

"Onward now! Onward for the mainland! Look, do you see? There is a nightgull hoping to steal food, and that splash off the starboard was a whittelfish casting about for darkshells or floating weeds; they greet us. And, do you see, the island is nearly out of sight in this dark. They can no longer see me, much less catch me. I am free! I am free! I am free!" He shouted this into the night until he was hoarse, then his voice fell and he said, "Ah, Magister! How I wish you could be here with me! Well, I will do as you asked, which is to say, I will put your lessons to good use; this much I vow on my hate for that accursed island and all who put me there."

The breeze stayed steady, and though hundreds of years had passed since he had sailed, and even then he had been far from the most efficient sailor, still he managed to keep her on course, his eyes no longer looking back, but fixed ahead, searching for the mainland. He kept the boat on course for the shortest distance he could manage, making as few adjustments as possible, his eyes never closing or deviating as the hours passed by, his spirits as high as the winds.

His straining eyes were able to pick up a dim, flickering light, then another. He steered for them, also easing off the rope to release some of the wind whose capture was propelling the vessel forward at such speed. He released more, and more, and then heard, rather than saw, the rollers finding the beach and breaking there with a soft hiss. He pulled the keel as if it were most natural thing in the world, and let the halyard fall for the jib, then the mainsail, and let the boat make its way onto the beach. It seemed too heavy to pull up by himself, so he dug the fluked anchor into the sand, jumped out, and his feet touched the mainland.

The last time his feet had felt the ground of the continent of the Empire had been in Northport, and then—

But no, he must move forward.

He seemed to be in a village the size of Wetrock. He could see, even in the dim light, where the altar must be, though not to whom it was dedicated, and there was the storm-house, yes, as big as the one in Wetrock, and, like that one, next to the one tavern, and, oddly for this time of night, the tavern was full of light, and as he walked carefully in that direction, he heard voices, some sounding frightened, some angry, most of them shouting. He hesitated. Fishermen woke early and set out at dawn if not before; it was as much a law of nature as water running downhill, the steward running the household, or Teckla running from a fight. What could cause an entire village—and from the sound, the entire village was in the tavern—to be awake, shouting and talking, in the middle of the night?

He approached cautiously. Would they recognize that he wore clothing from jail? He touched his hair, remembering from his last look in a mirror that his noble's point was concealed, and he could pass for a Teckla, but could he still? Did he want to? What did he look like now? How had the centuries aged him? A shiver went through his body; he ignored it and crept closer. Once more, he tried to recall the sensation of touching the Orb, to bring his connection back, but it was as if that part of him had been amputated.

His curiosity drove him toward the tavern, and yet there was also a certain cold practicality: He was aware that he had no food and no water, and that soon he would become hungry and thirsty. His plan to travel overland to the Valley of Dust was impossible without food and water, or money to buy them, or means to secure them. And so he pushed his ear against the wall of the tavern, and listened.

The voices were confused and difficult, and it was soon clear that everyone was afraid, but it took him a long time to determine the cause. At length, however, from a word here, half a sentence there, piecing it together, it became clear. Yet, even then he did not believe it, but listened more, until there could be no possible doubt.

It was not just he who could not reach the Imperial Orb; it was everyone.

He tried to struggle with the concept. Nothing had prepared him for such a possibility. Was it confined to this region? Had there been some sort of explosion, scattering Phoenix Stone far and wide? If so, how far? How far inland must he go? Or what if that was not it? What if the Orb was, well, *gone*? Was such a thing possible?

He left the side of the tavern, working his way behind it and along a path that paralleled the main road before heading off to the east. He passed by a cottage, and in the dim light saw a dog tethered to a stake, and a stylized Jhegaala above the door. A local merchant, no doubt; perhaps the very one who sold supplies to the prison. But, in any case, someone with more wealth than a peasant would have.

The dog began barking furiously as he approached the house, but he was well beyond the reach of its rope. He climbed into a window and looked around. It was hard to see, and he wasn't keen on striking a light even if he found one—the dog barking was bad enough. After some time, however, he managed to find a larder. Having no pockets in his jail uniform, he tucked in his shirt and stuffed it with a loaf of bread, a cheese, and some hanging sausages, after eating several of these until he was entirely satisfied. He looked for a wineskin that he could fill with water, but didn't find one, so he settled on a wooden pint-sized cup. He also looked around for anything that might work as a weapon, and settled on an iron fireplace poker. He slipped out the window, found the well and drank, then filled the cup, suddenly struck by the notion that, after spending hundreds of years in jail, he had now, for the first time in his life, broken the law.

He took the path to the main road, seeing no one, and continued out of the village. The road took him south and east, which was, it happened, the direction he wished to go. He had questions about finding his way without a compass spell, and questions about defending himself with only a fireplace poker, and questions about running out of food and water. But one thing he did not question: he was now free and on his way.

Ahead of him, the dawn began to break.

Chapter the Seventeenth

In Which Livosha and Kefaan Explore the Island

I feel odd," said Livosha.

"Yes," said Kefaan. "Something just happened. I cannot—"

"The Orb!" said Jerin.

"Yes?" said Livosha, taking her words as an expletive.

"No, it is gone."

"What?" said Kefaan. "The Orb cannot . . . wait, it is true!"

"I cannot feel it," said Livosha. "It must be some strange property of the island."

"That must be it," said Kefaan. "For, you perceive, it began as we came near. But apropos the island—"

"Well?"

"Let us not forget that there is a volcano."

"I had not forgotten."

"And then?"

"Let us go a little closer."

"Very well," said Kefaan, although it was difficult to detect any significant amount of enthusiasm in his voice.

"But slowly," said Livosha, a suggestion which was agreed to with an alacrity that couldn't be mistaken.

As they crept nearer (if the word "crept" can be used of the progress of a sailing vessel, a question which we have answered in the affirmative, although not, we confess, without certain misgivings), Kefaan said, "Is the mist clearing?"

Livosha peered forward and said, "Perhaps a little."

"It doesn't seem hot."

"That is true."

"Slightly warm, perhaps."

"I agree, perhaps slightly warm."

"I see no sign of a volcano."

"Nor do I."

"Nor an island."

"These may be related."

"It is possible."

"By which I mean, if we find the island, it may be that we will also—"

"Yes, yes. I understand."

They continued in silence for a short time more, then Livosha said, "I see something!"

"Well, but what is it you see?"

"Good Jerin, spill a certain amount of wind if you would, for I wish to proceed even slower now, for I believe I see an island."

"I agree," said Kefaan, sounding perhaps the least bit apprehensive.

Jerin did as she was told without a word. They came closer to the island—through the thick mist it appeared to be tall and without a trace of anything growing—expecting at any moment to be burned up in fiery ash or covered in molten lava. The mist was thick, as we have insisted, but broke here and there, and at one point they could see clearly that the top of the mountain—that is to say, the island, for it appeared that the entire island was only a mountain—was smoking.

Jerin, entirely on her own, let the boat slow even more; no one questioned this decision the Teckla did herself the honor to make.

Still, they came closer, and discovered that they were not immolated, and, moreover, they were not even so warm as to be uncomfortable. Still, something continued to produce the mist, or, at any rate, it would become thick enough to hide the island entirely, then clear somewhat, then hide it again.

"So then," said Kefaan. "Let us see."

"Well?"

"Suddenly, we have found we have lost our connection to the Empire."

"That is true."

"And we are sailing toward a volcanic island."

"That is also true."

"In order to search what may be an illegal prison, no doubt against the will of some number of persons who work there, and who may have significant interests in preventing us from learning what it is we wish to know, or, indeed, from ever leaving again."

"Ah, there I must disagree with you, my brother."

"Oh, and in what way have I erred?"

"From what you have told me, it is not an illegal prison, it is an illegal jail."

"Well," said Kefaan. "But in everything else?"

"In everything else, well, it seems that what you have said is true."

"That is good then," he said. "I merely wanted to understand."

"Look!" said Jerin. "Is that not a dock?"

"Where?" said Livosha. "Ah, the accursed mist closed before I saw it. Well, but steer as well as you can toward where you thought it was."

"I am doing so, my lady."

"There!" said Kefaan a moment later. "I see it!"

"And what else do you see?" said Livosha, looking anxiously.

"What else? Why, nothing."

"Nor do I."

"But, what else did you wish to see?"

"Not wish, my brother. I feared to see armed individuals who have arguments to make regarding our use of the dock."

"There seem to be none."

"So much the better. Here, Jerin. I will take the tiller. And you—"

"Yes, my lady?"

"You may practice your skill of jumping onto a dock and tying the boat up."

"I am prepared to show my lady that my words were not mere braggadocio."

"I am counting on you."

"There, you see? I am on the dock."

"Well, and the boat?"

"It is tied fore, and now, also aft."

"You have done well."

"I am glad my lady thinks so," said Jerin.

We have no doubt the reader has observed our use of certain terminology related to sailing. Should the reader be curious if our own personal background involved such matters, we will say that it did not, but, rather, we required ourselves to learn of these things in order the better to understand the development of the history we have the honor to relate. This willingness to study unknown material, we are forced to add, ought not to be considered a virtue. Rather, should a supposed historian fail to do so, as, for example, by attempting to discuss the cavalry charge at Sironwë while displaying an ignorance of the uses of horses as well as the particular terms used to describe the special maneuvers and evolutions of horsemen, this supposed historian will naturally make us question not only his abilities, but even his dedication to the truth.

Livosha and Kefaan followed the worthy Teckla onto the dock and looked around, as well they could in the thick cloud of fog that still enveloped them, and which occasional gusts of wind only broke up momentarily. During one of these gaps (known, we should add, as "flaws" to those accustomed to the sea, as well to those accustomed, as all historians ought to be, to call things by their right name, as sloppiness in the matter of terminology, for example by referring to the one-handed fighting axe used by Baroness Tuvin at the Battle of Rounded Bluff as a "great axe," indicates sloppiness in research, in verifying information, and in making deductions), they were able to spot a narrow path built of flagstones that seemed to lead up the mountainside.

"So then," said Kefaan, loosening his sword. "Shall we see where this leads?"

"I have no other ideas," said Livosha. "So I believe we should, and this very moment at that."

"Will you lead, or will I?"

"I would claim that honor."

"Very well. Then 'Climb, climb, good Kieron, for honor never lieth below.'"

"You have become very literary, my brother."

"Well," he shrugged, and followed Livosha up the path—the very path, we must observe, that Eremit had followed over six hundred years before.

"You perceive," said Kefaan, "that we can see neither to the one side, nor the other."

"Well, that is true."

"And we know that to the right, it is a long drop."

"I do not dispute you."

"I only mention this to suggest care."

"Oh, I am taking care."

"So much the better."

The path at length ended in a sharp turn to the left which led to a sort of covered archway, beneath which was a heavy door. Upon attempting the door, it was discovered not to be locked; indeed, a close inspection revealed that, far from being locked, it was not entirely closed, as if the last person to use it had not wished to take the time to pull it to the secure position. Livosha observed this, and, by a look, assured herself that Kefaan had seen it too. The latter shrugged, and Livosha led the way inside.

The reader, we trust, need not be reminded of the long stone stairway down, spiraling out around a great pit. Livosha led the way slowly, grateful for the hanging lamps that provided some light, but wishing there were more and regretting her inability to perform a light spell. At length, there was a door to the left. Livosha looked through it, and saw a cot upon which sat a elderly man. In prison garb and such dim lighting, it was impossible to guess his House. As they approached, he turned, and instantly—or, to be precise, as instantly as his age permitted—approached the door.

"Please, my lady. Can you tell me what is happening?"

"I? Well, but I had hoped you could tell me."

"You perceive, I am locked in here."

"That is true," said Livosha. "And yet, we have only just arrived."

"All I know is that there was a clang, and the jailers all went running, and I have not seen one since. And, as I am one of the guests who perform certain services in exchange for a cell with a window, well, I ought to have been let out to carry out my duties. I conclude, therefore, that something unusual has happened."

"I perceive the justice in your conclusion, if not in your position. How long ago was the alarm?"

"How to tell time? An hour, perhaps two, perhaps three."

"Very well. You perceive, even if I wished to let you out, I would be unable to."

"I understand that."

"Would you, nevertheless, be willing to answer certain questions?"

"More than willing, if for no other reason than the pleasure of conversation."

"So much the better. Then I will ask my questions."

"And I will listen to them, and, more than listen, if I am able to answer, then, cracks and shards, I will do so."

"Then here is my first question: Do you know a prisoner named Eremit, of the House of the Iorich?"

"Ah, no. That would be impossible."

"How, impossible?"

"Yes, for two reasons. The first is, we have no prisoners here. By order of the director, there are only guests."

"What is the difference between a guest and a prisoner?"

"Oh, none at all."

"Very well, then. I accept the term."

"And you are right to."

"But what is the second reason?"

"In addition to having no prisoners—"

"Yes?"

"We also have no names."

"How, no names?"

"None at all."

"But how are you distinguished, one from the other?"

"By the number corresponding our room."

"Room. Which is the same as a cell?"

"You have understood exactly."

"So you are only known according to the cell you occupy?"

"Precisely. I, myself, am number one. Now, if you were to tell me this individual's number, why, I could tell you where to find him."

"Well, but you perceive that is impossible, as until this moment, I had not been aware that he would be identified with a number."

"I understand."

"But, can you tell me the layout of this jail?"

"That I can do. And, not only can, but will, and with the greatest pleasure."

"Then explain. What is at the bottom of this stairway?"

"Three corridors. The one on the right leads to the kitchens, the storage areas, and the cold rooms. The one in middle to the offices, dining area, and living quarters of the hosts—"

"That is to say, the jailers."

The old man nodded his assent and continued. "And the one on the left to the various corridors where guests are confined."

"Very good, then that is where we will go."

"Yes, but—"

"Well?"

"You must have a key."

"Ah, that is true, and you are right to remind me of it. This is a jail, and jails have keys."

"Yes. Apropos, how did you get down here?"

"The door from the outside was unlocked."

"That is unusual."

"I do not question this."

"And the volcano?"

"There was a volcano?"

"Nearly. I watch the ash fall from my window."

"And is it falling now?"

The prisoner—or, if the reader prefers, the guest—left the door and came back in a short time. "It is not! I have never seen such a thing. And, moreover, the mist seems to be thinning out, which means there is less steam. Ah, ah, well, but that explains how you were able to arrive without burning up. For if you had burned up, well, I doubt we should be engaged in this diverting conversation."

"I am strongly inclined to agree with this conclusion."

"So then," put in Kefaan, speaking for the first time, "we must somehow find a key."

"I agree with this," said Livosha.

"The keys," said number one, "are in the offices of the hosts."

"So, then, it is the central corridor we seek."

"Yes, and I will give you further directions to the director's office, if you wish it."

"I wish it extremely," said Livosha.

"Then here it is."

He gave them precise directions, and even listened while these were repeated back, at which time he said, "Then I wish you success in your endeavors. Apropos—"

"Yes?"

"I hope you will not forget me."

"We will not," said Livosha. "And, moreover, if we find an opportunity to free you, well, we will do so."

"Ah, ah! Then it remains for me to hope such an opportunity arises."

"As do we, good, ah, sir."

And with that they left him there and continued down the stairway, passing several other prisoners with whom they did not stop and speak, until at last they reached the bottom. They approached the middle corridor and found a heavy door, wide open, with an unattended desk. They looked at each other, shrugged, and continued.

They followed the directions they had been given until, at length, they heard voices, and opening another unlocked door, they found themselves in what seemed to be a wide dining room with benches and tables, at which were gathered some thirty or thirty-five persons in uniforms of Iorich colors, a few of whom had marks of rank. They were all facing away from Livosha, except for one who was not in uniform, and appeared to be addressing them. As they entered, he stopped speaking and stared, whereupon everyone else in the room, following the direction of his gaze, did the same; thus did Livosha, Kefaan, and Jerin find themselves suddenly the center of attention.

There followed what can only be described as, at least to Livosha, an awkward silence. Then she cleared her throat and said, "Well."

"Who are you?" said the man in the front of the room.

"You must be the director," said Livosha.

"Why, I not only must be, but in fact I am. Yet, you perceive you failed to answer my question, which, far from asking about my identity, which barring certain unfortunate circumstances I cannot fail to know, in fact, asked you of yours. Moreover, as you are in my institution—proved by you having correctly identified me as its director—I think you ought to answer the question I did you the honor to ask, and moreover, without an instant's delay."

"I accept your reasoning," said the Iorich. "And I will answer you at once. I am Livosha, daughter of Cerwin, and this is my brother, Kefaan. There, do you agree I have answered your question?"

"Entirely. But now I must ask you another."

"Very well, I cannot stop you from doing so."

"I am glad you realize this. My question is, what are you doing here?"

"Ah, you wish to know that?"

"Indeed I do, and the proof is, I asked."

"Well, I am looking for a certain person I believe to be incarcerated here, and moreover—"

"Yes, moreover?"

"I wish to learn what has happened to cause such upset in your institution."

"You wish to know that? Well, so should we."

"How, you do not know?"

"It is what we have been discussing here; that, and how best to carry out our duties under these circumstances."

"Well, but what *are* the circumstances?"

The director frowned. "Surely you aware that we have lost our connections to the Orb?"

"But, I had thought that was only because we neared the island."

"Not in the least. We are accustomed to depend upon sorcery, above all to control the volcano, which is our best security device."

"So, you do not know what has happened."

"I say it, madam, and I even repeat it."

Livosha and Kefaan looked at each other, then back to the director.

The latter said, "However, we must now return to the matter of your presence."

"Very well," said Livosha. "Let us return to it."

"This is a secure facility, madam, and no one is allowed to see our guests without proper authorization."

"Oh, I understand that. Only—"

"Well?"

"How is it possible to get proper authorization for an illegal institution that is, itself, unauthorized?"

This remark was the cause (if we can assume cause, that is, by immediacy of the effect) of two distinct things: the first was such a remarkable flush spreading across the director's countenance that it was visible all the way in the back of the room, and the second was stir and hum of sudden conversation, of which Livosha could make out little except the occasional, "is that true?" and, "didn't I tell you?"

The director, it seemed, had a sort of baton, which he picked up and brought down sharply on the table in front of him, with the immediate result that the room quieted down and everyone's attention returned to him. We trust, in any case, that on this occasion there is no question of causality, which is to say, even those mystics who insist upon seeing history as a series of disconnected incidents, and whose favorite refrain appears to be a more-or-less triumphant "we cannot know!" to any suggestion of any causal relationship whatsoever, which opinion, we believe, ought to disqualify such an individual from daring to instruct anyone in anything, much less history, which is, after all, an unending chain of cause-to-effect-to-cause, cannot doubt that the room became silent because of the sharp stroke of the baton on the table, or even—for we do not fear to dare—to assign the action as being deliberately carried out to achieve this effect.

Once he had the attention of those in the room, and, to be sure, of Livosha, Kefaan, and Jerin (for let us never forget the brave Teckla who, at this moment, wished above all to be anywhere else), he said, "As to the question of the nature of this institution, I do not choose to comment at this time. However, it is certainly the case that you have no authorization to be here, and, moreover, that you are outnumbered."

"Outnumbered?" said Livosha, showing not the least trace of fear. "Then do you threaten me with violence?"

"Nearly."

Livosha and Kefaan touched their swords as one.

"Jerin," said Livosha. "Get behind us, and warn us should anyone come from that direction."

Jerin appeared unable to form words, but nevertheless did as she was told.

"Then, you mean to resist?" said the director.

"Well, if you attack, that seems to be the only option."

"Although," added Kefaan, "you perceive, as we have committed no crime, anyone who attacks us becomes, therefore, a criminal, and you may wish to consider what will happen if any of your fellows should ever decide to testify on the subject of an illegal attack to defend an illegal jail."

This shot appeared to go home, as the various jailers looked at each other showing signs of discomfort. The director said, "So, then, you wish to die."

"Not in the least," said Livosha. "But if living does not seem to be an option, well, I am not so attached to my life as to give it undue consideration. Perhaps I shall even find you on the point of my sword before I fall, which, you perceive, would not displease me in the least."

"Or you could surrender."

"Well, and then?"

"We would put you in one of our rooms."

"Cells."

He shrugged. "You say rainstorm, I say rainstorm[3]."

"If you wish to be done with words, well, give the order to charge. I promise you, we will happily defend ourselves to the best of our ability."

"I do not doubt you in this," said the director. We should add that Livosha and Kefaan had now placed themselves just on the other side of the door, which meant they could only be attacked by one or two at a time, a circumstance that was not lost on the jailers.

"You cannot win," said the director, though whether this was said in order to convince Livosha, or the jailers, or himself, must remain speculative.

"Perhaps not," said Livosha. "And yet, a cell does not appeal."

"What then?"

"If you permit us to find our friend, we will leave, and no more need be said."

"That is quite impossible. I have been entrusted with the care of my guests. I could not forsake this trust."

Livosha shrugged and her drew her sword; Kefaan did the same. "As you please," said Livosha.

[3] Ibid

Some twenty of the jailers also stood up; the others looked around as if uncomfortable. We should add that, of those who stood up, only half were armed, and these half drew their weapons, while the others looked around for something to fight with.

"Sister," said Kefaan. "You have more knowledge of such games than I do."

"Well?"

"Can we survive?"

"No," said Livosha.

"Ah. Very well. You perceive, I was curious."

"I give you a last chance," said the director. "Surrender, or die."

Livosha shrugged. "I say we die, then. It is all the same."

Kefaan shrugged. "I have said she had the lead, so then, well, now I must follow orders like a Dragon."

"As you please," said the director, who then raised his baton and cried, "Charge!"

It seemed at first as if Livosha were wrong, and they would not be overwhelmed: The first jailer to approach took her sword in his thigh, which caused him to fall into another, to whom Kefaan gave a good cut on the arm that made her drop her weapon. As the next attempted to find a way around her, Livosha's weapon struck like a serpent, first biting his shoulder, then giving him a good cut in the side of the neck with the same motion, making him drop his blade and clap his hand to the neck to be certain that she had not cut the vein. He thus got into the way of another, whom Kefaan managed to strike under the arm with such force that the blade emerged from the other side, and as this was happening, Livosha gave the next such a cut on her wrist that she was unable to hold her weapon.

All of this, be it understood, happened so quickly that the jailers began to wonder if they would able to win after all. It changed, however, with the attack of a certain Wosca, of the House of the Dragon. Wosca was, we must say, large. He measured well over eight feet tall, a full head taller than his nearest comrade, with such broad shoulders that he was often described as square. In addition to these physical attributes, he was known to be as impulsive as a constable who fancies himself treated without respect and as impatient as an author waiting to hear from his editor. For a moment, then, this man, who had no weapon at all, nevertheless looked for a way to approach the two Iorich who were defending themselves with such ferocity. At last, however, frustration overcame him, and he charged,

with the intention—insofar as he had an intention—of simply forcing his
way through the press of bodies.

The press of bodies, however, had no thought of permitting itself to
be forced through—so eager were the jailers to come to intimate quarters
with their adversaries, that the effect of Wosca's charge was to force them
all forward, with the result that Livosha and Kefaan suddenly found themselves at the bottom of a pile of bodies, unable to defend themselves, and,
indeed, unable to move at all.

To be sure, this was very nearly the end of them, as two of the jailers
who happened to be armed jumped up and raised their swords looking like
spear-fishers trying to spot their elusive prey, as they tried to see where to
strike without harm to their fellows, but at that moment, the director cried,
"Take them alive, and put them in a room. I wish to question them."

One of the shift captains picked himself up from the floor and said,
"Question them, Director?"

"Certainly. Consider what they said about the legality of our institution."

"Well, what of it?"

"I want to find out how they know of this, and, moreover, who else
does."

"Ah, do you think they'll tell you?"

"Oh, certainly, for I believe they truly are brother and sister."

"Well, if they are?"

"Then torturing one will surely convince the other to cooperate."

"Well, and then?"

"And then, once we have learned what they know, why, we can dispose
of them as we will."

"Very good, then. I shall have them placed in a room. Two rooms?"

"One. I wish to give them time to talk over their predicament, as it
cannot fail to make them more frightened and thus more easily persuaded."

"Then I will carry out your orders. But, apropos—"

"Yes?"

"What of those of our brothers and sisters who failed to support us?"

"Ah, yes. I will consider that matter as well."

"Very good, Director."

With these words, Kefaan and Livosha's weapons were taken from
them and they were brought to a cell, much as Eremit had been six centuries before. They were unceremoniously thrown in, and the door was closed

and bolted. After a moment, Livosha rose, went to the door, and looked through the barred window. "We are not being observed," she said.

Kefaan got to his feet and went over to the desk. "That's lucky," he said, sitting down.

"You heard what they plan to do to us?"

"Yes, I heard."

"Well?"

"I confess, I am not looking forward to it."

"Can you watch me being tortured and not tell them what they wish to hear?"

"No," said Kefaan. "Could you?"

"No. But if we do not resist, well, once they learn what we know, they will kill us."

"I must say, my sister, our fortune does not, at this time, seem so high."

"I cannot argue, my brother."

"So then?"

"You take the bed, I'll take the chair."

"Then you wish to sleep?"

"Yes, so that, when they come, I will be rested."

"Then you wish to fight them?"

"It seems to be our best choice."

"That is true. Perhaps they will kill us, thus saving us from the unpleasantness of torture."

"Precisely. And, who knows, perhaps we will emerge victorious."

"Perhaps we will. Have you a plan?"

"Why yes," said Livosha. "After a fashion. You will hit the first one over the head with the chair, and I will throw the bed at the second."

"With this plan, I agree."

"So much the better. Then let us rest."

"Very well, only—"

"Well?"

"You take the bed, I will take the chair. After all, it is to be my weapon, and, moreover, I am already sitting in it."

"Very well, I yield."

"Then let us rest."

This they proceeded to do, and, if they did not sleep, they at least took their ease, preserving their energy until it would be needed.

They preserved their energy, as it happened, for a long time; whether the director wanted to make them wait, or his efforts were taken up with other matters they could not know, but the hours dragged by until, at last, they heard a key fumble in the lock.

They caught each other's eyes and nodded. Livosha sat up and took hold of the bed frame, while Kefaan took hold of the chair. As the door opened, Kefaan stood up, raised the chair over his head, and stopped—

"Jerin?"

"Yes, my lord. I hope that I have not so displeased you as to cause you to hit me with a chair. You perceive, it would be humiliating, as well as painful."

"But, what are you doing here?" said Livosha.

"Rescuing you, my lady, if that is acceptable. If it will cause you distress to be rescued by a Teckla, I understand, and I will leave without a word of complaint."

"No, no. I am not concerned about that. You understand, as you are in my service, it is just as if I had rescued myself."

"I understand completely. Then here are your swords; I found them in the director's office when I was getting the keys."

"But how is it that you weren't caught?"

"Oh, in the simplest manner. When all of the bodies came tumbling down, I hid in one of the corridors. No one was looking for me, and so I wasn't found."

"It was well done."

"I am glad to hear you say so."

"Ah, I feel better already," said Livosha, strapping the sword on.

"As do I," agreed her brother.

"Well then," said Livosha, "what now?"

"You are our commander," said Kefaan. "Thus, you decide."

"Jerin, do you know your way around?"

"I have the honor to inform you that I believe I have been lost in every corridor within this mountain, or island."

"And have you explored all the cells?"

"Ah, no, but I have at least seen where they are."

"Then you will lead us."

"But my lady, whither am I leading us?"

"To find Eremit, of course."

"You perceive," said Kefaan, "that will require searching every cell."

"Oh, not every cell. For as soon as we have found him, well, we can stop."

"That is true," said Kefaan. "I had not considered this circumstance. Very well, then, let us begin."

"And if we find any of the jailers, well, I shall pass my sword through their bodies a certain number of times until they cease to be threats."

"A good plan, and I subscribe with all my heart."

"My lady—" began Jerin hesitantly.

"Yes?"

"I do not like to intrude with my suggestions—"

"Shards! I think you earned some intrusion when you rescued us before we were to be tortured! So then, what is it?"

"I did not see Eremit, but—"

"Yes?"

"I did see something odd."

"Well, tell us what you saw."

"There was a cell with a hole in it."

"A hole?"

"Exactly."

"But, to where did the hole lead?"

"I don't know, my lady. I saw at once that neither Eremit nor you were in the cell, and so I left to continue my search."

"Very well, bring us there now."

Jerin lead the way down several corridors in the apparently deserted jail until at last they came to a cell marked "81." Livosha looked inside, and, indeed, she could see that there was a neat, circular hole in the wall. Without hesitation, then, she opened the cell and stepped inside.

"Look!" said Kefaan, pointing to the top of the wall.

"Well, there are symbols there. And ancient Serioli, too."

"Ah, my sister. I never learned ancient Serioli, though I tried, as I knew you and Eremit would pass notes in that language, and I wished to read them for my own amusement, and perhaps to taunt you with."

"Did you?"

"I must confess it."

"Ah, well, we will not speak of that now."

"So much the better, but what do the symbols say?"

"They say, 'You need not find me, I will come back for you.'"

"Ah, a threat!"

"Well. Come, let us see where the tunnel leads."

"I am behind you."

In a few moments, they were out in the open, looking down at the Ocean-sea as the last of the mist blew away.

"There," said Kefaan. "Do you see? Tracks in the ground. Newly made."

"Come, then. Let us see where they lead."

They followed them carefully, until at last they saw before them the very dock at which they'd landed, although no sign of Eremit could be found. And, as Livosha looked, she realized that, not only was there no sign of Eremit, but, moreover, there was no sign of the boat on which they had hoped to escape.

Part II

MAGISTER VALLEY

Chapter the Eighteenth

*In Which Livosha and Kefaan, Having
Explored the Island to their Heart's Content,
Would Now Prefer to Leave*

My brother," said Livosha.

"Well?"

"Our boat is gone."

"How, gone?"

"Look for yourself."

"I am looking."

"And?"

"Well, what you say is true. It is gone."

"I am pleased that we agree."

"As am I, only—"

"Well?"

"You perceive that this is an eventuality I had not anticipated."

"So then, it will have an effect on our plans?"

"I think so. I had hoped to use the boat to leave with Eremit before the jailers discovered we were missing. But now—"

"No Eremit, no boat."

"Exactly."

Suddenly, there was a loud, deep peal, as of a large bell, that seemed to come from within the mountain.

"I believe," said Kefaan, "that our absence has been discovered."

"Then," said Livosha, "they will find us."

"That is not my preference," said Kefaan.

"Nor mine, if truth be known."

"And so?"

"We need time to think."

"Oh, I am all in favor of thinking, and even more in favor of time."

"Very good, then. Follow me."

They followed her back up the side of the mountain where they had come down, retracing the steps they had just made, until they came to the hole.

"You wish to go back into the cell?" said Kefaan.

"More than that, back into the jail."

"But, I fail to see how that will give us time."

"Soon you will."

"Very well."

Upon entering the cell, Livosha walked directly through it and to the opposite cell. "Jerin," she said.

"My lady?"

"Open the cell."

"Yes my lady."

As the door opened, Livosha received a curious look from a young woman of dark complexion like a Hawk, but blond hair, and features that made one think of the House of the Dragon. She rose and said, "What is this?"

"I am opening the door, madam, and then I am leaving. What you do is up to you."

"Then, they are releasing us?"

"Not in the least. I am releasing you."

"Ah. But, you are an Iorich."

"That is true, but I am not with the jail."

"So, then, you are releasing prisoners to create confusion to aid in the escape of some particular person you came to rescue?"

"You have understood exactly. The jailers are in confusion, and I wish to add to it."

"Very well. But is there a way off the island?"

"As to that—"

"Well?"

"Not as of yet."

"But then—"

"Come, I will make you a bargain. If I manage to escape—"

"Yes, if you manage to escape?"

"I will inform the nearest village that there are people who need rescuing, and, they being fishermen, who are always alert to anyone's need for rescue under any circumstances, they will likely bring boats out here and so help free you."

"So much the better. But what is my side of the bargain?"

"Take these keys and free everyone in this corridor, then, either continue to another corridor, or give the keys to someone else to continue the work. Come, what do you think of this bargain?"

"I accept with all my heart."

"Then here are the keys. I am Livosha, and this is my brother, Kefaan."

"I am called Kelsama."

"A pleasure to meet you, Kelsama."

"A pleasure indeed."

"And now, farewell, we must be away."

"Good fortune go with you."

"And you as well."

This done, Livosha, Kefaan, and Jerin returned to cell number eighty-one.

"Very good," said Kefaan. "With any luck, that will keep the jailers busy. Only—"

"Well?"

"How are we to escape the island?"

In answer, Livosha pointed to first the desk, then the bed.

"What of them?" said Kefaan.

"They are constructed of polished neeora wood, which ought to both float, and be proof against the water. We will, therefore, construct a raft, and use the blanket as a sail."

Kefaan looked doubtful, but said, "If you think it can work."

Livosha shrugged. "We will soon know."

"Very well. What must we do?"

"It is simple enough. We must remove the legs and drawers from the desk so it will fit through the tunnel, lay the desk on top of the bed frame. Then find another desk and do the same. The bed frame will hold our raft together, and two desks will provide enough deck area for the three of us."

"Then I," said Kefaan, "will find another desk, while you begin working on this one."

"Very well, with this plan, I agree."

It was harder than they had expected to remove the legs and the drawers from the desk, leaving only the surface, as the desk tended to fall to pieces from the strain. In the end, however, after having gone through six desks, they managed to achieve two completed ones. Then, Kefaan with one desk frame, Livosha with the other, and Jerin dragging the bed frame while holding the blanket, they made their way through the tunnel.

It was still fully dark, which surprised them, as it had seemed as if more time had passed. They were not, however, displeased by this, as the darkness would provide a certain degree of concealment.

They set the two desk-tops on the bed frame.

"It is not," observed Kefaan, "too stable."

"No," said Livosha. "We shall have to use our clothing to tie it together. But first, let us get it into the water."

They made their way carefully down the slope, as it wasn't easy burdened as they were, and at last came to the water. Livosha waded out first with the bed frame, the others coming behind.

"Well," said Livosha. "It has dissolved. Indeed, all of the wood has turned into small chips. I had not expected that."

"And," said Kefaan, "the desk-tops have fared the same."

"This is distressing," she said.

"And astonishing. For, you perceive, neeora floats."

"So I had thought."

"It is known, Livosha."

"Indeed. No doubt the jailers have used a polish that somehow causes this effect, though how it could do so is a mystery to me."

"Well, but we need a new plan now."

"With this I agree. But there is a fortunate side."

"Ah, well, if there is a fortunate side, so much the better. But, what is it?"

"If we had tied the desk-tops to the frame first, well, our clothing would now be wet."

"That is true," said Kefaan. "Yet I am scarcely consoled. What must we do now?"

"We must search the jail for something that will float, and hope the jailers or the other prisoners have not discovered it first."

"Very well, then. But let us hurry. You perceive, the dawn is coming, and with light, we will be more easily found."

"That is true."

They made their way up the hill and, yet once more, back into the jail, through what had been Eremit's cell, and into the corridor.

"Come, Jerin. Now you must lead. We must find our way once more to the barracks rooms; perhaps one of the tables there will not have been treated in the same way."

Jerin nodded, and at once set off. She flawlessly guided them past a number of turnings. At several points, Livosha observed fresh blood stains on the wall and floor, and so was not surprised when they came upon the bodies of two prisoners and a jailer. She was relieved to see that neither of the prisoners was Kelsama.

The Teckla continued leading them through the maze and confusion with a skill that did her credit, which credit, naturally, reflected on Livosha, though this observation was not made explicit. They continued in this fashion until they reached what Livosha recognized as the very corridor they had followed to first arrive at the dining hall, at which time she checked to see that her sword was loose in its scabbard.

"Do you hear that?" asked Kefaan.

"It sounds as if there is fighting."

"And no small degree of fighting. Even, perhaps, a pitched battle."

"And coming, alas, from the very direction we wish to go."

"And so," said Kefaan, "what then?"

How Livosha would have answered this question we cannot know, as, at that moment, there appeared eight or nine jailers, all of them armed, who were either running from something or to something, but, in any case, advancing toward them at a good pace.

"There are a large number of them," observed Kefaan. "And, you perceive, we have no convenient doorway to use to hold them off."

"That is true," said Livosha.

"And so?"

"I believe a retreat is in order, and, moreover—"

"Well?"

"A quick retreat."

"You, then, suggest we run?"

"You have understood me exactly. Come, what do you think of this plan?"

"What I think of it, my dear sister, may be deduced by the fact that I am already putting it into action."

"So much the better."

They ran the opposite direction from which they had intended to go, seeing, on the way, several prisoners who appeared to be lost, and all of whom chose to avoid what gave every sign of being impending violence, the more easily understood as none of them were armed.

After some period, they found themselves at the base of the long winding stairway they had taken down, but which now, for reasons that ought to require no explanation, led up.

"Well now," said Livosha. "Here is my plan."

"Very good," said Kefaan. "I am listening."

"Let Jerin past, for it is our duty to protect her."

"With this I agree."

"We will then draw our weapons, and defend ourselves as we back up the stairs. I believe that, by moving and using our weapons in a defensive fashion, we should be able to make it to the top."

"Well, and then?"

"Then, we will endeavor to go out the door and close it behind us."

"Well, but if we close it, I think they can open it."

"We will use your sword to wedge the door closed."

"And then? For, you perceive, we still have no way off the island."

"Then we will reflect. You perceive, we must first save ourselves from the most urgent threat before we turn our attention to the next, for if we fail in the first, there will be no need to consider the second."

"You reason like an Athyra."

"And so?"

"Very well. I accept this plan."

Thus they began their long, slow, dangerous way backward up the stairs, defending themselves furiously. Livosha saw that the director himself was there with a look of ferocity, but she was no more able to reach him than he was to reach her. As they were only concerned with defending themselves, they were unable to inflict damage beyond, on Livosha's part, a few insignificant nicks and cuts, but they managed to continue backward up the stair. Once or twice Livosha attempted to strike a blow that would send one of her opponents over the edge of the pit, but these opponents appeared unwilling to cooperate with this endeavor. Step by step they climbed, Kefaan against the wall, Livosha with nothing but emptiness to her side.

"My dear sister," said Kefaan.

"Well?"

"I confess, my arm is growing tired. It seems we have been at this for some hours."

"That is true. My arm grows tired as well. Yet, no doubt our enemies are experiencing something similar. Apropos, Jerin, how near the top are we? For if I should look myself, it might permit someone to strike me."

"Close, my lady. Only twenty or twenty-five more steps."

Kefaan grunted.

"Twenty steps, my brother? Can you do it?"

"I must," he said.

Kefaan proved himself equal to the task, and they succeeded, though not without effort, in reaching the landing. Jerin, following the plan as it had been outlined by Livosha, rushed to the door, stepped outside, and held it open, with the intention of shutting it the instant they were through. Alas, this plan, good though it was in conception, failed in the execution. The jailers were too close on their heels, and instead of being able to shut the door, found themselves flung backward as their enemies piled through.

"Run," suggested Livosha, which idea was accepted by the others without discussion or commentary. They rushed down the path until they reached the bottom, then, as one, they turned. The jailers stood at the top, preparing to follow them down.

"Jerin," said Livosha.

"Yes, my lady?"

"Permit me to suggest that this is a good time to draw your knife."

"My knife, my lady?"

"Exactly. For we are about to be attacked, and have nowhere to run save the dock, after which we stand to become tolerably wet, and more-over, have trouble breathing."

"Yes, my lady, only—"

"Only?"

"If I draw my knife while they are charging us, as they seem about to do, is it not the case that I might cut one of them?"

"You perceive, Jerin, that is the entire idea."

"Ah. I had not considered this circumstance. Very well."

With this, she drew her knife, at which moment there came the sound of a voice calling from behind them.

"Your pardon, my friends, but did you wish for transport to the main-land?"

Livosha risked looking around, and saw the Orca fisherman from whom they had first borrowed the *Carilia*, and, moreover, he was standing in the *Carilia* as he spoke.

Above them, the jailers began to descend.

"My sister?" said Kefaan. "I believe we should accept his offer."

"I nearly agree. Jerin, you first. Run. Kefaan, you after."

"And you, Livosha?"

"I am behind you."

"Well, and our enemies are behind you."

"So they are, and yet, now Jerin is in the boat. Follow her, and push off."

"And you?"

"I will jump."

"Very well. I have pushed free of the dock."

"I am jumping."

"There, I have caught you."

The fisherman, for his part, turned the rudder and pulled on the main-sail until he had snared the wind as if in a veritable net, from which the reader may deduce a certain expertise on his part, which deduction would be entirely correct, although, as we have established that he made his living on the sea, hardly surprising; the reader may have observed that we often gain great skill in matters upon which our livelihood depends, although, to judge by certain historians who have been placed, for unknown reasons, in prestigious positions, this is not always the case. Nevertheless, in the case of the Orca fisherman (whose name, alas, has not come down to us), the skill was not only great, it was, moreover, sufficient: the boat at once gathered way and took them out toward the open sea. Behind them, the jailers stood on the dock, shaking their fists; the director in particular seemed especially unhappy.

"But, how came you to be here?," asked Livosha as she settled into the boat.

"In the simplest way," replied the one who now could justly be considered their captain, as he was in charge of the vessel on which they were passengers. "This morning I looked, and the *Carilia* had returned."

"But, how did you know we had not returned with it?"

"Ah, as to that."

"Well?"

"All of us in the village have suddenly, since yester-day morning, lost our connection to the Empire."

"Yes, as have we. But how did this circumstance lead you to conclude that we had not returned?"

"Because, starting yester-day morning, and continuing to all hours of the night, the entire village had gathered in the tavern to consider the matter."

"Well, and?"

"In the first place, had you returned, well, it seemed likely you would have arrived there as well, at least to say the boat was undamaged."

"Yes, I see that. But you said in the first place. Then, there is a second place?"

"Indeed there is, and a most convincing one."

"Then I am anxious to learn it."

"Here it is, then: While we were in the tavern engaged in our conversation, which, I assure you, became tolerably loud—"

"I do not doubt this. While you were there, you say?"

"A local merchant's house was broken into."

"Well, and?"

"What was taken was some food and a large cup and a fireplace poker."

"So then?"

"It seemed the sort of things that might be taken by someone without money who contemplated a journey."

"I cannot argue with your logic. Go on."

"What if someone had been kept as a captive on the island, and had taken my boat as a means of escape, and feared there might be some pursuit, and so did not wish to be seen."

"You reason like an Athyra. And then?"

"Well, but that would mean you were still on the island, but with no means to leave. So I came out to discover if this was the case, and had barely touched the dock before I saw you running from several persons who did not look like they had good intentions toward you."

"Well, but, did it not occur to you that we might be lawbreakers, and they were attempting to arrest us?"

He shrugged. "Well, but if that is the case, is your money then no good?"

"Ah, you wish to be paid?"

"I shall return you to the shore, and if you choose to reward me, I will accept it."

"I think you may depend upon a reward, and a sufficient reward to show you that we are not ingrates. Moreover—"

"Yes?"

"We are not, in fact, lawbreakers. Just the reverse."

"So much the better."

"In fact, there are many persons, perhaps hundreds, who have been held on that island illegally."

"Shards! Is it true?"

"I give you my word. Can you, perhaps, enlist others to return to the island and help those who are trapped there? They cannot pay, at least at once, but it would be a kindness."

"If the wind holds, and it smells as if it will, we shall be arriving on the mainland at nearly the time many of us will be returning with our catch. I will spread the word among them as they return, and no doubt many will be glad to assist, simply from kindness."

"So much the better."

"But, what of you?"

"Ah, well, you see. The individual who broke into the merchant's home—"

"Yes?"

"He is the very friend whom we had set out to rescue."

"And so?"

"And so, we will search for him."

"I wish you all the best luck in this endeavor."

Livosha turned around and looked. The island had already all but vanished in the boundless sea.

Chapter the Nineteenth

In Which We Visit the Valley of Dust and Learn Why it Can No Longer be Found, at Least Under that Name

On a chilly evening six days after the sudden and shocking loss of connection to the Empire, Alishka sat by the fire while, for the thousandth time, the other eight in her band argued over what could have caused such a thing.

"It is simple," said Fagry. "The magic of the Orb could not last forever. It has exhausted itself, like a wineskin that has been drained, or like Jiscava's luck at dice, and soon the Phoenix and the Vallista and the Athyra will contrive to replace it, and all will be as normal."

"Ah, well," said Doro. "As you are so prescient, perhaps you can say when this happy event will occur."

"That is unlikely," said Liniace, whom everyone had thought asleep, as her eyes were closed and her boots so close to the fire one would have thought they'd be burning. "As he has, you perceive, predicted it would be no later than to-morrow on each of the last five days."

"And," said Fagry, "what then is your idea? Do you persist in your belief that the Easterners have conquered the Empire and taken the Orb for their own?"

"It is not a belief," said Liniace. "It is a possibility."

"Well," said Cho. "But in order to conquer the Empire and take over the Orb, they must first have taken over the Orb, which, you perceive, is impossible, as it violates the law of cause and effect."

"It is still more likely," said Liniace, "than the ground opening and swallowing the capital city."

"Why?" said Cho. "Is it not the case that sometimes the ground opens and swallows things? What makes it impossible in this case?"

"Shards!" said Liniace. "To begin—"

"Hssst," said Branf, and everyone fell silent as if it were Alishka who had spoken. In Alishka's case, it would have been because of the respect they had for their chief; in Branf's case, it was because of how rarely he spoke. They all looked at him in curiosity, even Alishka, and waited to see what he was about to say. In fact, he said nothing whatever, merely pointed. They followed the direction of his finger, and saw a figure approaching them, walking slowly.

Alishka rose. The stranger was a man, and dressed in filthy clothing that looked as if it might once have been white, and he appeared far too thin to permit him to live through the autumn this far north. In his left hand, he had what appeared to be a large drinking cup, and in his right was what was perhaps a stick. As he came closer, she was able to see that it was metal, and, moreover, had a point on the end. He was not only thin, as we have just had the honor to observe, but he also seemed, though he continued walking purposefully toward her, so weak as to be barely able to put one foot before another.

As he came near he said, "I bid you all a good evening, and wonder if I might have use of your fire for the purpose of warming myself for a short time."

"And that is all you wish?"

"That is my greatest wish, if not my only one."

"For, you perceive, for that, you do not require a weapon."

The stranger glanced at the object in his right hand as if he'd forgotten it was there, then elaborately looked at the individuals gathered around the fire. "Well," he said, "first, permit me to observe that the nine of you have little to fear from me, and, next, this is not a weapon, it is a tool." With this, he took two steps forward and used the object in his hand to stir the fire, causing sparks to rise into the air as if in celebration of his arrival.

"Then," said Alishka, "as the fire is here, it is here such a tool is useful; therefore, you need not carry it."

The stranger shrugged and let go of it. "There. Now, you perceive, I am unarmed except for a cracked wooden cup, which, I may add, is empty. In exchange for the tool, may I request some water, and a bite of bread?"

"So then, you are a beggar?" said Alishka.

"If a beggar is one who begs, well, perhaps I am an asker. But come, Alishka, you would not refuse food to a hungry man."

"How is it you know my name? Have you come from the authorities?"

"I do not believe there are any authorities left," he said simply, causing all of those present to look at each other.

"How, no authorities?"

"Well, we are in the county of Longview, are we not?"

"And if we are?"

"The county seat is Dachfe?"

"It is."

"The home of Dachfe e'Drien?"

"That is true."

"Well, his home is a pile of rubble, having, it seems, fallen from the sky a few days ago."

They looked at him in silence, then at each other. Then Nef rose to his feet and took a single flatbread from the bag. After a nod from Alishka, he handed it over. The stranger tore off a small piece, and bowing to them all, put it in his mouth and chewed it slowly. As he did, he closed his eyes and seemed to become unsteady on his feet.

"Please, sit," said Alishka, indicating that Fagry and Jiscava should move aside to make room on their log. "You did not tell me how you know my name."

"Ah," he said, sitting carefully. "So then, my guess was right." He tore off another small piece of flatbread and ate it.

"It is," said Alishka. "But, on what basis did you guess?"

"I was told of you by a friend, who was a friend of yours as well."

Alishka's eyes narrowed and she touched the hilt of her sword. "I have no friends."

"Alas, that is true," said the stranger. "But you once had one."

"I do not know of whom you could—" She stopped suddenly and stared at him, and her heart gave an unusual flutter. Then she recovered and said, "State his name."

"Magister," said the stranger.

"You are a friend of Magister? But, you say 'was.' Then—"

"Alas, he is dead. He died in jail, and, indeed, in my arms."

Alishka found herself sitting down with no notion of how she came to be. Her companions were silent out of respect for her grief as the stranger continued to slowly eat the flatbread, piece by piece. Branf passed him a wineskin; he nodded his thanks and drank.

"Is that why you came?" asked Alishka after a moment. "If you traveled here merely to give me this news, well, I am in your debt."

"I should admire to have you in my debt," acknowledged the stranger. "But, alas, I did not know you would be here. Magister said this was one place you could be found, but there are others, and it was to the place I came, not to see you. Although, in the first place, I am glad to see you, and in the second, I hope you will love me a little for my honesty."

"That depends," said Alishka.

"Well, let us see. Upon what does it depend?"

"Why are you here?"

"Ah, as to that."

"Well?"

He nodded to the cave. "Magister left me something in there and I promised him I would get it."

Alishka frowned, remembering well the cave, from having sheltered in it from rain and snow a thousand times over the years. "There is nothing in the cave," she said.

"Nevertheless. Do you object if I go in?"

"Not in the least."

"And may I have my stick?"

Alishka studied him. He seemed to be old, and yet it could be only the signs of having had a difficult life combined with the obvious distress caused by his recent travel. His eyes were confident, yet contained secrets. She felt inclined to trust him, but wasn't certain she should, in spite of his claims to have known her friend the Magister. "Why do you wish your stick?"

"Perhaps I am afraid of snakes. Or perhaps I wish to draw in the dust. Or perhaps, after walking such a distance without food, I would like to lean on it."

"You say 'perhaps' in a way that makes me think none of those is the real reason."

He smiled.

"Well," she said, "at least give me a name."

"Ah, you wish a name? Very well. This is the Valley of Dust, is it not?"

"Yes, and well named, too. But then?"

"Well, I claim it as my valley, so call me Dust."

"Your valley?"

"Needless to say, as you were here first, I will not dispute your right to occupy it as long as you wish."

"That is remarkably good of you."

"Well."

Doro, who was as close to a second-in-command as Alishka had, said, "Captain?"

"Well?"

"Do you believe we can trust him?"

"You think we cannot? What could he do in the cave?"

"I don't know, but permit me to accompany him."

Alishka turned to the stranger. "Do you object to company?"

"Not in the least."

"Then I shall go with you myself. When do you wish to go in?"

Dust put the last of the bread he had been given into his mouth, chewed it carefully, and swallowed. "Now," he said.

Alishka felt a sudden thrill shoot through her at this word, though for no reason she could name. She stood up. "Very well, let us go in then."

"And us?" said Doro.

"Wait out here. If it should chance that he comes out and I do not, well—" She shrugged. "—you will know then what to do."

"Indubitably, Captain," said Doro.

The stranger, that is to say, "Dust," as he called himself, had no reaction to overhearing these words, a reaction (for, as the reader knows, not to react is itself, at least at times, to react) that left Alishka uncertain if it was reassuring.

He bent down to the fire and retrieved, first, the fireplace poker, then a burning stick. "To light our way," he explained.

"Very well."

He led the way into the cave and so toward the back. Once there, he began kicking debris, rubble, and filth to the side.

"You're barefoot!" cried Alishka.

"That is true," said Dust. "But, you perceive, only because my shoes fell apart during the walk. They were not well made."

"Your feet are bleeding!"

"Not badly."

"If you wish, I will continue clearing the rubble myself, and thus spare your feet from further injury."

"Thank you, but I am nearly done. There, you see?"

"But—what is that? What is the design? I have never seen anything like it!"

Dust laughed, though it seemed to Alishka to be the sort of laugh that contains a mix of emotions that does not include amusement. "If you wish me to guess, my dear Alishka, it is nothing. Once, perhaps, when we could reach the Orb, it was something, and it is possible that it will be something again someday. But for now, I do not believe it is anything."

"But then, why are you here?"

"I promised Magister," he said with flat finality.

"So then, you walked, I don't know how far, days, with no shoes, no food, no water, all to come here to accomplish nothing, to fulfill a promise to a dead man?"

"I had food and water when I set out," said Dust. "And have not been without for very long."

"Nevertheless, why have you done this?"

"He was my friend," said Dust simply.

"Well, I honor you for it."

Dust shrugged. "We should both honor him, for he was worthy of honor."

"In that, I agree."

"And, moreover, though I have not said so, I honor you, for you saved his life."

Alishka felt the blood rising to her cheeks, and was glad they were in a dark cave. "Well," she said.

Dust abruptly sat down in the middle of the design.

"Now that I recall, this is where we first found Magister."

"Yes, so he informed me," said Dust.

"And he was sitting just as you are."

"Yes," said Dust.

"And was scratching marks with a sharp object, just as you seem to be doing."

"Yes," said Dust, and, with the fireplace poker, he scratched a single line, connecting two points, one near his right knee, the other near his right hip.

"What is that?" said Alishka.

"What?"

"Something under your shirt is glowing."

"How, glowing?"

"Yes."

He looked down and said, "Why yes, so it is. In time to my heartbeat if I am not mistaken. Well, I freely confess, I had not expected that. Indeed, I had not expected anything."

"But what does it mean?"

"I have not the least idea in the world, I assure you."

"But then—"

She stopped and stared for a moment. "What is that?"

He suddenly appeared to be in the middle of a tiny localized storm made up of golden sparks. "It is a signal," he said.

"A signal? But what is it signaling?"

"That it is time for me to stand up."

He rose and walked forward several steps. The sparks continued to occupy the area above the peculiar design for some few seconds, and then they seemed to be coalescing into a shape.

What at last emerged was a being. It was small—smaller than a human, or even an Easterner, though not, at least to believe the stories she'd heard as a child, as small as a Serioli, nor was it pale as those beings were said to be; rather its skin seemed to be a rich copper color. It had no hair, ears that flopped down, and large eyes that were red and looked perfectly round. Its mouth was also large, but it had no lips or teeth, and it had, for that matter, no nose. It did, however, have two legs, and, moreover, two arms, both of which ended in hands, which hands were supplied, as it were, with opposable thumbs and three fingers each.

"Cracks and shards!" cried Alishka, unaware that she'd even decided to speak. "It's a demon!"

"Well," said Dust.

The being within the design spoke. Its voice was high, and its speech was full of squeaks and whistles that quite startled Alishka, though not as much as when Dust replied in the same language.

"You speak its tongue!" said Alishka.

Dust broke off and said, "Magister taught me, although I had not until this moment known why," then returned to his conversation with the demon.

During this conversation the demon looked at her several times. At one point, Dust paused and said, "He has agreed that you are not to be a gift."

"That's lucky."

"Yes. Also, I assume you do not have an ovipositor?"

"I have never heard this word pronounced, and hence do not know what it means."

"No more do I. I shall therefore assume you are lacking one."

He returned to the discussion, nodding several times, although Alishka privately doubted that the being would understand the gesture. Then Dust said, "Well, I can settle the argument."

"I beg your pardon," said Alishka. "Argument?"

"As I approached the camp, you were arguing about the Orb, and why it was no longer possible to touch it."

"Ah, well, yes?"

"There has been an explosion, although the cause is not known. The city of Dragaera is gone, and there seems to be a sea of amorphia where it once was."

"Scrotums of the gods! Can it be?"

"So it would seem. He had no reason to lie. Indeed, as he is in some measure bound to me, I am not convinced that he would be able to lie if he wished to."

He went back to conversing in squeaks and whistles, while she tried to comprehend the enormity of what she had just learned. And what of her band, that it was her duty to protect? What would become of them? Would the highways become empty of fat merchants? Would they need to move near to a bigger town? And would they be safe even so? No, it was too much for now; she was going to have to consider the matter, talk about it with the rest. Yet it did not for an instant occur to her to doubt him, or the demon who had conveyed this intelligence.

She realized suddenly that the conversation with the demon had stopped. "I beg your pardon," she told Dust. "I must ask you to repeat what you did me the honor to say."

"I was thanking you for your hospitality and kindness."

"How, you are leaving?"

"Exactly. And I hope you will convey my gratitude toward your fellows."

"I will do so, only, well—"

"Yes?"

"How are you leaving?"

"As to that, well, we will see. But I trust S'rik'ki'ka, he seems to be a fine fellow for a demon. I will see you again."

With that, Dust set the glowing stick he'd used for light into the ground, dropped the fireplace poker, and walked forward into the diagram on the ground, and presently vanished in a shower of golden sparks. Alishka stood for a moment staring at the spot where he'd been, then picked up the fireplace poker and walked back out of the cave.

"Well?" said Doro.

Alishka shook her head and sat down in front of the fire. She absently stirred the coals with the poker and said, "Come, my friends. Gather around. We must have conversation."

Some two years after the events we have just observed, Alishka was in an inn at a hamlet some ten miles outside of Northport. The name of the hamlet has not come down to us, perhaps because it was so rarely used; to those who lived nearby it was, "I'm going to town," and to others it was, "that place on the road that goes by where the windmill burned down." In fact, there was little there except the inn, a house nearby where the innkeeper's son lived and grew malt and hops, a Chreotha who sold items from Northport on the back of his wagon and knitted blankets, and the house belonging to the innkeeper's husband who had been thrown out some years before and now made his living exchanging money for goods with the local bandits who frequented the inn, which he was not permitted inside of except before dusk on Endweek.

On this day, then, Alishka sat at her usual table. Doro and Fagry were at the next table, giving her a certain measure of solitude. She was nursing a beer, Doro was eating bacon and tubers, Fagry was drinking wine. The door opened, then, and a particularly unusual sight greeted her: a man who was dressed in white from head to foot—shirt, cloak, breeches, boots. He had a sword at his side held on with a white belt, and he wore a white sash over his shoulder, marked by the one splash of color he wore: a bright red ruby pinned to the sash. He walked up to her without hesitation, and, he not appearing hostile, Alishka waited. When Doro and Fagry began to stand, she motioned them to wait. He sat down without being asked and said, "I trust you are having a pleasant day, Alishka?"

She frowned. "Do I know you?"

"Evidently not," he said.

She frowned. "If you think to jest with me, sir, I must tell you my spirit is not of a jesting disposition."

"Perhaps this will give you a certain cheer," he said, placing a medium-sized uncut sapphire on the table.

She looked at it, and looked at him, and her eyes narrowed. Alishka had handled her share of jewels, but knew better than to consider herself an expert. She said carefully, "What do you pretend this is worth?"

"As to that, well, you must determine it when you sell it. There are honest jewelers in Northport."

"And your share, sir?"

"I have no share. I merely give it to you as a gesture of gratitude."

"How, gratitude? In what way have I been so fortunate as to deserve your gratitude?"

The stranger chuckled as if these words reminded him of something amusing. "Do you know your Ekrasan, Alishka?"

"A little."

"'You shared your fire when I was cold and your meat when I starved, and so you are my brother by steel or by blood.'"

"*Tears of the Heart*, Day Three, Act One, Scene Four," said Alishka. "That one is not difficult."

"Well."

"But I did not—"

She stopped and looked at him closer. "Barlen's farts," she said. "Is it you, Dust?"

"The same," he said, bowing from his chair.

She looked again at the sapphire. "Well, suddenly I am glad for my small courtesies. You perceive, matters have not been easy, and this will help."

"Perhaps," he said, "I can help more."

"You have my attention."

Dust waved it aside and said, "We will speak of that later. For now, I wish a bottle of as good a wine as this establishment can provide."

"That is easily done," said Alishka, and signaled to the host.

When the wine had been poured, Alishka said, "So tell me, if you would, how your fortunes have come to change so much in a mere two years."

"Ah, you see that they have changed."

"Nearly."

"Well, I do not deny it."

"And then?"

"You perceive, I had a demon bound to my service."

"I can understand this might give one certain advantages, if—"

"If?"

"That is to say, there are stories."

"Oh, many. There are countless stories. To which stories do you refer?"

"Of those who lose control of such beings."

"S'rik'ki'ka is a good sort, and I only required a few small services of him, and so we parted on good terms."

"He did not mind being summoned?"

"On the contrary, it appears I pulled him from an awkward social situation. While I never managed to understand the complexities, from the way he spoke of it, he was more than happy to vanish against his will."

"Ah, so much the better. But then, what services did he provide?"

Dust smiled a little. "As to that, well, it was not without value."

"From this answer, I deduce that you do not wish to discuss the matter."

"You are perspicacious."

"Very well. And other matters?"

"I happened upon a small fortune in gems."

Alishka looked at the sapphire that was still on the table. "So I perceive. And?"

"I have acquired land."

"You use the word 'acquired.'"

"Well, and is it not a perfectly good word?"

"Oh, I do not quarrel with the word. And yet it does make one wonder in what fashion you acquired it."

"In the simplest way. Shall I tell you?"

"If you please, for I find our conversation most agreeable."

"This is it, then. A distant heir of the e'Drien line of the House of the Dragon came to take possession of the County of Longview, she having been fortunate enough to be away when her castle fell."

"I understand this. And?"

"I was so fortunate as to be able to render her certain assistance in the construction of a new manor to replace the old castle. The new one, you perceive, being smaller and, moreover, at a lower altitude."

"I understand this. But then, you are a Vallista?"

"Not in the least. But I have learned something of the art of engineering."

"Well, and then?"

"My advice was so good, she rewarded me with a small barony on her land."

"Well, and where is this barony?"

"You know it well, my friend, for it was once called the Valley of Dust."

"Once called?"

"Yes, I have renamed it Magister Valley."

Alishka was surprised at the sudden tears that sprang to her eyes upon hearing this name, but she nodded and said, "That was well done."

"I'm glad you think so, for you are welcome there whenever and for as long as you wish, and with whomever you bring."

"I am grateful for your kindness. Have you improved upon the land?"

"It is, as you know, difficult to find labor in that region. Nevertheless, I've managed to have built a small home of six or seven rooms, much as a merchant might have, and there is water, and once the trees have grown there will be firewood for the winter."

"So now, instead of Dust, I may with justice call you Baron Magister?"

He shook his head. "I do not wish that name. We both know who we mean when we say Magister, and I should not like to introduce confusion."

"Very well, I accept this. I will continue to call you Dust."

"I am glad you agree. The house will perhaps be a trifle crowded when your band all arrive to escape from pursuers, but it is there, and, moreover, contains an excellent view and the security of knowing that there is only one direction from which it can be approached."

"It is good to know that it is there. And, moreover—"

"Well?"

"I compliment you, for you have been busy in the last two years."

"I was forced to remain inactive for many years, so, you perceive, I do not wish to waste time now."

"I understand that."

"And you, my dear Alishka? You say things have been difficult?"

"Let us not speak of that. Rather I have news that may interest you."

"Oh?"

"You were sought after."

"How, sought after?"

"Two Iorich came looking for you, only a day after you had left."

"Well, and?"

"We pretended we had never heard of you."

"So much the better."

Dust drank some more wine while Alishka studied him. He had certainly changed: he was clean, and the deep rings were gone from beneath his eyes. Those were the most obvious changes. He seemed younger as well; when she first met him, she would have guessed his age at between two thousand and twenty-five hundred, now she would have guessed that he could not be older than a thousand years, perhaps younger. And yet, she perceived, there was more: In two years, he had acquired a kind of confidence that was close to insolence, as if he felt immune to worldly dangers, or, even more, as if he were so much in control of his environment that nothing could happen around him except by his choice. Alishka found it disturbing, yet curiously intriguing.

"You are studying me, I see," said Dust.

"Well."

"What are your conclusions?"

"Shards! My conclusion is that, if you continue to wear white, Dust is a good name, for you will acquire much of it."

The other chuckled at this witticism Alishka did him the honor to share, then said, "But you see, because one wears clothing upon which dust doesn't show does not mean there is no dust, only that one has refused to acknowledge it."

"Ah, you become philosophical."

"And if I do?"

"Alas, my circumstances do not permit time for philosophical reflection."

"I must dispute you, my friend—for so I hope I may consider you. Philosophical contemplation need not be separate from activity, but on the contrary, ought to inform our actions, as our actions inform our philosophy," by which statement he proved he had given more careful thought to these matters than some who occupy important positions in which having given these issues due consideration ought to be a requirement.

Alishka, for her part, merely shrugged and said, "No doubt you are right. But you have been generous. You said, or, to be more precise, *hinted* that I could be of further service to you."

"You are not wrong."

"Then, what is it you wish me to do?"

"Journey to a place called Wetrock, five hundred or five hundred and fifty miles south of here on the western coast."

"Well, and?"

"Learn what you can of the local baron, and the fate of someone called Livosha, daughter of Cerwin, and her family, and the family of Baroness Sudora. Also of the local connections of authority, that is to say, who bows to whom? As much of the history as you can discover of what happened there some six hundreds of years ago. If you accept, this purse should provide sufficient expenses as well as payment. What do you say?"

Alishka took the purse he offered and weighed it in her hand; in addition to expenses, the payment would certainly provide for her band for some time.

"Livosha," she repeated. "It seems I have heard that name, though I cannot recall when."

"It is not an uncommon name," said Dust. "And the mission?"

"I accept with pleasure."

"Very good. Now let us see if you understand the task."

"You may judge: The barony of Wetrock, five hundred miles to the south. What happened six hundred years ago, Livosha, daughter of Cerwin, her family, the family of Sudora, the present lines of authority."

"You have it exactly."

"You perceive, it will take some time; a journey of such length is not completed overnight."

"I am in no hurry. I will meet you again in Magister Valley."

"Then that is where I will see you. I will not fail in this task you have done me the honor to give."

"I do not doubt you in the least."

"And if you will excuse me, I will, without wasting an instant, begin preparations for the journey."

"So much the better."

Alishka rose, secured the purse and the sapphire, collected Doro and Fagry with a gesture, and bowed deeply to Dust, after which, followed by her two subordinates, she walked out of the inn to begin gathering her band.

Chapter the Twentieth

In Which We Return to Those Unsavory or Unpleasant Persons We Saw Before, Who Now Have Their Own Problems

Some fourteen or fifteen years after the fall of the Empire, though chaos still reigned supreme, there were, here and there, signs of the development of a new normalcy, or, if the reader will permit us to borrow a term from natural philosophy, a new *equilibrium*. One of the first places to show these signs was the port city of Adrilankha. Though the port was all but deserted, save for the fishing boats, nevertheless the rice still grew beyond the jungles to the southwest, the wheat and maize was still collected in the flatlands to the south, the sheep and the cows still grazed the grasslands to the east, and so the city was as close to self-sufficient as it was possible to be at that time.

Of course, the money that Prince Traanzo had once counted upon from his estates had stopped with the fall of the Empire, either because his steward was too canny to trust a supply of gold on roads filled with bandits and no protection, or because he had foolishly done so. Traanzo himself, however, had, in the few hundred years before the catastrophic vanishing of the Orb, accumulated immense wealth in a number of ways, some of which, of course, he used to guard the rest, now depending on expensive locks and well-paid guards where once he had largely counted on sorcery; but this left him a considerable fortune even apart from what he received as the High Justicer for the county of Whitecrest. He was, therefore, as content and free from worry as anyone could be in those days of turmoil. More, he considered himself remarkably fortunate, as his interests as Heir had taken him often to Dragaera City, and it was only by a matter of days that he had escaped the destruction of that city, and this only because complications of the laws regarding Imperial Finance had driven him to seek the peace and quiet of his own home in order to work them out. While not especially superstitious, he nevertheless could not entirely rid himself of the feeling that he had been spared by the gods, which in turn made him feel that he had a sort of blanket of divine protection over him, which, even if his conscious mind did not entirely accept it, he found a not unpleasant sensation.

On the day of which we have the honor to write, he received word from his cloaklady (who, as we will be meeting him later, and as he has no important role in these events, we will postpone the introduction of) that a certain Iorich had arrived at the front gate desiring an audience. Upon being informed that this worthy only gave his name as "the director," Traanzo at once called for him to brought in.

The reader will, of course, recall the director from our earlier meetings, but the individual who now presented himself had little in common with that personage. He was, first of all, covered with the dust of the road. His hair was so disheveled his noble's point could not be distinguished. More significantly, he had a acquired a long scar that ran from the bridge of his nose to the point of his jaw, his left arm was in a sling, and he had a pronounced limp. Though he seemed to be on the very point of exhaustion, he nevertheless managed to bow deeply to Traanzo.

"Well," observed the prince. "You appear to have had certain hardships."

"I cannot dispute Your Highness," said the director. "Of the eight who set out with me fifteen years ago, three are dead, and one was so badly wounded I was obliged to leave her behind on the road. Nevertheless, as you see, I am here."

"That is true, and the fact that you are indicates that something urgent has happened with regard to Burning Island? So urgent, in fact, that you embarked on a fifteen-year journey just in order to tell me?"

"We were not, you understand, traveling the entire time. We stopped for several years in a village called Markingstone in order to work and gather resources, and then again in a place called Nuresit. Moreover, I must, for the sake of honesty, Your Highness, object to one word in what you have done me the honor to ask."

"What word is that?"

"'Just.'"

"Ah, so there was another reason?"

"There was, my lord, and a most pressing one for me, if not for you."

"Well, let us start with that, then. What was this reason?"

"I have nowhere else to go."

"I understand this reason. But then, let us move on to the other, that is to say, to the question of the island itself, and the jail upon it."

"My lord, you perceive that with the vanishing of the Orb, we could no longer control the volcano."

"Yes, I understand that."

"And, moreover, there was a certain amount of upset among the staff."

"By upset, you mean panic?"

"I do not deny it."

"Well, there was panic here as well. But, what then?"

"In the confusion, one of the guests managed to make his way out of the cell."

"Ah, and what prisoner was this?"

"Number eighty-one."

"Well, but you perceive, this number is not useful to me."

"Alas, I no longer recall his name."

"Very well, go on."

"Not only did this guest escape, but he somehow contrived to free the other guests."

"How is this possible?"

"He had assistance from two persons who arrived on the island with the intention of causing this disruption."

"Go on, then."

"And there was, in addition, a conflict among the jailers."

"How, a conflict?"

"Some of them feared betrayal by the others if word of this came to the Empire."

"But there is no Empire."

"This was not known at the time, my lord."

"That is true," said the prince, struck by the extreme justice of the observation. "So then?"

"Then, somehow, word came to the nearby fishing village that there were individuals trapped on the island, and so they brought their boats out to aid in the rescue."

"And what was the result of this rescue?"

"I do not exactly know, my lord. You perceive, I was obliged to accept a rescue myself, or else remain trapped on the island. The prisoners who escaped at once scattered."

"How many were there?"

"At least a score, perhaps three times that."

"Cracks and shards! And you do not know where they are?"

"Not in the least, my lord. I gathered the loyal jailers I could find and we set off at once to inform you of this circumstance. You perceive, with bandits, some of which are more nearly described as armies, we have had to go carefully, and finding supplies and provisions has not been easy. We stole some horses, but were unable to procure provender and so they died."

The duke nodded. "Very well. Then I will see to it your people are fed and lodged while I consider this matter, and what can be done about it."

"Thank you, my lord," said the director, bowing deeply. "I had known I could trust your kindness."

"Of course," said the prince, and dismissed him with a smile while he considered whether there was any reason not to have him executed.

One day some eighteen years after the fall of the Empire, that is, three years after the conversation we have just observed, the Lord Berwick, the Baron of Wetrock by appointment of His Benevolence the Count of Dorin, was taking his breakfast with his son. This was taking place, be it understood, in the very room in which, more than six hundred years before, Eremit had enjoyed a meal with the family of whom all save Livosha and Kefaan were now dead. The breakfast consisted of shredded beef wrapped in pastry, duck's eggs poached in red wine, and of course, legume pudding, although this was naturally prepared with more care and fresher legumes (as well as rosemary, stinseed, and tarragon) than that which had been served on the Burning Island.

At first, the meal was silent, as was usual, father and son having little to say to each other beyond observations on the food and intentions for the day, neither of which are of sufficient interest to be worth taking up the reader's time.

But then the son, that is to say, Yanis, happened to say, "My father, I am curious to know if there has been progress on the matter of raising Wetrock to a county."

Berwick, for his part, scowled with evident impatience. "Has it come to your attention, my son, that, some twenty years ago, events transpired that necessarily delayed all such matters?"

"And yet, with your inability to discover the location of the missing heirs, the urgency has not reduced."

Berwick's eyes narrowed. "I shall," he said, "ignore the barb implied in your use of the word 'your' and merely contradict you."

"How contradict me?"

"Yes, for the reason that you are incorrect."

"In what matter am I incorrect?"

"In the matter of urgency."

"You pretend that there is less urgency?"

"Certainly there is less urgency. The same catastrophe that has interfered with our plans, must necessarily interfere with any plans the pretenders—that is to say, the missing survivors—may have. That is, travel has become difficult and dangerous, likewise communication, and triply so with any possible legal action they may contemplate. Moreover—"

"Well? Moreover?"

"If they did nothing during the six hundreds of years before, what reason have we to think they will do something now, when every action they may attempt has become so much more difficult?"

"I do not deny the justice of what you say, and yet—"

"Well? And yet?"

"It is a matter that, you perceive, is unfinished."

"Nothing, my son, is ever finished."

Yanis brushed this aside with a gesture that, reflected Berwick, would have gotten him slapped six hundred years before. The younger man said, "I cannot help but observe that there were two tasks, my lord father. One was to make certain of those in Cryden House, the other those in Cerwin's family. You perceive, the first, that is to say, my task was completed, even though one of them unexpectedly arrived at the count's with an errand that could have ruined everything had I not had the foresight to put myself in a position to take the necessary action. It was the second task, that is to say, yours, my lord father, that—"

"I will interrupt you here because, even before continuing, you have fallen into an error."

"But, what error have I fallen into? It seems to me that everything I have said is true."

"And yet, we differ upon this subject."

"And will you do me the honor to explain in what we differ?"

"I will do so this very moment."

"In that case, I am listening."

"To begin, then, what you are pleased to call 'your task' was carried out with such clumsiness that His Benevolence the Count was forced to go through the motions of a full investigation on behalf of the Empire, with the subsequent delay in the reward we were promised, a delay that has extended even to the present day."

"Ah, you return to this again?"

"And if I do? You perceive, it is still the case that it happened, and, moreover, that three of them survived."

"Only one of whom was my responsibility, father, and he, that is to say, Eremit, was disposed of."

"But, you perceive, he was disposed of by being imprisoned."

"And then?"

"Imprisoned," repeated Berwick. "And yet, those imprisoned can be freed."

"Not from the Burning Island," said Yanis. "We have assurances on this from His Benevolence."

"Well, but it seems these assurances are not in all ways reassuring."

"My lord father, I do not understand what you do me the honor to tell me."

"Some two months ago a woman, that is to say, a stranger, arrived in Kartro, just a few miles from here."

"Well, and?"

"She settled there, taking a position as a servant to the Speaker, who is, as you know, my cousin."

"So then?"

"Four days ago she, having received payment, became drunk, and in the course of this, she told of having once been a prisoner in an island prison, protected by a volcano, off the northwest coast. She escaped, she said, in the confusion of the catastrophe eighteen years ago. My cousin, upon hearing this, questioned her, as he feared to have a felon among his servants. It seemed she was unaware of any crime she had committed, having only offended a certain Iorich by making insulting remarks about his character. She said, upon being questioned, that of some two or three hundred prisoners, at least two score had escaped, most of the rest having drowned or been killed by the jailers. It was only by accident I learned of this, the subject having come up with my cousin over our monthly game of Shereba."

"Well, but," said Yanis, though somewhat shaken by this intelligence, "is there any reason to believe that, of this two score out of three hundred, Eremit is one?"

"Is there any reason to believe he is not?"

"Well, but, is there any way to find out?"

"I have been considering this question."

"And?"

"I do not know."

"Ah."

"But I know who would."

"And that is?"

"His Benevolence. You perceive, it was the count who arranged for young Eremit to be imprisoned; if anyone knows how to determine what has become of him, that is who it would be."

"And so?"

"And so, my son, since you are so willing to bring up the matter of our long-delayed promotion, I suggest you prepare yourself for a journey and speak to the count himself.

"Very well, my lord father. If that is your wish—"

"It is."

"—Then I will prepare at once, and be gone by noon."

"And you will be right to do so."

"Then with your permission, I will excuse myself from the table, and begin to prepare my departure."

Berwick nodded, and Yanis stood, bowed, and left the dining room.

We trust the reader will remember Dorindom Castle, home of Count Dorin; we hope that the reader will also remember the count's private study, of which, to be sure, we have only had time to provide a glimpse before Eremit was struck senseless. At the moment of which we now write, just a little more than a day after the conversation between Berwick and Yanis, the latter, who had not been struck from behind or from any other direction, stood before His Benevolence, trying not to shift his weight from foot to foot in order to hide a certain nervousness. This discomfort was noticed with some amusement by the count.

At this point, we are forced to draw the reader's attention to the previous two sentences, as a special case in which, in order to convey significant information—specifically the matter of the shifting of Yanis's feet and the count's awareness of it—we have violated certain literary conventions. In particular, we have elected to first show the thinking of the younger man, and then, immediately, show the thoughts of the count. While it is the case that, in our role as historian, we are able to deduce with some certainty the ideas of those we examine, and thus discover them to the reader in good season, the difficulty arises with the disorientation that the reader will certainly feel when directed to shift so rapidly from the thoughts of one to the thoughts of the other. It is a well-established rule among those who work with the pen that to make such shifts willy-nilly is to damage the integrity of the narrative and do a certain amount of violence to the reader's ability to fully immerse himself in the text. We have, on this occasion, chosen to risk this confusion because we believe that, while Yanis's thoughts in this instance are sufficiently important that we would be doing the reader a disservice by failing to reveal them, nevertheless, we believe that the reader will best understand the events we propose to unfold if seen through the eyes, as it were, of the count. Thus, for the sake of brevity, we have taken the liberty of making this brief shift in perspective as the most efficient method of ensuring that the reader is fully aware of all necessary information.

With this understood, the count, who, as we have said, was amused to see Yanis's discomfort, at length invited his vassal to sit in a small, armless chair facing the desk behind which his Benevolence conducted his business.

"So, then," said the count. "You wished to see me. Have you blown up any more manors, or is it upon some other concern?"

Yanis flushed slightly, which amused the count even more.

"Your Benevolence, I have come to inquire about the young gentleman whom you caused to be arrested."

Dorin felt his eyes narrow, and felt a pulse throb in his throat. "Perhaps," he said in the voice that caused the courtiers to look at the floor and swallow as if something were lodged in their throats, "you wish to phrase that thought in a different way?"

Yanis looked at the floor and swallowed as if something was lodged in his throat. "My apologies, Benevolence. I meant to say, the young gentleman who, that is to say—" Here he dropped his voice and leaned toward the other, "a certain Eremit."

Dorin frowned and gestured for the courtiers to step back, after which he said, "Well? What of him?"

"We wish to determine if it is possible that he has escaped."

This time, the sudden "thud" of his heart was unmistakable. This was not only unexpected (he had thought the man had been sent to inquire about his father's promised county), but was disturbing. Could Eremit be free, and, if so, could he somehow be a threat? And yet, there was no Empire to which he could appeal, and no Orb under which he could testify. (We would mention at this point that Yanis observed the count's evident discomfort with a certain relief, but we are loath to risk disorienting the reader a second time.) Dorin felt the tension ease a little within him, and he said, "Come now, explain to me why you believe this man might have escaped."

"Willingly," said Yanis, and, without delay, described the information that had been relayed to him, and which, the reader already being cognizant of, there is no need to repeat.

When the other had finished speaking, Dorin took a moment to reflect on the unpleasant sound of the voice to which he had been obliged to listen, which managed to be simultaneously nasal and grating. When this contemplation had run its course, he considered the words he had heard, and, even more, the meaning behind the words, and concluded that it was a matter about which there was no question of joking. After giving the matter a certain amount of thought, he pronounced the word, "Well."

"Your Benevolence?" said Yanis.

"You may return to your home."

"Thank you, Benevolence. But as to the matter—"

"I do not give you accounts of my actions."

"No, Your Benevolence. Of course not."

"Nevertheless, I will say something for purposes of setting your mind at ease."

"Your Benevolence is, ah, that is to say . . ."

"Benevolent?"

"Yes, my lord."

"I will look into this matter. That is to say, I will discover if there is any reason to worry, and moreover, when I know, I will inform your father of what I have discovered."

"Thank you, Benevolence."

Dorin waved to dismiss him, not really paying attention as the other rose, bowed, backed up, and turned to leave. When he had gone, Dorin rang for his assistant and said, "Bring me Hadrice." This assistant, whose name, alas, has not come down to us, bowed, although Dorin noticed with some amusement that he appeared to shudder a little at hearing the name, and left to carry out this mission.

In a short time the door opened, and the individual referred to arrived. Hadrice, of course, was not her name at birth, rather, it is a contraction of two words in Lichachtra—that is, the most common language among the cat-centaurs of the northeast—the words being *hadrio diska*, meaning *silver knife*. And, indeed, the long dagger of pure silver on her right hip was the most outstanding feature of her gear, contrasting with the plain, businesslike sword of more than common length and weight that she wore on her left. Should the reader observe that it is unusual for a retainer to walk about armed, we will respond that Hadrice was no ordinary retainer. The fact that she was summoned was proof that the matter, whatever it was, had gone beyond words.

She was of shorter than average stature, and would seem to be thin and even *frail* to the casual eye, if such an eye failed to notice the confident ease of her stride or the cold detachment of her gaze. Her dark hair, darker even than her complexion, was always worn swept back and tied. Her leather garments defied any attempt to guess her House, and she wore no jewelry or sigil to supply a hint. She presented herself to Dorin with a deep bow, a gesture the count appreciated all the more as he knew no one else, even His Majesty were he still on the throne, would receive this degree of respect from her.

Whence she came no one knew, nor, indeed, why she had attached herself to Dorin; even the count himself didn't know. But she had presented herself to him and offered him her loyalty and her sword, and he had perceived at once that this was an offer worth more than gold, and so had accepted instantly. He had never had cause to regret this decision, although there were certain missions she had carried out that he disliked contemplating.

As was his custom when speaking with Hadrice, he used as few words as possible, both because he knew she preferred it that way, and to make the interview as short as possible, as in spite of her unquestioned loyalty, she made him feel as if he were in the presence of an unchained dzur who would devour him without a thought except for the circumstance that it happened not to be hungry. He therefore explained exactly what he wished in terms that left no room for doubt, including all of the possibilities of what she might discover, or answers she might be given. When he had finished, he said, "Have you any questions?"

She bowed to signify that, not only had she no questions, but she was ready to depart on the instant.

Dorin pulled up paper, and quickly wrote a note, which he sealed. "This is to be given his lordship to prove you are my emissary," he said. "And this," he added, handing her a heavy purse, "should prove sufficient to make the overland journey."

"Overland, my lord?"

"There are too many tales of pirates, marauders, and uncontrollable winds to permit me to recommend anything else."

"The overland journey will take some time."

"Yes, I am aware."

"Very good, Benevolence."

"Then go," he said.

Unlike any of the courtiers, she did not back up; she merely bowed once more, turned on her heel, and walked out. She made it seem as if it were the proper etiquette, and, even if it were not, there was no one willing to say so.

On this day, Traanzo's cloaklady, an Issola who was called Urastor, happened to arrive in the prince's parlor while his master was engaged in comparing the breeding records of certain mares to determine which of them to add to his stables. The prince looked up, frowned, and said, "Well?"

"Your Highness, there is an individual to see you."

Now, the prince understood that Urastor chose his words as carefully as an historian, and so the word *individual* caught his ear at once. A gentleman or a lady would certainly have been identified as such; a Teckla, if for some reason the Issola imagined the Teckla should be announced, would have been called by this name. So then, what sort of individual might, to the Issola, deserve the appellation *individual*? Traanzo asked himself this question, and, being unable to arrive at an answer, thought to interrogate his cloaklady upon the subject.

"You say 'individual,'" he said.

Urastor bowed, indicating that in his opinion, no criticism could justly be made of his lordship's hearing.

"But then, what sort of individual?" said the prince.

"She is armed, my lord, showing the sign of no House, but if I am any judge, she is very dangerous."

"Has she given a reason for wishing to see me?"

"She pretends to be a messenger for Count Dorin."

"And has she anything to indicate this?"

"A letter with his seal and signature."

"And this seal and signature, are they authentic?"

"Entirely. They are dated according to Tortaalik's reign, and indicate she has been traveling for nearly a year."

"And then?"

"My lord, she is dangerous."

The prince nodded, considering. After a moment he said, "You are, you say, convinced of the seal and the signature?"

"I am, my lord."

"Then send her in."

"Guards, my lord?"

"No, I will see her alone."

"Very well, my lord."

Urastor left, and in a moment, Hadrice entered, bowing to the prince in a way that could have been considered insolent if Traanzo were inclined to take offense which, on this occasion, he chose not to be.

"What is your errand?" said Traanzo without preamble, as he deduced, by the expression on Hadrice's countenance, that pleasantries would be wasted on her.

"My lord," she began in a tone indicating that, to her, these words were a tiresome necessity that meant nothing at all, an opinion that, while the historian will not directly comment on it, must be acknowledged as at least a stance with some justification. "A man named Eremit was locked in the secret prison to the northwest, and we must know if he is still there, if he is dead, or if he is alive."

"Jail, not prison," corrected Traanzo automatically, a correction that was entirely wasted to judge by the change, or rather, the lack of change, it produced on Hadrice's demeanor. The prince, in the meantime, tried to remember the name of this individual, and why he had been jailed, and whether he or his father had done so. At last he said, "Remind me of the circumstances."

"Six hundred years ago," said Hadrice with no hesitation. "By request of my lord Count Dorin, in exchange for certain considerations regarding mining interests in the southern portion of the western coast."

"Ah, yes. I am aware," said the prince, "that a certain number of prisoners escaped, but not who they are, and thus, I am unable to tell you if the particular individual in whom you are interested was one."

"Then I will discover this."

Traanzo shrugged. "You must understand that, first, there is no longer an Empire, and, second, that I am the Iorich Heir and High Justicer. Therefore, there can be no question of danger to your master, in that there is no one to prosecute him except me, and I, well, I would decline to do so."

"Nevertheless," said Hadrice. "I have been asked to find this person. Is there anyone who might have useful information?"

"The director of the jail."

"And where might I find him?"

"He is below, in one of the dungeons; I have still not made up my mind whether to execute him."

"May I request that your lordship refrain at least until I've spoken to him?"

"Of course."

"And may I request permission to see him?"

"More than that, you may talk with him, and use any methods you wish in order to get answers."

"So much the better. Then, with your permission, I will do so."

"But, do you not wish to rest from your journey and perhaps have a bite to eat first?"

"No," said Hadrice.

"Very well, then. I will give the necessary orders."

Hadrice bowed, then, and took her departure, the prince ringing for a servant to guide her to the dungeon where the director reposed.

Chapter the Twenty-first

In Which It Is Shown That, if All Roads Do Not Lead to Adrilankha, At Least Many Do

We must now, once more, look at events that have happened before those we have just witnessed. Upon reaching the shore— for as the reader will hopefully remember, we last saw Livosha and Kefaan arriving on the shore—Livosha at once made good on her promise to pay the Orca, parting with two good imperials out of gratitude for his rescue. Lest there be any confusion, we must observe that when we say "hopefully remember" we mean that, if we have succeeded in our intentions, the reader will not only remember our friends' arrival on shore, but will be feeling hopeful on their behalf. We apologize for the confusion that may be caused by this locution which we took, of course, for purposes of brevity.

Having hopefully arrived—which is to say, they, too, were hopeful— they stood on the shore and watched as boats, which had only begun returning with the day's catch, at once began to set out for the island with the intention of rescuing prisoners.

"What is your thinking, sister?" said Kefaan.

"Concerning what, brother?"

"As they rescue prisoners, they may also, in the course of things, rescue jailers."

"Well, if they do?"

"Are we interested in remaining here and meeting them?"

Livosha frowned and considered the matter. "I am not anxious to meet them again. But even more—"

"Well?"

"I am anxious to attempt to find Eremit. You perceive, that is why we came here."

"Oh, I have not forgotten this circumstance. But—"

"Well?"

"How do you propose to find him?"

"I shall begin by asking questions."

"Ah, that is where I do myself the honor to think you're wrong."

"In what way am I wrong?"

"In two ways."

"Let us see, then. What is the first?"

"You cannot ask questions now, as there is no one to ask. Or at least, very few, as most of them are on their way to the island."

"Well, that is true. And next?"

"You will not ask questions, our good Jerin will ask questions. If you remember her argument about things people will say to and around Teckla, I think you will come to agree with my position."

"In this, you are not wrong. I so much agree with you, that I am ready this very instant to send Jerin to ask questions."

"But not this instant. Rather, I suggest we find a place to sleep for a few hours until everyone is back."

"But then, you perceive, we stand to meet the jailers."

"Not if we remain somewhere out of town, and only send Jerin in to ask questions."

"You propose, then, to camp?"

"There are still merchants here who can sell us what we need to camp out of doors for a night, somewhere we will not be observed."

"Very well, Kefaan, I agree with this plan."

"And you, Jerin?" said Kefaan. "Are you ready to see what you can learn of where Eremit could have gone?"

"I give you my word, I will do my best."

"Then let us quickly find a place to rest, for I give you my word, I am near to falling asleep where I stand."

They managed to purchase a few blankets and some sail canvas that could be used as a tent from the very merchant whose home had been robbed the night before, and, folding all of this into a neat bundle (along with some dried beef and bread) to make it easier for Jerin to carry, they made their way a few miles out of town until they found a place sufficiently hidden by tall grass and brush of various sorts, at which time they set up the tent, climbed into the blankets, and slept for several hours. In fact, they slept through the night, and upon waking the next morning, discovered that Jerin had already left. They waited there, taking their ease, until nearly noon, when the Teckla returned.

"You have returned," observed Livosha.

"I thought it best to leave before the morning, so that I would have a chance to speak with the fishermen."

"That was well thought!" exclaimed Kefaan.

"I am pleased to learn this," said Jerin.

"But, did you discover anything?" asked Livosha.

"Nearly."

"Well, and?"

"You wish me to tell you what I have discovered?"

"You have understood exactly."

"Then I will."

"I am listening."

"He went inland."

"Ah, inland."

"Moreover, I know which direction he set out in."

"How were you able to determine this?"

"First, because he did not go along the coast by water, as is proven because no boats are missing."

"That seems to be a just conclusion."

"I am gratified you think so."

"And, as to the direction?"

"First, there is the road."

"Very well, the road. What next?"

"Next, he was seen on the road by a Teckla family whose cottage he passed."

"Very well. Is there more?"

"I followed the road for a certain distance, and saw footprints leading away from the road, and I followed them, and found this."

At this point, she held out a thin bit of canvas that had a tear along the side. Livosha took it and frowned. "Is this from a sail?"

"On the contrary, my lady. It is the sort of canvas that made up the shoes that were on the feet of the prisoners on the island."

"How," said Kefaan. "You noticed that?"

"I always notice shoes," said Jerin. "You perceive, I often have none, and indeed, I have none now. This has resulted in a curiosity about them in others."

Livosha was silent for a moment, then she said, "Very well. We must do two things."

"And what are they, sister?" said Kefaan.

"We must follow where our clever Jerin believes Eremit has gone."

"Very well. And after?"

"At the first opportunity, we must get Jerin some shoes."

It was a six mile walk back to the posting station, where they acquired not only mounts, but certain supplies of food, fodder, and other gear to make their journey easier, as they feared they would not be near civilization. With this excellent planning, they set out and made good time, although they stopped whenever they saw another piece of canvas, and as it became dark. On the second day, they found the remains of both shoes, and later that day they began to see blood.

"He has cut his feet," said Livosha.

"He isn't used to walking without shoes," explained Jerin.

They continued during daylight hours, the occasional spots of blood making it easy to see the trail, until at length they arrived in a long valley, at the end of which they found several persons taking their ease around a fire.

"May we approach your fire?" said Livosha.

The woman who seemed to be the leader stood up, glanced at their weapons, then at her own band, and signaled that they might.

"I greet you. I am Livosha, and this is Kefaan. We are seeking a friend."

"A friend?"

"Exactly."

"And the name of this friend?"

"Eremit."

"I fear I know no one of that name."

As they spoke, the bandits—for so Livosha was convinced they were as soon as she saw them—made room in front of the fire.

"Perhaps," said Livosha, "if I were to describe him?"

"If you do, I will listen."

"This is it, then. He is still young, perhaps seven hundred years in age. He has high cheekbones, a cleft chin, and little noble's point. He would be wearing dirty white, as is sometimes the case with prison uniforms."

The woman nodded thoughtfully, and said, "I am Alishka, and you have made me curious."

"Explain what you are curious about, and perhaps I will be able to satisfy your curiosity."

"That is my hope."

"Then I am listening."

"It is this: When I see two individuals of the House of the Iorich who are searching for someone in prison garb, well, I wonder if 'friend' is the most precise description of the relationship between them."

"I assure you it is. In fact—"

"Well?"

"Many years ago, we were engaged to be married."

The one calling herself Alishka shrugged like a Lyorn. "I was once engaged to be married. And so far from considering the man a friend, well, if I saw him again, I should spit him like a wild norska."

"We will pay for information," said Livosha.

"Oh, that is nothing. If we wish for your money, well, there are nine of us, and two of you, so, you perceive, we will simply take it."

"Perhaps not," said Livosha looking Alishka in the eye. The bandit chief held her gaze for a moment, then shrugged. "Well, in any case, we have not seen your 'friend' and we have no interest in taking your money, so you may as well be on your way."

Livosha looked at Kefaan, as if to silently gather his opinion on this subject. Kefaan shrugged. Livosha said, "Well, we have a certain quantity of wine. I have made trial of it upon myself and found it excellent. Perhaps you would care to share some of it, as a gesture in celebration of our acquaintance."

Alishka narrowed her eyes, convincing Livosha that she was no fool, but then she nodded. "Very well," she said.

"Jerin, fetch the wine."

"Yes, my lady," said the Teckla.

As Jerin handed her the wine, Livosha caught her eye for a moment, and had the sense that Jerin understood.

They sat and drank wine together, though there was little talk, and the silences were awkward. At length, Jerin came up behind Livosha and touched her shoulder, nodding.

"Well, we thank you for your hospitality."

"And you for the wine. I wish you luck in your search."

They mounted and slowly rode back out of the valley, Livosha alert to the sound of swords being drawn, but there were none. Once they were some distance away, Livosha turned to Jerin and said, "What did you learn?"

"He was there, my lady. They were whispering about it freely, and paid no attention to me."

"When?"

"My lady? Just now, when you were—"

"When was Eremit there!"

"Oh. I beg your pardon. Earlier to-day."

"Ah, to have come so close! Where did he go?"

"He vanished, my lady. Into the cave."

She drew rein and said, "Into the cave? Then he must be either in it, or through it!"

"Neither, my lady. He is gone."

"What do you tell me?"

"They were very clear about it. He and their captain went into the cave, and there, it seems, Lord Eremit summoned a demon, and the demon took him away."

"Impossible!"

"I only know what I was told."

Livosha considered. "And yet, I know he was there."

"I am curious how you know that, my sister," said Kefaan.

"One of the items stolen from the merchant was a fireplace poker, such as was lying next to the fire. It is an unusual piece of equipment for those camping out of doors. Moreover, as we approached, there was a considerable amount of blood in one spot just outside of their camp, as if someone had stood there, bleeding."

"So, he was there."

"But how could he summon a demon? You perceive, the Orb—"

"I know," said Kefaan.

"Well, there was something," said Jerin.

"How, something?"

"The cave ended after a short distance, and there was a glowing stick, as if someone had used it for light."

"Well, so they were in the cave."

"And a strange design on the ground."

"A strange design?"

"A pattern of some sort, scratched into the ground, some of it in gold lettering, some of it merely scratched on stone, and it had been cleared recently."

"And yet," said Livosha. "The Orb."

"Well," said Kefaan. "Jerin?"

"My lord?"

"Did anyone say anything about something Eremit was wearing?"

"Well, he had a sort of pendant or necklace with a gem on it."

"A purple gem?"

"My lord, how did you know?"

"My sister, it is all true," said Kefaan.

"How are you familiar with this?"

"There is a small but lucrative trade in purple stones among certain sorcerers."

"Jhereg."

"Yes."

"And I have been told the stones can be carved."

Livosha was silent for a moment, then said, "He could be anywhere."

"That is true," said Kefaan.

"So, we must decide where to go now."

"I learned one other thing," said Jerin. "He is no longer known as Eremit, he now goes by the name Dust."

"Dust," repeated Livosha. "Dust."

"I," said Kefaan, "do not care for dust. You perceive, it is too dry."

"So then," said Livosha, "we will go somewhere wet."

The reader will have no doubt noticed a peculiar confluence of events. That is to say, we have seen Eremit in Alishka's camp, and we have heard Alishka tell of Livosha's visit, and now we have seen that very visit as it appeared to Livosha herself. We have presented the information that we found ourselves required to convey to the reader in this fashion for the simple reason that it permits the reader to witness the events as they appear to those various persons with whom we have interested ourselves, and, as the action of each individual is predicated upon what that persons knows, believes, and understands, it cannot but help the reader's understanding of the development of our history to know the perceptions of these individuals.

The result of these perceptions and decisions, in the case of Livosha, is that she, Kefaan, and Jerin found themselves, a year and a half later, in the town of Rockwell in the County of Yisten on the south shore of Lake Guin. Yisten, we should say, had been seriously damaged by the fall of the Empire, as it had counted on the constant traffic along the Guinchen Canal that ran from Cargo Point to the Elbow River and thence south to the Ocean-sea. The loss of trade in this part of what had been the Empire was nothing short of catastrophic, and, while the region later recovered far better than many others, owing to not only fishing the lakes, but to the lush agriculture of the area, the immediate result was an exodus of river-men, lake-men, stevedores, and navigators.

Livosha had chosen the precise location of Rockwell when, as they had been moving south in the general direction of Guinchen, she had heard a rumor that all of the advocates had deserted the town. The rumor proved false, but only because there had been no advocate there in the first place, and hence there were none to leave. Livosha and Kefaan found a small house on the narrow main street not far from the road leading to the lake, and there they put out their sign, and settled disputes among the locals or represented them before Yisten. That they often did this in exchange for fresh fish, or vegetables, or such services as the locals could offer presented no difficulty while the pair waited to come up with another plan. Jerin, for her part, was hired as a groom at the town stable, and was happy enough with her horses.

Livosha settled in to wait, a wait that was made easier by frequent journeys made by Kefaan: to Cargo Point, to Yisten, even as far as Hartre. There was no need for Livosha to ask the reason for these expeditions, any more than there was a need for her to ask, when he returned, if he had met with success; he would tell her when he learned something.

To be sure, from time to time he would let fall a remark about having "met someone interesting," which Livosha considered a good sign. Still, as time went by with no results, she began to feel an impatience build, an impatience she endeavored to hide as well as she could. If Kefaan noticed this, he concealed it, which is to say, he did not bring up the subject. And yet, they were both aware of the passing of years and of the fact that they appeared to be getting no closer to their goal.

One day, some twenty years after their arrival, Livosha finished a conversation with two Teckla over who had the rights to a certain amount of seed produced by an area in which they both had interests. The discussion had been long, loud, and singularly unrewarding, although she had succeeded insofar as she had managed to send both of them away equally unhappy. She poured some tea into which she put a measure of the local equivalent of oishka, distilled from corn, and sat down in her favorite chair, reminding herself that this was far better than when she had been serving the countess.

At this point, she noticed that Kefaan, who had been away on a journey to Hartre, had returned, and was lying on the couch, his eyes closed. As she set her teacup down, he opened his eyes and said, "Good evening, sister."

"Good evening, and welcome back. I confess myself astonished."

"That I have returned?"

"No, not that."

"Well?"

"That you were able to sleep through the shouting in the other room."

"Ah, well, but I was not sleeping, I was merely resting my eyes."

"That explains it then."

"However, as you are here . . ."

"Yes?"

"I have learned something."

"And that is?"

"The Duke of Traanzo, now Iroich Heir and High Justicer."

"What of him?"

"It was his father who created the jail."

"Ah, ah! And it is he who is now responsible for it?"

"Exactly."

"Did you learn why it was created?"

"It was created during the last Orca reign, as a place to keep certain Teckla who had begun to agitate for a republic, but could not legally be detained."

"It seems not to have worked. Why was it continued?"

"The Teckla, it appeared, never learned of it, and so never shut it down. It was used after that for problems of a more personal nature."

"Well, we seem to have closed it."

"We, or the disaster that befell the Empire."

"Yes, or that. Where is the duchy of, what was the name?"

"Traanzo. It is east of the Pushta, but that is unimportant, for Traanzo himself is never there. He had a second home in Adrilankha, in the hills, where he was accustomed to escape the heat of the summer, and it has now become his permanent home."

"This is good to know, although it will not help us find Eremit, nor will it help us to exact our vengeance against those others who have wronged us."

"Ah, but it is there we differ."

"In what way do we differ, my brother?"

"In that I believe it will, indeed, help us to find Eremit, or to exact our vengeance, or, perhaps, both at once."

"If that is the case, then it must be that either my perception is faulty, or there is information you have not yet done me the honor to impart."

"It is the latter, my dear sister."

"Oh, so there is more?"

"Not only is there more, but it is significant."

"Ah, significant! Well then, will you tell me what it is?"

"I am prepared to do so."

"Then I am listening."

"So, shall I tell you now?"

"I have been waiting for you to do so for an hour."

The expression on Kefaan's countenance can best be described as *grim pleasure* as he said, "Do you recall the individual on the island who commanded an attack on us, that is, the director?"

"Nearly!"

"He has just been released from Traanzo's dungeons, where he has resided for the last five years."

"Shards!"

"There is more: he has been released in order to assist another in searching for Eremit."

"For Eremit!"

"And there is more."

"What, more?"

"Indeed."

"Then I am listening."

"The individual who has caused his release, and who is leading the search for Eremit, was sent by none other than Count Dorin!"

"The gods! But, how have you learned all of this?"

"In the simplest manner, my dear sister. You may recall my friend Tigra."

"I do."

"I have discovered friends of his in Hartre."

"By friends, you mean Jhereg."

"You have understood exactly."

"Well, and?"

"And these friends have friends in Adrilankha, some of whom work closely with Traanzo."

"But, how do they communicate? It is a long way from Hartre to Adrilankha."

"By messages on fishing boats, my sister. In fact, I am given to understand they are attempting to set up criminal enterprises that include both cities."

"And yet, are the waters safe?"

"For that, they collaborate with Orca who effectively control the sea-lanes along the shore, although not in the deeper waters. Also, it seems, Adrilankha has not been so fully ravaged by the fall the Empire, and many others have arrived, and are arriving. And some of these, my dear sister, are of no small importance to us."

"Such as?"

"My friend Tigra, for one, who has discovered much of this information for me. And for another—"

"Well?"

"The forger, Sajen!"

"Ah!"

"Also certain Jhereg with whom I have, here and there, had contact."

"To be sure, this is no small amount of news, and I commend you on your skill and patience in acquiring it."

"I do not deny that it has taken a considerable amount of time to make these connections, but fortunately I was able to be of service to these Jhereg in the same way as I was to Tigra. But come, sister, now that we know of these things—"

"Well? Now that we know?"

"What is it we must do?"

Livosha considered carefully for some moments. Then she said, "You say they are searching for Eremit. But, where and how are they searching?"

"As to that, I do not know."

"And how recent is your intelligence?"

"The director was released from the dungeon eleven days ago."

"In that case, the trail is still warm."

"And then?"

"Come, let us prepare."

"For?"

"A departure. We will take only what we need."

"Then, you propose to go after them?"

"I nearly think I do!"

"Very well."

"And do you disagree with this plan?"

"Not in the least."

"And then?"

"As you say, let us prepare our departure, for I, for one, am anxious to be in action. You perceive, six hundred years is long enough to wait."

"I could not agree more. Apropos, we must put a sign to say that we are no longer accepting clients."

"Hardly a loss."

"As to that, I agree."

"How much money do we have?"

"Let us see."

They emptied their purses on the table and counted. "Four imperials and three silver," said Livosha.

"That will get us to Adrilankha," said Kefaan, "and even supply a day or two's food and lodging. After that, I do not know."

"But I do," said Livosha.

"Ah, you have a plan?"

"I do. But it will require five silver coins to put into action."

"Then it will be hard to reach Adrilankha, but we can still do it. But come, tell me your plan."

"As to that, you will soon know what it is. For now, you must come with me."

"But, where are we going?"

"To a dressmaker."

"You require different dress, my sister?"

"No, dear brother. You do."

"How, I?"

"Exactly."

"Very well, I am in your hands."

"Then hurry. The outfit will cost three silver, and it will be another to have good Tsika finish it by to-morrow morning."

They left their house, and an hour later they had returned.

"My sister," said Kefaan. "I fail to understand the need for the clothing with which I was just fitted, and for which we paid."

"I will explain in good season. For now, there is no time to lose."

"Very well, then, you pack, and I will consult such maps as I can find and determine the best route to Adrilankha."

"I will be ready to depart by to-morrow's morning."

"And by then I will know whither we are bound."

As promised, they set out the next day, stopping to collect the clothing they had ordered the night before, and leaving behind such property as would weigh them down and a sign upon their door wishing the best of fortune to all of those who came by and urging them to calm and patient conversation in all disputes.

This done, they pooled what money they had and purchased a pair of horses for the three-hundred-mile journey to Floodwater, where they were able to find a barge headed downriver to Windy Bay, which, if it was no longer a bay, was at least still windy. From here, in exchange for agreeing to work, they found passage on a large fishing vessel of the type known as a coastal brig that brought them, after the long voyage up the bay, to the mouth of the Adrilankha River, and thus to the future Imperial capital itself.

To Livosha, it seemed as if setting her foot onto the solid land of the greatest city then remaining in what had been the Empire was as if she had stepped into another world, as in one of the stories of a Serioli who takes a child on an enchanted journey through lands of wonders and marvels. But here, instead of flying trees and singing mountains and rivers of jewels and castles of fire, the wonders were less obvious, and yet struck deeper into the heart. The sweeping wings of the cliffs above them seemed like a bird that brought her, and the entire city, under its protection. The white stone stairways climbing up from the port to the market level seemed like veritable gates to a land of dreams. The Tower of Corn and the Prince's Citadel looked down as if they were benevolent gods. The mouth of the river emptying into the bay spoke of constant renewal, as if the city were saying, "Take what you need, I will never run out." For a time, even her mission was driven from Livosha's mind, and the thought grew in her, *In other circumstances, I could live in peace here.*

They stood for some moments staring around them, then Kefaan said, "Come, my sister. Our path lies ahead."

Livosha nodded and they began the long climb up the white stairway to the city.

Chapter the Twenty-second

In Which Livosha,
Though Unaware of Doing So, Asserts Causality
and Certain Other Philosophical Principles

Three days later, the euphoria that had overcome Livosha on her first view of Adrilankha, while it had not vanished, had at least sensibly diminished. This diminution had been caused by several factors: the first being when the wind shifted and brought the stench from the slaughterhouses (not, to be sure, nearly as active as they are in our own day, but still sufficient to be noticed), next by the crowds of Teckla flooding the streets that were oppressive in their sheer number, and next by the sight of rickety-looking wooden structures that did not seem as if they would survive a good storm, and next by, in fact, a good storm that struck early in the morning and left the streets full of mud, soaked their clothing, and would certainly have given them the cough if a tavern keeper had not invited them in to share his fire.

Their circumstances—that is to say, their supply of coin—had now become so acute as to cause them some embarrassment: no money for food, no place to stay; indeed, matters looked to be dire. And yet, it was at that moment that Livosha said, "Come, my brother. As we have the shelter of a fire to wait out the storm, let us do so where it is dry and warm."

"Well, but then?"

"Then, did I not promise that you would see?"

"You did. And then?"

"Well, I now repeat it. You will see."

"I trust you entirely."

"And you are right to do so."

Once the weather cleared, Livosha stood up and said, "Do you wait here, while I set out upon an errand."

"You fill me with curiosity."

"It will soon be satisfied."

"Very well, then I trust you entirely."

"I will return soon. And when I have—"

"Yes, when you have?"

"Well, you will see."

She set out at once, pausing only to thank the host, who pretended he was pleased to have the nobility among his clientele, and promised to keep Kefaan well supplied in exchange for a promise on her part that they would speak well of his establishment. This is a case where, as so often among various sorts of small entrepreneurs, the value of word-of-mouth, or, in the commercial lingo of the time, *exposure*, is so highly valued, that many merchants of various sorts are happy to give away their goods to nobles, craftsmen, musicians, or artists, merely on the condition that those who have received the goods promise to praise them to their fellows. Indeed, the reader is invited to make trial of this with such local merchants as may be nearby in order to prove the veracity of the author's thesis.

And so, Livosha set out into Adrilankha, and it was there that, we must admit, she made a mistake that, while understandable, could have upset her undertaking with catastrophic results. It was understandable because, at the time of making the plan, she had had no true conception of the size of Adrilankha, the largest city she had seen until that time being Candletown, and Adrilankha, even then being far greater both in area and in population, those two measures that are customarily given for the size of city, instead of statistics more important but difficult of measurement, such as number and skill of artists and the number and assiduousness of scholars. The result of this—that is to say, the result of Livosha's unfamiliarity and incomprehension of a city of this size—was that asking for directions did not produce the expected results: instead of being told where the object of her search was, she received blank looks, shrugs, dismissive gestures, polite embarrassed smiles, or apologetic bows, according to the House and disposition of the individual who was unable to answer her question.

At last, however, she met a complaisant Lyorn who said, "An artist? You will mostly find them near Favintoe Market, where lodgings are not as expensive as other places, yet close enough to the wealthier areas to give them hope of making a sale or receiving a commission."

She thanked the Lyorn kindly, and followed his directions to the area known as Favintoe, which still exists to-day, although its characteristics have undergone considerable change: at the time, the Favin Canal (*toaino* in the ancient language of the Tiassa) was still operating and thus providing a continuous stream of goods directly to the district from the fisheries, from the slaughterhouses, and from the wagon roads to the west. As a result, the district grew into an area full of markets, which multiplied as good markets will: the merchants drawing in custom, which custom, in turn, draws in merchants, the entire process of which not only asserts causality, but displays the continuous transformation of cause into effect into cause that forms no part of, and is therefore denied by, the mystical philosophy adhered to by certain academics whom the author will not name out of respect for the reputation of the institution that has misguidedly employed them. The over-all high quality of goods resulted, by the beginning of the Seventeenth Cycle, in the nearby districts being settled by those who enjoyed fineries, and even in considerable new construction projects being begun as those moving in were unsatisfied with the dwellings they'd been left by those moving out. Of course, the filling in of the canal during the Interregnum at the direction of the Countess of Whitecrest, who pretended stagnant waters led to disease, changed all of this, but that had not yet happened by the time of which we have the honor to write.

Upon reaching this district, Livosha at once began asking her questions again, and, as evening was setting in, at last she was directed to a small, plain tent in front of which was a man painting in oils the portrait of a young Dzurlord who seemed to be anxious about the exact angle of his chin, continually readjusting it. The artist endeavored to conceal his annoyance at this behavior, and presently the Dzur inspected the painting, grunted, handed the artist a few coins, and promised to be back after the work had dried, demanding that, by then it be matted and framed according to some agreement previously entered upon.

Once he had gone, Livosha, who in fact had no more understanding of "matting" than certain so-called historians have of the economies of markets, approached, bowed, and said, "My good Sajen, may I have a few moments of conversation within the privacy of your tent?"

"Of course, my lady. And yet, it seems you know my name."

"That is true, and the proof is, I have just pronounced it."

"And yet, how is it you know my name, when I am unaware of yours?"

"All will be answered soon."

"Very well."

He led the way into the tent, inviting her to sit on the cushions, of which he had several, all of which attempted, if the reader will forgive a figure of speech that appears to assign motivation to inanimate objects, to make up in bright colors what they lacked in comfort. "Well?" he said.

"I am Livosha."

"My lady."

"I have a commission for you."

"Ah, a commission! So much the better. Would you do me the honor to describe this commission?"

In answer, Livosha removed a parchment from her pouch, and handed it over. "I need this," she said, "to be in written in the hand of Count Dorin of Westward, with his signature. I have with me a sample of that hand and signature."

"But my lady, that is illegal!"

"Well."

He cleared his throat. "I have heard," he said slowly, "that those who are willing to do such things charge a great deal for the service."

"That may be, and yet, I think you will find it in your heart to do it for nothing."

"For nothing? And yet—"

"As you have said, good Sajen, it is illegal. As is putting the signature of my mother, Cerwin, and my father, Tiscara, on false deeds claiming to have sold their estates to an Orca named Berwick. If you have suddenly been overpowered by your conscience and wish to confess your crimes, then I am certain that I could arrange a meeting with the Countess of Whitecrest, who, I am informed, has lately returned from the duchies, and we will see what she has to say. That the Empire itself has fallen does not, you perceive, mean that the duchies have, or that there is no longer any law at all. So, shall I arrange this meeting?"

Sajen, whose countenance had undergone several severe and even drastic changes during this discourse, cleared his throat and said, "I'm certain that won't be necessary."

"Then you have what needs to be written, and here, as I have promised, is a sample of Dorin's hand, and his signature. You see that I always do what I say I will; it has become a habit."

"Very well. If you give me a day—"

"No. Now. I will have it in my hand when I leave this tent, or we will go together to see the countess."

Sajen nodded and at once set to work. In an hour, it was done, sanded, and ready.

"I hope you are satisfied," said the artist.

"We will see," said Livosha. "If there is a problem, you may expect to see me again."

"There will be no problem."

"So much the better. Then I will inform my brother and his associates— by associates, you perceive, I refer to various Jhereg of his acquaintance—

that there is no need to go to the countess on my behalf, which they are prepared to do, should I suddenly, for some reason, vanish unexpectedly."

Sajen turned pale and said, "I believe we understand each other perfectly, my lady."

"I am glad that we do. Apropos, it would be best if you forgot that you had ever seen me."

"I have a very poor memory, my lady."

"That is well, then."

With the necessary documents in her possession, she returned to the inn.

"Ah, has everything gone as you expected?"

"Not only as I expected, my brother, but even as I wished."

"So much the better. But, what now?"

"Now it is time for you and for me to find a place of privacy in which to change into the clothing we purchased before setting out for this city."

"Very well, we will change clothing. And then?"

"And then, my brother, it will be time for us to seek employment with Prince Traanzo. With these recommendations from Dorin, we can hardly fail to be hired."

It fell out exactly as Livosha had said: that very day, Livosha found herself working as an assistant advocate, doing much of the paperwork that the prince's affairs generated, as well as filing and copying documents. We hardly need to add that, as she was filing and copying documents, she was also reading them. As for Kefaan, with the word of Dorin behind him, and new clothing of gray and black, he stepped into his new role of Traanzo's contact with the underworld, a position easier to carry out as he had sufficient friends among real Jhereg that he could fulfill such requests as the prince might have for such persons—intimidating competitors, securing the best fees among competing Jhereg for legal protection, even providing some of his own ducal guard, known formally as the Breakwater Battalion and informally as lock-knees for their way of standing while on duty, to arrest, threaten, or beat those working for one Jhereg when another had paid him more. Kefaan, in the event, was able to complete all of these tasks to the complete satisfaction of the prince.

Livosha and Kefaan, though of course unable to admit being brother and sister, presented themselves as friends, letting those who believed them secretly lovers to continue to think so, as this permitted them to acknowledge each other and even meet openly. The first such meeting (and, as it happened, all such subsequent meetings) took place on the terrace in the back of the manor. The advantage of the terrace was that it was impossible for anyone to approach within listening distance without being seen.

"And so, my brother, is everything going according to our plan?"

"If by 'going according to our plan,' you mean have I learned anything, then yes."

"Then tell me what you have learned."

"The director is still here."

Livosha frowned. "From the island?"

"Exactly. You perceive, he can identify us."

"Tell me everything. What is he doing here?"

"He was put in the dungeons and tortured for his failure."

"How badly?"

"Not as badly as some."

"Very well. You perceive, I am not shedding tears for his suffering."

"No more am I, my sister."

"But then?"

"He was released at the request of Hadrice."

"Who is Hadrice?"

"The servant of Dorin I mentioned before, the one who has been tasked with finding Eremit."

"Ah, then we have a similar mission."

"Although opposite motivations."

"That is true. What do you know of her?"

"Nothing, except that I saw her once."

"Well, and?"

"From her countenance, I judge she is single-minded, and dangerous, and I beg you not to take her lightly."

"Very well. And have you seen the director?"

"No, for you perceive I have been avoiding him lest I be recognized."

"Very well. I will attend to this matter."

"I trust you entirely."

"We will speak again soon."

Livosha, having settled on the course she would pursue, wasted no time in turning thought into deed, for it is well known that, however powerful we might consider thoughts, while they remain merely thoughts they cannot have any effect on the world. Indeed, this is the very subject of a letter this author recently had the honor to send to Pamlar University's Department of Historical Studies observing that were it in fact the case that history flows from idea to idea, then there would be no need for activity at all;

whereas if history flows from action to action, as it does, then in addition to a rational basis for understanding history, we have also a rational basis for understanding ideas as the product of activity. That certain supposed scholars who believe that the human mind contains the beginning and end of history, without, in turn, explaining whence this mind is filled, need to have *rationality* explained is an irony that is, we trust, not lost on the University, nor on the reader.

Livosha, while giving no thought to such matters of epistemology as we have had the honor to set before the reader, nevertheless understood them, as it were, instinctively, in that, as we have said, once her plan was formed, she at once put it into action, and in so doing provided herself the opportunity to fulfill her plan while simultaneously making a firm if unconscious statement about the relationship between the idea and the world whence it comes. She did this by at once discovering, by means of asking various servants, where the director might be found. She was soon informed that he had been given chambers on the third story, far in the back of the servants' wing. This was, in fact, only one story above where she, herself, was quartered; it was only fortune, she realized, that had prevented them from meeting sooner, before she was ready, which might have had results that were unfortunate to her plans, if not, indeed, her life.

She considered for a moment that her plan required lying, but, after a certain amount of inner conflict, she concluded that lying to an Iorich who had so dishonored himself as the director had was not significantly different from lying to a Teckla. Upon reaching this conclusion, she armed herself with a poniard and set off to the stairway. Upon reaching the third floor (or the fourth, depending on one's method of counting) she went at once to the room described, stood outside the door, and clapped.

The question, "Who is there?" came from inside the room. Livosha said, "An old acquaintance," and waited.

When the door opened, she pushed hard, forcing her way in so suddenly that the director stumbled backward, catching himself on the small desk with which the room was supplied. She drew her poniard and placed the point under his chin, while, in a low tone, reciting the words, "Make a sound and you are a dead man." In fact, the director did make a sound, but as it was merely a squeak, and not especially loud, Livosha decided that, on this occasion, she could let it pass without taking the action she had threatened. She kicked the door shut with her heel and said, "Good day, Director. Do you recognize me?"

At first, he seemed confused, as well as frightened, but then his eyes widened and he nodded as much as he could without driving the point of the knife into his neck—it was a small motion, yet clear enough.

"Good," she said. "I have a problem that, perhaps, you can help with, if you would."

The director swallowed with some difficulty, as if his mouth had become dry. Livosha continued, "The problem is, there is someone here who would recognize me and my brother from an earlier encounter, and it would be inconvenient if this were to emerge. I feel that I can solve this problem by pushing this poniard—you are aware of it?"

The director indicated by certain gestures that he was, indeed, not unaware of the sharp object pushing against his neck.

"Yes, I can solve my problem by pushing this poniard with a small amount of pressure and thus puncturing an assortment of vessels and organs that I am convinced you would prefer to remain whole. I am curious, however, if you might suggest another solution. If my understanding is correct, you have an interest in such a solution being discovered, hence it seems only reasonable to ask for your opinion on the matter. You understand my thinking on this?"

"Entirely," said the director, though it seemed to Livosha as if it were not easy for him to express this thought.

"So, then, have you any suggestions?"

The director managed to gasp, "I could leave!"

"Well, yes, that is true. And yet, how could I know you would do so? With my knife no longer at your neck, you could have a change of heart."

"My word of honor?"

"Feh. You operated an illegal jail. How could I trust your word?"

"Well, but—"

"Yes?"

"Surely we can find something?"

"Oh, I am entirely willing to find something. I merely wait upon your suggestion."

When the director's mouth had opened and then closed again some number of times without a word, or, indeed, a sound emerging from this vocal aperture, Livosha said, "Well, I am beginning to wonder if, in fact, you have any suggestions at all. And yet, I give you my word, I would prefer to secure your willing cooperation than to provide what Ekrasan called, 'the ultimate proof of your mortality.' Not," she added in something of a conversational tone, "that you do not deserve to have a significant length of steel penetrate your neck, mouth, and brain; for an Iorich who would knowingly cooperate in such an unjust, illegal, and ignoble activity as the perpetuation of illegal confinement disguised by false legality certainly deserves whatever punishment he might receive. Don't you agree?"

Whether the director did or did not agree was difficult to determine from the sounds he made, although his distress at the question could not be mistaken, which, Livosha concluded, may itself have been an answer.

"You have nothing to say?" she said. "Then I must kill you? Is that your belief?"

"Please," he managed.

"Ah," she said. "You say 'please.' I nearly think you would prefer to live."

Once again the director made a gesture that would have been a nod if he had been able to so without the possibility of causing his own death, which would have been acting in direct contradiction to the very question to which he was attempting to give an affirmative answer. We would be lying if we did not admit that Livosha took a certain cruel—albeit just—pleasure in the gentleman's predicament.

Livosha said, "It is possible you can live," she said. "If you wish to be my friend, for I have firm principles about friendship. Would you like to hear them?"

"Yes," he managed.

"Then I will tell you. I believe friends do not hold knives at other's throats, that is the first thing. Do you agree?"

The director indicated that he did.

"Moreover, they help each other. Do you agree with this as well?"

The director appeared unwilling to dispute this simple proposition.

"Well then, if I remove the knife from your throat, can we be friends?"

"Oh, yes!" he said.

"Are you certain? I would not like to think you would change your mind about something as important as friendship."

"Oh, I wouldn't!"

"Because if you did, my other friends would be disappointed."

"Other friends?"

"Why, yes. I made many friends in the jail. I did so in the simplest manner: I set them free. They have long memories, and no small amount of gratitude for this service. We have formed a sort of community. They wanted to come and visit you, to have a conversation with you about their illegal imprisonment, but, you perceive, they were unable to do so while you were locked in the dungeon. Then, once word got out that you were free, they began making plans on how best to communicate their feelings to you. I intervened on your behalf, saying that you would like to be a friend. They were skeptical, of course, but I gave them my assurance of your good intentions. Come, was I wrong?"

"How . . . how many of them are there?"

"Only ten or fifteen that I know of in Adrilankha. Perhaps there are more elsewhere."

"I . . ."

"Yes?"

"I would like to be your friend."

Livosha removed the weapon from his throat and put it in her belt. "I am pleased that I have not been proved wrong. We meet every few days, you see, and every few days, I will give them assurance of your continued friendship. Of course, if I were to find myself unable to meet with them, well, I do not know what would happen. So I will work very hard to keep myself safe, for your sake."

The director rubbed his throat. "You are very kind."

"You would do the same for me."

"Oh, without a doubt!"

"Well, you see, I have already shown you friendship in two ways. First, I have convinced my friends not to have the conversation with you they wished to—and I give you my word, you would have enjoyed it less than you think. And, second, I have removed the knife from your throat. Come, is it not true that I have proven my friendship?"

He nodded carefully, still rubbing his throat, and for the first time she studied him. He had changed in the last twenty years: he seemed shrunken, or perhaps *diminished* would be the more precise term (for Livosha, trained as an advocate, valued precision as much as historians do, or rather *should*), and the air of command that had once defined him was entirely missing. Moreover, he had developed an odd sort of twitch or tic with his left hand that compulsively drew in on itself and opened again like a suckersnail inhaling elegans.

"Then, will you prove your friendship for me?"

"Of course!" he said quickly—perhaps, it seemed to Livosha, even eagerly.

"You are working with Hadrice to attempt to trace a certain Eremit, are you not?"

He nodded and said, "Yes," then added, "my lady."

"And what have you learned?"

"Very little, my lady. We have been attempting to track down where the escapees went, but, to this point, we have not even assured ourselves that number eighty-one, that is to say, Eremit, even survived."

"I see," said Livosha, who, though more than willing to receive information, felt otherwise about giving any. "How are you searching?"

"Hadrice has sent agents out to the northwest, each of whom has a sketch I have supplied based on my memory of number eighty-one."

"Ah, then you do remember him?"

"He came to mind eventually."

From the way he pronounced this sentence, Livosha concluded that various means had been used to stimulate his memory, but chose not ask for details. "Well," said Livosha. "I will speak with you from time to time, and discover what you have learned. Until then, I am glad to have made a friend."

"As am I, my lady, I promise you."

Livosha left him there and returned to her duties within the manor.

After careful consideration, Livosha came to the conclusion that, except for the meetings she would, from time to time, insist on with the director, they see each other as little as possible, and that she see Hadrice even less. She met with Kefaan every alternate day, but for the most part, they only spoke of trivialities after assuring each other that there was, as yet, no news.

This continued until a winter day when they met on the terrace, both muffled in heavy cloaks. Livosha, who had arrived first, turned around upon hearing footsteps, and was greeted by her brother with the words, "So, it would appear that this time you have news."

"Ah, is my countenance then so easy to read?"

"Well, I have known you all of my life. Perhaps you would be more a cipher to those who knew you less well."

"I hope that is the case. At all events my brother, you are right. I have news."

"Then tell me at once, for I am bursting with impatience."

"There has been progress on finding Eremit."

"Ah, ah! Where is he?"

"We do not know exactly, but one of Hadrice's agents traced him to a place called Magister Valley."

"I am not familiar with such a place."

"And yet, you have been there."

"I?"

"Yes. At the time, it was called the Valley of Dust."

"Ah, well, yes, now I recall. What of it?"

"In the valley is a cave."

"I remember."

"On the floor of the cave is scratched a design."

"I remember that there was a design"

"The agent thought to copy the design."

"Well, and?"

"And the design happened to pass through my hands on the way to Hadrice."

"And you copied it?"

"You perceive, copying things is part of my job."

"And I do not question your skill in it."

"You are right not to."

"Well, but what of the design?"

"I contrived a certain matter of property that would take me to the home of a certain Athyra named Jima, all as part of my duties, of course."

"Of course."

"And, while there, I asked him if he knew anything of this design."

"And did he?"

"He recognized the type, and the function."

"Well?"

"Shall I tell you what it is?"

"Bah! You see me dying with impatience!"

"Then I will not keep you longer in suspense. It was a glyph used in the forbidden sorcery of the ancients, which, when given power, can open a path to another world, and draw through it—"

"Yes, draw through it?"

"A demon!"

"Cracks and shards! So then Eremit, or, rather, Dust as he now styles himself—"

"Summoned a demon, who, presumably, carried him away."

"Willingly, or unwillingly?"

"I will believe it was willingly, as he had summoned the demon, and I hope I am not wrong."

"But, how could Eremit have learned this skill?"

"As to that, I cannot say."

"Well, and where did he go?"

"I do not know the answer to that, either."

Kefaan considered, then nodded. "Well, in any case, it is certainly more than we had yester-day."

"I am glad you think so."

"But, do we have any way of discovering where he might have gone?"

"It is possible," said Livosha.

"Possible is good. Not as good as certain, but far better than impossible, do you not agree?"

"Oh, entirely."

"So, then, what is this possibility?"

"The Athyra has said that, if we can bring him to the place, and find him a similar enchantment to what was used, he might be able to determine where the demon took him."

Kefaan frowned. "My sister. Are you aware that you are talking of a journey to the far edge of the Empire, over seas filled with marauders and roads filled with bandits, using illegal magic that we may never find, on the slim chance that we can learn whither to go next, which might be as far away again, and then discover that, in twenty years, he has left for somewhere else, by some other means? Is this truly what you propose?"

"Oh, not in the least, for you have misstated the position."

"If I have, I should be glad to be corrected."

"Then I will correct you: with the fall of the Empire, the fact that such sorcery is illegal must be considered moot."

"Well, that is true, I must concede the point."

"And then?"

"Nevertheless, there remain the other issues."

"I do not dispute the other issues."

"Yet, if you insist upon going, I will accompany you."

Livosha considered the arguments her brother had brought up, and also considered the age and health of the Athyra wizard, which made no promises of surviving such a journey. "Well," she said at length. "Let us reflect."

"I agree with reflecting," he said, Livosha observing his efforts to hide the relief this answer gave him. *And yet,* she thought to herself, *he is not wrong. It is a desperate enterprise. Are we yet sufficiently desperate?*

We must mention in passing that the reader will have noticed that we have related a conversation in which Livosha described certain events that were not witnessed by the reader. We have made this decision for the simple reason that, knowing we must both inform the reader of the events that took place—that is to say, Livosha's conversation with the Athyra—and the transmitting of this information from Livosha to Kefaan, there was no requirement for the reader to receive this information twice. The question then presented itself to the author: What would be the best way to communicate it? That is to say, we might as easily have shown the reader the conversation between Livosha and the Athyra, and then, by merely setting down a phrase such as, *Livosha explained to her brother what she had learned* we would have discharged our duty equally well. In general, one may say that each method is as good as the other, but, having in previous chapters of our history, used the latter method, we thought, on this occasion, that by using the former we would not only discover to the reader all necessary information, but, in addition, display something of the historian's art in demonstrating (*demonstrating*, the reader must understand, being nearly always superior to *stating*) the different methods by which necessary material may be disclosed to the reader.

Once this information had, in fact, been so disclosed, Livosha said, "And so, my brother, have you, on your part, any news?"

"In fact, Livosha, I do have some."

"Well?"

"I have been given a task that may prove interesting."

"If it is interesting, well, I am interested."

"By definition, my dear Livosha."

"Go on, then."

"You are aware of pirates?"

"I know they exist."

"In fact, I know of three bands."

"You know more than me, for in truth, I had not even been aware that 'band' was the collective noun for pirate crews."

"In honesty, I am not certain that it is. What I mean is, different pirates prey on shipping in different parts of the coast, and the ones I know of make harbor in three places, these being Far Harbor in Zerika's Point, another on Silver Island, and a third at Sandy Point in the Shallow Sea."

"So then, there are three bands, if they are properly called bands, and if they are not, then there are three of something else. I understand. Go on."

"These bands must have ways to trade their goods for gold, or other things that are useful to them."

"That is but natural."

"Thus there are those who work with them."

"I understand. And then?"

"His Highness, that is to say, Prince Traanzo, is concerned with the nearest band, that is, those who work from the Shallow Sea, and harass shipping and trading and, when desperate, even fishing near Adrilankha."

"I understand why he would be."

"He thus set me to discover, through my contacts, who trades with them."

"Did he do so in order to stop this trading, or to profit from it?"

"As to this, I do not know the answer."

"Very well. But, did you discover who was trading with the pirates?"

"That, and more."

"Ah, well, now I am more than interested, I am eager."

"I eventually discovered a certain Orca who trades with the pirates who harbor at Sandy Point. But I did not stop there."

"I recognize you so well in that!" said Livosha admiringly.

"I thought to look into this particular Orca's business arrangements and found that he has partners all along the south, and that among them is—"

"Yes?"

"Dorin of Westward!"

"Ah, our old enemy!"

"Exactly."

"But, what is the business between this Orca—apropos, what is his name?"

"Rennis."

"What business is there between Rennis and Dorin?"

"I do not know, but it seems to me—"

"Well?"

"If I can provide information that proves Dorin is working against Traanzo's interest, that cannot fail to help us."

"I think you are in the right of it."

"So then?"

"Keep looking!"

"That is my plan."

"And?"

"We will speak again the day after to-morrow," said Kefaan.

Livosha nodded.

Chapter the Twenty-third

In Which It Is Demonstrated that the Merchant Is the Connection Between the Bandit and the Pirate

At roughly the same time as the events we have just had the honor to relate were occurring, there was a clap outside of a house in what had once been called the Valley of Dust, but was now known as Magister Valley.

Alishka nearly jumped at the sound, which had not been preceded by any sound of footsteps, which was unusual because of the silence that surrounded the house, and because of the flagstones Alishka had had installed all around it for exactly this purpose. Recovering, however, she called out, "Who is at the door?" at the same time reaching for the sword that was never far from her hand, in case the answer was not to her liking.

The answer was the single word, "Dust."

She leapt from the chair and, crossing the distance in two steps, flung open the door.

"It is you!" she cried.

"Well," said Dust.

"Come in, come in! It is, after all, your home. Alas, all I have to offer is wine, too pale and too young, and the remains of this fowl I snared, too thin and too old."

"I didn't come for refreshment, my friend, though I will be glad for a cup of wine."

"I will fetch it. Please, sit, sit!"

Dust sat, and Alishka brought him wine. He nodded his thanks and said, "I am astonished that you are here alone. What has become of your friends?"

"Well, let us see. Doro is with Jiscava and Cho watching the road over the hill to the east, where sometimes merchants attempt to sneak through. Fagry, Nef, and Liniace are in town trading some of our goods for necessities and even luxuries. Kitescu and Branf are in various rooms behind us, sleeping, as they had business that kept them up late. I hope that answers your question, my lord."

"Ah, let there be no 'my lord' between us, Alishka. And yes, my question is fully answered."

"I am glad that it is, for it permits me to ask one in my turn."

"Ah, you have a question then?"

"Indeed, would you like to hear it?"

"Certainly, Alishka, and this very moment. And once I have heard it, well, I will do my best to answer it."

"So much the better. Here it is, then: To what do I owe the honor, and, may I say it, the great pleasure of your visit?"

"Ah, that is your question?"

"Well, if it is not, I ought not to have asked it."

"That is true," said Dust. "Very well, but, can you not guess?"

"How, guess? When I have not seen you in—how many years? Seventeen? More? And you suddenly appear, how can I guess as to your motives?"

"And yet, when we last met, what was the subject on which we spoke?"

"Ah!" said Alishka, suddenly comprehending. "There was a mission you did me the honor to entrust to me."

"That is exactly the case."

"And, no doubt, you wish to learn of the results."

"No one can question your comprehension, good Alishka."

"You are kind to say so."

"Not in the least. But then?"

"You wish me to tell you what we learned?"

"Nearly."

"And yet, this is difficult."

"Oh? What is the nature of this difficulty?"

"You must understand that we carried out this mission nearly eighteen years ago!"

"Well, and?"

"And I don't remember it!"

"But, my dear Alishka, did you not take notes?"

Alishka frowned, struggling to remember. "Why, yes," she said at last. "I did. I am certain of it."

"And then?"

She rubbed her temples. She could remember the return journey, there had been a blizzard, and her horses had died, and she had to walk, and yes, she remembered tumbling in the door with Fagry and Cho—what had she said? "You two start the fire, while I place these notes . . ." Where?

"Ah!" she cried, suddenly standing.

"You have remembered."

Without responding, Alishka rushed into the bedroom she had been using, the one that would have belonged to Dust if he had been there, and opened the door to the built-in wardrobe. At the top was a small box. She worked the mechanism, and the door to the box fell open. She reached in and—yes! A moment later she returned in triumph, in her hand the sheaf of notes she had collected from that small village, what was it? She glanced at the top page. Wetrock. Yes. She sat down, smiling.

"I deduce," said Dust, "from the expression on your countenance that you have found the notes."

"I have. I discovered them, as so often happens, in the very place I had left them. You perceive, it was only necessary for me to recall what that place was, and to go there, and here they are."

"I follow your reasoning exactly."

"And now that I have found the notes—"

"Yes, now that you have them?"

"There is no reason I cannot give a report on the mission, explaining what I learned."

"So then, you will do so?"

"With the greatest pleasure."

"Then I am listening."

"Do you wish me to begin now?"

"My dear Alishka, it is an hour since I wished for anything else."

"This is it, then."

As the reader is already familiar with the substance of the events that Alishka discovered, having observed them at the same time as Livosha, we do not see a need to take up the reader's time by repeating them, as it is well known that repetition, or redundancy, or iteration, can by its nature, indeed, by its very definition, do nothing to advance understanding, and, hence, has no valid place in any work that purports to further human knowledge, however this ingemination or replication is presented. We hope the reader will have taken care to note this artistic law, as we will not, of course, be saying it again.

She then informed Dust of the attack on Livosha's home, and of the explosion of Cryden House, in short, of the murder, the treachery; during all of this, Dust listened without a word, and watched her without a flicker of expression. When she had finished, he said, "What were the names of those who escaped?"

"*May* have escaped," corrected Alishka. "Kefaan and Livosha."

As this last name was pronounced, it seemed to Alishka that, for the first time, Dust betrayed some flicker of emotion, but it was too subtle for her to read, and gone too quickly for her to be certain.

"You've done well," said Dust. "And I thank you. Moreover, here is the rest of the payment I promised you."

He set another uncut sapphire on the table. Alishka said, "I believe you are mistaken, Dust. You promised me nothing. On the contrary, you paid in full before we set out."

"Perhaps you've forgotten," said Dust.

Alishka felt her lips quirk, bowed her head, and put the sapphire into her pouch. "Perhaps I did," she said. "At all events, I am pleased to have been able to perform a service for you, and I hope you learned something of value."

"In fact, I did. So much so that it is possible that there is another service you could perform for me."

"Well, I am more than happy to perform any service within my power."

"You have spoken of certain of your band—that is to say, Fagry, Nef, and Liniace—trading goods for supplies."

"Your memory is far better than mine."

"Well, but the length of time over which my memory was required to work was, you must see, considerably less than that demanded by yours."

"That is true," said Alishka. "But then, what of the matter?"

"I wonder if it is possible that some of the goods they are trading have been acquired by means that are less than honest."

Alishka shrugged. "That is possible."

"I further wonder if those being traded with are aware of this."

"I do not say they are not. And then?"

"I cannot help but wonder, good Alishka, what sort of people will knowingly trade in stolen goods."

"Well, you perceive, sometimes it is only those with criminal disposition, other times, why, almost anyone. It is a question of how hungry one gets, for as the belly becomes empty, standards become lower. When hunger reaches the point of desperation, one might engage in all sorts of acts to fill it, where when it becomes so full that all memory of hunger is gone, one might then speak freely of the moral depredations of crime."

"You speak as one with experience of your fellows, Alishka."

"I do not deny it."

"My question, then, is this: Have you had dealing, in the course of exchanging those items you have for those items, be they coin or goods of more specific use, with any Jhereg in Northport?"

"I confess that, from time to time, we have had commerce with a few of them, my dear Dust."

"I am pleased that this is the case."

"I am glad to have pleased you."

"Oh, you have, I assure you. And you could please me more by introducing me to one of these."

"How, you wish to meet a Jhereg?"

""My dear Alishka, I have said it before, and now I repeat it: No one can question your comprehension."

"Well, I can think of two, no, three Jhereg in Northport who may be suitable. It is possible that, if you tell me more of why you wish to involve yourself with them, it will make it easier to choose among them."

Alishka suddenly, for the first time, felt the full weight of Dust's gaze, as he looked at her without expression, yet with a cool, detached appraisal that made her feel as if she were a bottle of wine being considered for purchase. "I believe I will not," he said.

"Of course," said Alishka.

"So, will you write me a letter?"

"Better than that, my dear Dust, I will take you there, and perform the introduction in person. You perceive, that is more likely to have an effect, especially as none of them know my hand, and so might not be persuaded a letter came from me."

"You will, then, travel to Northport with me?"

"With all the will in the world. When would you like to leave?"

"To-morrow morning."

"In that case, may I suggest we get a good night's rest? It is a long journey, and a tiring one. I must give orders, and make explanations to my band, so I will be up for some time writing. You, of course, will take the bedroom that is yours, and I will, when I am ready, take the remaining bedchamber, and thus we can enjoy the luxury of each having our own bed, which is especially valuable to me, as certain of my compatriots are known to snore."

"With this plan I agree," said Dust, and rising, he drained the rest of his wine, and, without another word, retired into the bed-chamber.

Alishka, for her part, did exactly as she had said, writing out instructions and explanations, and, when she was done, gathering what she would need to travel, and then, going into the other bedchamber, stretching herself out fully with a contented sigh that indicated that, even after several years, she still appreciated the luxury of sleeping without the company of her comrades.

The next morning they set out for Dinshouse, the village at the very northern tip of the Cold Sea, where they could find a ship to take them to Northport. In our opinion, the events of this travel, and then, later, of the journey across the Cold Sea, can have little interest for the reader, and to detail the events of this journey can only cause ennui. That this is the sensation primarily experienced by Alishka, in response to Dust's general laconicism and unwillingness to explain his errand, is hardly an excuse to require the reader to suffer such a fate. That art (and, as we have insisted, the propounding of historical truth is an art) is necessarily based on mimesis is undeniable; yet mimesis, like historical absurdism (a term this author has himself coined as the most apt description of certain approaches to understanding the evolutions of the past) has its limits. There is, we insist, no more reason to subject the reader to an experience that can only provide annoyance without corresponding edification than there would be for a prestigious institute of higher learning to reject the advice contained in a helpful and informative letter from a noted scholar speaking on a subject that falls within that scholar's area of expertise. That such things as we have had the honor to refer to will occasionally happen, is no excuse to compound the error, that is, to subject the unfortunate reader to the anguish felt by such a hypothetical scholar.

The reader will then, we are certain, understand if we have elected to next look in on Alishka at the time the ship, called the *Leundir III*, arrives safely at Northport. Now we should say that Alishka, who had many talents and skills, some of which we will not be required to explore by the needs of our history, did not number among them the various abilities associated with sailing. In fact, so far was she from having this skill, that she quite nearly contrived to drown herself by ignominiously falling from the boat that was being used to bring her to shore from the *Leundir*'s anchorage. However, between the skill of certain sailors and Dust's alertness, she made it safely, if not dryly, to shore.

"Come," said Dust. "Now we must hurry if we are to find you warmth and shelter before this air causes an illness that will prove difficult of treatment."

Alishka, whose teeth were chattering with too much energy to permit speech, and who felt herself shivering to a degree she could not remember experiencing even during several long winter nights waiting for the passing of a merchant's cart, contented herself with nodding, and leading the way to the Altar and Cup, an inn that was conveniently placed next to a shrine dedicated to Trout.

Having arrived at their destination, and Dust having arranged for a seat by the fire and a bottle of the best and strongest wine in the house, she at once began to feel better. "It is good," she remarked, "to be on land again. Had the voyage gone on much longer, I am uncertain if I would have lived."

Dust shrugged, "While it is possible to die from the discomfort caused by a sea-voyage, it will, as a rule, take a more severe case than you experienced to accomplish this feat, not, you understand, that I wish in any way to dismiss the unpleasantness you have undergone. The pirates were the greater danger, I think."

"How, pirates? There were pirates?"

"Indeed. They chased us for several hours, and even looked to be gaining on us when, by some fluke, the breeze failed for them but not for us, and so we were able to get away."

"That is well, then."

"I agree."

"Do you know, Dust, there were things I wished to speak to you about during our journey, but my illness prevented it."

"Well, now you are not ill. Of what did you wish to speak?"

He was facing the fire, not looking at her, though he must, she decided, be aware of the intensity of her concentration on his countenance. After some moments of silence, she said, "What, exactly, did you receive from the demon, my dear Dust?"

He turned and looked at her briefly, then returned his gaze to the fire, though in fact she had the impression he was seeing something that was far away. "We struck a bargain. That is to say, I had a certain amount of control over him which he would prefer I not have, or at least not use."

"And then?"

"We agreed that he would perform three services for me. It seemed a reasonable number, and, after all, when dealing with a demon, it is just as well to have him kindly disposed, don't you think?"

"Oh, I would never dispute that! But—"

"Yes?"

"What is it he did?"

"For the first service, he brought me to a place where I could rest, recover, and gather an immense number of sapphires."

"Where is this place?"

"As to that, well, I cannot say, as it was not of our world."

"Very well. And what was the next service?"

"Let us say that he took steps to improve my health."

"Your health?"

"I am not likely to age as quickly as you would expect."

"He gave you more than that, I think."

Dust smiled briefly at the fire. "Perhaps he did."

"Well, and the third service?"

"Ah, the third service. That one we have not yet agreed upon. But I can call him when I need him, and I believe there will come a time for it. But may I suggest you find an empty room and change into dry clothing?"

"With this plan, I agree." She went off to do so, thinking, *I would like to learn your secrets, my friend. Or would I? Might it be better not to know? Perhaps, yes, it would be better not to know.*

Once properly dry and clothed, they left the inn and Alishka took the lead after Dust said to find them the best lodgings, and, from having been in Northport so many times, she was able to do so with no trouble, bringing them to a long, low structure directly on the road that seemed to have been added to many times, and bore a sign that attempted to show three happy fish jumping out of the ocean, but thanks to a certain lack of skill on the part of the artist, they appeared less happy than prepared to leap out and bite the viewer's throat, hence, the inn became known as the Angry Fish, a name which the host, after several hundred years, accepted rather than ordering the sign repainted. The Angry Fish, as we shall call it, gave the lie to the general rule of hostels that says, "slipshod on the outside, discomfort on the inside." In fact, the rooms were all clean, well appointed, and had mattresses with that mix of goose and clackbird feathers that results in such perfect luxury. There was a small common room where meals and wine and beer were served, but it was, as a rule, only attended by those guests who had just arisen or were about to retire, gaining little custom from local traffic.

They spent, therefore, a peaceful and restful night, broken only once for Alishka when something awakened her, and she saw that Dust, next to her on the bed, was staring up at the ceiling with his teeth and fists clenched. Presently, he relaxed and closed his eyes, and she returned to sleep without giving the matter any more thought.

The next morning, they had a leisurely breakfast in the common room, as Alishka pretended that those whom Dust would want to meet would be unavailable until late in the morning. They therefore had salmon omelets, legume pudding, and several cups of klava.

"So then," said Dust at one point. "Have you decided to whom you wish to introduce me?"

"I have not," said Alishka. "I have been turning the matter over in my mind, and it seems to me that, instead of choosing, I should tell you something about the three Jhereg I know, and you may then decide among them."

"Very well," said Dust. "I agree to this plan."

"Then, if you like, I will begin."

"If, as you say, it will still be some hours before we are able to see any of them, then I can imagine no better use of this time than what you propose."

"I am about to speak, then."

"Do so; I am listening."

"First, there is Orlith."

"Very well, Orlith."

"His income used to be untaxed gambling, but, now that there is no Imperial tax (as a natural consequence, you perceive, of there being no Empire), he has expanded his business interests to include loans, and protection services."

She observed a flicker of expression, as of distaste, cross Dust's countenance when she pronounced, "protection services," but she did not cease her narrative.

"Next," she said, "there is Turod."

"Turod," he repeated, as if to commit the name to memory.

"Turod," she continued, "is the one I most work with, as he will buy and sell, and arrange the buying and selling, of any goods with no question. He has friends among several of the pirate crews that shelter among the Fingers to the northwest."

He nodded that he understood, and indicated that she should continue.

"The third," she said, "is called Keen. His business is a combination of the two others: that is, he deals in stolen goods, runs gambling games and brothels, and gives loans."

"Very good. Now tell me, what are they like?"

Alishka felt herself frowning, suddenly feeling as if she were being somehow tested, a sensation she did not care for.

"Orlith is quiet, and you feel as if he is always listening. Moreover, you will never know what he is thinking; I believe that, should he decide to kill me, he would bow politely and give the order when I had left, still smiling."

Dust nodded and said, "Well, and Turod?"

"He talks a great deal, and wishes to appear cheerful, as one who has not the least care in the world, but he is, I think, always weighing and evaluating like an Orca."

"Very good. And last, Keen."

"Ah, well, Keen is young, and seeing him in his surroundings you would think him poor; why he wishes to convey this I do not know, but I have had his private home pointed out to me and it is lavish. I do not enjoy speaking with him, for I fear that, at any moment, I might accidentally enrage him and he would have me beaten or worse."

"Yet," said Dust, "he has never done so?"

"Not so far," agreed Alishka.

Dust fell silent and seemed to be considering matters. After a moment he said, "Well, my dear Alishka, I must compliment you on the summaries you have shared."

"Then, they were useful?"

"Oh, to be sure. I found them precise, and you have told me what I wished to know."

"I am pleased to have done so. And then, have you made a decision?"

"Oh, certainly. How could I have failed to make a decision when you have presented the three choices so clearly they might as well have been in front of me?"

Alishka, though not entirely certain Dust was not making game of her, only bowed her head and said, "Then?"

"Is it now time?"

Alishka looked out the window and attempted to judge from the amount of light (the various timekeeping methods that came into being during the Interregnum, as imperfect as even the best of them were, had not at this time even begun to be developed). "I believe it is close enough," she said.

"Then come, let us go."

"I am ready."

"Then I am following you."

"But, you have not told me which one we are to visit."

"Can you not guess?"

"I assure you, I am as ignorant as an Easterner."

"Well, as I have not told you why I wish to speak with a Jhereg, it is reasonable that you are unable to determine this."

"I am pleased to hear you say so. And then?"

"Take me to Keen."

"Very well, I will do so," said Alishka, although she was, in fact, not eager to meet with this individual.

She led the way out into the cold of Northport's winter and, knowing the path well, made her way down the street. After some time, she turned onto a road called Shepard's Climb, after which, in a few steps, they reached the door of a small cottage above which hung a sign that said, "Furrier." Alishka clapped, and there was an answering grunt from within which she, from familiarity, took as a sign to enter. She did so, Dust following behind her.

Against one wall were barrels filled with furs from various animals, directly in front was a long board set up on two more barrels, and upon this board were a few pieces of fur and some long scissors and sewing equipment. There was a door behind the table that, she knew, led to a workshop and another door, beyond which—that is, a considerable distance beyond which—was another house where the tanning took place. On this day, by good fortune, the wind was blowing from the other direction, and so the stench of the tanning room only lingered slightly. Alishka worked to ignore it; Dust appeared not to notice.

In addition to the furnishing, the room also held certain persons, and as for the most part the *people* in history are more interesting than the *things* (because, of course, individuals are capable of actions without things, but things are unable to act without individuals) we will now hasten to inform the reader of them. There were, then, four persons in the room: one was a large man with thick fingers wearing the black and brown of the Chreotha, and, at present, sitting at the table working with a large piece of fur and a diagram which he consulted repeatedly. From this, the reader may deduce that, when the door opened, he did not so much as look up from his work, and in this the reader would be correct. Two others wore the black and gray of the Jhereg, and, moreover, full cloaks suitable for concealing weapons (although it must be added that the shorter of the two, at least, was unconcerned with this concealment, to judge by the fact that his cloak was pushed aside, and a sword and two daggers were evident on his belt). These two were seated on barrels, and, though giving the impression of taking their ease, nevertheless carefully observed Alishka and Dust as they entered.

The remaining man sat on the only chair in the room, in the far corner from the door. He was between six hundred and seven hundred years of age, wore black and gray garments that seemed well made, and did not, at least at first glance, appear to be armed. Alishka greeted him with a bow that was polite, but not overly subservient, and said, "My greetings to you, Keen."

"Alishka," said the Jhereg, then turned his eyes toward Dust, as if waiting for an explanation, or introduction, or both.

"This," she said, "is my friend Dust. He is trustworthy, and is, moreover, the source of that sapphire I placed into your hands some years ago, and which I think you may remember."

Keen shrugged. "I remember there was one. What then?"

"He would have words with you. I promised to make an introduction, and, you perceive, I have now done so."

"Well," said Keen, shrugging. "You have introduced us. What then?"

"Then," said Dust, "I wish to speak to you about a matter of business."

"Speak then."

"Certainly," he said. "Will you cause someone to bring me something to sit on, or will you stand?"

Keen's eyes narrowed, and Alishka felt her breath catch. Dust, for his part, seemed perfectly plussed (a word, as the reader ought to be able to deduce, that means the opposite of the more usual "nonplussed." We have chosen to use the less common word here in the service of brevity), merely awaiting an answer. After a moment, the Jhereg shrugged and gestured with his chin to one of those seated against the wall, who then got up and moved the barrel over in front of Dust.

"Well, and for my friend?"

"She can stand, or wait outside."

Before Dust could respond, Alishka put a hand on his shoulder. "Come," she said. "I wouldn't miss this conversation for anything."

Dust shrugged and sat on the barrel. "So, then," he said. "We will speak."

"I would guess," said Keen, "that you have an offer for me."

"You are perspicacious."

"Then let me hear it."

"First, here is part of my offer." He reached into his pouch and removed a large, uncut sapphire. Keen picked it up and studied it with an expert eye. "Well, I admit, that is a good start."

"So much the better," said Dust.

"And next?"

"Next, I will keep you as my lieutenant."

"As your lieutenant?"

"Precisely."

"I do not understand what you do me the honor to tell me."

Dust shrugged. "It is simple enough. This business is now mine, but if you accept the sapphire, you may continue under my orders."

Keen stared at him for a moment as if uncertain if the other did him the honor to jest. Alishka, who knew Dust rather better than Keen did, took a step back. As she did so, and, indeed, as she began to reach for a weapon, Keen rose and gestured to his two compatriots, who began at once moving toward Dust.

"Kill him," said Keen.

Dust, for his part, remained seated. As the two rushed at him, he drew his sword, which, though Alishka had not noticed it before, was of tolerably good length. With a movement of his wrist too quick for Alishka to follow, he beat the blade of one of the Jhereg into the blade of the other, then, still without stirring from the barrel, and with the appearance of having as much time at his disposal as a warboard master contemplating his next move, deliberately ran the point of his blade through each of their hearts, after which he turned back to Keen and, very slowly, brought the point of his blade toward Keen's eye. The two others sighed and fell over in place.

"*Tsi garra*," murmured the one called Keen in the language of the Serioli, proving he was educated. "*Nis ta'arks!a ðiafan quo!*"

"So, then," said Dust, who either didn't understand the murmur or chose to ignore it. "Do you wish to accept the payment? You perceive, I am anxious to come to agreeable terms with you."

From where she stood, Alishka could observe Keen's countenance as he attempted not to display shock at what he had just seen, an attempt that, in the end, failed, as the Jhereg cried out.

"Who *are* you?"

"My name is Dust," said the other coolly. "Come, my friend. Will you work for me?"

Keen looked at the two bodies on the floor, then nodded.

"In that case, take the sapphire." Here he placed it on the table once more, and added, "Perhaps you can buy something nice with it."

The furrier, Alishka noticed, had at some point risen and pushed himself against the far wall; he now, looking at Dust as if he were a snake that might suddenly bite, gingerly took his seat again and returned to his work. Keen swallowed, then picked up the sapphire. He stood up and walked around the end of the table, and, bowing, indicated the chair he had just vacated. Dust nodded, himself went around the table, and sat in it.

"Where shall I begin?" said Keen. "No doubt you wish a report of assets?"

"There will be time for that," said Dust. "First, you are to write two letters."

"Two letters? Well, I can do that. To whom shall I address the first one?"

"To your contact among the Pirates of Icolev."

"Ah, you know of this?" He looked over at Alishka, who shrugged.

"Very well," said Keen. "I admit, I know certain individuals in Icolev. What is the letter to say?"

"It is to introduce me, and to inform them that, from now on, I will be speaking for you, and representing the interests that you had hitherto represented."

"What is the other letter?"

"To a prince, or a duke, or, if necessary, a count of the House of the Jhereg. Whoever has the most authority in this region."

Keen coughed. "My lord Dust, I must explain, with the Jhereg—"

Dust held up his hand. "I understand that titles of nobility within the House are meaningless regarding the, ah, the activities of some members. Nevertheless, that is what I wish."

"Very well," said Keen. "That would be the Duke of Quanoth. What shall I say to him?"

"Say that, for the price of five hundred imperials' worth of uncut sapphires given into his hand, you are, through his offices, granting me the title of baron within the House of the Jhereg. He is to have all necessary papers filled out and delivered here."

"I . . . my lord Dust, the House of the Jhereg, well, we do not sell titles."

"We do now," said Dust.

Chapter the Twenty-fourth

In Which Is Demonstrated the Theater Adage that Two on a Mark Means a Tangle of Limbs

Before entering into the substance of the events to which this chapter of our history is dedicated, it is necessary to describe a certain series of incidents that fall somewhat beyond the boundaries of our narrative, in that they involve individuals with whom we have not, until now, spent any time. We might well expect the reader to be astonished at such a decision, as our hypothetical reader is no doubt aware, both because of the over-all shape the combination of incidents has acquired, and because of the easily observed number of pages remaining, that we are farther, or, perhaps *deeper* into the text than would usually accompany introductions of previously unknown persons.

The reason for this decision, unusual as it is, is easily explained. What we have earlier referred to as the *substance* of this chapter will inevitably raise questions in the mind of the reader, which condition is, of course, quite normal, and requires us to mention that among the skills that are necessary in order to effectively communicate historical understanding is the ability to rigorously maintain an awareness of questions raised in the reader's mind, for the simple reason that, should there become too many of these questions, or should they remain unanswered for too long, there is a certain strain on the mind that is as antithetical to clarity and antagonistic to comprehension as would be a single sentence that is extended beyond reason—which confusion can best be remedied by, in the one case, the answering of the question, and in the other, by coming to the end of the sentence, or, if the reader prefer, in the latter case by failing to extend the sentence beyond what the reader's awareness is able to hold, and in the former case by means of answering the question *before it is asked*, a method that, as the reader has no doubt deduced, we have chosen to employ in this instance (the issue of the length of a single sentence, which we had the honor to use as an example, can be considered moot due to the author's habitual terseness).

The small matter that must be understood, then, is quickly explained by directing the reader's attention to a rundown cabaret in the hamlet of Dinshouse some ten or eleven days after Alishka and Dust took their departure on the way to Northport. While we need not explain exactly what happened, trusting the reader's perspicacity to draw the necessary conclusions, we must, by way of providing the necessary foundation for these conclusions, explain that two men were sitting at a small table within this establishment. One of these men the reader has seen before, albeit briefly: this was Kitescu, one of Alishka's band. With him was a man of middle years and dark complexion whose House, owing to his leather traveling garb, could not be determined. On the table with them were two cups, and four bottles of wine, three of them empty.

We will not stay with this pair for long, as the reader will be able to determine the substance of their conversation quickly. The man in leather continued to buy wine, Kitescu continued to drink it. The conversation gradually turned from affairs of the day, comparisons of their respective home towns, discussions of the various child-rearing methods practiced upon them, and hopes for family, to a discussion in which the unknown asked certain questions which the bandit answered.

After some time, Kitescu ended by putting his head down on the table and commencing to snore, an event that, evidently, the other considered the end of the discourse, whereupon, inquiring of the host, he was supplied with pen, paper, sand, and pounce (the latter because, since the fall of the Empire, paper had been in short supply, produced locally, and was therefore frequently of poor quality). The unknown made use of these items to write a letter, which he sealed with a ring he wore, and then went down to the pier to hire a ship or a boat that would be willing to carry the message.

At this point, it becomes important, indeed, indispensable to say two words about communication, by which we mean, the exchange of thoughts or information, particularly over vast distance. The difficulties involved in this are something the modern reader may have difficulty in comprehending. To-day, of course, such communication is simple: providing that no material object need be transmitted, one can exchange thoughts with a close acquaintance nearly without effort, merely by casting a spell so simple that few are even aware that a spell is being cast. In order to get a message to someone one does not know well, one can, for a price, visit any of several services that connect all of the major cities of the Empire and, indeed, many of the minor ones, and a hand-written message delivered to such a service will become a hand-written message in the possession of the recipient in a matter of few hours, or, if in an outlying duchy, a few days. Beyond this, and for a smaller payment, we have the Imperial Post, which stations post riders at such numerous places that a letter going from one end of the Empire to the other will arrive within a few days of its being sent (a system that, admirable as it is, will in this historian's opinion have entirely vanished within a century owing to the ongoing reduction in cost of commercial psychic communication).

Before Adron's Disaster, the Interregnum, and Zerika's reemergence with the Orb and all of its new powers—that is to say, in the old Empire— the only one of those systems in place (with the exception of those individuals with the skill and knowledge to touch each other's minds) was the post system, which was nowhere near as well developed as in our own time, which meant that a message could take a month or more to reach its destination, which meant, of course, double that if a reply was required. That this was a limiting factor in the growth and prosperity of the Empire is well known.

All of which is to say that, with the fall of the Empire, communication became so slow and cumbersome—and sometimes dangerous—that it is difficult for to-day's reader to imagine. When it might take most of a year for a message to be received—if it ever was—and then as much time for the answer to return, the reader should have no difficulty understanding why decisions that would normally be based on communication and information became less reliable. It should be added for the sake of completeness that a message sent from one port city to another might arrive faster than one sent overland, but there was even less certainty that it would arrive at all.

This is one (although certainly not the only) cause of what has been described by historians as the "splintering" that began thirty or thirty-five years into the Interregnum, when various sections of the Empire either set up as independent kingdoms, or were torn apart during an effort to so establish themselves. As a point of interest, Northport itself was heavily involved in such a conflict, as the effort was made, first, to create a Kingdom of Zerika's Point, and then to carve various pieces out of it. Although beyond the scope of our present work, the author would like to take the opportunity to recommend Chersa of Cuttertown's excellent study of this phenomenon, which in the end turned into an impassioned dispute among two dukes and a prince over who would be able extract the most value from the local peasants (which peasants, who were of course drawn into the conflict, for reasons that are difficult to understand failed to declare a clear preference among the contenders).

This, however, is beginning to stray from the point, which, however tempting, we should prefer not to do. The point, then, is, quite simply, that it took some twenty-two days for a particular message sent from North-port to reach Adrilankha. This message, which the reader has already deduced is important to our history, was sent by an agent of Hadrice to Traanzo's manor.

This message was at once placed into Hadrice's hand, after which Hadrice called for the director and showed it to him. And so it was that, a few hours later, Livosha heard about this message.

As to the contents of the message, which we are aware we have not as yet discovered to the reader, it was simplicity itself: "The one called Eremit now styles himself Dust, and can be identified easily as he dresses himself in white. He is in the company of a bandit chief named Alishka, and they left for Northport 12 days ago. I am now going to Northport to look for them." It was signed with the letter "L" which was either the first name of the individual sending it, or a special designation, a matter of which we must confess our ignorance. It should be noted, in passing, that this is an example of a matter—small, it is true, and arguably insignificant—that this historian has not discovered. We hope the reader, and, even more, any who wish to study the art and science of history, will take a lesson from this: there are things we may be unable to discover, and, upon coming across such matters, the honest historian will say so forthrightly rather than, as we have seen from certain supposed academics who disgrace the name of "scholar" as they shame the institution that awards them such prestige, obscuring one's lack of knowledge by obfuscatory prose or, worse, by out-right fabrications, such as inventing the name and history of an unknown drummer-boy at the Battle of Shining Mountain. It should be obvious that, to the serious historian, there can be no greater crime than this.

Livosha and Kefaan met that evening on the terrace, and Kefaan said, "Well, once more I perceive there is news."

"And once more you are right, my dear brother."

"Well, and then? You do not propose to keep me waiting, I hope."

"Not in the least. And the proof is, I am about to tell you."

"Then I am listening."

Livosha, no more inclined to waste words than this author, quickly described the message she had learned of.

"At last, we have certain word," said Kefaan with evident satisfaction.

"Yes, although—"

"Yes?"

"He calls himself Dust."

"Well, this was something we already knew."

"And he wears white."

"That is also true."

"I cannot help but wonder what has happened to him."

"We will find him, sister, and then we will know."

"Then, you propose to set out after him?"

"The trouble," said Kefaan, considering the matter, "is time. We could spend a hundred years following him to one place only to learn he has come to the very place where we would have seen him if we had waited, and if we wait, why, it may be that he will remain where he is, and so we could have found him."

"That is true," said Livosha. "How then shall we address this conundrum?"

"You must make the decision," said Kefaan.

Livosha nodded, accepting this. They stood in silence while she considered all that she knew, contemplating her options the way the author of a fiction might consider the possible twisting and turning of the plot. At last she said, "Very well, I have decided."

"I recognize you so well in that," said Kefaan. "But, what have you decided?"

"For now, we will remain here."

"So, we wait?"

"Not entirely," said Livosha. "We will do more than wait."

"Ah, and what else will we do?"

"You, my brother. Have you contacts among the Jhereg of Northport?"

Kefaan considered this question. "It may be that someone I know knows someone who knows someone else."

"Attempt to discover this, then. And if possible, learn what you can. Is Eremit, that is to say, Dust, still in Northport? And what is he doing there?"

Kefaan nodded. "I understand, my sister."

"And your affairs? That is to say, the matter of Rennis the Orca and the pirates and Count Dorin?"

"I have made certain small advances."

"Well?"

"I have learned something of the nature of the association among them, and, I assure you, it is tolerably complex."

"Well?"

"In simple terms, that is, as simple as I can make it, in order to deliver gold, goods, and even messages along the coast, it is necessary to convince the pirate ships to leave one unmolested. There is, I am told, a significant danger that one will encounter a pirate or two when sailing along the coast between Adrilankha and Hartre, or between Hartre and White Harbor; no doubt it is also true if one were to continue to Northport, but I have no knowledge of this."

"Your knowledge, my brother, is extensive. Go on, and discover more of it to me."

"But here is what I learned from my friends in the Jhereg: If one encounters a pirate, let us say, when setting out from Adrilankha, one might, with a sufficient ransom, or tribute, be released."

"I had not known pirates accepted such tributes."

"It is what I have learned, and it is, moreover, the custom all along the southern coast. Though the quantity of bribes varies among the bands—"

"If that is the word."

"—if that is the word, and even among ship captains, the custom is inviolate among the pirates. And there is more."

"Well?"

"Well, it seems that all of the captains within a band are known to each other, and, if one pays the proper ransom to a ship, one is given a certain note, signed by the captain, and if one is stopped a second time, why, one need only show that note, and one is at once released. It is this that has allowed trade to resume, at least in a small way."

"I understand. But does this have an effect on our plans or intentions?"

"As to that, I am uncertain. I hope to receive news to-day or to-morrow that will make clearer Count Dorin's role in the matter. In the meantime, I am keeping Lord Traanzo abreast of what I have learned, but, so far, he has not displayed the hoped-for animosity toward Dorin."

"Very well, then. I think we are done for now. We will meet again the day after to-morrow and see what we have learned."

"Until then, my sister."

"Until then, my brother."

Livosha embraced her brother and left the terrace to return to work. The next day it was still early in the morning when she heard a clap outside of the closet where she was accustomed to perform her duties. She opened the door at once, and, to her shock, found Hadrice there.

Livosha had seen Hadrice from time to time, but they had never had occasion to speak; upon seeing the strange woman there now, the thought immediately grew in Livosha: *We are discovered. It is over.* She did not, however, permit this thought to express itself on her countenance; she bowed and said, "My lady, how may I—?"

"I am not your lady, call me Hadrice," said the other coolly.

"As you please, Hadrice. I am—"

"Nedyrc, I know." We apologize if we have not, until this time, mentioned the names under which Livosha and Kefaan—that is to say, "Nedyrc" and "Arin," concealed themselves; we have, until now, had no occasion to bring the matter up, and so we made the decision to withhold these statistics out of a desire to avoid requiring the reader to keep in mind information that could be, until now, of no use.

Nedyrc—that is to say, Livosha—curtsied and said, "How may I be of service, Hadrice?"

"You are the assistant advocate, are you not?"

"I am."

"You can attest to a witness statement?"

"I can."

"Then come with me. I must speak with someone. I will be questioning him later, in detail, but he may make important utterances when I first speak with him, and these may have legal importance."

"It is, then, to be an arrest?"

"Exactly."

"I am trained in recording such events, though I have never done so. May I know the name of the individual to be arrested?"

"Sajen."

It was a stroke of luck that, as she pronounced these words, Livosha was gathering paper, pen, and ink from the desk and preparing them for transport, for her face was turned away, and thus the expression of shock that, she had no doubt, flashed across her countenance was concealed. She merely said, "Very well," and continued her preparations, after which she said, "Permit me, then, to get my cloak."

"I will meet you outside of the east door."

"You will not need to wait long."

Livosha returned to her chamber, threw on a hooded cloak, and gathered what she would need to record conversations. She wrote a note to her brother, using the language of the Iorich and also certain codes known to the two of them to tell him to be ready to depart in an instant. She left the note in his chamber, and then went down to the east door where Hadrice waited with three horses.

"Do you ride?" she asked.

"I do. But, will there be no others to help with the arrest?"

"No one else will be needed. Come, let us go."

Livosha hung back slightly as they made their way north through Adrilankha, afraid that she might accidentally turn onto the right street ahead of Hadrice, thus inspiring questions she would not care to answer. As they rode she said, "Hadrice, if there is to be violence—"

"Well?"

"I beg you to observe that I am unarmed."

"I beg you to observe," said Hadrice coolly, "that, were you armed, I should disarm you for fear you would cut yourself, or me, by accident."

"Very well," said Livosha, clenching her teeth and fists. She pulled her hood over her head, hoping to avoid recognition by Sajen.

Hadrice nodded and the journey continued without conversation.

At one point, they turned away from the Favintoe district, and Livosha nearly asked if he had moved, but caught herself in time. Somewhat later they entered a part of city she had never seen before, with narrow, curving streets paved with stones that had been laboriously planed flat. The street they were on at once began to climb as well as turn until Livosha lost all sense of direction, and looked around hoping to spot the harbor to give her a sense of where she was; the houses, most of them three stories tall and built of stone, were too close together—some of them actually touching—to permit much of a view.

From this street they turned onto another that was so similar, in width, style, and in the sorts of structures built along it, then she became even more confused. At one point Hadrice stopped, looked carefully around, consulted a scrap of paper in her palm, and continued, though what she could have been looking for Livosha could not imagine. After climbing for some time, they started down the still-curving street, and shortly after that they stopped outside of a building that, to Livosha's eye, had nothing to distinguish it from a hundred she had just passed.

Hadrice dismounted and hobbled her horse and the one she was leading, there being nothing apparent to which to tie them.

Livosha said, "Do I wait, or come?"

"Come, but remain behind me."

"Very well," said Livosha, who then dismounted, hobbled her own horse, and followed Hadrice to a stone stairway of four steps ending in a door. While Livosha remained at the top of the stairs, Hadrice went down to the door and clapped sharply. Livosha was unable to distinguish the words from inside, but Hadrice answered them by saying "water and wine," which Livosha assumed was a kind of password.

The door opened, and Hadrice put her shoulder to it and pushed in quickly. Livosha, startled by the movement, took a moment to follow her. By the time she got there, she discovered that Hadrice had drawn a weapon and there were three individuals, all of them wearing black and gray, on the ground, bleeding, writhing, glaring, and gasping in various ways, until one of them stopped moving and stared upward with glassy eyes, a pool of blood still spreading from his neck. It seemed to be a small apartment, with a bedroom and its own kitchen, but mostly a single room with chairs and couches. The couch was occupied by an individual whom Livosha at once recognized as a very frightened Sajen. She started to raise the hood of her cloak, then realized it was already up. Either the hood was working, or the forger couldn't pull his eyes from Hadrice; in any case, he gave no signs of having recognized Livosha.

Hadrice, in the meantime, was raising her sword and pointing it at Sajen. When this was accomplished (with, in Livosha's opinion, an admirable amount of drama), she said, "I have a writ of arrest from the Countess of Whitecrest on the charge of forgery, and must beg you to come with me to answer certain questions."

Sajen's eyes were as wide as the gap between certain academics avowals and their results; his mouth opened and closed, and at last he said, "My lady, I—"

"Don't call me my lady. My name is Hadrice, and I arrest you in the name of the Countess of Whitecrest."

"How did you find me?" he said, which abruptly reminded Livosha that she should be marking down anything he said, which she immediately began to do.

"As to that," said Hadrice, "why did you suddenly leave your home and find Jhereg to hide, or to," she paused and looked around, "protect you?" There may have been a certain ironic emphasis on the word "protect."

"Oh, well," said Sajen, and coughed. "I was, that is to say, I was visiting friends."

Livosha wrote that down.

"Are many of your friends Jhereg?" Hadrice wanted to know. "And do you visit them often, suddenly, bringing with you a satchel containing changes of clothing?" Hadrice was, at this point, looking in a corner of the room where there was, indeed, a sort of tote bag with the top open next to a square case, presumably containing Sajen's art supplies.

"Oh, that," said Sajen. "Well."

"Yes?"

"I do not believe I wish to continue this conversation."

Hadrice shrugged. "Then take your things and come with me."

Sajen, obviously not at all happy, picked up his two cases and started toward the door. He noticed Livosha for the first time then, and attempted to peer under her hood, but evidently could not, for no sign of surprise or recognition appeared on his countenance.

As they left the room with two wounded men and one dead man, Hadrice turned to Livosha and said, "Can you lead on the way back?"

Livosha shook her head.

"Very well," said Hadrice. "Did you record the conversation?"

"Yes," she said.

Hadrice nodded and led the way out. As they mounted their horses, Hadrice said, "Sajen."

"Well?"

"If you attempt to escape I will catch you, and then I will break both of your legs. Do you understand?"

The forger nodded.

"Good, then. Get behind me, and Nedyrc in the rear."

In due course, they made their way back to the duke's manor, at which time, though there had been no conversation until that time, Sajen said, "But, that is not Whitecrest!"

"Well."

"Where are you taking me?"

"Do not worry, though not the estate of the countess, it is under her authority, and, moreover, there are secure dungeons there, so you need have no fear for your accommodations."

He fell silent after that, although Livosha guessed he was not reassured. Once they had dismounted, Hadrice took Sajen by the arm and, turning to Livosha said, "Have the transcript to me by to-morrow morning."

Livosha, not wishing to speak more than necessary, lest Sajen recognize her voice, merely bowed, and Hadrice led Sajen inside.

Once she was on her own, she threw her hood back and closed her eyes, leaning against the manor next to the door and letting the cold breeze buffet her face. She shook for some few moments before she was certain that she was able to walk. Having come to this conclusion, she entered the manor and at once made her the way to the library, where Kefaan often spent his time when not actively engaged in service to the duke.

He was, in fact, there, and as he looked up, she nodded to him, accompanying this gesture with a significant look, and at once made her way to the terrace. In a few minutes, Kefaan arrived, and said, "I received your note, and I have prepared for a departure if it is necessary."

"It is necessary, I assure you."

"Then, we are discovered?"

"We are about to be, and no artifice can prevent it. The forger, Sajen, has been taken, and he will soon tell everything he knows, and that must necessarily include us."

"Shards!" said Kefaan. "I perceive that there is no question of joking."

"None at all. And yet—"

"Well?"

"I cannot help but wonder why the forger was taken, and, moreover, how he came to be found."

"How, found?"

"Yes, for he had hastily left his old quarters, and was now staying in a new part of the city, protected by three Jhereg."

"What do you tell me?" cried Kefaan, turning pale and displaying evident excitement.

"Why, only the truth, my brother. He had recently, I think within a day, left his previous domicile and relocated among three Jhereg in a part of the city with which I am unfamiliar. But this intelligence seems to disturb you."

"Ah, ah! I spit upon all the gods!" cried Kefaan. "Which is only just, as they all seem to have chosen to spit upon me!"

"But come, calm yourself and explain."

"Calm myself? I do not believe I am capable of this exertion!"

"Nevertheless, you must try, because, if you remain in this distressed state, your explanation must necessarily suffer, and I suspect that it may be important for me to comprehend."

"Well, I will do my best, then."

"That is all I can ask."

"And you wish me to explain?"

"Nearly! The way you carry on fills me with curiosity."

"Then I will tell you the entire story."

"That is what I wish."

"You know that I have been keeping in touch with various Jhereg."

"I am aware of this."

"And, moreover, my assignments from His Highness Traanzo also require such intercourse."

"Assuredly. It was because of your knowledge of these persons that I thought to arrange this position for you."

"And so I have been carrying out these duties."

"Well, and?"

"You may remember that I spoke of certain orders from his lordship Traanzo to discover who was trading goods with the pirates who operate out of the Shallow Sea."

"Indeed, I remember that exactly. So well do I remember it, that I remember you found such a person. And the proof is, he is an Orca named Rennis."

"No one can question your memory, my sister."

"That is good, for I have come to rely on it. But go on."

"After the last time we spoke, I learned something important: in order to save money for ransom, Count Dorin and Rennis had come up with a scheme to save the tribute money."

"Ah, ah. Well, what was this famous scheme?"

"Instead of paying the first ship to catch him, and receiving a note stating that the ransom had been paid—"

"Well?"

"He simply had someone forge those notes at a cost of one or two Imperials each, and then put them into the hands of his captain, who would pass them off as if received from a pirate. That is, should he meet Captain Tall—"

"Is there a Captain Tall?"

"I do not know, my sister; I am merely making up a name for the purposes of illustration."

"I understand. Should he meet Captain Tall, then—?"

"He would give him a note that seemed to be from Captain Short. And if he happened to meet Captain Short, well—"

"He would give him a note as if from Captain Tall. I see that. And, moreover, I see something else: you said a forger. Could it be—?"

"Not only could, but is, my sister! Of course, I hadn't even guessed it might be the one we knew."

"Well, but what happened then?"

"Upon learning of this scheme, Lord Traanzo admired it so much, he thought to do the same himself, and the easiest way to become involved was to have the forger work for him."

"Well, but how did Hadrice become involved?"

"Ah, ah! I did that, fool that I am! I learned that the forger—you perceive, I had not been told his name—"

"Yes, yes, I understand that."

"I was told that he had learned inquires had been made of him, and, fearing arrest for forgery, he had gone to the Jhereg who had first hired him and asked for protection. Well, when I learned this, I thought that the simplest way to advance his lordship's interests would be to have him brought in. His lordship thought the same, and ordered his arrest."

"And then?"

"It seemed to me that if I could gain information from this forger before his lordship did, it might provide useful information for us in our quest for vengeance."

"That was not badly thought, I admit. And so, after thinking this?"

"After thinking this, I told Hadrice—"

"Yes? What did you tell her?"

"Ah, it is to weep! If I had a beard like an Easterner, I would tear it out."

"Go on, go on! What did you tell Hadrice?"

"I told her that this was the very forger who had been previously hired by Dorin, and so she must arrest him to keep her master's secret safe!"

"But it *was* the same forger!"

"I know! If I had suspected that it was, I never would have said so!"

"Well," said Livosha thoughtfully. "It is unfortunate. How did you not tell me about it? For I had spoken to Sajen, and might have made the important connection."

"It was yester-day, Livosha. We were not to meet until to-day."

"Well, that is true."

"I have been foolish."

"Not in the least, my brother. For consider, if we had known who the forger was, what could we have done? You might have put his lordship off the scent for a while, but that is all. We might not have needed to run at once, but we still would have had to run."

"You are good to say so, Livosha. But, as you say, now we must run."

"Yes, before this forger talks and reveals who we are, as he certainly will."

"But, run to where?"

"Why, Northport, of course. We will once more attempt to track down Eremit!"

Chapter the Twenty-fifth

In Which the Author Says Two Words about Pirates

At this point, it is necessary to make a few observations about piracy. The reader, no doubt, has at least some familiarity with the concept of plunder on the high seas. There is also little doubt that the reader has many misconceptions about this sort of criminal activity, but we will say frankly that it is not our task in this brief work to correct these. To the reader who wishes to make a serious study of the matter, we cannot too highly recommend G'Wulf's excellent survey in fourteen volumes called *Liberty Cove*, which, although focusing only on one place and within a relatively brief span early in the Fourteenth Cycle, lays to rest many false impressions and communicates important aspects of the historical reality of sea-going crime in all of its depredation and barbarity.

For our purposes, it is sufficient to point out that the fundamental nature of piracy changed abruptly with the fall of the Empire. Until then, it had been an enterprise in which the term "cut-throat" might justly apply; with the Imperial Navy always on the watch, pirates had to strike fast and hard and finish their bloody work quickly, thus many of the stories of pre-Interregnum piracy, such as "Song of the Red Wench," and *Hard Onto the Rocks* and *Run for the Dawn*, as well as the popular theatrical production *Lanterns in the Crosstrees* have surprising elements of truth in them, if, indeed, they do not understate the violence and brutality of which these lawless elements, rejecting the submission to authority that is the first requirement of civilized behavior, were capable.

The changes caused by the fall of the Empire were sudden and vast. First, much of what had been the Imperial navy at once turned pirate, and, in many cases, these newcomers were not treated kindly by their old enemies. Elde Island, which had been the abode of pirates unable to find bases on the mainland, was abruptly deserted. Crews were changed, new ships captured and used, old ships abandoned, new ports and hiding places discovered. More significantly, with the pirates now having unfettered control of the seaways, to the point where they were able to prevent the very trade on which they had depended, a new balance between trade and theft, or between organism and parasite, had to be struck, which, though in no case arranged deliberately, seems to have been well in place by the tenth year after the fall of the Empire. The nature of this new balance the reader may deduce by the conversation on the subject in the previous chapter of our history: the various pirate bands both tended to respect discrete areas (although this was by no means complete: the nine-hour battle between the *Lamplighter* and the *Emperor's Arse* is justly legendary), and, more significantly, cooperated with each other within a band, each band working to enforce its own laws and regulations that would permit enough trade along the coast for there to exist something worth robbing and ransoming. Some ships, to be sure, attempted to avoid the pirates by sailing far out into the Ocean-sea, beyond Elde, which was not unsuccessful, but, as we know, carried its own risks with the difficulty of navigation now that there was no longer an Orb.

Thus, peculiarly, with the fall of civilization, piracy, which represented one of the least civilized aspects of society, quickly became more peaceful and more law-abiding than it had been hitherto. What lessons there may be in this fact we must leave to the moralists.

With this understood, we turn our attention to Northport, and then still further north, into the area known as the Fingers (which name they acquired in the Sixth Cycle from an Athyra called Lady Veshika, who created the first truly reliable levitation spell, and thus saw the region from a considerable height and named the area before later cartographers confirmed her vision). Among the Fingers, roughly halfway between Tree-By-The-Sea and the Narrows, is a principality with the fanciful name Mermaid Cove, the traditional home of the Tiassa Heir. It is a region protected from the worst of the storms by tall, grass-covered hills full of goats and squirrels, an area with thick forests, orchards of fruit trees (including the most northern orchards of limes and avocados known anywhere). The sea near-by is full of sea-otters, porpoises, jackfish, and sturgeon, the latter two of which provide a large part of the diet of the locals. Fresh water is found in abundance, both from springs and from the various streams flowing down from the Knuckle Mountains further north, and even from two respectable lakes, one called Rice Lake, named for that oddest of grains known as northrice that grows naturally around it (in addition to various sorts of mushroom), and further inland, Duckling Lake, which was near soybean and scorchroot fields.

The chief town was known as Icolev, and was one of the larger cities (if we may use the word, which has a certain validity by way of comparison, and, moreover, prevents us from repeating the word "town" within a sentence, which sort of recurrence is so often annoying to the ear of the reader) in the sparsely settled north, boasting some six thousand residents, and also something of a trading center.

It was here that, some four years after the fall of the Empire, a certain very large, broad-shouldered pirate known as Captain Sheen anchored his ship. His name, we should add, was given him by his crew as a gesture of affection in honor of the gleam from his carefully shaved head. Upon arriving, he at once determined it would make an ideal base for his crew, and so he established himself there, arranging with certain local Orca for supplies, and with a Jhereg who happened to live there to trade his goods, and with the peasants and free-holders to keep his crew supplied with wine and oishka, both of which were produced in great quantities by all of the locals, who argued incessantly as to the comparative quality of their products.

There are many tales of battles for dominance among pirate captains who wished for control of their base, but nothing like that happened in this case: as word of the base at Icolev spread and other ships drifted in, they found the arrangement so easy and profitable, that no one challenged Captain Sheen, who, for his part, was content to mostly let matters sort themselves out, provided the gold continued to flow into his coffers, which it did in, if not a flood, at least a steady stream. He spent much of his time on his ship, the *Raptor*, even when in harbor, and conducted the business of the base—such as it was—from his great cabin.

One day, several years after he had established this base, just past the noon hour, he received word from the speaking tube that a stranger had come aboard looking for him with a message from Keen. Sheen disentangled himself from his current activity, put on a nightgown (in fact, a red silk robe with gold tracings), and took himself onto the deck. Facing him was a man who was dressed entirely—even to his boots—in pure white. Sheen attempted to guess the man's House, but failed; possibly Yendi or Jhereg, then, though his short, compact build might indicate Iorich, although he lacked the sharp angularity of face. Perhaps Tiassa, to judge by the cheekbones.

The other, who had been giving Sheen the same scrutiny Sheen gave him, bowed and said, "I am called Dust. I have a missive for you from Keen." He removed a folded and sealed paper and handed it over. Sheen accepted it, broke the seal, read it, then said, "Do you know what it says?"

Dust shrugged. "It either says that I am trustworthy, and will be guiding the business arrangements between us from now on, or it says that you are to kill me. I hope the former, for I believe Keen can be useful and I should dislike to have to replace him."

"No," said Sheen, "the former, although he adds that you are dangerous."

Dust shrugged again. "I think you are as well, are you not?"

"Who I? I prefer not to need to be."

Dust nodded. "Don't we all."

"Well, come down to my cabin and we'll talk."

"Very good."

Sheen led the way, startled to suddenly realize that he was nervous having his back exposed to the stranger; he ignored the sensation, entered the cabin, and sat behind his desk; from the practiced way in which Dust ducked coming down the stairs, as well the way he walked and held his right hand—half extended as if about to reach for support should the ship make an unexpected lurch—as he came down the stairs, Sheen determined that he had spent some time aboard ship.

Sheen turned his head and said, "Business." Acilla yawned, rose from the cot, put on a robe, kissed the top of Sheen's head, nodded to Dust, and went up on deck. Sheen automatically followed her with his eyes, then turned back to his guest.

"So then," he said. "You are the new business agent for Northport."

The one called Dust bowed his head in agreement with this statement.

"Do you propose any changes in the arrangements?" Sheen kept his voice carefully neutral during this, but Dust appeared to understand his meaning, to judge by the small quirk of his lip.

"No," he said. "And yes."

"Well," said Sheen, shrugging. "Between the two answers, I nearly think the possibilities have been exhausted."

"I do not propose changes in arrangements between you and me," said Dust. "But I hope to expand my business, and perhaps yours with it."

"Go on," said Sheen. "You perceive, this is the moment when I listen to you. Should there come a time for you to listen to me, I suspect you will know it, and if you do not, well, I will inform you."

"That is right," said Dust. "I wish to involve myself with those in Far Harbor."

"That is a long way," said Sheen. "I don't travel that far south."

"No, but you know some of those who do."

"You think so?"

"It seems likely."

"I know Captain Nosaj. They sometimes call him 'Tooth.'"

"Does he bite?"

"I regret that I am unaware of the origin of the name."

"But, he makes his base in Far Harbor?"

"Yes."

"Then you can introduce us."

"I could."

"You hesitate."

"I reflect."

"You worry?"

"I consider."

"You consider risk."

"And reward."

"They often correspond."

"I do not deny it."

"And then?"

"What are the rewards?"

"Here are some," said the one called Dust. He then emptied a purse onto the desk, revealing five uncut sapphires. Sheen picked them up one at a time and examined them.

"Keep them," said Dust. "They are yours. And there are more."

"I do not deny," said Sheen, holding them in his hand, "that you make a strong argument."

"Well?"

"And yet, you perceive, wealth is not what motivates me."

"I had not thought it was, and yet, do you deny that it makes things easier?"

"Not in the least."

"Therefore?"

"But if, in order to acquire wealth, I must sacrifice my goals, that makes it a bad exchange, does it not?"

"I do not dispute you. So then, let us examine these goals, and we will see if my proposals will aid them or hinder them."

Sheen nodded. "Very well, I agree."

"Then I am listening."

"To begin, I will not bend my knee to anyone, nor will I ask those who sail with me to."

"Even you?"

"Even me. We decide together. I'll do nothing to threaten that."

"I understand, and I even admire it. Next?"

"Next, we must have supplies and shelter."

"You perceive, wealth would make these matters easier."

"I do not deny it."

"Very well. Freedom, a base. What else?"

"Third is safety, which, as you know, is always the third consideration."

"How, safety?"

"Yes, that is to say, I wish to keep my crews alive and healthy and not permit them to be massacred."

"That is but just."

"I am pleased you agree."

"I more than agree, I think I can assure you that assisting me will not work against any of the goals you have done me the honor to outline."

"Well, but, without meaning to give insult—"

"Yes, go on."

"I must assure myself of this circumstance by learning something of what you intend."

Dust appeared to consider this for a moment, then he nodded. "Very well. Something, not everything."

"Tell me what you care to, and then we will see."

"I accept this."

Sheen then listened as Dust outlined his plans, which information we have chosen to withhold from the reader at this time, both in an effort to create a certain suspense (which we are aware some may object to as contrived, but we believe falls within the bounds of the liberty we have granted ourselves in our capacity as entertainer as well as historian), and, moreover, because, as we are required to reveal the details at a later point, to do so now would necessitate describing them twice, which could not but prove annoying.

When Dust had finished his discourse, Sheen considered carefully what he had heard. Then, after due consideration, he said, "Very well, I agree. We sail to-morrow morning, if the wind is fair."

"In that case," said Dust. "I hope the wind is fair."

"We always do," said Sheen.

In the event, the winds were so fair that in less than a month they saw before them the gentle beaches and low houses of Far Harbor. They had arrived without incident not only because of the winds, but because they flew the gray flag with upraised dagger that is known as the symbol of pirates.

They did, indeed, encounter three others, who, not recognizing them, demanded their harbor and chief; but in all cases the response, "Mermaid Cove, and it is I, Sheen," was accepted, particularly when accompanied by the hoots, cat-calls, and obscene gestures that were the accepted means by which pirate crews greeted one another.

This having been done, as we say, they arrived in Far Harbor, and dropped anchor in the sandy bottom some hundred fathoms from shore. Dust, who had handled himself aboard the ship well enough convince Sheen that his impression of the man's seamanship was correct, followed Sheen into the longboat. As they pulled away, Dust said, "Who is it we are to meet?"

"Captain Nosaj."

"What can you tell me of him?"

"He used to be part of a theatrical troop in Wirav."

"An actor?"

"No, everything else. That is to say, he gathered the properties, painted the sets, arranged the lighting, built the stage."

"Ah, well, and that prepared him for piracy?"

"Not in the least. But his troop did a production of *Repel Boarders* and he was required to do the sets and acquire the properties, and, in the course of studying for this, he became so fascinated by the life, that he abandoned his career and joined a pirate crew. He proved to be so skilled in the art of piracy that soon he was elected captain, and eventually came to be the one that everyone came to for counsel and to settle disputes."

"As you do in Mermaid Cove."

"Exactly, though it must be said, where there are eight ships, including my own, that harbor in Mermaid Cover, there are three times that number in Far Harbor."

"Very well, I understand. And you know him?"

"We have had the opportunity to meet, and, moreover, to drink together a certain spirit made on Elde Island from molasses, which, when consumed in the proper quantity, is useful for solidifying an acquaintance-ship and curing melancholy."

"And when used in improper quantities?"

"It will cause fights and lead to the headache."

"I now understand. And, apropos Captain Nosaj, you can introduce me?"

"I can. And, moreover, I can supply a certain amount of the spirit to which I have just alluded to help make the introduction proceed smoothly."

"That is all I need," said Duot, and the longboat continued toward the shore.

And now, with the reader's permission (or, if we are to be honest, without; alas, the reader is, by the very nature of the process of historical exposition, unable to register an effective protest, although we nevertheless express the wish for this permission as an acknowledgment that we are taking a step that the reader may potentially find distasteful, thus indicating our respect for the reader's inclinations), we will turn our attention to a place several hundred miles from where we were, and a time nearly a month later.

The place is one we've seen before: a small village in Zerika's Point known as Wetrock, or more precisely, a certain estate on what was now called Berwick Road, from which the reader may deduce the name of the house, that being Berwick Estate. It has, since the reader first saw it at the beginning of our history, changed little. The astute observer might notice that the northern side has sunk a little into the garden, so that the stalks of cindle now, it being high summer, peek over into the dining room window as if to beg for crumbs and the ivy on that same side has climbed high and made certain small inroads into the wall; the chimney on the west side has developed a long diagonal crack for about half its length; the walkway up to the doors on the south is now covered with grass and weeds, the door itself being boarded shut. Yet other than these few changes, it is much the same.

At the very top of the structure was a door that led up from the master bedroom, and was where Cerwin and Tiscara had been inclined to watch the town and beyond to the Ocean-sea on fine days. This was one custom that Berwick continued, often coming to enjoy the view of his land, his town, his people. It must be said that the last six hundred years of prosperity had been good for him, advancing him with dignity into late middle age, still with all his faculties, with keen eyes, and his wit undimmed. His only son, Yanis, stood next to him on this occasion, as he often did, Berwick dispensing advice, Yanis sometimes listening, sometimes not. Berwick could not, he admitted to himself, always tell.

Must the reader hear of the subjects discussed? We may say that finance provided a good portion of it, how to protect one's capital while taking certain risks with selected portions, how to convince others to shoulder this risk, the proper rate of expansion of commerce, the balance of manufacturing, trade, and land, and so on. If it was said by Clostin that obsession with commerce is the death of fine feeling (and we assure the reader it was, although the context indicates it was meant more metaphorically than literally), then Berwick seemed determined to prove it beyond any doubt.

On this occasion, the subject was marriage—that is to say, Berwick's. His son, Berwick decided, was attempting to prevent the conversation from turning to his own marriage, or advice of other sorts, by striking first, suggesting that the older man find a bride and produce more off-spring. "After all," he said, "I am hardly immortal, father. We live in a world where accidents are possible."

Berwick, as always when his son made such an effort, found himself in that tangle where amusement wars with annoyance, and was groping for a response containing the proper proportions of wit and contempt when he heard footsteps behind him.

"My lord?" said his attendant, Lan.

"Well, what is it, old man?"

"You have a visitor, m'lord."

"A visitor? How? I saw no one."

"He arrived at the front door, my lord."

"The front door? Then, it is a nobleman?"

"After a fashion, m'lord."

"Speak plain, you fool. Is it, or isn't it?"

"It is a Jhereg, my lord."

Berwick frowned. A Jhereg? At this point, Lan handed him a palm-sized card on which was written, in a precise and elegant hand, "The Baron of Magister Valley," and the symbol of the Jhereg. Well, certainly a Jhereg, then. Why? A message from Dorin? But then it would be a liveried messenger. What then, someone wishing to exploit the fall of the Empire to carve into the still lucrative sealstone business he had built with his own hands? If so, the Jhereg would feel the teeth of the orca! He had over a hundred men-at-arms, he had friends among the marauders of the coast, he could call on Dorin, and even, perhaps, Traanzo himself. Let this Jhereg try his oily insinuations!

But no, he told himself. Let us not jump to conclusions. *We will listen to this Jhereg and see what he says, and then, well, we will see.*

He turned to his son and said, "Go downstairs with Lan and be certain this Jhereg is well treated. I will be down shortly."

"Why, father?"

Berwick shook his head and sighed. "The one who makes the other wait shows power. Whatever this Jhereg wants, we must establish that he is the supplicant. Now go."

Berwick remained on the roof for what seemed to him a good length of time, then took himself down to the withdrawing room, where Yanis stood near the door while a stranger in black and gray sat in one of the chairs against the far wall, somehow appearing, in spite of his back being perfectly straight, both feet flat on the floor, and his arms on the armrests, to be entirely relaxed. He rose as Berwick entered and gave a bow that was exactly correct, saying, "My lord Berwick, thank you for agreeing to see me."

Berwick gestured for Yanis to leave; the younger man shrugged and did so, with an insolent shake of his head. Berwick then turned back to the Jhereg and said, "You have wine, I perceive?"

"Yes, and I find it excellent."

"You are a judge of wine, then?"

"I have had the honor to taste a number of vintages, and thus have developed an awareness of what pleases me."

Berwick poured himself a glass, shrugged, and sat down. The other did the same. "Well, it is easy to know what pleases us."

"Is it?" said the Jhereg.

"I seem to know what pleases me, at any rate."

"Do you indeed? Well, so much the better. As I am here in hopes of making arrangements that will please you, it will make it easier for me if you know what that is."

Berwick wasn't certain how, but he had the uncomfortable feeling that the conversation had somehow gotten away from him. "You have business with me then?"

"It may be," said the Jhereg.

"Then please be so good as to state it."

"Since you are kind enough to ask, I will do so, and in terms that leave no room for doubt."

"That is the best way," said Berwick. "Believe me."

"Oh, I believe you entirely. This is it, then. You have made certain arrangements with the, ah, let us call them *sailors* of Far Harbor. I know this because I have also made arrangements with them. Your arrangements involve shipping steel and manganese to the forges in Aussiar and the canal in Candletown. My own—"

"These pirates," said Berwick. "They talk too much."

"Oh, my lord, your pardon. It was not they who told me of this."

"It was not?"

"No, my lord. It was merely observation; watching the loading of ships and wagons, noting their directions."

"Well, go on."

"My own arrangements with these individuals—"

"Pirates."

"As you say, Lord Berwick. My arrangements are of a more directly commercial nature. They supply me with goods for sale, I supply them with what they need. It is beneficial to all concerned."

"Well," said Berwick. "And what has this to do with me?"

"It seemed to me that you could benefit from such commerce."

"You are offering me your business?"

"A part of it."

"How much, and in exchange for what?"

"How much is a seventh part. I promise you, it will be a tolerably round figure."

"And what would you need of me?"

"As of now—nothing."

"Nothing?"

"Almost nothing."

"Do me the honor of telling me of this 'almost nothing.'"

"I have always had a dream."

"A dream, Baron Magister?"

"Please, call me Daifan."

"Very well. A dream, Daifan?"

"A dream, a wish, a desire. Shall I tell you of it?"

"If you wish, I will be glad to hear it."

"This is it, then. Later, when I am old, and rich—for, you perceive, I desire that, when I am old, I shall have wealth to go along with it."

"That is but natural."

"At that time, when I am old, and rich, I would wish above all to find a peaceful, quiet village on the seashore."

"Well, and here it is."

"But there is more."

"I am listening."

"I should like then to live without servants, without pomp, passing my wealth on to any children I might have acquired, and retire to a quiet, peaceful inn or tavern in such a village."

"Ah, in fact, we have one. It is called the Wriggling Dolphin. Or, did you know this?"

"I did, in fact. And I know that, the owner having been unable to meet his debts, because of the loss of custom in the last six hundred years, you have acquired it, opening its doors only occasionally, keeping the old owner on as a paid caretaker."

"You are well-informed."

"My lord, I always try to learn what I can before any business venture."

"Very well. But what of it?"

"I wish it."

"My lord, you must know that its value, if it has any, can be measured in a few imperials."

"So much the better, for you will not feel the loss, especially as I will not want the transfer to take place until you have received the first payment from me, and even then, you will have the right to change your mind about the sale and keep the payment."

"Keep the payment."

"It is a gesture of confidence, my lord. I am so certain that you will be delighted with our new arrangement, that you will want the sale to go through in order to keep the payments coming to you, the more-so as you need do so little to earn them."

"It seems to me, Baron Magister, that you are being extraordinarily generous."

"It is not generosity, my lord Berwick, it is self-interest."

"I fail to understand what it is you do me the honor to tell me."

"Then I will explain."

"I am anxious for you to do so."

"I have studied you, my lord Berwick."

"Studied me?"

"Indeed. Moreover, I admire you."

"Well."

"I learned how you came into possession of this wealth you now enjoy, and of the various combinations you have employed. Someone able to pull off such a coup is someone with whom I wish to ally myself, and so I have chosen to begin this alliance by showing my generosity."

Berwick stared at him hard. "You say begin, but what will then follow?"

"As to that, who can say? It may be that at some future time you will be able to be useful to me. When that day comes, I will speak with you, and we will expand our business relationship. I cannot know what that arrangement might be; you perceive, without the Empire, everything changes so quickly. But this is a time when opportunities may appear at any moment, and when such an opportunity arises, I wish to be ready."

"You have a head for business like an Orca," said Berwick.

"I cannot express the pleasure this compliment gives me."

Berwick bowed. "Will there be papers to sign?"

"Only the transfer of the Wriggling Dolphin, which I will have drawn up and sent to you for your signature and witnessing along with my first payment. Other than that, there will be no papers. I will merely see that your portion is delivered to you every quarter."

"Then it seems that you have come here, not with a business proposal, but with a gift."

"It may seem that way, my lord."

"Well?"

"I give you my word, I am engaging in this for my own benefit."

"Then I believe you."

"And you are right to."

"Well, I accept your offer."

"I am gratified that you have done so."

"May I convince you to stay for dinner?"

"Thank you, no, my lord. I am otherwise engaged."

"Then I bid you farewell, Lord Daifan."

"Farewell to you, Lord Berwick."

Once Lan had shown the Jhereg out, Berwick sat for some moments considering the matter, then called for his son.

"Yes, father?"

"The Jhereg who was here, his name is Daifan, Baron of Magister Valley."

"Well?"

"He has made a business proposal that sounds to be very profitable, and yet—"

"Well, and yet?"

"I wish to know more of him. See what you can learn."

"I will do so at once."

Chapter the Twenty-sixth

In Which Livosha and Kefaan Attempt to Reach Northport

There were, at the time of which we have the honor to write, four methods of arranging transport by water along the coast. The first method was the simplest: one might find a ship that had a full load of cargo and was going in the desired direction, and either pay or work for passage. Second, one might, if one were sufficiently wealthy, hire such a vessel. Third, one might convince a fisherman that such a journey was worth the risk, as pirates habitually ignored fishermen, or sometimes even purchased from them, unless the pirate had had such hard luck as to be prepared to prey on anything afloat. Last, of course, if one had certain skills as a sailor, one might steal a boat.

This last method, we must say, Livosha rejected out of hand, as, having had a certain experience with being the victim of boat theft, she was naturally unwilling to inflict such suffering on another. While it can sometimes be the case that the victim of a particular crime, in anger and despair, will justify perpetrating the same crime on others, we insist that it is also the case that, in many, that peculiar quality called *empathy*, in which we, by a sort of inner transference, feel what another is feeling, or at least what we imagine another is feeling, will provide a sort of moral constraint or compulsion that will make such an act abhorrent. That Livosha was such a one is proved by the fact that the idea of stealing a boat never so much as occurred to her. Of the other methods, those that required a supply of money were, of course, impossible; the wages they received from Traanzo being sufficient, as the saying is, "to keep the sky off one's head," but hardly enough to pay for passage in these times when passage money must necessarily include a portion of the cost—either in ransom or in risk of loss—that might be incurred by encountering pirates.

This left them with the need to work for their passage, which, thanks to the experience of the last six hundred years, was not as abhorrent a concept as it so often is to those who, though once high-born, find themselves unexpectedly cast low. Those like the Teckla who are born to toil, and those who like the Dragon, the Lyorn, and the Athyra in our own happy age need never give such matters consideration, can never understand the difficulty of those whom circumstance brings to such an unexpected pass. Indeed, it is exactly here—in this lack of understanding and the remedy thereof—that the true value of the art of history and the science of history join together in common cause: for is it not the case that the highest goal of both is in the transformation, in exactly such a manner as to permit one to enter into the life of another? While a clearer understanding of the motions of history is of course, desirable, and while a pleasurable experience on the part of the reader is a necessary precondition for the reader to continue "turning the pages" as is said by the lettered, yet when they come together, it is possible for the reader, to partake of the experience of another. There are, to be sure, many other benefits: it has been suggested by some that merely accidental coincidence of cosmetic similarity between a particular reader and a certain historical character will provide a valuable point of identification that can be inspiriting to that reader. That this happens cannot be denied, any more than can the pleasure it gives the reader, and, should he hear about it, the author, when it happens to occur. And yet, underneath (or, perhaps *above*) such matters, we find that, regardless of secondary questions of appearance, what provides the most value is for a reader to enter fully into the thought processes of those figures from history who view matters in a way, and have had experiences that, are so far removed from those of the reader, that, without the intervention of the author, the artist, the historian, the scholar, no comprehension between them would be possible. Thus, the creation of empathy, the sharing of experience, moving beyond secondary issues of geography, of House, or even of Time, can provide us a deep, fundamental connection that could exist in no other way. When combined, then, with what this author believes is the other task of the historian, that being to expose truth that, though part of our experience, and even vital to it, nevertheless normally lies hidden within the complexities of life, we have laid out before us the highest goal of those who dare to lay the fruits of their artistic labor before the eye of the public.

We must now observe to the reader that, among these virtues of the greatest works of art and history, virtues for which we must all strive in our own way and with the abilities we have learned and the talent we have been granted by the beneficent gods, certain things never appear. Among these are the humiliating scramble after critical acclaim, the craving for high position within the academy, the disgraceful groveling after public applause, and the pusillanimous sacrificing of truth upon the altar of common prejudice. Should an otherwise honest and beneficent institution fall into the error of advancing to distinguished position one who openly strives for those very goals that ought never to be listed among the desired ambitions, we can only hope that, in time, such an institution will come to a better awareness of its duties and obligations, and more, we must as well as possible help it, in our small way, by appeals to the finer sensibilities of its guides, to come to such an understanding.

Livosha, then, as we have said, was perfectly willing to work for her passage, as was her brother. This willingness, while opening the possibilities, did not actually go so far as to secure the needed transport. The two of them, therefore, addressed this problem in the most direct way: they went down the long white stairway leading to the harbor, and began asking after any ships that were soon to depart for the west and might need additional hands. They discovered the problem with this plan nearly at once: they met a ship captain, a weathered-looking woman of the House of the Orca with a long scar above her eye, who listened to them, and then said simply, "Show me your hands." When they had done so, she said, "No."

They walked off and Kefaan said, "Perhaps we will meet a captain who won't think to look at our hands."

"Do you think that's likely?"

"It is possible," said Kefaan.

"How possible?"

"Not very," admitted her brother.

"Then we are agreed, for that is my opinion as well."

"Well, what then? Between us we have five imperials; once that would have bought us a berth, but, alas, no more."

"Then we must discover a different plan."

"Very well, I agree. But, what plan can we discover?"

"Let us reflect."

"I agree with reflecting."

"I will reflect as well."

"Upon what will you reflect, Livosha?"

"Upon how to find a ship or a boat that will take us west. And you?"

"I am reflecting on purchasing horses."

"It is a long way on horseback."

"But we will get there."

"There are bandits."

"But no pirates."

"Also, it may be harder to get out of the city."

"Harder, but possible."

"Also—"

"Well?"

"That stairway."

"That is true," said Kefaan. "Climbing those stairs again, well, the idea is daunting."

"I am fatigued merely considering it."

"And yet, we must escape the city. Traanzo will be looking for us."

"Well, then I must make my last throw."

"My sister, I do not like the sound of that."

"There is nothing else to do."

She returned to the scarred captain with whom she had just spoken, and, removing the pendant from her neck, held it out. "Will this pay for our journey to Northport?"

The captain took it, studied the rubies, ran gnarled fingers over the inlay work, and said, "It will, and a cabin of your own and good meals besides."

"Then we are agreed."

"We sail in two hours."

"With your permission, my brother and I will board now."

"So you are not seen by whoever is looking for you?"

Livosha started to speak, but the captain waved her hand. "Never mind, I'll not require you to lie to me, it is of no importance." Then she waved again, this time getting the attention of a man who seemed to be a male version of herself and was taking his ease on a pile of damaged fishing nets. Once the other nodded, the captain held up two fingers, pointed to Livosha and Kefaan, and then to the ship. The two Iorich then (for Kefaan had changed his garb, and no longer seemed to be a Jhereg) took their satchels and followed him onto the ship, and so below decks where they would not be seen. An hour later, they were settled into a cabin, nervously hoping they'd be under way before Traanzo started looking, or at least before he had the ships inspected. It was, to be sure, a long hour that followed, but at the end were the squeaks of wood and shouting of orders and tramping of feet and clanking of chains, and they felt the ship gather way and begin the long journey down the Funnel (as it was known in those days) and out into the open sea.

With Livosha and Kefaan, if not safe, at least having escaped the more immediate danger, permit us to say two words about the ship that was, they hoped, conveying them to safety. The *Hartre's Kiss* as she was called was of the type known officially—that is to say, by the shipyard—as the White Harbor Sweeper, but unofficially as the Bucking Crate, that is to say, a two-masted, square-rigged ship, one sail on the foremast, two on the mainmast, designed to carry as much freight as possible and as few hands as possible, resulting in an unweatherly, cranky ship with a wide beam and a deep hold and, as her crews often said, "A nose like a bloodhound for a lee shore." Or, as they also said, "What she lacks in speed she makes up in bulkiness."

Still, the size of the hold did permit a great deal to be carried at once, and, moreover, she was comfortable far out from land, both of which were advantageous to her owners, the former because, if she got through without encountering pirates, they stood to make a small fortune with each trip, and, second, because the further from land, the less chance there was of encountering the water-borne marauders. With this, and the winds they encountered once clear of the Funnel, they had, after thirty-four days, gone south of Elde and west of Greenaere, and were heading northward toward the mainland.

It was at this point that, in the cabin where they were spending most of their time so as to avoid getting in the way of the crew, that they suddenly heard the stamping of feet, and the ship heeled alarmingly, which would have caused Kefaan to spill his wine had not Livosha saved it with a quick grasp. Livosha handed it back and said, "This could be trouble."

"The weather seems fair."

"I agree. It is not the weather."

"The crew appear competent and the captain skilled."

"So it is not an error by the crew or the captain."

"Therefore?"

"Pirates?"

"So I would guess, sister. And also hope."

"Hope?"

"Better pirates than Prince Traanzo having gone to such lengths to find us."

"That is true."

"Shall we, then, go on deck and offer our assistance?"

"Let us first arm ourselves."

"I agree with this plan."

They found their swords still where they had stowed them, strapped them on, and climbed onto deck, where the situation was instantly clear from the sailors, though attending to business, all looking off the starboard beam (we should explain that starboard is a nautical term that means the right-hand side of a ship when facing forward. Its opposite, larboard, re-fers, obviously, to the right-hand side of a ship when facing backward). Following this gaze, then, they could clearly see a ship, close enough to tell that it had two masts, and was fore-and-aft rigged; this was, in the opinion of Livosha, too close.

They found the first mate, the same fellow who had first conducted them on board, who was busy directing the sails be adjusted to attempt to get a little more speed. In between orders, Livosha said, "Where would you like us?"

"Below," he said, without turning around.

"We can fight."

"In fact," said Kefaan, "it would be more precise to say *she* can fight. Nevertheless, I do have a weapon."

The mate spared them a glance, grunted, and said, "They'll be board-ing us on the larboard side aft. Find a place between there and the main-mast, that's where they'll press us."

"The larboard side? And yet, they are coming up on the starboard side."

"Well," said the mate, who evidently was not inclined to explain.

"Do they kill everyone?" said Kefaan. "I ask, you perceive, only out of a certain unimportant curiosity."

"Some do, some don't. Some only do if you annoy them." He looked out at the approaching ship, now, it seemed to Livosha, noticeably closer than it had been. "I intend to annoy them," said the mate.

"And yet," said Kefaan, "I was told they accept ransom."

"They do, most of them."

"Well, and?"

He shrugged. "Our owner doesn't choose to pay ransom. He considers it beneath him."

"Ah, well. And where is he?"

"Adrilankha."

"That is but natural," said Kefaan. "But isn't it a poor business deci-sion?"

"Perhaps. And yet, we have made nine journeys to Northport and nine back without incident."

"Nothing lasts forever."

"That is true," said the mate. "If the Orb does not, what can?"

Gradually, the pirate ship came closer, until Livosha was able to see the flag, gray with upturned dagger. "What is that in front of it?" she asked.

"A ram," said the mate, who was now methodically, and with no sign of distress, directing the crew to defensive positions, save for those who remained aloft or ready to haul on a rope.

"A ram? But, correct me if I'm wrong, if they strike us with the ram, will we not sink?"

"It is almost a certainty."

"Well, but, if we sink, will they not be unable to retrieve the cargo?"

"Oh, no. A ram that size will not tear such a large hole. They will almost certainly have an hour or two to transfer the cargo."

"Ah, I see. And will the captain prevent them from ramming us?"

"She means to. If the *Kiss* were a little more nimble, I'd put odds on her, she knows some tricks. But as it is, well, we shall see."

As the ships came closer, Livosha felt herself grow at once more tense and less tense, an odd feeling that she could not recall having experienced before. It was, she thought, a result of impending danger, which she had also not experienced before; the danger she had encountered in the past occurring suddenly. *How odd it would be,* she thought, *to discover myself skilled in facing a surprise attack, yet unable to face an attack I knew was coming.* And yet, though observing herself as if she were a stranger, she did not believe she would have this problem; her hands felt light, her feet seemed attached to the deck, her mind was clear, and her eyes sharp.

Quite suddenly, there was crisp word of command from the captain, and the crew, that is to say, those who were not standing ready to defend against the boarders, sprang into action. Even Livosha, with all of her experience on the western coast, could not follow the rapidly unfolding events as the ship heeled, seemed about to turn in one direction, then, in a way that no ship ought to be able to do, especially one as unwieldy as the *Hartre's Kiss*, she came about the other way, and she was suddenly next to the pirate ship, then they touched, the pirate's ram making a sound like a wounded darr as it scored the side of the *Kiss*, but failed to penetrate.

The pirates, wearing all the colors of all the Houses, and (as the saying is) "a few for the future," leapt aboard, their weapons as numerous as their colors, shouting and yelling and making all manner of sounds that had nothing in common except volume and the quality of fear they inspired.

Livosha was busy, then. She had fought before, but never been in anything that could be called a battle, in which she was pushed and jostled a thousand times in a thousand directions, in which by the time she had determined if the person before her was friend or foe that person's face was gone, another face or back or axe or foot in its place. She was never after able to recall most of it, nor guess how long it went on, but suddenly she found herself and few others in the center of a ring of enemies, bodies moaning on the deck, a few of them not moving. She looked for Kefaan, and found him not far from her, on one knee, holding his arm with blood leaking through his fingers. He caught her eye and winked at her.

One of the pirates, who seemed to be in charge, said, "Lay down your weapons and we will spare your lives."

There were the sounds of swords and axes falling to the deck. A moment later the pirate looked at Livosha and said, "Well?"

"Bah," she said. "I am uncertain if I wish my life spared."

"That is up to you," he said. He was a squat, bandy-legged man holding an odd, long blade with a backward curve of a type Livosha had never seen before. "But, you perceive, I do mean it about sparing your life."

"Well, that is good, and yet, spare it for what?"

"Why, whatever you wish. We will relieve you of your cargo and send you on your way, and even supply a letter saying that you had received us as your guests, which will prevent any further trouble from our friends."

"And yet—"

"Well?"

"I like this sword, having had it for so long. I should hate to give it up."

"You perceive, if you attack us with it, you will die, and then someone will take your sword just the same."

"You make a good argument."

"And then?"

Livosha sighed. "Very well, then." She dropped her sword and shrugged, then went over to see to her brother who, at that moment, fell over onto his face. With a cry, she turned him over, and saw that not only had he the wound in his arm, but also a gash low on his abdomen, and he was very pale.

She looked around to see if anyone might assist her, but there were too many wounded. She did what she could, however, tearing clothing off dead men and attempting to slow the bleeding. Sometime later, perhaps an hour, perhaps two, she felt someone standing over her. She turned, and it was the pirate captain, looking concerned. "Who is it?" he asked.

"My brother."

"He needs attention."

"Indeed he does."

"I have a physicker on my ship, and, moreover, we are only a day's sail from our harbor, whereas this ship, wherever she may go, will be days."

"And then?"

"If you wish, I will arrange transport for you and your brother to our port, and do what we can to help him."

"And, in exchange for this?"

"You fought well to-day. You wounded at least four of my men, and one of them may not recover."

"Well?"

"Would you like your sword back?"

Livosha felt her eyes narrow, and waited. At length the other said, "Have you ever considered piracy? I would like you to join my crew. I can promise good accommodation, wealth, and above all, freedom. Moreover, of course, we will do all we can for your brother."

Livosha looked at her brother, pale and still bleeding. She was aware of her hand trembling. He opened his eyes at that moment, and silently mouthed the word, "No."

"But my brother—"

He coughed and managed to whisper, "You know you cannot. If you do, who are you? And who am I?" Then he shuddered. The rise and fall of his chest continued, but seemed slower and more labored.

Livosha rose and looked at the pirate. "Your name, sir?"

"I am called Nosaj. And you, madam?"

"I am Livosha, and I fear I must decline your offer. I am an Iorich, and, as my brother has done the honor to remind me, I must remain one. You perceive, to rob and steal and kill for money those who have done me no harm, well, I confess I am more likely to seek you out than to join you."

Nosaj sighed. "Well, I understand. It is a shame, however. You'd have made a good pirate. Apropos, if you choose to come looking for me, well, I am easily found. My port is Far Harbor, and I will do my best to entertain you, although you will understand if, for the moment, I do not return you your sword."

"I'll find another."

"I do not doubt that you will."

There was then the sound of a new voice, cutting into the conversation. "I think, my dear Nosaj, that you are incorrect. On the contrary, as these are the very two for whom I have paid you, I believe that, by our agreement, you will return her sword, and, moreover, bring her brother to your base, all without extracting a promise of any kind."

These words were said in a low tone that could be best described as conversational, yet had, at the same time, an air of authority that could not be denied. Livosha looked up in curiosity, and saw a figure dressed in the colors of the Jhereg. She next observed that she, herself, was the object of the Jhereg's scrutiny. She studied his countenance, then, and, without being aware of making any decision to move, she found herself on her feet, staring.

"Eremit!" she cried.

"Well," said the Jhereg.

Chapter the Twenty-seventh

In Which Dust, Livosha, Alishka, and the Author Discuss Vengeance

L ivosha stared, her mouth open; her feet seemed to be veritably frozen to the deck, and she was most keenly aware of the pounding of her heart. Eremit gazed back at her with something of a smile playing about his lips, and then he abruptly turned to Nosaj. "Well?" he said.

"This is part of the payment to you?"

"Let it be all of the payment."

"As you say, then" said the pirate, bowing to the Jhereg. "Return her sword, and some of you help bring this man aboard the *Cat*. I warn you I will take a piece of skin the size of an orb for each bounce or jostle. Smooth and handsome, now. That is right."

Livosha accepted her sword without being aware who had handed it to her, still staring at the man in Jhereg colors. "Eremit!" she said at last. "How came you here? Are you now a Jhereg? A pirate?"

"I am many things at once," he said. "But come, let us go aboard the *Creeping Cat*, where we can attend to your brother. Apropos, have you anything to take from the ship?"

She shook her head. "I have my sword, nothing else matters."

"Then let us be on our way."

"Yes, of course," she said, still too astounded to do more than follow the pirates onto their ship. Once aboard, as the crew was separating the two ships that had been lashed together with thick rope, she went down to where a woman she didn't recognize was examining Kefaan and cleaning his wounds. Livosha was about to ask what she could do when the woman opened up a cupboard and began removing bandages—clean linen bandages, Livosha noted. She began laying them out next to her brother. She said, "Tell me, is he—"

"Hush," said the physicker.

Livosha nodded and began to assist. Kefaan seemed unconscious, although he did moan softly when the physicker sewed up his wounds. When he was bandaged, the physicker supported his head and forced some sort of dark, thick liquid into his mouth, rubbing his throat like a baby's until he swallowed it. "There," she said. "He will sleep now."

"Will he—"

"I don't know. He is strong. He lost a great deal of blood, but nothing vital was punctured. We will have to wait and see."

Two pirates came in, then, and moved him, while others brought in another, who had been pierced in the neck. Livosha thought she recognized him, and wondered if she'd been the one to do it. Unsure of what else to do, she remained and assisted. She continued doing so as others came in. The most difficult case was one whose foot had been caught between ships and had to be amputated. Livosha and Eremit helped hold him down, though Livosha kept her eyes closed during the procedure.

At length, after the last patient had been seen, Dust showed Livosha to an area just abaft the captain's quarters that had been quickly turned into a cabin just big enough for a cot for her brother and a hammock for her.

"Eremit, we must talk. I have a thousand questions."

"Sleep now, you are exhausted. We will talk to-morrow."

Livosha wanted to protest, but she suddenly felt her eyes closing on their own, and nodded. She climbed into the hammock and was asleep before she knew it.

She was awoken by the familiar sounds of a ship dropping anchor and sails being taken in. At first she was bleary, but then she remembered, first her brother, and then Eremit, and was instantly awake.

Her brother still seemed pale, and there was an unhealthy haggard look to him. As she stood over him, wondering if she should find him some water, two crewmen came up and announced that he was to go on the first boat to shore, and did she wish to go? She did, and as they put him on a piece of bulkhead and carried him to deck, she was behind them, and then accompanied her brother onto the boat, watching closely to see he wasn't jostled.

She hardly noticed the village, although, in truth, there was little enough to notice beyond the vast expanse of beach and the oddly low houses, which had been constructed in that fashion by the Vallista Lady Dymbra in the Seventh Cycle, so that all of the hovels, cottages, houses, and manors had a view of the bay, which she believed everyone would find as enchanting as she did. How many did or did not share this opinion lies outside the scope of our history, for which we need only observe that Livosha paid it no attention.

Her brother was brought to one of the small cottages and set on a soft bed, while lamps were lit and another physicker, a man, looked him over carefully, removing the bandages and inspecting the stitching. At length he grunted and prepared a poultice. He applied it to Kefaan's wounds, then looked up at Livosha and grunted. "Husband?"

"Brother."

He nodded. "He should do well enough."

She nodded and reached into her purse.

"No, no," he said. "We work together here. I patch them up, the others tear them apart, and we split the gold. It is a most beneficial system."

"Well, I thank you for your skill."

She bowed and left the cottage, then, once outside, leaned against it, closing her eyes.

"My lady Livosha."

She opened her eyes again. "Eremit."

"I no longer go by that name."

"What then?"

"I have a number of others. Most call me Dust."

"Dust. Why that name?"

"Perhaps because I make people feel unclean. But come, let us find a place to sit. It has been, well, it has been a long time."

"I cannot dispute this intelligence you do me the honor to share."

"Then here, these chairs serve us as an open-air inn, although we must fetch our own refreshment. Do you still drink wine, preferring the full reds?"

"Your memory is without peer, my friend."

"I have trained it."

He went into a nearby cottage, emerging with cups and bottles. He poured wine from one bottle that he had somehow already opened and sat down across from her.

"Livosha," he said.

"That is still my name, though I used another for a time."

"Yes. Nedyrc."

"You knew?" she stared at him.

"You took the name of my house and reversed it."

"But how did you know?"

"I have many friends, and they have eyes."

"But if you knew where I was—"

"Well?"

"Why didn't you find me? Cracks and shards, did you not know how hard I was seeking you?"

"I did."

"Well?"

"Each day there was a chance of you being recognized, of Kefaan being recognized. Were I with you, it would have put you at too great a risk."

"You think I cannot determine what risk I wish to take?"

"It is all the same risk. If you fall, I fall. I am not willing to take a needless risk that might cause you and your brother to fall."

Livosha fell silent for a moment, her head spinning, trying to decide what to ask. "When did you find out where I was?"

"I had been watching Traanzo for some time. It was there I found you, shortly after you began working for him. And may I say—"

"Well?"

"That was well done. You have almost certainly learned things I have not."

"That is possible. I learned, for example, every name of everyone who had been incarcerated on Burning Island."

"How, you did?"

"Many things I memorized, but that list I copied, and I keep it with me in hopes—"

"Well?"

"In hopes that someday the Empire will be restored, and it will be used to get justice for you, and for the others. There was one called Kelsama who helped us. Perhaps she is dead."

"Helped you?"

"In our escape."

"Escape?"

"Did you know we tried to rescue you?"

"From the island?"

She nodded.

"I did not. When?"

"The day you escaped. We borrowed a boat and sailed out to release you."

For the first time, an expression of astonishment came over his countenance. "The day I escaped? That is to say, the day the Empire fell? And the day the prisoners got free?"

"Yes, well, we did that too."

"Shards! So then, the boat on which I escaped—"

"Yes, that was the one we brought."

"My dear Livosha—"

"Think nothing of it, my friend. After all, we brought the boat with the intention of rescuing you, and, well, that is exactly the use to which it was put."

"And yet—"

"Besides, as you returned it intact, it was then able to rescue us in turn."

"And was it able to navigate itself?"

"No, but for that, there was help."

"It is always good to have help."

"Eremit—that is to say, Dust—"

"Well?"

"What happened to you?"

Dust looked away. "Don't you know?"

"You were imprisoned, and somehow you summoned a demon, even after the Empire had fallen."

"I met a man in jail who trained me in such arts."

"And the demon transported you."

"Yes, to a place where I could recover, and where I had the peace to practice what I had learned while in jail, and where, moreover, there was plentiful supply of uncut sapphires, which I could turn into money, which has proven very useful."

"Where is this place?"

"Far from here, my dear Livosha. On another world."

"So, you are able to travel to another world?"

"With help."

"From the demon?"

"He has been very helpful. More wine?"

"If you would."

"There it is."

"Thank you. What you have been doing?"

"The same as you: I have been preparing vengeance against our enemies."

Livosha nodded. "Then we should discuss what we have learned."

"Yes. And, we should discuss other things."

She looked at him, at the sunken hollows of his eyes, the pout of his lips, his disheveled hair, and, once more, at his eyes. "No, my dear Dust, there is nothing else to discuss. Eremit has gone away, and Dust has returned. An Iorich is gone, before me is a Jhereg. Perhaps, when we have done what we must, there will be other things to discuss. But not now."

Dust bowed his head.

"Eremit?"

"Well?"

"Do you remember when we watched the Furnace sink into the ocean?"

"Livosha, there were days in my cell when I remembered nothing else, not even my name."

Livosha reached over and took his hand. "Come, my friend. Drink more wine, we must exchange information, then make plans."

Dust nodded. "Forgive me, Livosha. I have not asked: how fares your brother?"

"We will see. I am hopeful."

He nodded. "Tell me, then, how did you escape from the attack on your home?"

"You wish to know that? Then I will tell you."

She explained about the tunnel, and about Riffetra, and the treachery of Gystralan, and of Lady Ficora. He listened carefully, his eyes fixed on her, taking in every word. When she had finished, he said, "Well, I compliment you on your escape."

"As you perceive, I had help."

"And now that we are together, you have more."

"And so?"

"Shall we destroy our enemies?"

"Oh, certainly."

"Then let us make plans."

"I think plans are necessary. Berwick has four score of men-at-arms, and Dorin ten times that number."

"I am aware of this circumstance. Whatever we contrive, we will not be able to assault Dorindom. You perceive, we lack an army."

"I know a forger. Can we entice Dorin out of his castle?"

Dust considered. "Forgeries can be detected. I am loath to depend entirely on one with the knowledge that, should it fail, our quarry will escape us."

"With this I agree. Can we count on the pirates to assist us?"

"We can count on a pirate captain named Sheen, but his band is small."

"And Captain Nosaj?"

"If he is to assist us, he must have a reason."

"Wealth?"

"He, like Sheen, is less driven by wealth than by other matters. I have convinced him to let us use his base as our sanctuary, and a certain number of sapphires sufficed to arrange for the freedom of you and your brother, but to risk his crew will require a greater inducement."

"What then?"

"I believe," said Dust, "that I have an idea for how to enlist his help."

"Very good. But, what of Dorin?"

"That will be difficult. It may be that his weakness is Traanzo."

"And yet, Traanzo has even more forces at his disposal than Dorin."

"Yes, but he also has a weakness. He is in Adrilankha, which still has, thanks to the Countess of Whitecrest, laws."

Livosha frowned. "Can we exploit those laws against Traanzo? I must observe that the creation of the jail on Burning Island was a crime against the Empire, not the county, and Whitecrest has no authority."

"That is true."

"And then?"

"It will not be easy," said Dust. "And it will take considerable time to prepare—that is to say, at least several years."

"Then let us begin," said Livosha. "We require a plan. And, I give you my word, it must be a good one."

"Then let us consider the matter."

It seems unlikely that, by now, the reader is unaware that our history concerns itself, above all, with revenge—that is to say, with the infliction of harm done for a wrong suffered. This work, of course, is far from the only one to treat of such matters; indeed, revenge has been a theme of history, of literature, of art, of the theater, as long as these have existed, and has been a subject of inquiry at least as far back as Ekrasan's Third Discourse. And in all of these works, the condemnation has been quite nearly universal.

Why? The reasons are many and nearly as diverse as the motives for revenge. It damages the soul, say the mystics. It threatens the respect for authority that is required for society to function, say the civicists. It too easily leads to abuse, say the moralists. It inspires further and unending revenge, say the fatalists. It is the proper domain of the Lords of Judgment, say the pious. It is a waste of one's own life, say the humanitarians. And so on.

And yet, reply the historians, and yet, it is always present. In art, from the mighty sculpture by the unknown artist called the Hammer of Bre'in (lost, alas, in the Fall of the City), to Rahera's epic poem, *Homecoming of Sitrata*, to the nine-day play *The Fall of Nileesitac*, nothing stirs the blood like a tale of one who was wronged, standing up and, with his own hands, taking justice as if in defiance of the gods. However often we are told of the evils of vengeance (sometimes in the very tale, be it understood, that we are enjoying for the vengeance it purports to condemn), still, we return to this form of tale more often than any other, save perhaps the love story.

This historian has no intention of adding to the mountain of critical studies condemning the tale of revenge, nor, for that matter, any interest in defending such tales; as we are now writing history, it would seem that expressing our own approbation or disapprobation as to the actions of these historical figures would be to take onto ourselves that task of judgment and evaluation that properly belongs to the reader. Rather, it is our wish to take a brief moment to ask what it is in such tales that appeals so strongly. Why do we return over and over to this sort of tale to such a point that it is necessary to expound against them at such length?

In the opinion of this historian, it is the very unfairness of life that generates the appeal. It is not only the sense of helplessness that oppresses us, but the sense that, as good people (for, as Magister pointed out early in our history, we all believe that we are good people), we deserve better, we deserve not to have to suffer the ill-fortune caused by fate, or by the hand of another who disregards us in pursuit of selfish interests (for although, as we have said, we all believe in our own goodness, we are not so sanguine about the goodness of others).

Even this historian, when faced with a palpable injustice caused by malicious and slanderous gossip, has felt a desire rise in him to seek vengeance, not for himself, but for the innocent young lady whose sensibilities have been so callously disregarded. Of course, we do not pursue these goals, contenting ourselves merely with the occasional letter in hopes to bring a small gleam of the light of justice into the darkness of self-interest.

We hope the reader has not objected to this digression, which we have engaged in for what seemed to us two good reasons: first, because we wish the reader to consider these matters as our history works its way toward its climactic moments, and, second, because we are now required to see matters through, as it were, a different pair of eyes, and, as we have already had the honor to mention at an earlier moment, such an abrupt transition can be disturbing, and cost the reader that enjoyable sensation of immersion, in which the experiences being related feel as if they are a part of the reader's own experience, and it is our wish to permit this to continue as long as possible, and thus we have elected to separate this transition in order to prevent the reader from being forced into awareness of narrative, rather than, as both author and reader prefer, the *contents* of the narrative. With this understood, we now continue.

Alishka spotted Dust seated at a table outside of the wine-house along with a stranger who, from what she could see, was a not-unattractive young woman of some seven or eight hundred years. Seeing this, Alishka hesitated for a moment, but Dust saw her and signaled her over, standing up as he did so. The woman he was with also stood up, turned, and seemed about to bow when her eyes suddenly widened as if in recognition. At the same moment Alishka, who had thought the woman familiar looking, suddenly remembered where she had seen her before.

"You!" they both cried as with one voice.

"Ah, then, you have met?" said Dust with an ingenuous air.

"Nearly," said Livosha. "We traced you to her camp, after the island."

"Yes," said Alishka. "She and another Iorich were chasing you for the jailers."

"Not for the jailers," said the stranger.

"Then why?"

"To rescue him."

"How, rescue him? And yet, he was already rescued."

The Iorich looked at her with an expression of bewilderment, as if at a loss to explain. Dust said, "Come, Alishka. Get a cup and have some wine."

When she returned, and Dust had poured her some wine, he said, "So, it would seem some explanations are required."

"I admit," said the woman, "to some curiosity."

"I share this with you," said Alishka.

"Well then, to begin, Alishka, this is Livosha, my friend, and, indeed, betrothed from when I was young and happy and foolish, and this, Livosha, is Alishka, a friend whom I acquired when I was older and grimmer and perhaps a little wiser. I beg you to be friends, as we will, I hope, be working together."

"Working together?" said Livosha, just as Alishka had been about to.

"So I hope."

"But," said Alishka, "in what capacity?"

"Well," said Dust, "Livosha and I were just making certain plans."

"Do these plans include me?"

"They could," said Dust. "If you wish them to, and if Livosha is agreeable."

"But," said Livosha, "if I may ask without giving offense, what does she bring with her that will assist us?"

Dust smiled. "A small but very loyal band who all have certain skills acquired on the road. Although, it must be said, one of them speaks too much when drinking."

Alishka felt herself frowning. "What is this?"

"Kitescu," said Dust. "Permitted himself to become intoxicated, and answered questions put to him by an agent of one Hadrice, who works for a certain Dorin. Apropos, should you meet Hadrice on the street, let her pass; she is no one to be trifled with, I give you my word."

"Well, I will have words with Kitescu."

"And I," said Livosha grimly, "will have words with Hadrice."

Dust nodded.

"So then," said Livosha, "these plans. How does Alishka fit in?"

"As to that," said Dust, "it is up to you, of course, whether we choose to use her talents, but I will tell you what I had envisioned."

"I am listening," said Livosha.

"You were betrothed?" said Alishka.

The other two turned and looked at her, and she felt herself flushing a little. "It is just that, well, she is Iorich."

"So was I, at one time," said Dust.

"At one time? Then, did the House expel you?"

Dust frowned and considered. "In fact," he said, "it would be more precise to say that I expelled them. That is to say, I became aware of certain activities carried out by some of them, and chose not to associate myself with them anymore."

"And so," said Livosha, "you became a Jhereg?"

Dust shrugged. "I became many things."

Alishka looked back and forth from one of them to the other, wondering at what was unspoken between them, but concluded that it was not her affair.

After a moment, they returned to discussing their plans, plans which, we assure the reader, will not be long in being revealed, as putting them into practice began the very next day, when the three of them set off in three different directions to begin the preparations.

Vokra of Mudrun came home from drinking with friends at the Sailing Muffin in White Harbor. He had not overindulged that evening—he rarely did—so other than a certain artificial cheerfulness, he had all of his faculties about him. He closed the door, hung his sword on its peg next to the Kinship Blade, lit the lantern, and closed the door. He set the lantern down in the kitchen and worked the pump, pouring himself a cup of water to wash the taste of dust out of his mouth—the last few weeks had been unusually dry for a seaport, and those who take pleasure in making dire predictions predicted that at last with the fall of the Empire, the good weather it had produced would now vanish to the ruin of all. It is, we should add, only natural that, with any cataclysmic event, there are some who will assign it to impossible causes, others who will propound impossible effects, and some who will do both. While Vokra gave such predictions no more attention than they deserved, he nevertheless drank water to relieve the dryness of his throat.

"Good evening, Vokra."

He turned quickly, his hand automatically reaching for a weapon.

"There is no call for that, Vokra. If we are to fight, which I admit is very possible, though I hope we do not, I will permit you to get your weapon. Either weapon, in fact."

Vokra picked up the lantern and carried it with him. The figure seated on one of his chairs was not holding a weapon, and seemed to be dressed entirely in white.

"Who are you, and what are you doing in my home?"

"I am called Dust, and I was waiting for you in order to have a conversation with you, and, now that you have arrived, I am having exactly that conversation."

"Is it your custom to break into people's homes?"

"Your door was not locked."

"Is it your custom to walk into people's homes?"

"Only the homes of old friends."

"Old friends? You perceive, we have never met."

"On the contrary, Vokra. We met, and spent many days in each other's company."

"And yet—ah!" He felt his eyes narrow. "You were someone I once escorted?"

"You have understood exactly, my dear Vokra."

He glanced over at his weapons, estimating distance and time, but Dust said, "I told you, my friend, you needn't worry."

"You have said so, and I even heard you. And yet—"

"Well?"

"And yet, I wonder what business we could have that does not involve some sort of vengeance."

"Oh, but it does involve vengeance."

Vokra nodded, and, in spite of the other's words, prepared himself to reach his weapons.

"Not, however," continued Dust, "vengeance against you."

Vokra felt himself frowning and said, "No?"

"Well, you were carrying out orders that, to the best of your knowledge, were entirely legal, is that not the case?"

"It is."

"Then no more need be said about that."

"But then, what is there to talk about?"

"Look on your table, Vokra."

"There are papers there."

"Are you a lettered man, Vokra?"

"I am an Iorich."

"Then read the papers."

Vokra hesitated, then picked up the papers and held them near the lantern. "A list of names," he said.

"Yes."

"Many names."

"More than seven hundred in all."

"I don't recognize any of them."

"Keep looking."

"Ah, well, there's one I know. Yes, and another. Perhaps a third."

"And?"

"They were all prisoners I escorted."

"Escorted where?"

"I am not permitted to say."

"Why not? It no longer exists."

"No longer exists?"

"Its magic failed when the Orb failed, then the jailers rioted, and the prisoners—some of them—escaped."

"Including you?"

"Including me."

"Well, what of it, then?"

"The jail was illegal."

"Illegal?"

"It was a jail for those whom certain powerful people wished forgotten. No one incarcerated there ever received a trial."

"I don't believe you."

"How many prisoners did you escort there?"

"Thirty-one."

"How many did you escort back?"

Vokra found himself unable to speak. The other remained silent, letting him consider this matter.

"Who has done this?" said Vokra at last.

"A certain Duke Traanzo. Or, rather, his father; the son then continued the work after his father's death. I have no doubt you recognize the name, as he is, in fact, your prince. That is to say, the Iorich Heir."

"Why would he do this?"

"Influence, power, money."

"How much do you know," said Vokra, "about the Kinship of the Mask?"

"I was once an Iorich."

"Once?"

"Then they betrayed me."

Vokra nodded. "We volunteer for the Kinship at a young age. I was eighty. Do you know why we volunteer? You're an Iorich, you must, therefore, know what it is like to be raised by one."

"I do not believe, my dear Vokra, that they are all the same."

"No? Perhaps not. I'm given to think so, because all of my kindred told the same story. But then, perhaps, if they were all the same, all children would join the Kinship."

"Perhaps."

"But we speak of justice, Dust. That is what we learn, that is what we eat with our pap, drink with our water. Fair is fair and right is right and that's an end of it. But it isn't, is it, Dust? Sometimes justice isn't enough, and sometimes it is too much, and so what the Iorich teach their children is too much and too little."

Dust shrugged. "Well, Dragons may teach their children to be too warlike, the Lyorn to pay too much attention to duty, the Athyra to spend too much time in contemplation."

Vokra nodded. "Some accept, and become advocates and justicers. Some of us rebel, and become landlords. And some of us accept too fully, and that means we turn away from our family, and so find another. And our new family is held together, not by ties of blood, or of affection, but by shared duty, and the knowledge that we are serving justice. We do not think about it, Dust, we live it, it is in the air we breathe. And now you tell me that our order has been used as a tool of injustice."

"I do not take any pleasure in telling you, Vokra."

"I understand."

"And, moreover, what I offer is a chance to correct this injustice. At first, only in a small matter, a brook that trickles off from the river. But if that goes as I hope it will, well, then we will see."

Vokra nodded. "Well. I must determine the truth of what you tell me. If you are lying to me, I will not take it kindly."

"I would expect nothing less of you. And when you have made this determination, gather some others who feel as you do, you must know some."

"We are in touch. What then?"

"Come and find me in the pirate encampment at Far Harbor. I will be waiting."

"A pirate encampment?"

"Yes."

Vokra considered this, then shrugged.

"Very well. You will not wait long."

There is a place on what is usually called the Laughing River but is known to the locals as the Deepwater about a hundred miles above where the Yendi River joins it. Here, along the banks, there is a village called Rafts, overlooked by a tall castle. The local count being a Dragonlord, and the baron being a dzur, and the duke, also a Dragon, having been in Dragaera City at the time of its fall, it was a region that, during the whole of the Interregnum, saw no shortage of skirmishes, battles, and outright wars. "Peace" in this region meant that those guarding the baron's castle needed to be alert for nothing more than raiding parties, carried out in revenge for the raiding parties sent east, and that the dairy cattle, beef cattle, and kethna were the only ones whose allegiance might suddenly change from day to day.

Those who had guard duty in this castle must, nevertheless, retain their vigilance; although Doscava, Baron of Raft, was not unusually cruel, neither was he well disposed toward those who were careless or neglectful of their duty. Thus it was that Livosha, riding up toward the main gate, was hailed with challenging words while still some distance off. She continued, ignoring the challenge for another fifty yards, at which time she stopped and called back, "I give you my word, I would have replied to the question you did me the honor to ask, but from that distance I could distinguish nothing you said. But if you will be so good as to repeat it now, well, I will answer as best I can."

There was a pause, then an answer: "I beg your pardon, madam, I am suffering from a slight cough that has taken up residence in my throat, which restricts the volume I am able to achieve."

Livosha looked in the direction from which the voice came and said, "Ah, well, I know a certain herbal tea that may be of some assistance, and I believe I have a small bag of it with me, as I have sometimes had this very ailment, and I prefer to be prepared."

"You are very kind, madam. But permit me to repeat my question, now that you can hear."

"I am listening."

"Who are you, and what is your business here?"

"I am Livosha, daughter of Cerwin, and I am here looking for a certain friend. You perceive, I am alone, and thus it is unlikely that I am a significant threat to your high walls and your halberds."

"Well, if you give me the name of your friend, I will learn what I can."

"She is called Kelsama."

"How, Kelsama? The guard?"

"That is she."

"Ah, well, if you are her friend, and I am her friend, then we are very nearly friends as well."

"Then may I speak with her?"

"I am unable to give you permission to enter, but I will give her your name, and see if she wishes to come out."

"That is all I can ask," called up Livosha, who wondered at how the other managed it with a cold, as her own throat was already beginning to feel rough.

She waited for some few minutes, until at length the heavy gate swung open and a figure came out. Livosha dismounted and led her horse forward until they met.

"Kelsama! I am so happy you escaped."

"And you, Livosha. But, how did you find me?"

"Ah, as to that, well, I have a friend who has eyes everywhere. We have been seeking you for three years."

"Ah! You are determined!"

"You perceive, it wasn't easy. But we managed to find a list that had the name Kelsama e'Kieron on it and the number seventy-two."

"And then?"

"We saw that you were a Dragonlord, and learned of your birthplace. We thought you might return to your home, or near it, and after that, we looked until one of our spies found your name on the roll of guards."

"And then you came here."

"Yes."

"All of this to thank me, when you had, in fact, already thanked me when you opened my cell door?"

"That, and other things."

"Well, what other things?"

"Do you enjoy hunting, Kelsama?"

"Hunting? Yes, sometimes."

"You know the pleasure of stalking one's prey, then?"

"I think so. And yet—"

"We know who created that jail, and why."

"And?"

"Would you enjoy stalking him, running him down, and then having a conversation with him about it?"

Kelsama turned and began walking back to the gate.

"Where are you going?" said Livosha.

"To turn in my resignation and beg the use of a horse."

"In that case—"

"Well?"

Livosha dug into her pouch. "Here."

"What is it?"

"Tea. Give it to the gentleman at the gate. It will ease his throat."

"I will return soon," said Kelsama.

Chapter the Twenty-eighth

In Which An Argument Is Made That the Pirate and the Bandit Should Be Friends

Evening was just setting in when Riffetra heard the sound of the clappers he had installed below. He frowned, because it had been so long since he had heard them, that he didn't realize they were still functional. Then he wondered if there was some sort of mistake. He waited, and a few minutes later the clap was repeated.

He shrugged and went down the stairs. He was no longer a young man, which fact was impressed upon him as he noticed how long it took— for we are, by nature, more aware of the passing of time when we know that someone is waiting for us. At last he reached the bottom, pulled open the door to the common room, and then worked the bolt on the door to the outside. At last he threw it open, and felt his jaw drop.

Outside the door was the most remarkable figure he had ever seen: a man clothed, except for a red jewel, entirely in white from head to foot, even to his boots, so he seemed to shimmer in the fading light.

"Riffetra," said the man, his voice low and melodic. "Would you permit me to come in and exchange two words with you?"

After a moment to recover himself, he said, "Who are you?"

"My name is Dust, and I give you my word, I come as a friend."

"Well," said Riffetra, "it is so long since I've had a friend, I no longer quite know what to do with one. But come in. The ale and the pilsner are long sour, but there may be a bottle of wine that is still good."

"There is no need," said Dust. "I brought a bottle."

"Bringing a bottle of wine to an inn? Well, that tells us how things have been, does it not?"

They went inside and Riffetra lit a lamp. Old habits came back, and so he wouldn't permit Dust to sit until he had wiped off the chairs and the table, and cleaned a pair of cups. He poured coals for the wine brazier, feeling a certain nostalgia for the thousand thousand times he had done so in the past. Then he stopped and said, "I have no ice."

"Break the neck."

"Very well," he said. As a host, he was skilled at breaking the necks of wine bottles when, for some reason or another, the tongs couldn't be used; but, as a host, he disliked doing so. He managed it cleanly, however, and brought the bottle back, setting it before the man in white, who gestured for him to sit.

When they were seated, Dust poured the wine. Riffetra tasted it, and said, "This is quite remarkable."

"Thank you. It is from my own vineyards."

"Ah, you are a wine grower!"

"No, but I bought some good wine land in near Lake Chen, and hired a vintner. It is remarkable what one can do with money."

"Is it, my lord?"

"Not my lord. Just Dust."

"An unusual name."

"I get through small openings, and you can never be entirely rid of me, and sometimes I can keep you from breathing."

"Well," said Riffetra, feeling suddenly uncomfortable.

"I'm sorry, my friend," said Dust, his voice suddenly warm. "You have nothing to fear from me. On the contrary, you risked your life to perform a service for someone I care deeply about, and I am grateful."

Riffetra frowned. "I cannot imagine what you mean, my—, Dust."

"No? You cannot? Well. I know pirates, my good Riffetra, and I know Jhereg. And I know Orca, and I know Teckla. I give them money, and they tell me things, and I remember what they tell me. After all, what is dust? It is the name we give to all the small particles that come from everything and everywhere; we never know whence came each speck, nor whither each goes. Dust can be moved from place to place, but never destroyed. It doesn't have memory, you see, it is memory. So you may not remember this service you have done, but I am Dust, I remember, and that is why I am giving you this."

As he made this remarkable speech, he pulled out a rolled scroll and handed it over.

"What is this?" said Riffetra.

"It is the Wriggling Dolphin. You own it again. And here—" He set a purse on the table. "This should be enough to buy supplies and get it running again. The custom will be poor for a while, but I think that, soon, Wetrock will prosper again. So repaint your sign, oil your woodwork, polish your cups."

"My lord!"

"Just Dust. And, if you would, there is a small service you might do for me. To be clear, my good Riffetra, there is, in this case, no condition. All that I have given is yours whatever you decide. However, knowing that you have a good heart, a kindness for those I have a kindness for, and a resentment of injustice, I think that, after I have explained what I wish, you will readily agree."

Riffetra opened the purse and stared at the bright imperials inside, and he unrolled the scroll, and read it, then read it again, and yet again. He set it down, trying to control the trembling in his hands and the pounding in his heart.

"I don't care what it is," he said. "I will do anything you wish."

The city of Aussiar in the Zerika's Point region had changed considerably since the fall of the Empire. Wooden structures, built with the timber that grew so plentifully outside of the city to the north and west, had burned or collapsed or simply fallen apart, and few had been rebuilt. Much of the economy, that is to say, that which was based on pearls and iron, had either collapsed or at least been crippled, and many artisans and tradesmen had moved away, as well as some of those who supply them. Livosha could see the difference as she moved through streets that had once been crowded, but were now, if not deserted, at least more easily navigable.

She stopped and spoke to an elderly Teckla woman. Livosha had the fanciful thought that this woman might be same Teckla her brother had spoken to six hundred years before, but there was no way to know (nor, indeed, is there any way for the author to know, yet it is pleasant to think she is right, for it provides a sort symmetry or correspondence that, although generally lacking in history, is an agreeable feature in works of art). Livosha (who, we should add, was on foot on this occasion), said, "Your pardon, auntie, but where can I find Gystralan the money-lender?"

The woman stopped, made an obeisance, and said, "Rocksalt Lane, my lady, on the north side next to the luthier."

Livosha handed her a coin, saying, "I hope you will do me the honor to take this and use it to drink my health."

The Teckla smiled, accepted the coin, and bowed. "Then that I will do, and the blessing of Barlen go with you on this day. Ah, and before I carry out this request with which you have not only honored me but also provided the means, I will add that Rocksalt Lane can be found by following this street to Imperial, turning there to the right, and continuing for only a short distance, until you see a narrow unpaved street winding to your left. That is Rocksalt." With this, she bowed once more and continued on her way.

As the reader is already familiar with the process of following a Teckla's directions and arriving at a certain destination, having observed them on our previous visit to Aussiar, we do not see a need to take up the reader's time by repeating them, as it is well known that repetition, or redundancy, or iteration, can by its nature, indeed, by its very definition, do nothing to advance understanding, and, hence, has no valid place in any work that purports to further human knowledge, however this ingemination or replication is presented.

She found, then, a low structure of brick that seemed in remarkably good repair compared to those around it. She continued past it to an empty lot a short distance further down, a lot that, to judge from the wheel ruts and other impressions in the ground, occasionally served as a market. There were a few tree stumps here and there that had been smoothed off to serve as chairs. She sat in one and waited.

Two hours passed, then three, then four, and still she waited. The light began to fail and a chill set in, and just as she was noticing this and wishing her cloak were heavier, the door she was watching opened and a man came out. Though she only had a glimpse of his face, it was enough to recognize him as Gystralan even with the extra years. He turned and walked down the street away from her. When he was out of sight, she came back. She was about to clap, but noticed a sign nailed to the door that said, "Please walk in," so, without hesitation, she did so.

At a small desk with a few candles, a figure was hunched over. His pen made a steady *scratch scratch scratch* over paper as he worked, not even looking up when the door opened.

Livosha cleared her throat.

"Oh I beg your pardon, my lady," said the Tsalmoth, standing suddenly. "I had thought . . ." He coughed in embarrassment. "How may I serve you? Alas, my master—"

"Has left. When the door opened you thought he had returned, and dared not look up lest he scorch you with his tongue."

"And his stick, my lady. How may I—" He stopped and squinted. His eyes seemed to be permanently red, and there was a bow to his shoulders that had not been there before. "Your pardon, my lady. Do I know you?"

"Perhaps you do. At all events, I know you. It is hard to forget a man who saved my life."

"Saved your . . . my lady, I do not understand what it is you do me the honor of telling me."

"No? Well, that is unimportant."

"Yet—"

"I am here on business."

"As I have said, my lady, my master has left."

"My business is with you."

"How with me?"

"Exactly."

"But, what business could you have with me?"

"I must make a payment on a debt, my dear Emeris."

"Ah, well, that is different. I will accept the payment in my master's name, and record—"

"But my dear Emeris, the debt is not owed to him, it is owed to you."

"My lady, that is impossible."

"Not in the least." She pulled her head back and bowed. "I am Livosha, daughter of Cerwin, and if it were not for you, I would be dead now."

Emeris sat down, apparently without deciding to, and his mouth fell open. Livosha smiled. "Come, my friend. I am here to thank you, and to give you a commission."

"A commission?"

"First, a partial payment." She tossed a purse onto the desk, pleased at the way Emeris's eyes widened at the agreeable, heavy thump it made.

"There will be plenty there to see you safely to Candletown."

"Candletown, Lady Livosha?"

"Yes. In Candletown, I repay the rest of my debt to you."

As this conversation was taking place, the one called Gystralan was continuing his walk home, reflecting on how his enterprises seemed, in spite of the interruption caused by the fall of the Empire, to be gradually improving. It had been difficult for a while; in fact, if he hadn't had the foresight to take one particular calculated gamble, as he thought of it, which permitted him to quickly accumulate a great deal of capital, he might not have weathered the storm. But he had, and now, Empire or not, things were looking up. Soon he might have to hire an assistant. That is to say, a second assistant, unless he could manage to get more work from the Tsalmoth. Perhaps he could; things were so difficult right now, that the threat of being sacked could do wonders. Yes, perhaps he should try.

He reached his house, opened the door, stepped inside, and turned around to find something sharp at his throat, which, upon examination, proved to be a long piece of steel, at the other end of which was a man in the gray and black of the Jhereg, who gave no overt indications of having a sympathetic attitude.

"What—"

"Please do me the honor of wearing this, my dear Gystralan."

"Who are you?"

"Call me Daifan."

"What is that?"

"A hood. If you would be so kind as to put it on." He prodded a little with the point of the sword.

"I can't see."

"You perceive, if I had wanted you to see, I wouldn't have had you put on the hood."

"And yet—"

"Now turn around, and put your hands behind your back."

"What are you going to do?"

"Tie them."

"But, if I don't want my hands tied?"

"I will tie them anyway, unless you resist."

"And if I resist?"

"Then I will push a certain number of inches of good Aussiar steel up under your chin and into your brain, which, I give you my word, will make it more difficult for you to calculate interest."

"Very well, here they are."

"There, it is done."

"Well, what next?"

"Next we will sit here, like good companions, for a short length of time, at the end of which a coach will arrive. We will get into the coach and go for a long ride."

"To where?"

"A ship."

"And then?"

"Ah, if I were to tell you everything, you wouldn't be surprised, and that would hardly do after I've gone to all of this work for your entertainment."

"I have money."

"That you do, my dear Gystralan."

"I could pay you."

"Well, first I will perform the service, afterward you can decide if you wish to pay me. Ah, and there is the sound of the wagon. Come, I will guide you carefully."

Gystralan sighed and went along.

A small vessel, that is to say, a boat with a single mast and two sails, arrived in the harbor at Adrilankha during the last hours of the day. Her crew consisted of a captain and a mate, and she carried seven passengers. As the vessel approached one of the long piers with which the harbor was then supplied, as there was at the time no division among fishing boats, sailing ships, and yachts, the captain, whom the reader will recognize as the pirate known as Sheen, spoke to one of the passengers, saying, "You perceive, should I be recognized, well, you may succeed in your mission and yet have no way to escape, for there are a certain number of people in this city who would love to see me strapped to the executioner's star, and will be happy to assist in this endeavor."

"Well," said the passenger, who was, in fact, none other than Alishka. "And then?"

"I will, therefore, remain belowdecks until you return, and thus will be unable to assist."

"I understand," said Alishka. "The seven of us will, I hope, manage."

"You can find it? This is a large city, and I am told it can be hard to find one's way around."

"I can ask directions."

"Ah," said Sheen. "You are pleased to jest."

Alishka shrugged. "Dust gave me precise instructions, as well as certain devices he pretends will enable me to complete the mission, and I have allowed extra time. You perceive, I am not worried about becoming lost on the way there; I am worried about becoming lost on the way back, as that would be embarrassing."

"I should hate for you to be embarrassed. We are, after all, in much the same line of work, although the highways I work tend to be wetter."

"So then, I will go slowly on my way there, making notes, so that, above all, the return will go smoothly."

"And once you have returned?"

"Perhaps all we be well, but perhaps we will be pursued, so it would be best if we were ready to leave on an instant."

"I promise you, we will be."

"Very good, then. I see that we have arrived."

"If you will be permit me to tie us up, well, you can be off."

"Then we will go."

"Best of luck to you."

"I will see you soon, Captain Sheen."

The seven of them stepped onto the pier and began walking in single file toward the city. Sheen watched their progress for a short time, although he could not, in all honesty, have said why. There were several children playing Cats Will Scamper around some of the piles of cargo, and, as he watched, one of them stopped and waved at him. He smiled, as one does, and waved back, after which he turned back to his mate.

"Come," said Sheen. "Let us go below. As there is nothing else to do for some hours, we will sleep."

"This had better work," said Fagry.

Alishka heard the thud as Doro hit him. This was, Alishka reflected, the seventh or eighth time he had made this observation, and whereas it had been too obvious to require expression the first time, the seventh or eighth was quite sufficient. The first time, Alishka had replied, saying, "Dust says it will work; do you doubt him?" There had been no answer from Fagry, but then there had begun to be regular repetitions. She was inclined to forgive him, because his job tonight was the hardest, and because she did have doubts of her own.

Alishka kept her doubts to herself, which doubts, in fact, were not related to Dust's promise, for she had no question on that score—if Dust said it would work, then it would work—but rather on her own band. She missed Nef, who had fallen to his death from a cliff near Creigshead, for his steady sword, sharp ears, and dry wit, not to mention his singing voice. She missed Liniace, who had retired from the life to seek her fortune in the east, for her calming presence. Now they were only seven, and, if truth be told, not all of them were as young they were: Branf, in particular, was slowing down.

But that was her band, and now was too late to worry. She had agreed to do what was asked, and they were now huddled against a wall at night, wearing black, the light-skinned among them with faces blacked, weapons blacked, waiting either until the moment it was time to move, or until they were discovered and must abandon the plan and try to escape with their lives. Alishka hoped for the former; she did not wish to disappoint Dust.

When it happened at last, they quite nearly missed it, there was no flash of light, no explosion, almost nothing at all, in fact, except a quiet *pop*. Alishka's first thought, when she realized it had occurred at all, was that it had failed, but then she saw a crack appear in the block at her feet, and spread, and continue spreading until, in what seemed to be hardly more than a minute, the entire block had crumbled to nothing, leaving a hole in the wall big enough for a man to fit through.

"Doro," she whispered.

Doro nodded, drew a knife, and slid through the opening. An instant later she whispered back, "It is good, Alishka."

"Kitescu,"

He nodded and, without a word, followed Doro in. He would wait there while Doro would move further in, find the lone guard who should be on duty at the intersection, ensure his silence with a sharp blow to the head if possible or a knife to the throat if necessary, and come back. In the meantime, Alishka kept sending the others in, until everyone except she and Fagry had gone into the hole.

She turned to Fagry and said softly, "You know your job?"

He nodded. "I will sit here, as if drunk, my back covering the hole. When you return, either successfully or because of something going wrong, I will assist you, one at a time, out of the hole. If I am disturbed while waiting for you, I will quell the disturbance."

Alishka nodded, gave his arm a reassuring squeeze, and slipped down the hole. She found herself in a long corridor with the rest of her band. She moved past them and took out the lightstick, rubbing it against the stone walls next to her until its soft glow began. At that moment, Doro returned and nodded.

Alishka led them forward. Just past the intersection they saw the guard, who was bound, gagged, and also appeared unconscious: Doro, we perceive, was that sort of individual whose boots are held on with straps over the lacings. She left Kitescu there both to guard and to give warning in case of trouble and continued, turning right at the intersection.

The doorway yielded to the key supplied by Livosha's brother, who was now recovering, although, having come so close to death, he was still weak. They were now in a torture chamber, filled with the usual implements of that grim and barbaric work, but it was unoccupied. This was, reflected Alishka, both good and bad; good because it increased their chances of success with the mission, bad because, ever since she had been questioned at the age of one hundred and ten about the name of her companion after her first theft, she had taken an especial delight in slaughtering those who used such implements. She did not examine the implements closely, therefore neither will we.

Immediately beyond this room were the cells.

"Jiscava and Cho," she said.

The two named went to the end of the corridor. Cho quickly looked through the barred door, then turned back to Alishka and nodded, then, along with Jiscava, took up a position on either side of the door. They each drew their sword and waited.

Alishka led the other two, Doro and Branf, to the third cell on the right-hand side. She withdrew the other key she'd been given and tried it. It went into the lock but wouldn't turn, which Livosha's brother, whose name she could not quite recall, had said might happen.

Well then, there was nothing for it. She removed the key and took out a tube filled with a composition Dust had made that included, Dust claimed, metals taken from minerals mined in Wetrock. She poured the powder into the keyhole and whispered, "Look away, everyone. And Jiscava and Cho, be ready."

She held the lightstick against the lock and waited. Dust had warned her it could take time, but, it must be said, it seemed to Alishka as if dawn would come before anything happened. And then there was the hiss she'd been told of, and she barely managed to turn her eyes away before such a brightness filled the room that she could see it through her tightly closed eyes.

There were voices from down the hall, but that was not her affair; she opened her eyes, turned, and kicked the cell door open. Two strides, and there he was, withered, haggard, but, from the description she'd been given, it was him.

"Can you walk?" she said.

"I'm blind!"

"It will pass. Doro, Branf."

They came forward. Branf took his arms, Doro his legs, and they carried him out of the cell even as the door into the area opened. Jiscava and Cho struck, and it was over.

Perhaps no alarm had been given, but it would be a mistake to count on it, therefore, time was now all that mattered. Doro and Branf led the way, with Jiscava and Cho behind them; Alishka herself took the rearguard.

Kitescu fell in before her, and they reached the exit where Fagry waited, Alishka's ears straining to hear sounds of pursuit. The prisoner was pushed through, with Fagry's strong arms doing most of the work, he then helped the others through one at a time, and last of all Alishka.

"Come," she said. "To the harbor, the boat awaits."

"I think I can walk a little," said the prisoner, "though I still cannot see."

They put him on his feet, but he fell over at once. Alishka cursed, and they picked him up again. Just to be sure, she said, "You are the artist called Sajen?"

"I am," he said. "And, the gods, you have rescued me from Prince Traanzo's dungeons!"

Alishka shrugged. "So much the worse for you."

They continued down toward the harbor where the pirate would see them to safety.

Chapter the Twenty-ninth

In Which the Kinship of the Mask
Demonstrates Repentance

The morning after the events we have just witnessed, we will use our powers of apparent omniscience to look in on someone we have, hitherto, only seen briefly, that being Hadrice. The reader must understand that when we say "apparent omniscience" we are, in some measure, speaking ironically. Although it is true that in any history the author will quite naturally present the appearance of being able to see any and all of the incidents that are being displayed for the reader, and, moreover, to see any detail within them that the author may choose, in fact, as a moment's thought will reveal, this is not the case. The process of historical study in all its painstaking assiduousness must still fail, not only to *describe* all of the facts, but to *know* them, for the simple reason that facts are infinite, and books—even though certain works by tedious, ignorant academics of the mystical persuasion may seem infinite when the reader is forced to wade through them like Jigrae Lavode through the Ramshorn Swamp and may seem unending—are nevertheless finite. Thus the task of the historian lies not only in gathering facts, and selecting them, but in drawing conclusions from them. This takes on an importance when the reader, or, worse, the historian, is unaware of the difference. Facts, as we all know, are abstractions from the world, in which we isolate a particular facet of an object to consider: for example, to state that the Orb measures nine inches in diameter is to state a *fact* which is gleaned by ignoring all of the complexities of the real and mystical, of the motion, the color, the makeup, except for one, which is, its diameter. To state that, for example, the mouth of some particular desert-born scholar is two inches in width is to abstract from all that the scholar is, the one matter of interest, that being the width of his mouth, which is also thus a *fact*. To say that the Orb would not fit within this mouth, or some other aperture we might consider, is *not* a fact, although it is true; rather, it is a *conclusion drawn from facts*. Its truth, of course, we could prove through experimentation, but this circumstance is beyond our point, which is, simply, that the historian works from facts and from conclusions drawn from facts, and that the reader must always bear in mind which are which. That one might make a casual and informal statement in which the word *fact* is used to mean *a thing that is true* (which in truth we have done often in this work, and will continue to do), is, naturally, perfectly acceptable in certain circumstances; we must insist, however, that the careful study of complex aspects of history does not qualify as one of those circumstances. That a student, or, still worse, someone who holds himself to be a scholar, might confuse these two concepts—the fact and the conclusion drawn from facts—would provide the explanation for any number of errors that would otherwise baffle us. Lest the reader fall into this error, then, we have taken this opportunity to make clear that, while a great deal of what passes before his eyes consists of facts, a great deal more consists of conclusions that, using the strict rules of deductive logic, have been drawn from those facts.

With this understood, then, we turn our attention to Hadrice. She very carefully studied the crumbling stone where the wall was breached, then interrogated the guard who was knocked senseless, the one of the two who had fought the bandits who was able to speak, and examined the cell door, and the cell itself, managing to reconstruct the entire affair with the accuracy of an historian recreating a battle from an examination of the ground, the reports of officers, the notes of observers, and the letters of survivors. Then, as she inspected the cell, looking in the dust to reconstruct where the prisoner had been taken by the arms and the legs, she suddenly knelt down, seeing a small scrap of paper.

She held it up next to her lantern, and saw that it was, evidently, a piece of a note, torn off, no doubt, in the commotion of the escape. It read: "mber 15, Highstep Road. He escaped from the Burning Isl."

She took it upstairs. So, then, one of the escaped prisoners was in Adrilankha. It may be that Eremit was not in touch with this prisoner, but then again, it might be that he was, or this prisoner, at any rate, could have useful information.

She found the director in his room, where he spent most of his time, being afraid to set foot out of doors, and said, "Come with me."

"Where are we going?"

"Out," she said.

The director chose not to press for more details, and so threw on a cloak and followed her. In ten minutes they were mounted, and riding through Adrilankha. Highstep Road, on the edge of the Little Deathgate area, was not an area to be entered lightly, but then, neither was Hadrice to be dealt with lightly.

They found number 15, a tall, thin building of red bricks, with a convenient hitching post in front of it. The buildings on either side were too far away to be useful for anyone trying to escape, and the street was wide enough that the coach-and-four on the other side was not in the way. Hadrice judged that the building was broken into flats, three on a side, two stories, perhaps another one or two in the basement. There was some worry about someone escaping out the back, but she was confident she would be able to catch anyone who tried to run.

She dismounted and said, "Come."

"What—"

"We are going to look through this building until you recognize someone."

"But who?"

Hadrice climbed up the brick stairway, opened the door, and took herself to the first flat on the right. She clapped, and heard a gasp next to her, while at the same time something very sharp pressed against the back of her neck.

Someone said, "Hold still, or I will sever your spine." At that moment, the door at which she'd clapped opened and facing her were two individuals in gray outfits, gray masks, wearing badges of the House of the Iorich, and each was holding the massive sword that was the mark of the Kinship of the Mask.

Hadrice did not feel any special fear, but she was also aware that there were now at least three and more likely four weapons a few inches from her, and if she resisted, she would certainly die. Therefore, she remained still and waited.

One of the Kinsmen moved to the side, and she heard the director say, "Wait, wait, where are you taking me?"

She listened carefully, and heard three sets of footsteps walking away, one of which was certainly the director's. With the blade she could still feel on the back of her neck, that meant there were two. She remained still, and waited.

After a short time, the pressure on the back of her neck eased. "All right, we are going to let—"

Hadrice dropped to the floor, drawing at the same time. With the same motion as the draw she cut the leg of the one in front of her, then rolled and came to her feet. The Kinsman was already closing with her, swinging hio maooivc weapon in a cross-body motion. Hadrice continued forward, coming inside the swing while cutting at his shoulder. He cried out and his weapon fell to the ground, and without hesitating she ran out of the door.

She looked down the street and saw a coach rolling away. It was only then that she realized the horses were missing. She considered going inside and finishing the two Kinsmen, but then shrugged. She cleaned her sword, sheathed it, and began looking for a hack or a pedicab to take her back to the prince's manor.

Livosha pulled on a certain rope outside of a certain gate, and waited. If memories of the last time she had pulled that rope, and of various events that had transpired since then went through her imagination, well, we do her the kindness to leave them there, trusting the reader will accept that even historical characters may, from time to time, have thoughts upon which we ought not to intrude. Presently, there came an elegant chaise drawn by a white horse. It pulled up, and an elderly man climbed out slowly, as if moving caused him pain. He shuffled up to the gate and opened his mouth to speak, but Livosha spoke first, saying, "My dear Biska, you should not still be doing this! You should be cared for in honorable retirement, with grandchildren climbing on your knees while you drink cups of mulled wine and eat raisin cake."

The old man stared at her for some few moments, then his face broke into a smile. "Is it you, Livosha?"

"The same. Come, how are you, my friend?"

"As you say, I am old, old."

"But, why are you not retired?"

"Alas, my mistress pretends that should I retire, I will be cut off without a penny and left to starve."

"She is not remarkable for her kindness."

"I will not dispute you, Livosha, though there is not another in the world to whom I would dare speak these words, save perhaps one other."

"One other, my old friend?"

"A new servant, a stable girl. She has been very kind to me, sometimes easing the knots in my muscles and seeing to it I am kept warm."

"I am glad you have this friend. In fact, I wish to see her, and thank her. Come, can you let me in?"

Biska frowned. "Have you business with her ladyship?"

"Oh, yes. Yes I do. I have such business with her ladyship as will astound you. But first I wish to meet this stable girl."

"Very well, then I will open the gate."

"And you will be right to do so. There, I will close it for you, and assist you into the chaise."

"You are very kind, Livosha."

"Bah. Someone must be, sometime, or what sort of world would we have?"

"A poor one, I fear."

He drove her up to the front gate. "If the countess asks," she said, "tell her that it is I, and I will be along to see her shortly. And when my friends arrive, please be so good as to let them in."

"Friends?"

"The first two you will of course let in, but the third, I would take it as a kindness if you would show him in to see the countess."

"I do not understand."

"It will all be clear soon."

She left the carriage and walked around back to the stables, where she saw a familiar figure polishing a bridle that did not require polishing, while, it seemed, having some sort of conversation with a dun mare.

"Hello, Jerin."

The groom looked up, and her face broke into a smile. "My lady Livosha! I was told you would arrive! You see, I still have the knife you gave me."

"A pleasure indeed, my dear Jerin. I trust you have been well?"

"Ah, the lady of the house is impossible, but it has only been a year, and one can stand anything for a year, is it not so?"

"Perhaps it is. And your work, is it done?"

"I have completed everything my lord Eremit—that is to say, Dust, or is it Daifan?—requested of me."

"So much the better. How did he find you?"

"I do not know, m'lady. I was working, and he rode up and asked if I remembered him, and I said I did not, and he said he was Eremit, and I said that did not seem possible, and he gave me a sapphire to thank me for assisting you, my lady, although I insisted it wasn't necessary, that I was honored to have been able to perform a small service for such a noble, beautiful, intelligent, talented, proud—"

"Yes, yes. I understand, good Jerin. And then?"

"He asked if I would like to perform a further service for you, and I said yes and he gave me instructions, and I turned in my notice, and here I am. Apropos, m'lady, how is your brother?"

"He was wounded some years ago, but has quite recovered."

"I am glad to hear it."

"So, then, the papers?"

"I have kept them safe, in my loft above the stable."

"Fetch them, then. And have you anything clean?"

"Why yes, my lady."

"Change into it. We are about to have a conversation for which you will want to look your best."

Half an hour later, they stood in the front hall. Biska shuffled toward them. "Livosha? Jerin? I perceive you have met."

"Good Biska," said Livosha. "As I have said, you are about to have visitors who must be admitted. When they arrive, please send them in at once. Apropos, where is the countess?"

"Her salon, Livosha. She is auditioning a trio of musicians for an entertainment she is planning. And yet, who—"

He was interrupted by the sound of the clapper. He looked at Livosha, then at the door, and shrugged and set off to his duty.

"Come, Jerin. It is time."

Livosha and Jerin walked into the countess's salon without clapping. There were, in fact, three musicians there, in the middle of a song. Livosha had intended to wait for the music to end, but as they came in, the countess frowned and gestured the musicians to silence. "What is the meaning—"

Livosha threw a small purse to the musicians and said, "Leave here." Whether it was the purse or the manner in which she spoke, the musicians immediately packed up their instruments and left.

"Who are you," said the countess, putting down her tea cup and rising to her feet, "to—"

"You are a fool," said Livosha. "One can act the cruel, disdainful, arrogant, haughty, egotistical potentate who generates hatred and contempt every time she opens her mouth, or one can engage in highly rewarding criminal activity. But only a fool attempts to do both at once."

"How dare—"

"Be quiet, Countess, and listen. I have been prevailed upon by a man who is kinder than I am to offer you a means of escaping utter ruin. But if you continue in this manner, I will not make the offer, and the Countess of Whitecrest will hear how Morganti weapons are making their way so freely to the Jhereg."

The countess sat down. "I deny any—"

"I do not," said Livosha, "care what you deny, and what you admit to." She nodded to Jerin, who withdrew from a box she was carrying a set of papers and laid them, not without a certain flourish, upon the countess's tea table.

"What are these?"

"The first set of documents is a carefully and laboriously compiled list of the sea captains, Jhereg, merchants, and traders showing exactly how you arranged for the acquisition and shipping of these illegal—"

"Illegal! There is no Empire!"

"That is true, and we will return to it in a moment. For now, I will merely observe that, difficult as this was to put together, it would have been impossible were it not for the fact that your household staff, and, indeed, everyone who has had any intercourse with you, hates you and wants to see you fall. Of course, the real credit must go to our good Jerin, who is skilled in finding things. Now this next set of documents describes all of your holdings, financial dealings, and caches of treasure, including copies of deeds and summaries of debts."

"Why would you—"

"Hush. You may have a small amount to take with you, and you may keep your property outside Figshole. The rest is forfeit. If you decline this offer, there is this." She opened the pouch at her side and removed a rolled-up parchment. "This authorizes me, as advocate to the Duchess of Briatha of the House of the Iorich, to have you taken up by the Kinship of the Mask and brought to her private dungeons, where she will then decide what to do with you."

"She has no authority here!"

"You think she does not? Well, let us see if all agree with you."

She clapped her hands, and two individuals came through the door, both them dressed in gray, with gray masks, massive swords slung over their backs.

"The Kinship!" cried the countess.

"Is this the one we are to escort?" said one.

"That is uncertain," said Livosha. "Bide, please, and we will see. Now, Countess, do you sign?"

"It is unjust!"

"'Discontentment with one's place has never led to happiness,'" quoted Livosha. "'Nor has begging. I despise beggars. Don't you?'"

At that moment Biska arrived, bowed, and said, "My lord Emeris has arrived."

"Him?" cried the countess. "Send him away!"

Biska started to turn, but Livosha said, "Biska, do please bring him here. We have been awaiting him."

Biska looked at her, at the countess, then back at her. "Very well," said the countess.

An instant later Emeris arrived, still bent, his eyes still bloodshot, but a look of curiosity on his countenance. He started to say something, but Livosha said, "My dear friend. Your aunt is just about to sign over to you her estate, her titles, her wealth, and her goods. While you cannot, as beneficiary, be a lawful witness, you can at least sign your own name beneath hers, to complete the transaction."

Emeris looked from the countess to Livosha to the two Kinsmen standing cool and detached. His mouth worked, but no words came out.

Livosha walked over to the desk and found the gilded quill, dipped it, and returned, heedless of the ink that dripped onto the floor. She extended the quill and said, "Countess?"

With a sob, the countess accepted the quill.

Livosha smiled at Emeris and said, "I congratulate you on your new fortune, my lord. Kinsmen, we will not need your services, it seems, but please be so good as to escort the countess, ah, that is to say, this freewoman from the grounds before she can prevail upon the kind-hearted Emeris to let her stay, for, if she does, I must trouble myself to call you again. Come, Jerin. I believe we are finished here."

Chapter the Thirtieth

In Which the Dancers Take Their Places and the Music Begins

S ajen the forger blinked, woke up, and looked around. He was in a long, narrow room that he had never seen before, and either he had walked in and seated himself without remembering it, or someone had placed him in a padded chair. He was not bound, however, and he felt as if, when he was not so dizzy, he might be able to stand. To his left, was a door, and to his right—

"Ah, you are awake, I perceive."

Sajen squinted. The man who had spoken was dressed in the colors of the Orca, sitting in a chair quite like his own, and seemed familiar. He tried to speak, but found his mouth too dry. He tried to remember how he'd arrived there, but still could not.

"There is a cup of wine by your hand."

He looked, found it, drank. Then he tried speaking again, successfully managing to say, "Sir, do I know you?"

"Perhaps," said the other. "I have, at any rate, been attempting to determine the same thing. That is to say, if I know you; I have not been as concerned, hitherto, with whether you know me. But, perhaps we have done business together? I live in Aussiar."

"I passed through there, many years ago."

"And your profession?"

"I have the honor to be an artist of commissioned portraits and landscapes. Although I'd have remembered you if I'd painted you."

"Well, and I'd have remembered if I'd been painted."

"How did you come to be here?"

"In a hood, with my hands bound. When the hood was removed, you were already here."

"Who brought you?"

"Someone I don't know."

"Were you given a reason?"

"Not in the least."

"Nor was I."

"What do you remember?"

"I was rescued from a dungeon."

"Ah, you were a prisoner?"

"I was."

"Of whom?"

"An Iorich named Traanzo."

"The Heir?"

"The very one."

"How had you offended him?"

"Perhaps he didn't like one of my paintings. Who have you offended?"

"I? No one."

"No one, well, let us see. As you are an Orca, you are, then, involved with commerce?"

"Well."

"And is it possible one of your customers felt you had cheated him?"

"All of my dealings have always been fair and upright."

"Indeed, all of them? That is unusual."

"You give me the lie?"

"Not in the least."

"Well."

"But you must admit, for an Orca, it is surprising."

"We do have a reputation."

"But, in your case, not deserved?"

"Not at all."

"Very well. I am Sajen."

"And I am Gystralan."

"I have heard that name pronounced."

"It is a tolerably unusual name."

Sajen leaned over and studied his face. "I am certain that I know you."

"Perhaps you saw in me in Aussiar."

"Or you saw me when I lived in Candletown."

"Candletown? I've not been there since—gods! You are the forger!"

"Hush, then."

"We are alone."

"Well. It is true I have—ah, ah. You hired me to put the signature on certain documents! All is explained!"

"Explained? What is explained?"

"Do you remember the name of the lady we cheated out of her inheritance?"

"Cheated. It is a hard word."

"Duped? Bilked? Robbed?"

"Never mind the word. I do not recall her name. What then?"

"Her name is Livosha, and she found me in Adrilankha, and she threatened me."

"Threatened you?"

"She threatened to expose me to the Countess of Whitecrest if I failed to perform certain services for her."

"Did you perform the services?"

"I did."

"And did she expose you?"

"She did not."

"Well?"

"But I was discovered by Traanzo."

"Tell me the truth, then: What is your connection to him?"

"If you must know, he was the object of my little deception for Livosha."

"Ah, that must have been uncomfortable."

"The last few years have not been my most pleasant. He had me questioned, and he was not gentle about it. In the end, I told everything about Livosha and her brother, and I would have told him about you, except—"

"Well?"

"I didn't recall your name."

"Ah, that is good, then."

"For you. But, as I said, it was an unpleasant experience altogether. I had no paints and no paper, so I drew in the dirt on my wall. I even forged an order for my release from Traanzo on my wall, but no one would come into my cell to look at it. Still, I think it was good work."

"Well."

"But you see, that is who we have in common. Livosha."

"Well, that is true."

"You perceive, you hired me—"

"Yes, yes. I know." Gystralan sighed. "I still don't know how she got away. She was waiting in my offices, and Berwick's men were coming, and then she was gone."

"Perhaps she was warned."

"There was no one who would have warned her. Only I and my worthless assistant knew about it."

"Well? This assistant?"

"I give you my word, he is too frightened of poverty to betray me."

"Well, then I don't know."

"It is unimportant," said Gystralan with a dismissive gesture. "What matters is, this Livosha."

"Yes, it is true. But, has she any authority?"

"I don't know," said Gystralan, "because I don't know where we are. However, I know what we must do."

"If you know what we must do, and I do not, then I am prepared to listen to you."

"So much the better: this is it, then. We must not admit to anything. If we are accused, we must deny it."

"Is that sufficient? What if we are questioned? What if a question is a trap?"

"You don't know me, we have never met until this moment. With what can we be trapped?"

"Very good, then. I agree."

One might argue that now, as the winds of story carry our ship of history gradually toward the harbor of culmination, is an unusual time to introduce the reader to someone new. Indeed, were this a matter of literature, instead of history, one could very well point to such an event as a violation of the laws of literature laid down by Ekrasan and expanded upon by Pashiva so long ago. Nevertheless, we must insist that, exactly because we are speaking of history, we are not only relieved of the obligation of, in Pashiva's words, "planting the seed before plucking the flower," but, on the contrary, to actually plant such seeds before they have been brought to our attention, not by artifice, but by the actual events as they took place, is to sacrifice the very veracity that is the foundation of any study of the past.

Thus we argue that it is permissible to call onto our stage someone new, and, more than permissible, if it helps to make clear the unfolding of the events we have made it our duty to relate, it is even necessary.

Thus we now present, entering the room in the company of Livosha, the one known to history as Daro, the Countess of Whitecrest. (As before, we apologize for any confusion caused by the similarities between her name and that of one of Alisha's band; in fact, though euphoniously similar, the names have significantly different origins, Daro being from the now disused language of the Tiassa and meaning "bright blooming" and Doro being from the equally disused tongue of the Dragon and meaning "one who strikes hard." We may also add that Daro was given her name at birth, whereas Doro was given hers on the occasion when a particularly intoxicated Dragonlord failed to show sufficient respect for her physical boundaries. Also, as before, we assure the reader that these individuals will never appear so close to together that there is any danger of confusion.)

The countess, then, walked away from the hole through which she had been observing the Orca and the Chreotha whose conversation we, in our own way, have also been observing. As she led Livosha out of the tiny observation room and up the stairway to the manor proper, she remarked, "Well, Lady Livosha, I cannot deny it. You are right about the two of them."

"Yes, Countess."

"But, you perceive, these crimes were committed far from my holdings. I could go to the Empire to report them, but there is no Empire."

"Ah, but Countess, there is a matter you have not considered."

"Well, and that is?"

"You have just heard them commit the crime of conspiracy to circumvent justice."

"That is a crime?"

"It is. It is rarely prosecuted, because in order to prove it, one must also prove the crime the accused is attempting to circumvent. It is mostly used before the justicers in order to be able to read out a longer and more impressive list when pleading for an indictment."

"Well, in this case, we have no justicer, nor will there be an indictment."

"No, but neither are needed for what I have in mind."

"Ah, you have something in mind, Lady Livosha?"

"I do, Countess."

"I would suspect that this idea involves having your lands and title restored?"

"Eventually, yes, I should like that. But I beg you to believe that that is not my first consideration."

"What then? Justice?"

"Countess, I am an Iorich."

"I do not deny it."

They reached the countess's sitting room, and Daro gestured Livosha to a chair, then sat herself.

"Tell me," she said, "what you have in mind. And I give you my word, I will assist you if I can. For though not an Iorich, well, I would not mind seeing a little justice in these troubled times."

"It may be unpleasant."

"How, unpleasant?"

"Our plan, that is, the plan in which we are hoping to enlist you, would require you, first, to enforce the law of the city."

"Well, I am attempting to do that already. And then?"

"And then, in certain cases, to cease enforcing it."

"I do not care for that as much."

"And yet, it is in a good cause."

"Very well, then. Tell me everything, and I will judge, and hope to be as fair and impartial as an Iorich."

"I will explain to you at once," said Livosha.

Sajen and Gystralan were sitting in silence when the door opened, and a man walked in dressed in the livery of the House of the Tiassa, with a sword at his side and a halberd in his hand. While the halberd was, we must say, largely symbolic of his position as one of the countess's guards, the sword had nothing symbolic about it. Following him in was the countess herself; upon seeing her, they recognized her at once from the quality of her garb and the medallion of office around her neck. As they stood, she said, "Gentlemen."

"How can I help you, my lady?" said Gystralan. "I do not understand how I have come to be locked in this room with this person whom I have never met."

"Never met?" said the countess. "Ah, well. And you," she said, addressing Sajen. "Have you ever seen this man before?"

"Never in life until this very hour," he said.

"Well, then come with me, for I wish to discover something to you that I'm sure will be of interest."

She led them out of the room, around a corner, to a wall with a hole in it. She pointed to the wall and said, "There, do you see? This is where I was standing while you were inside having your interesting conversation about claiming not to know each other."

They looked at each other, both of them turning pale, then the Orca said, "My lady, I—"

"Well?"

His mouth opened, but words failed to emerge. At length, perhaps upon realizing this condition was unlikely to change and that there were, in fact, no words available for this circumstance, he closed his mouth again.

"What you have engaged in," said Daro in tones that might bring to mind ice, or stone, or some other hard, unyielding substance, "is a crime known as conspiracy to circumvent justice, and for this, I could lock you both away in my dungeon for a considerable length of time, for you have engaged in it, not only in my county, but in my very house."

"My lady—" said Sajen.

"However," said the countess.

"Yes?" they said, "however?" in a tone that suggested this had suddenly become a word of which they were both extremely fond.

"There is an alternative."

"We are listening, Countess."

"Then, in order to explain it, I will bring in a friend."

At her signal, Livosha appeared. "You!" said Sajen.

"But who are you?" said Gystralan.

"It is her, it is Livosha!"

"Well," said Livosha. "If you are to save yourselves, I will explain what you need to do."

"We are listening," they said, and no one who heard them could have doubted the sincerity in their voices.

"The Baron of Magister Valley," pronounced the one called Halvar, reading from the card.

The other bowed his head.

"You perceive, I have never heard of Magister Valley."

"That is not surprising for two reasons. First, because it is far in the northwest, where there are few people and much that is only poorly mapped. Second, because I named it myself."

"Those are two good reasons," said Halvar with a shrug. "But, I am a Jhereg, and you claim to be a Jhereg even if I have never heard of your supposed barony, so I will at least listen to what you have to say."

"It will not take long."

"So much the better. Am I to call you Magister?"

"Daifan. Those Jhereg with whom I have worked in the northwest gave me the name, and I confess I find it pleasing."

"Very well, Daifan. I am listening."

"Might we find a place to speak that is more conducive to such matters as hearing each other?"

Halvar looked around and shrugged. They were in a large tavern whose sign depicted the rudder of a sinking ship surrounded by floating cups, and that was called The Flotsam. It was early evening on Endweek, and very busy; servers running about, customers shouting out orders, barbacks running up and down from the storage cellars, hosts pouring pitchers and cups and opening wine bottles. "There's a room in the back," said Halvar. He collected his two bodyguards with his eye and gestured them toward the back; the other either didn't notice or ignored it. Halvar picked up his wine cup, the other did the same, and the bottle as well, which was just; as Daifan had requested the meeting, he had purchased the wine.

When they were in the tiny room, the bodyguards holding themselves as far back as they could to pretend they couldn't hear the conversation, Halvar said, "Well?"

"The countess has returned."

"My dear Daifan, if that is what I am to call you, the countess has been back for ten years now."

"Well, but she is more than back, she is becoming active."

"How, active?"

"She is hiring constabulary, specifically for the city."

"Ah, that I did not know. You are certain?"

"I am."

"May I ask for the source of this intelligence?"

"You may."

"What is the source of this intelligence?"

"I do not wish to tell you."

"You perceive, that makes me question it."

"Well."

"What are these supposed constables to do?"

"Collect taxes, of course. On brothels and gaming rooms first, other places after."

"So then, if I believe this, what is it you wish? You perceive, I suspect you have come to me for other than altruistic reasons."

"You are perspicacious."

"And then?"

"I can reduce this problem. I can see to it your area is not a priority for these constables."

"And you will do this for a price?"

"Of a particular kind, yes."

"Well, let us see. Before we come to the matter of this price, to which you allude so obliquely, I must have some reason to believe what you tell me."

"I am not unaware of this circumstance."

"Is it your intention to settle this matter?"

"It is, and in the most convincing way."

"Well, what will you do?"

"Nothing."

"Nothing?"

"Nothing."

"And yet, I fail to perceive how I am to be convinced by nothing."

"I will not convince you, the countess will convince you. And, when she has done so, I will return."

"Well, I understand what you have done me the honor to tell me."

"So much the better."

"Then I will see you when you return. Until then, Lord Daifan."

"Until then, Lord Halvar."

"It would seem, my friend, that everything is in place," said Livosha. She and Dust sat in his cabin on the *Raptor* and drank wine as the ship rocked gently at double anchor in Mermaid Cove.

Dust nodded. "Everyone except Kelsama, who, of course, cannot take her place until you have created it."

"An activity, I do not deny, that I have been looking forward to for some considerable time."

"I understand. We have made what preparations we can, now it is a matter carrying through."

"Let us see then. The Jhereg?"

"Awaiting actions of the countess."

"The countess?"

"Has agreed."

"The director?"

"When this ship has brought you to Wetrock, I will continue to Adrilankha."

"The Kindred?"

"Two were wounded by Hadrice, but Vokra has found others to replace them if they are needed."

"Then all appears ready."

Dust nodded his agreement. "And you have the first dance."

She nodded, thinking about what he had been pleased to call "the first dance." Livosha said, "How many men have you killed?"

"Two. And you?"

"I don't know. At least one, but sometimes in a melee, you perceive, you run your sword through someone and do not know how severe the wound is."

"I have never been in a melee. How was it when you killed the one?"

"It happened quickly. Two or three days later, well, it was not so easy for a while. You?"

It seemed to Livosha as if Dust was looking over her shoulder. "I felt nothing," he said.

Livosha nodded. "The tavern is now open again?"

"For the last two years."

"And the one we seek goes there?"

"Two or three times a week. You may, you perceive, have to wait a day or two."

"I have waited six hundred years and fifty, I can wait another day. And Riffetra knows?"

"Yes, he knows. He has consented to help, and, indeed, with some eagerness. I do not believe he likes our enemies. Of course," added Dust, "if they were likable, they would not be our enemies."

"That is true."

"I must add that, when I first began to put matters in place, I returned the Wriggling Dolphin to Riffetra as part of making my arrangements, but learning how he assisted you, it pleases me very much that we were able to reward him this way."

"We are in perfect accord, my friend."

Dust nodded. "Then we will bring you to Wetrock, and I will make the final arrangements with Captain Sheen."

"Apropos, these pirates."

"Well?"

"Do you trust them?"

"More than I trust the Jhereg, and we must deal with them as well."

"You perceive, that is not reassuring. I must put my life in their hands."

"I trust them."

"Then I will trust them as well."

"Then I will go upstairs and give the order to sail for Wetrock."

Ten minutes later, the *Raptor,* sails set, gathered way and began the journey south.

Livosha heard Riffetra slowly climbing from his tavern to his quarters, sometimes mumbling loud enough for her to hear, cursing his legs for their weakness and his back for its aches. He reached the top, opened his door, walked in and bowed.

"My lady," he said.

"I have told you, Riffetra, you need not call me that."

"I understand, my lady."

"Well?"

"You spoke of one called Fidra?"

"That is right."

"He is here."

She rose to her feet as if on a spring. "What, now?"

He nodded assent.

"Describe him?"

"Eyes like a Dzurlord, face like a Tiassa, but he wears the colors of the Orca, of course, as befits one of Berwick's guards. He has a mark of rank on his right shoulder in the form of a pin. Six and a half feet tall, hair pulled back into a tail bound with a red ribbon. He carries a longsword on a harness over his back, has a scar across his nose, and is missing a lower front tooth."

"Very good. You have horses?"

"I do."

"Then send a boy on one to Sheen on the *Raptor*. Tell him to have the longboat ready, and to be prepared to set sail in an instant. Also, have another horse saddled and ready for me."

"I will do so. And you?"

"I will wait ten minutes, and then the dance will begin."

"Is that enough time?"

"If the boy and the horse are fast enough."

"You could wait longer."

"A horse that is saddled and ready can attract attention."

"That is true. Very well. I am leaving now. But remember, I do not walk fast."

"I understand."

She waited what seemed to her to be ten minutes, then she waited a little longer, knowing that her excitement would cause her to misconstrue the time. Then she stood, made certain her sword was loose in its sheath, and went down the stairs into the tavern.

Only one table was occupied, and she spotted him at once from Riffetra's description. She approached the table slowly, letting them all get a good look at her.

"I beg your pardon," she said. "But are you the one called Fidra?"

He looked up at her through narrowed eyes and said, "What of it?"

"I have a question, and I believe that, as a sergeant in Lord Berwick's guard, only you can answer."

"Ah, well, if it is an official matter, I am off duty. See me to-morrow at the barracks behind the manor."

"Oh, I beg your pardon, but it is not in the least official."

"Oh, it is not?"

"I give you my word, it is quite personal."

He shrugged. "Well?"

"I want to know if it is true that you are useless in a fight except when outnumbering an unarmed enemy ten to one. I have said that no one could be that much of a coward, and yet I have heard—"

That was as far as he got before Fidra roared, stood, and drew his sword. Livosha smiled, drew, and put herself on guard. "Oh," she said. "I beg your pardon. I have failed to introduce myself."

At that moment, she stepped in as smoothly as an Issola, beat aside his blade with a movement too quick for the eye to follow, and ran her sword directly through his heart. She did not stop there, however, but continued, pushing her blade all the way into him until the crossguard was against his chest, most of the blade protruding from his back, and her mouth was near his ear. She whispered, "Livosha, daughter of Cerwin and Tiscara, sister of Nira. May you find a purple robe cut to your size, you foul, murdering worm-snake."

The others at the table were too shocked to respond for an instant, and before they could stand, Livosha took the sword from the dying man's hand, and, even as he slumped to the floor, she held it with her left hand to the neck of the man nearest her. "If any of you stand up, I will remove this man's head from his body."

No one doubted she meant it. They froze in place, and, as Fidra's body slumped down, she put her foot on it and withdrew her sword. Then she said, "I do not promise to kill the first one of you to go through that door, but I do not promise not to, either." Then she saluted them, dropped the other sword, turned and walked out the door. By the time they had risen to their feet and followed her out, she was mounted on a horse and headed toward the shore, where Sheen and his longboat awaited her.

This time, when Halvar saw the one called Daifan enter The Flotsam, he did not hesitate; on the contrary, he at once got to his feet, saluted, and gestured toward the small room in which they had spoken before. This time, moreover, it was Halvar who ordered the wine, signaling for two cups, and he shook his head at his bodyguards, indicating that he would speak with Daifan alone.

Once they were seated and each had wine, Halvar said, "Your prediction proved accurate."

"Well."

"There has been an increase in arrests, and a corresponding rise in the bribes needed to prevent them."

The one called Daifan nodded.

"So, then, you pretend you are able to repair this state of affairs?"

"I believe, my good Halvar, that I can instruct you in the steps necessary to remedy the matter, or, at the least, alleviate it."

"Then you perceive you have my attention."

"You know who Prince Traanzo is?"

Halvar narrowed his eyes. "What of him?"

"You have had dealings with him."

"You think so?"

"I am convinced of it. Indeed, if you need to be reminded of your own business arrangements, well, I will be glad to assist. There was a Jhereg known to you as Arin, who worked for His Highness. Arin arranged for certain of the prince's business dealings, of which you were the beneficiary. This excellent arrangement came to an abrupt end some two years ago, and you have not heard from Arin since that time. Come, is my information good?"

"Perhaps too good."

Daifan shrugged. "You perceive, I have sources. If I did not, you would not have consented to see me."

Halvar nodded slowly. "Well then, what is it you wish?"

"I should think that you have a certain loyalty to Arin. He is, after all, one of us." Daifan accompanied this statement with a singular smile.

Halvar ignored the smile, not entirely certain of its meaning, and said, "We do not betray our own."

"Well, but what of His Highness?"

"I do not understand the question you do me the honor to ask."

"You can stop the persecution of your operations by speaking to the Countess of Whitecrest and giving a statement, for the record, of the illegal activities in which His Highness was engaged. You perceive, the prince is not one of us."

"That is true, and yet—"

"Well?"

"I am having a certain difficulty in understanding how I am to testify about the prince's illegal activities without, at the same time, testifying about my own—not, of course, that I have ever engaged in such. But if I had, this would be a conundrum."

"And here is a way out of it," said Daifan. Moving slowly—a courtesy Halvar appreciated—the other reached into his cloak and pulled out a rolled-up paper. He removed the ribbon, unfolded it, and held it out.

Halvar took it, and said, "But what is this?"

"It is a document signed by the countess and by two witnesses stating that you will not be prosecuted for any crimes to which you allude during any testimony against His Highness, and that, moreover, no information gained in such a way will, in any way, at any time, be used to hinder your activities. It will be, my dear Halvar, as if you had never spoken. You must know an advocate; I suggest you bring that document to your advocate and get an opinion of someone you can trust."

"Well, and if I sign it?"

"Then, should you testify against His Highness, the persecution of your enterprises will stop, or at least be significantly reduced, for some period of time."

"That is sufficiently vague."

"It is what I can offer."

"Very well, I will bring this document to my advocate."

"And if he says to sign it?"

"Then I will sign it. And then?"

"Present yourself at the home of the countess, and give your name. You will be escorted within, and your testimony taken, and a time appointed for you to return and deliver it officially."

"And will His Highness know of my testimony?"

Daifan shrugged. "Do you fear him? I give you my word, once this is done, he will be in no position to harm you."

Halvar nodded. "Very well, Daifan. I will consider this. Apropos—"

"Well?"

"What is all of this to you?"

"I am paying a debt," said Daifan.

In the middle of a pleasant summer Farmday, at the newly built and, we must admit, not aesthetically displeasing barracks on the property now belonging to Lord Berwick, there came a clap as of someone requesting entrance. Within (for our attention is directed, at this point, inside the structure, and we apologize if our delay in making this explicit has led to any confusion) the barracks, which consisted of a number of identical beds, certain rooms for entertainment, and an office shared by the sergeant and the commander, inside this structure, we say, a man nicknamed Ironhead and a woman called Istamar looked at each other in some confusion. "Who," said Ironhead, "claps at the door of a barracks?"

"I give you my word," said Istamar, "I have not the least idea in the world, unless—"

"Well?"

"It is someone who is unaware that it is a barracks."

"Ah, I had not considered that possibility. So, then, a stranger?"

"It is possible."

"Well, shall we learn the answer?"

The two of them were closest to the door, and none of the others, who were resting, or engaged in quiet conversation, or engaged in loud conversation, or were gambling with dice, seemed to have any interest. Istamar shrugged. "If not, well, we will never know."

"That is true," said Ironhead. Then, in a louder voice, he called, "Please come in, and be certain to greet the lord and lady of the house, and to give your wet garments into the hands of the servant."

Upon completing this speech, he looked around to see if others found it as amusing as he did, but, alas, except for Istamar, no one else had heard it. She, at least, was polite enough to smile at his witticism. This small exchange having been completed, they turned their attention to the door, and saw a woman wearing the colors of the House of the Dragon coming toward them. As she approached, she said, "Well, I admit, there is little on the outside to indicate what it is within, but then, I have served lords about whom the same thing can be said, sometimes to the good, sometimes not. I am Kelsama. Whom do I have the honor of addressing?"

The other two rose and bowed politely. "I am Istamar, named for the waterfall in Ramshorn Peak in the Kanefthali Mountains. This is my friend Ironhead, and, while I will not explain whence comes his name, permit me to recommend that, if you should brawl with him, do not count on knocking him senseless."

Kelsama returned the salute and said, "I will remember this advice, should it ever be required. But, is there an officer with whom I can speak about employment? I was on my way to Zerika's Point to offer my services to the provost when a sudden shift in the wind caused our ship to run aground near a small hamlet some four miles north of here. This being the first sizable town I've found, I thought to offer my sword before moving on."

"In fact," said Ironhead, "it may be that there is such a position, as we have just lost a sergeant, and Noffin there having been promoted, the watch is now one short."

"Do you lose sergeants often?"

Istamar shrugged. "He is not lost, precisely. I was using the term, you perceive, only in the general sense of no longer a part of the guard."

"He resigned?"

"He was killed. And, you perceive, once someone is dead, well, he is then unable to perform his duties, and so is no longer a part of the guard."

"How did he die? I ask because, while I am quite content to rent out the use of my sword, and even the arm that goes with it, well, naturally, the more fighting I expect, the more danger I anticipate. And the more danger I anticipate, the more I will expect to be paid, for as you are aware, those of us who sell our ability to commit violence feel we must have sufficient recompense to equal the value of the risk."

"Oh, I understand completely," said Ironhead. "I have often made the same remark, have I not, Istamar?"

"You have, and the proof is, I have heard you make it."

"Well, but as for your sergeant?"

"As for Fidra," said Istamar, "it was the product of some old quarrel. I am unaware of the details, but he was run through quite effectually. Then the woman who killed him escaped on a pirate ship, so I do not think we will ever know."

"And here," added Ironhead, "well, it is such a sleepy village, and so much in the control of his lordship the baron, we have nothing to do but stand guard duty and play dice."

"Well," said Kelsama, "while I do not wish to appear to take advantage of another's misfortune, I am happy to take advantage of another's misfortune."

Ironhead nodded to signify he understood this reasoning perfectly. "Go ask Noffin," he said.

"I will do so, and, should I be hired, well, I give you my word I will buy the first round."

"In that event," said Istamar, shrugging like a Lyorn, "I hope you are hired."

In all of this, it may be the reader has forgotten the director, who was taken by a pair of Kinsmen and put into a carriage and driven away. If the reader has forgotten him, rest assured the author has not, and the proof is, we will now discover to the reader what has become of him.

He was put into the carriage with one of the Kinsmen who blindfolded him, and who said not a word the entire time. After a drive of over an hour, they at last came to a stop, and he was roughly guided from the carriage and down a short stairway into a musky-smelling place that he concluded to be a basement.

He was forcibly seated on a hard chair and his blindfold was removed. It was dim, but his eyes had become accustomed to this from the blindfold, so he was able to see that he was, indeed, in a basement, along with two Kinsmen and a very remarkable figure, dressed all in white, who looked down at him with a sardonic smile.

"Who are you?" blurted the director.

"Call me Dust, Director," he said. "Although you once knew me as number eighty-one."

"You!"

Dust bowed. "But I beg you to understand that I am not your concern. Your concern should be these gentlemen, who feel you have betrayed them. They were in favor of cutting you into a certain number of pieces and bringing you in a bag out onto the Shallow Sea and gambling about how many sharks you would attract in that condition, but I prevailed upon them to listen to you first, and so they have agreed, being kind-hearted gentlemen. I suggest, therefore, you speak quickly, but also choose your words with care. If it is hard to do both at once, well, I apologize."

The director's mouth opened and closed like that of, if not a shark, at least a fish. At length he said, "What do you want of me?"

Dust shook his head. "Not a good answer." He turned to the two Kinsmen. "Do you think it's a good answer?" They shook their heads. Dust returned his attention to the director.

"I don't know—"

"You worked for Prince Traanzo before; you work for Prince Traanzo now," said Dust coolly. "For hundreds of years you have been his dog. Well?"

The director nodded and sobbed. None of those around him appeared to be moved by this display of emotion.

"There is only one question to which we want an answer: will you work to make amends?"

"Anything!" he cried. "Anything I can do!"

"Will you," said Dust, "help us destroy His Highness?"

The director looked up, then, and it might be said that, for the first time, a certain light came into his eyes. "With the greatest will in the world," he said.

Chapter the Thirty-first

In Which His Highness Yields to Force and Berwick Yields His Supper

It was Prince Traanzo's custom, on the first Marketday of every month, to visit the local market in person. He chose Marketday for this activity for reasons that should be clear without the need for an explanation. When he made this sojourn, in which he was always looking for especially good seafood and weaverfruit, which he pretended kept him in a state of robust health and improved his prowess, he would always bring along two servants to carry his selections, as well as two of his guard to ensure he was not jostled by peasants as he engaged in his perusals.

On this occasion, however, he failed to purchase anything, for the simple reason that his excursion was interrupted by some eight armed individuals, all wearing the blue and white of the House of the Tiassa, who surrounded him as he was about to enter the market. One of them, who seemed to be the leader, said, "I beg Your Highness's pardon, but if you would be so good as to accompany us, my mistress Whitecrest begs a word of you."

Traanzo frowned, looked at his two guards, then at the eight in Tiassa colors, and said, "Begs?"

The other bowed assent, agreeing that this was, in fact, the word she would choose.

"Well, and if I refuse?"

"I will be required to insist," she said.

"And yet, I am a prince, and she is a countess. So by what right, then, does she insist?"

"Your Highness must understand that he is in the County of Whitecrest."

"Well, and then, am I under arrest?"

"Your Highness has understood exactly."

"And my guards, may they join us?"

"If they surrender their weapons, they will be most welcome."

"But I? Am I to surrender my weapon as well?"

"If Your Highness would be so kind."

"But, this is intolerable! Upon what charge am I arrested?"

"As my instructions are to bring Your Highness without delay into the presence of her ladyship, well, I am convinced this question will be answered quickly."

Traanzo glared, then, unbuckling his sword belt, said, "I yield to force, but under protest."

"Your Highness's protest is noted, I promise."

"Very well," said Traanzo. "Then I accompany you."

"There is a coach around the corner, so you need not be seen walking under arrest."

"The countess is thoughtful," said the prince.

In due course, the carriage rolled up to Whitecrest Manor, the door was opened, and Traanzo emerged, his teeth clenched, his hands in fists. He was duly escorted inside, through the front door as if he were a guest, yet with a pair of the countess's guards ahead of him and behind him. He was brought through the house and out to her study, where, as he entered, the countess rose and bowed.

"Your Highness," she said.

"What is the meaning of this?" said the prince.

"Please, sit down, Your Highness."

"I will not. I demand to know why I am here."

The countess shrugged, remained standing herself, and nodded to one of her guards who had been positioned by the door the entire time. The guard left, and, in a moment returned with three individuals: one was a Jhereg, the second appeared to be a Chreotha, the third an Orca.

"This," said the countess, "is Halvar, of the House of the Jhereg. He is about to testify to illegal activities carried out for you, through an intermediary known as Arin."

"Arin! But, he used forged papers to gain employment with me!"

"Indeed, and here is the forger, Sajen, whom no doubt you recognize, as he spent some time in your dungeons. He will testify, moreover, to having worked with this man, Gystralan, as part of a plot to defraud an Iorich of her land and titles."

"But," said Traanzo, "it wasn't my plot! This Gystralan, well, I have never seen him before!"

"No," said the countess. "But you know the others. And here is someone else you know."

At that moment a man in Iorich colors came in, arms held by two guards, who seemed, in fact, to be there less to guard him than to keep him from falling over.

"The director!" cried Traanzo.

"I'm sorry," he said, "they made me!"

"Ah, if we are having a reunion," said the countess, "here are some more."

At that point two others came in, both of them wearing the colors of the House of the Jhereg.

"Arin!" said the prince. "But who are you?"

"I am called Daifan," said the other.

"Well?"

"Once I was called Eremit of Cryden House. Ah, I perceive you recognize the name?"

The prince did not respond at once, but then, at last, he emitted the word, "You!"

"Why yes, it is I. I have much to say about the jail in which you illegally detained me for a number of years."

"That . . . there is no Empire to indict me for that!"

Eremit shrugged. "But there is a countess to indict you for the criminal activity between you and Halvar, to which both Halvar and Arin can testify. Arin, moreover, can testify to more than that, as he is, in fact, Kefaan, son of Cerwin, one of those against whom you conspired with Dorin. And, of course, you know very well what the director can tell. Shall we begin reciting our testimony before the countess, Your Highness? Because, once this recitation has begun, well, it will not stop until you are stripped of all land, all titles, all holdings, and all monies, and cast into the dungeons beneath this very room we now occupy. Or—"

"Yes, or?" said the prince, unable to disguise the eagerness in his voice.

"There is another possibility."

"What is that? You perceive, I am listening with all the ears of my body." And, it seemed, he was doing just that; at any rate, he was leaning forward, perspiration glistening on his face, his eyes wide, and his face going through remarkable changes in color as, in the space of a few breaths, it would become flushed, then drained of all color, then flushed again.

"Your Highness," said the countess, observing this remarkable phenomenon, "may I bring you some wine?"

"No, no! No, my lady, thank you, but, I must know, what is the 'or' of which I have heard spoken."

"Ah, you wish me to tell you that?"

"The gods! I think I do!"

"Then shall I tell you now?"

"If you do not, well, I will veritably swoon in this second, and then will be unable to hear."

"Ah, well," said Daifan. "Here it is, then. You give up your title as Prince, and your house here in Adrilankha you sign over to me. All of the wealth you have stored in this city, and all holdings, will pass to Livosha and Kefaan, and you will retire to your duchy, which, I am certain, would be overjoyed to see you. And, in addition—"

"Well?"

"You will send a trusted messenger, who is someone well known to Count Dorin, to that person, demanding he come and see you by the quickest available means."

"That is all? And I can keep my freedom and my life?"

"Your freedom, certainly. Your life, well, I only promise you are safe from me, from the countess, from Halvar, from Kefaan, and from Livosha. That is to say, if there are others who discover you, some of those who have, perhaps, escaped from the island, well, I can offer you no promises on that score."

"Yes, yes, I understand."

"Then you accept?"

"I accept, I accept! Ah, I have had a terror of being imprisoned since, well—"

"Since you learned of the illegal jail?"

He nodded.

"Then," said Daifan, "here are the papers, and we have witnesses; come, let us begin the ceremony. And when we are done, we will escort you to your residence—or, that is to say, my residence—and you will select someone to carry the message to Dorindom."

"I know just the one," said Traanzo. "Her name is Hadrice."

Once Traanzo had signed the papers, and left in the company of the countess's guards to ensure he did what he had said, the director said, "What of me?"

Daifan considered. "Yes, you. Do you remember number seventy-two?"

"I do. I remember all of my guests."

"Your what?"

"My prisoners."

"Yes, well, number seventy-two, her name is Kelsama, and she is a Dragonlord."

"Yes?"

"She is far from here now. But she is coming this way. Wherefore—"

"Yes, wherefore?"

"If I may do myself the honor to give you some advice—"

"You may! You may!"

"Run."

The director's eyes widened, he stood up, made a perfunctory bow, and ran from the room.

"Do you think," said Kefaan, "that Kelsama will chase him?"

Daifan shrugged. "In truth, it is none of my concern."

The next time there came a clap outside the barracks door, Ironhead, who happened to be taking his ease with Istamar and Kelsama, said, "My dear Clapper (for this was the nickname they had given Kelsama), if you are here, who would clap at a barracks door? And if you are not here, how am I speaking to you?"

"You have set a pretty mystery," said Kelsama. "I confess, not only am I unaware of the answer, but thinking about it threatens to make my head spin as if I were again playing that game to which you introduced me at the Wriggling Dolphin, and which, I promise, I will never play again."

"For my part," said Istamar, looking at the door, "I think there must necessarily be two of her, and one is so pleased with our company that the other will also wish a post."

"Well," said Ironhead, "but there is no post, and so, she shall have to share it."

"With herself," agreed Istamar.

"This will certainly confuse me," said Kelsama. "In fact, I have no doubt, it will confuse both of me."

"I wonder which one it will confuse more?" said Istamar.

"Come now," said Ironhead. "Surely if there was ever a question to which the answer is moot, it is that one?"

"Perhaps you are right," said Istamar.

"Or perhaps," said Kelsama, "we should call to whoever is at the door to enter. For my part, I am most anxious to learn if I am as attractive from a distance as I am from near-by."

"With this plan," said Istamar, "I agree."

"Very well," said Ironhead. Then he called loudly, "Come, and be one of our troop. You may join us in being given extra duty for striking a comrade by the sergeant, having your wages suspended for cursing by the lieutenant, and being cursed at and struck by the lord for whom we are pledged to risk our lives in exchange for wages that are too small even when not reduced."

"Well said," murmured Istamar.

This time, when the door opened, it was, in fact, a Teckla who stood there, a woman rather younger than middle years, and with her, as if it were a companion, was a large cask. She stood in the doorway, appearing uncertain what to do. Istamar stood and said, "Well, girl, who are you and what is that and what are you doing here?"

"I am Jerin, my lady, and this is wine, and my master Riffetra said it was his best, and I was to deliver it to the manor."

"I haven't seen you before," said Ironhead.

"I am new, my lord."

"Well," said Istamar, shrugging. "This isn't—"

"Any too soon!" interrupted Kelsama. "Just bring it right in."

Istamar frowned at her, and said, "And yet—"

"Hush," she whispered. "A keg of Riffetra's best wine? Delivered to us? If your enemy were to spread his arms and cry 'strike!' would you hesitate?"

"But," whispered Istamar, "the manor will not get its wine."

"And then? Riffetra will get a tongue lashing, and this girl will get a beating. Meanwhile, we will get a keg of excellent wine."

This logic proved too powerful to refute. "Yes, Jerin," she said. "Roll it right in, and we'll be sure to see that it gets where it is going."

"You are very kind, my lady."

"It is nothing," she said.

Jerin bowed, turned, and left.

Just past the tenth hour after noon on the second day of the month of the Issola in the thirty-eighth year after the fall of the Empire, Berwick set down his cup, rose from his dinner table, and said, in exactly the words used by the prince the month before, "What is the meaning of this?" This is a question that, as a rule, is not one requesting an answer, but rather is a statement in the form of a question, which is to say, it is a means of asserting that, whatever is, in fact, happening at that moment is displeasing to, and does not have the approval of, the speaker. In this case, however, that is to say, upon the date and at the time to which we have already referred, it could also have been interpreted, quite reasonably, as a question, in that the event that had just transpired was one that could not but be puzzling.

Should the reader wonder to what event we, and Berwick, are alluding, we will answer at once: A broad-shouldered man with a shaved head, wearing brightly colored silk clothing of red, yellow, and blue, appeared at the table unannounced, holding in his hand a glistening curved blade.

Although Berwick's remark could with great justice be considered a question as well as a declaration, he did not wait for an answer, but instead at once asked another question: "Where are my door wards?"

"They are occupied."

"How did you get in here?"

"A few of us came in from upstairs, through a tunnel that you would have discovered if you had explored the manor thoroughly. Once in, and once we had rendered your guards unable to resist and locked your servants in the cellar, the rest of us came in through the front door, like gentlemen. Apropos, I am called Sheen, but you may address me as Captain if you prefer."

Sheen approached the table as Berwick, standing, watched him with his mouth open; Berwick's son, we should say, had not stood, therefore his mouth remained open while he sat. Sheen looked over the contents of the table, and selected some roasted kethna. He picked it up, bit it, chewed it, swallowed it, then reached over and took Berwick's cup and drained it. "I am told," he said, "that undercooked kethna may cause stomach upset, or sometimes even violent illness. And yet, is it truly necessary to burn it black? It hardly seems respectful to the kethna, who, after all, gave his life for this exact purpose."

"What are you doing in my house?" demanded Berwick.

"Plundering it," said Sheen.

At that point, a woman in similar garb to Sheen's, and also carrying a sword, appeared and said, "There is jewelry of various sorts in the cabinet of the south bedchamber, Captain. Also, some small supplies of coin here and there. So far, no more than that. We are continuing to look."

Berwick suddenly flew into action, which action was to reach for the pull rope next to him. He grasped it and pulled, and as he did so there was a flash from Sheen's sword, and he discovered he was only holding the end of a rope in his hand.

Sheen picked up a piece of bread and remarked, "In truth, my dear Berwick, I don't know why I did that. The few of your men who are awake have already been dealt with by my crew, and it will take more than a bell to wake the rest, who, with what was put into the cask of wine we gave them, would sleep through a cataclysm." He bit into the bread.

"What—"

Sheen held up his finger. When he had swallowed, he said, "What was the question you were about to do me the honor to ask?"

"Why are you doing this?"

"Why? My dear Berwick, you must know that you have a reputation for wealth. And there are so many pirates operating along these coasts that soon we must begin to steal from each other, which would be humiliating, as well as difficult."

"Well, but—are you going to kill me?"

"Oh, it is unlikely it will come to that."

"How, unlikely?"

"Why, yes. We want your treasure. Once you give us that, why, we will be on our way."

"But, I have no treasure!"

"Bah. You perceive, it is impossible."

"I have considerable funds, but they aren't in gold."

"How, not in gold?"

"No, they are in the form of drafts on the Imperial Treasury."

"But, there is no Imperial treasury."

"Perhaps someday there will be. Also, I have some amount invested with a business partner."

"That is all very well, except—"

"Well?"

"I don't believe you."

"It is true!"

"Well, well. You perceive, there is nothing to be concerned with."

"How, nothing?"

"I give you my word. We will look through the house until we find the treasure, then we will leave you alone."

"But there is no treasure!"

Sheen shrugged. "We will lock you and your son in an upstairs room while we search, and, if we do not find the treasure—"

"Well, if you do not find it?"

"We will encourage you to tell us where it is."

"But—"

"Don't worry, my friend. No doubt we will find it on our own, and there will be no need for matters to become unpleasant." By this time, several more pirates had entered. Sheen signaled for a few of them and said, "Escort these two to one of the upstairs bed-chambers and lock the door. Not the master bed-chamber, as I may wish to rest. One of you remain outside the door, and another outside of the manor beneath the window. And, just in case the treasure is hard to find, prepare the questioning devices."

They immediately carried out his orders, and he sat down at the table, looking over what more there was to eat.

Chapter the Thirty-second

In Which Berwick Wishes to Visit Dorin Who Wishes to Visit Adrilankha

Once they were in the room, Yanis, on whose countenance distress could be plainly read, said, "Father, what are we to do?"

Berwick, who was himself not free from dismay, as proven by his drawn features and trembling hands, said, "I don't know."

"Will they find the treasure?"

"Bah. I told the truth, there is no treasure."

"So much the worse, for then they will torture us."

"I know, I know! Let me think!"

"As long as you are done thinking before they are done looking, my father, well, I have nothing to say about it."

"You perceive, you are not helping."

"Nothing would help, except a way out of this place!"

At these words, Berwick raised his eyes, which had been up until then fixed on the floor, and said, "Wait! A way out!"

"Well, what of it?"

"Weren't you listening? That fool of a pirate said there is a secret tunnel."

"But father, it is secret. You perceive, that means we don't know where it is."

"We can discover it."

"But we are confined to this room."

"Perhaps it is in this room."

"Why would they put us in the room with a passage to a tunnel?"

"Did you attend, my son? Most of the pirates came in through the front door."

"Well?"

"If the ones who escorted us to this room came that way, then they could have put us in the one with the tunnel in it. You remember he said not to use the master bed-chamber. I am certain if there were a secret entrance there, I'd have found it. And if it had been yours, you would have found it. There are only three other rooms, of which this is one, thus, we have odds of one in three that there is a secret entrance in this very room. It would be foolish indeed not to search for it."

"Very well, I agree with searching."

"Then let's be about it. You start there, move the furniture and look under it. I will start in the closet."

It took ten minutes to determine that there was a passage there, and another hour to find the catch, but at last they did. They pulled open the trap door.

"Quickly, get a lamp. It is liable to be dark."

"Do we know where it leads, father?"

"No, but it must lead away. This must be how those two children escaped us. We will be careful. But hurry, we must be gone before those fools come looking for us."

They climbed down the ladder, Yanis pulling the door closed behind him. When they reached the bottom, they lit the lantern and set out as fast as they could.

Soon they reached a ladder, and stopped and considered it. "The tunnel continues, but the ladder goes up," said Yanis.

"That is true. And then?"

"Which way should we go?"

"Let us see whither this ladder leads. Then we can decide if we should continue."

"With this plan I agree, only—"

"Well?"

"You say 'us.'"

"And is it not a perfectly good word?"

"Oh, Father, I say nothing against the word. But I wonder if its use means you wish us both to climb."

"As for that, well, you perceive you are younger than I am."

"That is true. And then?"

"You climb up, look around, then report what you see. But remain quiet!"

"I will do my best to."

He climbed up, and in a short time (although, in truth, it felt considerably longer to Berwick, who was perspiring and shifting his feet the entire time) he returned and said, "It is a stable, and there are horses."

"Any sign of pirates?"

"None."

"Can you saddle a horse?"

"I think so. Can you?"

"I used to know how."

"Come, let us try."

It took them some considerable time, and no small amount of noise—indeed, were the exact motions and remarks reproduced it would be an effective scene in a Commoner Alley farce, for which reason we will not reproduce them, as historical events ought not to become the subject of vulgar humor—they managed to get saddles and bridles on two horses, and even, after a certain amount of effort, mounted them, after which they went racing out of the stable, down the lane, and away.

As soon as they were gone, the pirate who'd been watching from the house returned to Sheen, who still waited at the table, treating himself to nuts and raisins.

"Captain."

"Well?"

"They are gone."

"They found the horses?"

"They did."

"And saddled them?"

"Eventually. Although—"

"Well?"

"If I knew a sailor who handled a ship as they handled horses, well, I should not let him aboard."

Sheen shrugged. "As long as they managed. Did they head out of town?"

"They did."

Sheen nodded. "Very well, we will wait for an hour to give them a good start, and then return to the ship."

"Understood, Captain."

"The last one out is to release the servants. Do we have the valuables?"

"There is little of value here, Captain, but what there is we have taken."

"Very good, then." He finished the wine and said, "We have done our part, my friends. Now it is up to Dust."

Berwick and Yanis took significantly longer to cover the distance between Wetrock and Dorindom than Eremit had seven hundred years before for several reasons. Chief among them was that, instead of a post system, they had to make the entire journey on one horse each, and, second, the quality of their horsemanship was not of the highest caliber. Nevertheless, at last they arrived in time, exhausted, frightened, and relieved all at once.

Upon approaching the gate, they were challenged by a guard who, to Berwick's eye, was impartial, professional, and more than a little intimidating, which is to say, while Berwick was used to such challenges as a formality, a part of the process by which one was admitted to the presence of the powerful, he was not accustomed to the sensation that, if he answered wrong, he ran the risk of having violence done to him. Nevertheless, he managed to give his name, and his son's, and to say that he wished to see His Benevolence Count Dorin on a matter of the greatest possible urgency. The guard, who upon hearing this name pronounced made an effort to appear agreeable, an effort that was appreciated even if not entirely successful, had the message transmitted.

The reader may have observed in all of this a change from our last visit, and, if so, we compliment the reader on his perspicacity. Since the fall of the Empire, the traffic at the gate had diminished to a trickle, each of these being carefully questioned. Similarly, the market area outside the castle itself was sensibly reduced and business there was transacted always under the eye of several guards positioned high on the castle walls and ready to signal an alarm of any disturbance.

In due time, word came back that he was to be admitted at once. It was with no small relief, then, that Berwick saluted the guard and went into Dorindom proper. The Issola—that is, the old gentleman who had spoken so kindly to Eremit so many centuries before—was not on duty at present, but another Issola was there, who greeted them and directed them to the count's private study. The count was there, seated at his desk. Next to him was someone Berwick had never seen before, a woman, openly wearing a sword in Dorin's study, and looking calm and, indeed, imperturbable. Berwick and Yanis made their obeisances, and the count nodded. "It has been some time, my dear Baron," said the count. "While it is always a pleasure to see you and Yanis, I cannot help but wonder if there is some particular or urgent cause for this visit."

"Oh, there is, Your Benevolence, and I give you my word, it is most particular and extremely urgent."

"Well, sit down then, my friends, and let us see. What has happened?"

"What has happened? My home was invaded!"

"How, invaded? By an army?"

"By a band of pirates! They were about to torture me when I escaped."

"Us," muttered Yanis, but the others didn't hear him.

"I am sorry for your trouble," said Dorin. "It sounds quite alarming."

"Alarming? I think it was!" said Berwick. "You perceive, I am alarmed, and, moreover, distraught. Can you do anything?"

"What is it you wish me to do?"

"Send men!"

"Haven't you your own?"

"They were drugged by the pirates."

"Well, no doubt they are fine by now," said the count complacently.

"And yet—"

"You must know," said the count, "that my time is not my own. I have been summoned to Adrilankha."

"How, summoned?"

The count nodded. "I received the message yester-day, sent by Hadrice, whom I trust entirely. I am packing to-day, and will depart to-morrow."

"To Adrilankha?"

"To His Highness."

"And yet, pirates."

"You are an Orca, and you are afraid of pirates?"

"Your Benevolence, it is because I am an Orca that I am afraid of pirates."

"Well." He shrugged. "Come along with me, see His Highness. He has profited from our venture, and so should be well disposed toward you. Perhaps he can use his influence to raise your barony to a county when he raises my county to a duchy, thus putting us both in a better position, both offensive and defensive, against our enemies."

"Perhaps it would be better for me to wait here."

"If you wish. I will give the necessary instructions."

"You will speak to His Highness on my behalf?"

"With the greatest pleasure, Baron."

"And yet, my home."

"Father," said Yanis.

"Well?"

"If His Benevolence will loan me a hundred troops, I will return to our home and secure it. And if the pirates are still there, well, I will endeavor to give them a lesson in manners."

Berwick considered for a moment, then looked an inquiry at Dorin, who said, "A hundred troops? Very well. I will write the order."

Berwick nodded at Yanis, considered him for a moment, then said, "Very well, I leave it in your hands."

"I will do my best not to disappoint you."

"Very good."

Yanis accepted the note from Dorin, bowed, and left the room, a certain eagerness apparent in his step.

Berwick then turned to Dorin and said, "Very well then, Your Benevolence. When do you depart?"

"With the dawn. I will be surrounded by two hundred horsemen for our journey to the coast, which will take three days. Then I will board a ship I have reserved, and, with fair winds, I will be in Adrilankha in a month."

"Then it remains for me to wish Your Benevolence a safe and productive voyage, and I look forward to seeing you on your return."

"I will have someone show you to a room."

Berwick bowed his understanding, and, when the servant had come, followed him to his appointed room. Yanis, meanwhile, went down the stairway and outside to take charge of the hundred troops that had been placed at his disposal.

The *Abi's Love* caught the wind and left the harbor at Zerika's Point (by which, of course, we mean the town) on a Skyday morning and attempted to work her way around Zerika's Point (by which, on this occasion, we refer to the geographical feature). The wind seemed determined to run her onto the rocks on the northern coast of Greenaere, but at length she managed to come close enough to the wind to permit her to slide down, as it were, northeast of that island until the she was able to turn to the open sea.

The third day of the journey, the wind turned, coming right on her beam, and they were able to begin making up lost time. Dorin spent the greater portion of the first couple of days in his cabin, sick at first, then recovering; after that, however, he was nearly always on deck (to the annoyance of the sailors in whose way he frequently was), sometimes looking aft at the schools of porpoises that might be following them, or just at the wake, flowing out in a smooth line; sometimes all the way forward as if peering into the future.

On the fourth day, Dorin was on deck when he caught sight of the coast again, first called by the lookout, then apparent on deck as dim, uneven ridges that could have been mountains, clouds, or something else entirely.

"What is that?" asked Dorin of the sailor who was closest to him.

"That is the coast, south of Ridgly, leading to the Elde Island Channel, which, though seventy miles wide at its narrowest, is nevertheless—"

The sailor's discourse was cut off by a call from the lookout who had not only been the first to see the coast, but was now the first to descry a set of sails, and then another.

"Pirates?" said Dorin, sounding worried.

"It is unlikely, my lord," said the sailor confidently. "You perceive, pirates by their nature do not cooperate, and thus do not sail in company. Moreover, what would be the good of such a combination, when they would only have to divide such treasure or ransom as they acquired among more crews?"

The lookout, meanwhile, called yet another set of sails, and still more, which appeared to lend credence to the sailor's argument.

"But then, what is it?"

"No doubt merchants from Adrilankha, who are sailing together to provide mutual protection from—"

"Pirates," called the lookout.

The sailor looked up angrily, as if the lookout had contradicted him for no reason, then he looked back, his eyes growing wide, even as the captain came up with his glass.

"Pirates?" said Dorin.

"And yet—" said the sailor.

"A veritable fleet," said the captain. "All flying the gray dagger."

"Will there be a fight?" asked Dorin.

No one answered for a minute, then two, then three as the captain kept his eyes on the approaching sails. At last he lowered his glass and said, "No, there will be no fight," and walked back to give orders to the crew.

"But then," said Dorin, "we are to surrender?"

As the crew was now busy for some time, no one answered him, but presently the activity—which, we should say, we are unwilling to describe in detail for the simple reason that, it being unfamiliar to Dorin, to give such information would be to give the reader knowledge that was denied to the individual whom we are watching, and, more, through whose eyes we are observing the unfolding of events, thus, though we would provide *more* information by doing so, in its most important features it would be wrong, or at least misleading—the activity, we say, lessened and Dorin repeated his question to the nearest sailor.

STEVEN BRUST

The sailor shrugged. "No doubt they will extort ransom from us, or take whatever cargo the captain happened to put on board."

Hadrice came up next to him, standing silent, a hand on the hilt of her sword, which made Dorin feel somewhat less concerned.

At length, the entire fleet was around them and presently a longboat came up and gently kissed the side of the *Abi's Love,* and then another from the other side. A dozen or so pirates came aboard from each, and spoke quietly to the captain. Dorin noticed that, all around them, in the pirate ships, of which there were at least half a dozen, were hundreds of pirates gathered at the rails, watching closely. He turned his eyes back to the captain, just as this worthy took a step back, as if startled, then he shrugged, turned, and pointed at the place where Dorin and Hadrice stood.

"What is this?" said Dorin. "Why was he—"

He stopped as a group of five individuals approached. "What is this?" said Dorin again.

"Ah," said one, a bald-headed man holding a curved blade. "I am Sheen of the *Raptor*, and this is the end of a chase. We thought we had lost you. The captain informed me you had been driven far south out of your way. When you failed to arrive, we had to make the best time we could to beat you to the Channel. For someone who didn't know he was being chased, well, you ran very effectually."

"Chased?" said Dorin. "Me? Why?"

"Well," said another, "perhaps I can answer that. I am Nosaj, captain of the *Creeping Cat*, at your service. And you, I presume, are Dorin?"

"*Count* Dorin," said His Benevolence.

Nosaj shrugged. "If you would be so good as to accompany us."

"Accompany you? But, why do you want me?"

"Ah, you ask that? Is it not the case that you have been profiting from forged letters of passage? A clever plan, I admit, provided you aren't caught. Come, do you deny it?"

If Dorin had had any thoughts of denying the charge, his face, which went through numerous changes of expression and color in a remarkably short time, at once demonstrated the futility of such an effort. Realizing this, he said, "But, how did you know of that?"

"Oh," said another of the band. "I'm afraid I told him. My name is Dust."

Dorin looked at him: A man with deep-set eyes, dressed all in white save for a red gemstone on his breast, who was now looking at the count with his head tilted, as if the one called Dust were a natural philosopher, and Dorin were an odd specimen found in someone's garden.

"Why?" said Dorin at last.

The one called Dust smiled. "You do not recognize me?"

"We have never met before!"

"On the contrary, I have had the honor of speaking to Your Benevolence on a previous occasion, some seven hundred years ago. On that occasion, however, I had a different name, and wore different clothes."

"But, what was your name then?"

"I was called Eremit of Cryden House, son of Nessit," he said.

The name hit Dorin like a blow. He quite nearly staggered, and stared at the other. "You!" he said at last.

Dust bowed.

"So then," continued Nosaj. "If you will be pleased to accompany us, we will discuss exactly what to do with you."

Hadrice, who had been standing imperturbably next to Dorin the entire time, upon hearing these words, moved forward until she was between him and the pirate.

"Well," said Nosaj. "What is this?"

"This," said a fourth individual, now stepping forward, "is my affair."

"But who are you?" cried Dorin.

She bowed. "I am Livosha, daughter of Cerwin. Next to me is my brother, Kefaan. We are aware that you have been looking for us, and no doubt feel a certain frustration at having failed to find us for so long. Yet now, I hope, your frustration is soothed, for if you still have not found us, well, we have found you. And," she added, drawing her sword and saluting Hadrice, "I believe you and I have some matters upon which to converse, do we not?"

Hadrice, for her part, had nothing to say, but she drew her sword, made a perfunctory salute, and put herself on her guard.

"Livosha," said Kefaan.

"Well?"

"I should prefer you not be punctured in this matter."

"Shards, I nearly agree with you! But have no concern, this is my affair."

"Very well."

"As an Iorich," remarked Livosha to Hadrice as she made a short lunge, tapping the weak of her opponent's blade with the weak of her own,

"I must express my pleasure, on this one occasion, that there is no Empire, and, thus, no need for the tedious formalities of dueling. We can simply slaughter one another as we please, and there is no one to say anything about it, don't you agree?"

Hadrice beat aside Livosha's blade and thrust, but the Iorich turned her body and stepped to the side, at which point she made a good cut at Hadrice's head, which the latter only avoided by the smallest margin.

"Ah, you are fast," said Livosha. She drew a dagger, an action that was matched by her opponent. "Apropos," she continued, "I beg you to observe that, should I happen to cut you, well, it will not be an accident."

Hadrice ignored these words and made another lightning-fast attack, attempting to knock both of Livosha's weapons aside with her dagger as she struck with her sword, this time coming close enough to cut a tear in the left sleeve of Livosha's shirt. "Oh come now," she said. "This is a favorite shirt. You perceive it is silk? Had I wanted a tunic, well, I should have ordered one in the first place."

Hadrice attacked once more, this time both blades weaving in a complex pattern, but once again Livosha slid to the side, and as she passed, she made a cut with her dagger for her enemy's throat that came close enough to cut a lock of her hair.

"There," said Livosha, "that looks better, don't you think? Shall we stop and beg the use of a mirror?"

Hadrice scowled, the first sign of emotion Livosha had seen her display. "Do you know, I would be throwing spells at you right now if the Orb were still active. Well, and if I knew how to throw spells."

Hadrice, still scowling, started another pass, but this time Livosha, instead of moving to the side, slid inside Hadrice's guard, bringing her sword in a quick circular motion that deflected both Hadrice's dagger and the sword, and, with a distance of only a few inches separating them, Livosha plunged her dagger to the hilt in Hadrice's throat.

Hadrice seemed startled, and she opened her mouth as if to speak, but only blood came out, and then she crumpled to a heap onto the deck.

"Well," said Livosha. Once Hadrice had stopped moving, she picked up the dead woman's dagger, which, the reader may recall, was silver, and said, "I believe I shall keep this, if no one objects."

Chapter the Thirty-third

In Which the Reader's Patience Is Rewarded as at Last Justice Is Served

Dorin stood with his mouth open until two of the other pirates came and escorted him into the longboat, which, once they were seated (a somewhat difficult and tedious proposition on Dorin's part, as he didn't seem to know how to navigate the rope ladder) they pushed off for the *Creeping Cat*. The process of getting Dorin onto the deck proved more difficult than getting down, and by the time it was finally accomplished, *Abi's Love* had already set her sails and was gliding smoothly away, with the air of a servant whose master had changed his mind about a beating and wishes to be far away before the matter is reconsidered.

Once he was safely aboard, he was brought to a place just abaft the foremast. He was not bound, it is true, but he was surrounded by a band of armed pirates who did not, to his eyes, appear sympathetic. He looked around for a means of escape, but, short of jumping into the Ocean-sea, none presented itself.

"So then," said Nosaj. "You have cheated us repeatedly for many years. In all fairness, we are not in the least outraged, or even offended by this action, but, alas, you have been caught, and thus we must find a means of satisfying ourselves, for the notion of being practiced upon fills us with sorrow, and, well, when we are sad, we have all agreed that we must find a way to be happy again."

The one called Sheen, standing somewhat apart, said, "You perceive, this is none of my affair, as I have never had the good fortune to be cheated by you. I simply watch to see that everything is carried out in the proper way."

"Well," said Dorin. "Of what does your happiness consist?"

"As to that," said Nosaj, "there has been a great deal of debate among the various crews about what sort of recompense to demand. Some of them want you to be cut into as many pieces as there are crews. Others want to just put two or three cuts in you—enough so you'll start bleeding, you understand, and then throw you into the water where sharks like to hunt. Still others—"

At this point, Dorin heard a rushing in his ears and the world seemed to spin. He next became aware of cold water in his face, and found that he was lying on the deck and there were several pirates who, in addition to cuffs, laughs, and harsh words, gave him assistance to his feet.

"Now, where was I?" said Nosaj blandly.

"Can't I pay you?" cried Dorin.

"How pay us?" Nosaj looked around elaborately at the other pirates. "I am uncertain. Have you enough? You perceive, while I am inclined to generosity, some of my companions, well, they fail to see the humor in the matter, although I have attempted to explain it to them. No, I think you don't have enough."

"I do, I'm sure I do!" cried Dorin.

"Well, let us see. How much do you have?"

"My fortune is—is nearly forty thousands of imperials."

"Another thing we were considering," said Nosaj, "is to attempt to see if the bloodfish off the coast of Zerika's Point can be induced to entertain you. If you are unfamiliar with them, they are unique in that they draw the blood from the larger species directly through their skin, using—"

"Eighty! Eighty thousand!"

"—a particular tube designed by nature so as to penetrate the skin in a way that, I am told, is excruciating to the victim. The experience, I have heard—"

"One hundred and forty thousands! It is all I have, every copper! I swear—"

"And your house and land?"

"Take it!"

"And you will give up your title to another?"

"Anyone you name!"

"And your interests in the sealstone operations?"

"All of it! All of it! Just let me live!"

"Very well," said Nosaj. "We accept your terms. Here is a note to your various bankers requiring them to remit the funds to us. This document is for the transfer of your land. This one is to your House, surrendering your title, and this one—"

"The gods! You have them prepared!"

"Well," said Nosaj, shrugging. "Kefaan, Livosha, and Dust will be good witnesses. There is a desk in my cabin. Would you care to begin signing?"

We must now, albeit briefly, risk jarring the reader's awareness to direct the reader to something taking place an hour later, and which we must
observe through the eyes, as it were, of a different person. The reason for
the first is that we do not believe it is useful to describe for the reader how
Dorin executed each letter of his signature, nor how the witnesses did the
same, therefore we will simply be acknowledging that this happened and
turning our attention to the next moment of import. The reason for the second is that this moment, which, we believe, is vital for the reader to witness
in order to understand the further developments of our history, cannot be
seen from the perspective of Count Dorin for the simple reason that, when
it took place, he wasn't there.

In fact, the only ones there (by "there" in this case, we mean the deck
of the *Creeping Cat*, which we would have mentioned earlier if we had not
first to establish the reason for the sudden change in time) where Livosha
had just emerged with Dust. Livosha was, at this time, holding a thick
sheaf of papers.

"You must guard those carefully," said Dust. "They will not be easy to
replace."

"Oh, there is no question of anything happening to them; I am fully
aware of their value."

"Very good."

"But next?"

"Well, next, you must return and take possession of your new property, while I—"

"Yes, while you?"

"I have business in another direction."

"I am aware of that, my friend. And yet, it took longer to capture the
ship than we had expected; will you still have time?"

"I think so. But you are right, I must not wait any longer."

Livosha looked around. "Well, but you must at least wait until the ship
arrives in port, must you not?"

"Not in the least."

"But then, what will you do?"

"Ah, you wish to know that?"

"Certainly, and the proof is, I asked."

"That is true," said Dust. "Very well, then: observe."

As he spoke, he put his hand inside of his white shirt, wrapping his fist,
it seemed, around an object that she could see was hanging by a cord around
his neck. In a moment, she perceived a purple glow coming from his hand.

"But," she cried, "what is—"

She broke off her sentence, failing, as we see, to complete it (which we expect the reader has understood already from the marking on the page, in which a line is used to convey a sentence that stops abruptly, whereas it is the typographical custom to use another symbol entirely for cases where, instead of breaking off, the sentence gradually ceases to move forward without finding its proper end, as an exhausted runner gradually slows before stopping), because of the remarkable event that occurred before her eyes, that being the sudden appearance of a shimmer in the air, as if in a tiny area of the deck there was a whirling of golden snowflakes, if the reader can imagine such a thing. These snowflakes gradually coalesced into a figure, and a figure, in fact, such as Livosha had never seen before, and which we would describe in some detail were we not certain the reader remembers as the strange being that Dust had first summoned so long ago.

"A demon!" she said.

Dust smiled, turned to the being, and began speaking in an odd, incomprehensible assortment of sounds, in which, after a moment, Livosha became convinced she could almost distinguish words. She listened and watched in amazement as they carried on their conversation, until Dust turned to her, smiled, and said, "I will see you soon, Livosha," and, before she had time to reply, both he and the creature dissolved in the same swirling gold-colored snowflakes in which it had appeared.

She remained fixed in the spot for some moments, until she noticed a sailor not far from her, who was also staring, her mouth open, at the place where the pair had just vanished.

"Did you see that?" asked Livosha.

The sailor closed her mouth, looked at Livosha, and said, "My lady, I would prefer not to say."

Some four miles northeast of the village of Hargon's Point—which is to say, less than thirty miles southwest of Wetrock—there is a place where the road makes a sharp bend around a peculiar hill—peculiar, first, in that it is remarkably steep and tall, and second, because it is the only hill within twenty miles in any direction. It is, in fact, the very Hargon's Point for which the village was named (the village having been built nearby for the reason that construction on a particularly steep and narrow hill was considered too difficult). After the turn, the road continues through a lightly wooded area for some two or three miles, at last emerging into grasslands.

It was here that Yanis, riding at the head of his troop, noticed someone standing on the roadway.

He frowned, but continued. As he came closer, he observed that the stranger was dressed entirely in white. The next thing he noticed was that the stranger didn't appear about to move, which was puzzling, as there were a hundred men-at-arms bearing down on him and he had not so much as drawn his sword.

A gust of wind came up, carrying dust into his eyes. He shut them, and the wind increased, and then increased more, until his horse began to shy, and he cried, "Hold!" His horse reared, and he fought to stay in the saddle, but it then seemed as if it were about to lose its balance, and so he leapt clear and rolled, coming to his feet with his eyes still closed.

At this moment, the wind began to die down, until, in a few seconds, it was only a light breeze. Yanis opened his eyes. The first thing he saw was the man in white, now only about twenty yards away, and, moreover, now holding a sword. It was only then he realized that, somehow, he was no longer where he had been—he was in a glade surrounded by poplar trees, and except for the man with the sword, he was utterly alone.

His mouth opened and closed a few times, as if the words he had generated were taking longer to emerge from his throat than he had expected them to, no doubt because they were entangled with each other in his trachea and had first to decide amongst themselves the order in which to proceed. At last one of these words, as if it were an advance scout for the sentence that still remained unable to extricate itself from a snarl of its own making, egressed: "How . . . ," he said.

"I desired a private conversation with you," said the other coolly. "I thus arranged for this privacy."

"Who *are* you?"

"You do not recognize me?"

"I have never seen you before!"

"Oh, this I know not to be true. You saw me in Dorindom Castle, the very day you arranged for me to be taken away, and on the day you arranged for my home, that is to say, Cryden House, to be destroyed, killing all of my family with it. I recognize that these are small, unimportant incidents in your life, yet, I am certain that with work, you can call them to mind."

"Eremit!"

"That was my name. I now go by Dust. And if you would do me the great honor to draw your sword, I would like, if you are agreeable, to change the nature of our conversation."

"Well, but. . . ."

"Yes?"

"If I am not agreeable?"

"Then I will run my sword through your body. And then I will do so again. I will repeat this exercise until it begins to bore me, which, I believe, may take some considerable time. Come now, you must choose. I do permit you to make the choice; you see I'm not a bad fellow."

"And yet—"

Dust moved closer and raised his sword. "I give you my word," he said in a tone that indicated the time for joking or banter was past, "I will kill you where you stand if you do not draw."

Yanis drew his sword and placed himself on his guard.

At this point, the author must render an apology. In our history, it would, in our opinion, be more satisfactory if we were able to present to the reader a contest of swordsmen that might produce anxiety, and fear for the safety of the individual we have been following so closely, as well as a certain degree of suspense, always so rewarding in its resolution. Alas, history, in this case, as so often, has failed to adapt itself to the wishes of the historian, but has, instead, determined to take its own path without consulting us.

Dust beat Yanis's blade aside and ran his sword through the other's heart.

"You have killed me!" cried Yanis.

Dust shrugged. "It would appear so."

"My father will avenge me!"

"Your father, I fear, has his own problems."

"The count!"

"The count is in our hands, and is, at this moment, begging for his life and giving up everything to save it, including, I may add, your father."

"The prince!"

"The prince has resigned his title and left Adrilankha in hopes of escaping the wrath of those he had falsely imprisoned."

"Jailed," corrected Yanis.

"I accept your correction."

"It is unfair!"

"Oh, there I must disagree with you. It was entirely fair."

"I was only doing what I had to!"

"So was I," said Dust.

He then withdrew his sword from the other's heart, at which time Yanis emitted a cough, a pleading look, and a sigh, and fell flat upon his face.

In Dorindom Castle, some four days later, Berwick was awoken by a commotion—which is to say, the tramping of feet, the calling of voices, and even the squeak or creak of heavy furniture being moved. He put on a dressing gown and slippers, and walked out with the intention of determining the cause of this disturbance, and, moreover, with the intention of having sharp words with whomever had caused his sleep to be disturbed.

The first thing he saw were a pair of servants carrying a large chair down the hallway.

"You there!" he said.

They stopped. "My lord?"

"What is going on?"

"We have been tasked to bring this chair into the master bedroom."

"And is that all?"

"No, my lord. There is a vanity that must be moved, as well as a certain amount of clothing to pack up, and—"

"But, who has given these orders?"

"The countess, my lord."

"Well, but why . . . stay, did you say count*ess*?"

"Yes, my lord."

"So, then, His Benevolence has married?"

"Not so far as I know, my lord."

"And yet . . . where is this countess?"

"In her study."

"But where is her study?"

"In the same place the count's was."

Berwick, feeling as if he had suddenly entered a dream, began walking to the study, but then he stopped, looked down at himself, and returned to his chamber. He rang for a valet to help him dress, and was so distracted that he made no remark about the valet's tardiness.

When he was finally ready, after looking at himself in the mirror without actually paying attention to what he saw, he took himself, after asking for directions of a servant, and in fact requiring a servant to repeat these directions twice, to what had been the count's study. It must be said, in all fairness, that the sight that greeted him upon his arrival in this place did nothing to calm his nerves. A woman he didn't recognize was seated at the desk, and standing over her were two other individuals. One, like the woman who was seated, wore the colors of the Iorich, the other, a man, appeared to be a Jhereg.

Berwick opened his mouth to demand answers, but before he could speak the woman behind the desk looked up and said, "Ah, my dear Berwick. Your timing is excellent. You were, in fact, the very subject of our conversation."

"But—"

"First, here, this informs you that your title, lands, and rights to Wetrock have been revoked. Fortunately, as you are an Orca, there are no legalities that would require delays in executing this, as the policies of the Orca are explicit on the subject of the rights of the county." As she spoke, she patted a book on the table before her, which was Dorin's edition of Plofer's *Case Studies in Entitlement Conflicts Among the Great Houses Volume I.* "If you were a Dragon, or, gods preserve us, a Lyorn, we might choose to go to war as being the easier solution compared to untangling the legal requirements. Apropos, we have confiscated the interest you had in Dorin's funds, and also those in Traanzo's, as well, naturally, as removing you from the ownership of Wetrock Sealstone Endeavors, as I believe you called it. Now, as to—"

"Who are you?" burst out Berwick, whose head was now spinning so much he was unable to fully grasp what was happening.

She frowned. "Ah, did I fail to introduce myself? I have the honor to be Livosha, daughter of Cerwin, and this is my brother, Kefaan, and this is Daifan, the Baron of Magister Valley, although you may best remember him as Eremit."

Berwick stumbled against the wall behind him.

"Perhaps you would care to sit," said Kefaan politely.

"Let him stand," said the one called Daifan.

"With all due respect, my dear friend," said Livosha, "we must have words with this individual, and if he swoons, well, the words will be wasted."

"Very well, then," said Daifan, and made no more objection as a servant, a Teckla woman wearing Iorich livery, whom he had not noticed before, found a chair and assisted Berwick into it.

"So then," continued Livosha as if there had been no interruption, "the question was what to do with you? Kefaan wants to see you prosecuted, and, indeed, we have four Kinsmen awaiting in case that is the decision.

You remember the Kinsmen, Baron—ah, that is to say, Freeman Berwick? Dorin made certain use of them on your behalf, and they are not pleased. Now Daifan no longer considers himself an Iorich, but rather, a Jhereg, and, as such, it is his wish to simply kill you out of hand. For my part, well, as you were personally responsible for ordering the death of those I loved, I am less kindly disposed than they are."

"Less kind?" repeated Berwick faintly.

Livosha nodded. "It is my wish to simply send you forth, as you are, penniless, landless, broken, and let you live out what pathetic life you have. Perhaps you can find work on a fishing boat. I should avoid attempting to join a pirate crew, however; they are not well disposed toward you."

"As we are unable to decide, we have left the decision to our good Jerin." Here she indicated the Teckla. "She, also, has a certain grudge against you, although because of you she about to achieve her dream of becoming stablemaster, so perhaps this will influence her vote. But before she decides, you may speak, if you have anything to say."

"You should also be aware," said Daifan coolly, "that your son is dead."

This last blow proved too much. The room seemed to both spin and contract upon him, and for a while he knew no more. When he awoke again, at first he was confused, for he was out of doors. He stood up, looked around, and saw that he was now outside of the gates to Dorindom Castle. Next to him was a sort of horse, that is, a tired, yellowish nag, and upon its back was his own satchel.

He stared back at the castle for a moment, then he mounted the horse and began riding south, toward the town of Zerika's Point, where there was no shortage of fishing boats.

Chapter the Thirty-fourth

Conclusion

Daifan—that is to say, Eremit—studied his friends, wondering if the peculiar mix of elation and exhaustion he observed on their countenances was also evident on his own.

"And so," remarked Livosha. "Let us see. Berwick, Yanis, Dorin, Traanzo. Who is left?"

"Sajen and the director," said Kefaan. "But perhaps they have been punished enough?"

"That is my opinion," said Daifan.

"I agree," said Livosha.

"And," added Daifan, "you are now the Countess of Westward, a pretty pin to add to your dress."

"And you, my friend," said Livosha. "You will take back your interest in the sealstone trade? It is, after all, yours by right."

He shook his head. "I wish no part of it. It is yours."

"And yet," said Livosha, smiling sadly, "what will you think when the Empire is restored, and sets out eastward armed with weapons made from these minerals?"

"I will be pleased for you," said Daifan honestly.

"But then, what are you going to do?"

After an instant's thought, he concluded that, after everything, he owed her a truthful answer. "Me?" he said. "I will have Captain Sheen transport me to Adrilankha, along with my friend Alishka and her associates, who I think would be happy to be done with life on the road, and I will take up residence in the very nice home that was given to me by the complaisant Traanzo and I will set about in, well, in business."

"As a Jhereg?"

"I have some thoughts on the matter."

"And I, my dear sister," said Kefaan, "intend to assist him."

"What, you, my brother?" cried Livosha.

"If the Empire is restored, either by this Kana, or by someone else, a Jhereg will need a good advocate, and I find I like walking between the worlds—that is to say, yours and Daifan's."

"And does this decision," asked Daifan, assuming an air of innocence, "have aught to do with certain looks I may have seen exchanged between you and my friend Alishka?"

"Oh, as to that—"

"Why, my brother," said Livosha. "You are positively blushing!"

"That may be," he said, although whether this was in answer to Daifan, Livosha, or both, he did not make clear. "However," he went on, as if determined to change the subject, "I will visit you often, you have my word." He paused for a moment, and then said in a lower and more serious tone, "But even were there no understanding between me and the lovely Alishka, well, you must see that I cannot return to Wetrock."

Livosha sighed and said, "I understand. But I will hold you to your word on the matter of visiting me."

"And you, good Jerin?" said Kefaan.

The Teckla bowed. "The stables await me, and I am eager to take up my duties."

Livosha's countenance brightened at this, which, in turned, pleased Daifan. But then she turned to him. "You perceive," she said, "that Traanzo is still alive, as are Berwick and Dorin. Might they not wish for revenge?"

Daifan shrugged. "Traanzo will be too busy running from Kelsama to seek vengeance, and Berwick is too broken. As for Dorin, well, let him try."

"Come," she said suddenly. "Let us walk in the garden. That is, my garden."

She took his arm, and they strolled together down the stairs, and (directed by the complaisant Issola who had been so kind to young Eremit so long ago, who was still on duty and appeared utterly unconcerned about the turmoil around him), found the gardens in the back. Daifan, with some difficulty, did not show the emotion that surged through him at the pressure on his arm, a pressure in which there was friendship, but no hint of possessiveness.

"So then," said Livosha when they were alone. "You are not to come back to me?"

"My Levoshirasha—"

"Ah, you call me that!"

"I remember a boy who was eager, full of life, as innocent and helpless as a Jhegaala nymph. And I remember a girl who was strong, and who laughed, and who gazed into the future as if eager for it to challenge her."

"I am still that girl."

"I know it well. But I am not that boy. Had we had the chance to change together, to grow, well, who knows? But with me, you will always seek that boy, and he will not be there. I will always wish to become him for you, and will always fall short. You will come to loathe me, and I will come to loathe myself."

"Your words are too strong. I could never loathe you."

"Too strong? Perhaps you are right. And yet I still love you, my Levoshirasha, and should we be together, that love would die, and it is the best part of me. I cannot permit that."

She sighed. "You are right, my friend. But it is difficult to accept."

"For me as well," said Daifan quietly. "But had I not said that we could not be together, well, you would have had to say it, and I will not ask that of you."

She pressed his arm and they continued walking. "When you take up residence in Adrilankha, will you give yourself yet another name?"

"I believe," he said, "I will stay with Daifan. It seems appropriate."

"How, is it? I am unfamiliar with its origins."

"It is ancient Serioli, and it means Demon."

"I understand," she said, and pressed his arm again.

And it is here, in the garden, that, with a certain bittersweet pleasure, we will leave the reader, as well as those persons we have been following during this brief examination of history. Whether the matter has, in the case of any individual reader, been instructive, or rewarding in any other way, is something for which we may hope, but cannot know, as the barrier between author and reader by its nature prevents any such knowledge, save occasionally for those works of criticism that might come across our desk, and which we will then file unread to avoid undue influence.

As for this desk, to which we have just had the honor to refer, we would be remiss in our duty if we did not inform the reader of its new location, that being the Office of the Chair of Interregnum Studies in the Department of History of Pamlar University at Adrilankha, which position we have only just accepted upon learning that the previous occupant of that prestigious office has been dismissed on charges of plagiarism, the greatest crime there is to an academic. While we cannot deny our pleasure at this unexpected change in our fortunes, we are sorry that it has come at the expense of a scandal befalling such a fine institution, and pledge at this moment to do our utmost to remedy any ill odor—which term we use in its metaphorical sense—that may have attached itself to the department.

And so, as one blows out a candle upon leaving a room, the light of which may seem to linger for a moment in the eye even after the flame is gone, permit us to blow out the candle of this small bit of history with our friends Daifan—that is to say, Eremit—and Livosha, though no longer lovers, at least friends, and each in a position, and perhaps with the wisdom, to create a future. For it can be said, we believe, without fear of contradiction, that it is in our individual and combined effort to create for ourselves the future we wish that we find cause for the study of the past.

*Acknowledgments**

{* Type-master, move this section to after the rest of the text. There is, I am certain, no need to discuss it with our esteemed author }

It is, we are told, the rigorous custom of that branch of commerce known as *the publishing industry* for an author to not only publicly thank those who have aided him in the completion of a work—a custom that, so far as it goes, we find reasonable and even laudable—but even more, to set this inevitable section of any history in a particular place, that is, at the end of the work in question, and nowhere else. If we have chosen to violate this custom, it would seem incumbent upon us to give some sort of explanation for this decision.

According to conventional wisdom (while "wisdom" is, perhaps, a dubious term, this is the idiom employed, and while engaged in questioning the customs of an entire industry, we do not choose to simultaneously question the parlance with which we refer to it, as this could only result in needless confusion), as well as we can determine from our conversations with such professionals as have done us the honor to speak with us on the subject, something like this: As the reader, that is to say, the presumed reader, is marked by a short attention span, a tendency toward ennui, impatience, and a generally hostile attitude toward learning, therefore, the argument runs, before thanking those who have been so kind as to aid a writer in the preparation of the work, one must first be absolutely certain the reader wishes to have this information, which certainty can only be achieved by the knowledge that the reader has reached the end of the work in question and is, presumably, still reading.

Needless to say, our own view of the reader, both from principle, and from our happy experience with encounters with such readers as have, from time to time, crossed our path, has nothing in common with this preconception. On the contrary, it has been our experience that our readers have been intelligent, eager to learn, and entirely willing to accept such wisdom as our poor efforts have been able to set forth.

We have, therefore, chosen to place these comments here, at the beginning, in part as a gesture of faith, as it were, in the positive attributes of our audience, and yet, in addition, for a second reason, which is as follows: A discourse on history may be viewed as educational, yet it simultaneously partakes of art, in that it attempts to engage with both the mind of the reader, and, if you will, his heart. With this latter aspect in mind, one important facet of such a work is the nature of the emotion one is left with upon completion of the work; that is, like a well-planned repast, the flavor that is left in one's metaphorical mouth must be considered vital. And, in our opinion, to leave the reader with such dry and uninteresting matters as a list of names, more or less notorious, cannot but have a detrimental effect on the feelings of the sensitive reader.

With this firmly understood, we would like, at this point, to thank those who have done us the kindness to assist, in one way or another, in bringing the present humble work to fruition.

We must begin, alas, with one who has moved on from this life, and whose passing we can say that we, and everyone whose life he touched, bitterly regret. We refer here to Ivan Székly, a very dear friend, and, moreover a man of letters whose knowledge was boundless, whose interests and passions incalculable, and whose skill with the written word marked him, although largely unknown to the public, as one of the greatest who ever set pen to paper in the Northwestern language. Those of us with the honor to have known him treasure each hour we were able to spend in his company, and still, years after his passing, feel undiminished sorrow that there will be no more of these hours, and that his pen, to the anguish of us all, is forevermore silent. In addition to all of this, for his kindness on behalf our own humble efforts, we render his memory now our sincere thanks.

Next, we must speak of the Dean of Pamlar University, who has displayed not only wisdom and kindness, but selflessness, putting significant effort into a task for which she was not only uncompensated, but even unacknowledged until this moment. We can say without hesitation that should letters produce more such as she, our culture would be the better for it. And we must add, in all fairness and honesty, that her works, while criminally under-represented upon the shelves of the common bookshops, are well-known to incite a deep and richly deserved passion in all who read them. For those who have been kind enough to single out this historian's skill with words for compliments, we can only say, with all sincerity and no false modesty, that in this matter in particular the Dean of Pamlar is our master, teacher, inspiration, and guide.

A particular Magian known as Ilen has proven to be extraordinarily generous with his time, providing much needed criticism to help the work, wine to help the historian accept the criticism, and good klava to counteract the wine. On a personal note, we must also say that this Magian's stunning successes with the public are an ample counter-argument to those philistines who insist that popularity is incompatible with quality. While it is not uncommon to speak contemptuously of "sell-besting," we have in Ilen's experience definitive proof that style, wit, depth, and power are not necessarily lost on those who love to read. He brings us tears and laughter, and, if we bring him a certain degree of success, it can only serve as a useful reminder that the public can demonstrate more appreciation of the sublime than the elitist who scorns it. More cannot be said on this matter.

Our dear friend Lord Shetwil is that rarest of curiosities, a Dzurlord poet. Whether he became a poet in order to provide greater opportunities for duels from those who mocked him for his profession, or whether this was merely a happy accident, we cannot say; in spite of our long friendship, it is a question we have never quite dared to put to him. Of course, Lord Shetwil is more than a poet, he is, in addition, a writer of moving and exquisite prose, the sort that grip one's senses in the moment of reading, and give cause for reflection for years thereafter—a goal which, in the opinion of this historian, all of those who seek to delight us with their tales ought to aspire. Beyond this, I have known him as a loyal and steadfast friend, as quick to defend a friend or a worthy cause with his wit as his blade, which, we are forced to say, is as unusual in a Dzur as the profession of poet. And yet, it is none of these characteristics which cause us to mention him in these lines. Rather, as sharp and piercing and precise as his wit, his use of prose, and his blade, even more sharp and piercing are his remarks on the works of others, in particular, those of your humble author. The time and effort he has put into a careful study of this historian's own efforts in order to suggest improvements would be worthy of praise even were they not as astute and, ultimately, useful as they have invariably been—useful, we are forced to add, in the immediate sense of the better casting of a particular thought or rendering of an image, but also and even more in his remarkable ability to generalize from a particular literary or historical issue to the general law that applies, and from which one would need to be utterly oblivious to fail to profit.

To us, as, indeed, to all who have had the pleasure of working with her, a special place in our hearts belongs to Her Eminence, C. Sophronia Cleebers, who was first provided to us by Glorious Mountain Press for the purpose of guiding an earlier work through the tedious process of publication. Imagine our surprise on discovering that, under her direction, the process was not tedious, but, on the contrary, stimulating, as she helped us discover that to make a book is a craft quite like no other, in the myriad number of skills it brings together, all so different, yet all working in harmony. Moreover, it must be said, her ability to grasp the essence of an historian's intent, and to, if the reader will permit, *tease out* the underlying meaning in such a way as to make it clear to the meanest understanding, and, indeed, in some cases to the historian himself, unaware as he was of what he was writing, provides a particular sort of joy, a satisfaction, that is only rivaled by the satisfaction of seeing Her Eminence's skill with the refining of a sentence, in which, more than once, this historian was prevented from putting, in a single thought, matters too complex to contain it, and which would have caused the reader to inevitably become lost in a tangle of clauses and subclauses to the ultimate confusion of said reader and, indeed, to the detriment of the work. To find someone so skilled in the understanding of *text*, at every level, is, or ought to be, the dream of everyone who works with the written word.

My first encounter with Adain of Arylle came when I happened across his observations on my work in a small publication distributed mostly in Candletown and with a circulation that failed to reach the 500 mark. How it came into my possession is a tale not worth the effort of recounting, but I will say that I was intrigued by his remarks on my first work, *Three Broken Strings*, which, if said remarks were not kind, neither were they entirely without merit—a rare gift in a critic. At this time, I became curious about the individual, and learned that he was well known in certain sections of Adrilankha as one who spent most of his time indulging in brothels, dreamgrass dens, public houses, klava holes, and shereba rooms, as well as playing obscure music on the sithara. By the time of my next work, which he also reviewed, he had stopped frequenting the brothels, but his pen had become sensibly sharper. When my next work appeared, I read his comments on it (he had, by this time, given up the dreamgrass), and began to wonder why, if he held such strong opinions of my literary endeavors, he continued to read them, much less write about them. When my next work appeared, he had stopped drinking ale and wine, but continued the criticism. Eventually we met in a klava hole (though by this time he was no longer drinking klava), and I found his company most agreeable. Since then, I have gone to him on more than one occasion to request his thoughts on my work, my belief being that these remarks would do more good before publication than after, and found his advice on this, and, I may add, on shereba, far from useless. I am, therefore, duly grateful, and must add that I have spent time listening to his music on the sithara (which vice, as of this writing, he has not given up) and found it, if not great, at least good.

I should also mention here those kind souls whose patronage, over the years, have permitted me to continue my work. Beginning with Lady Parachai of Redstaff, and the Marchioness of Poorborn (and of course Her Highess the Tiassa Heir), and to all who have so generously aided me in getting my small efforts out before the public, you have my humble thanks.

Last, I cannot end this brief discourse without an expression both of gratitude to and admiration for Luchia of North Leatherleaf. While modestly referring to herself, at one point, by the term "publisher," such an appellation is no more accurate than if, when discussing the Ocean-sea, we should observe, "It contains water." Indeed it does, and yet, so much more! Luchia is, in addition to a publisher, also a singer, a musician, a poet, a playwright, and an author, as well as, no doubt, possessing several other skills that have temporarily slipped from our attention. And in each of these, she defines mastery. Indeed, among those such as myself fortunate enough to know her it is a common jest that she is unable to throw the light discus, the explanation for the jest being our knowledge that she can do everything else, and do it so well as to leave us amazed. Her friendship and company are gifts to treasure, and it is our sincerest hope that more of the fickle public will come to know (and thus, inevitably, to love) her work, and more good companions will come to know her.

[A letter from Genphala of Mermaid Cove, addressed for some reason to the accounting department of Glorious Mountain Press]

Good gentlemen, I hope this missive finds you well. Certainly the ledgers I recently received detailing the status of my own small investment give some indication that your business matters have taken a turn for the better. Presumably this circumstance is due to the rampant profusion of the arts taking place under her most magnanimous majesty, Empress Norathar, and not my own small assistance. Truly such a trifling sum as what I have invested in your publishing house could not have been the means of its salvation, and I have said so to my clerks and my husband when they thought otherwise. It is *very droll* at times to hear them speak of it! One would think they forgot that I am Heir to an *entire House*—and not the least noble or the lowest on the Cycle, either—and therefore must be more knowledgeable than most about such weighty matters as the intersection of business and culture. You may be assured (as though such assurances would be necessary between such friends as we have become!) that after my laughter had ceased, I took them all most severely to task for their little jokes about "sinking a ship in a mountain range."

Now, speaking of sinking ships, it is my understanding that the reading public have been all over dying for more swashbuckling sorts of tales. I do so envy those who have fewer *worldly cares* than I, and can make time for the perusal of novels, for I can hardly take a moment away from all the dull business of lands and House and what-not that never seems to cease. But my dear friend Viasyl and my sweet little sister Jane have been in raptures lately over titles such as *Pirate Team: Endgame* and *The*

Skylark of the Ocean-Sea, so I know from them that the appetite is unceasing.

I am certain then that you will be delighted to have a look at the enclosed manuscript, an early draft taken from the notebooks of Lord Paarfi of Roundwood. Whatever has transpired in the past, you cannot but jump at the chance to read this latest bit of business from his pen. Indeed, it is only as a mark of the *kind esteem* between us that I have judged it right to forward this copy to you and avoid any undignified bidding between yourself and other houses (as I am assured would be the case should I permit him to work through the usual channels for such things).

Now, the story of how this manuscript came to be is nearly as thrilling as the one it tells, and I could wish my own *poor talents* were equal to relating it, but of course the man himself is too modest to think it worth telling, so I must try my very best.

First, I will set the scene for how I chanced upon the work. Some years ago, I was taking a *rare break* from my business in Mermaid Cove. "Genphala," my husband had said to me, "do take a little break and get into the Ocean-sea," or something like that. He's always so full of jokes, you know. But he offered quite manfully to see to my affairs as well as he could if I would go, and we parted amiably, knowing that on my return we would have such a nice reunion! So off I went to Adrilankha, and a year or so later I was enjoying one of those little soirees given by that blond marchioness whose name I never remember as it takes so long to recover from them, when who did I see looking downcast in the corner but Lord Paarfi!

It took a few cups but fewer minutes for me to winkle the tale out of him (for I am a monstrous good winkler when I choose to be), but I will only summarize it here for you, as the man himself is so skilled with words that he is known to be a bit loquacious, and I am loath to take up too much of your time. He told me that he had been passed over for some sort of honor or bit of furniture at his university, and they were lifting up some fellow who tends to lies or mysticism or something in his place. It didn't seem to signify much to me, because I thought all novelists were good at lying, but he informed me it wasn't a matter for joking so I let it drop.

Now we come to the real reason he was dragging a gray cloud amongst our jolly crew. It wasn't that a rival had beaten him, for

ACKNOWLEDGMENTS

Lord Paarfi is of that sensitive sort of disposition that always must feel strongly for his fellows, so much so that he would sooner pardon a thousand wrongs done to himself than see a bit of harm come to anyone else, could he prevent it. And so, to increase the prestige of the very institution that had slighted him, he had veritably thrown himself into his researches, which at that time were to do with a few Iorich who did something or other during the Interregnum.

At least, I believe that's when the events took place. For myself, I have *no head at all* for history, with all those dull dates and names lined up in unfeeling rows, stirred about here and there by a battle or a beheading. *Ghastly* stuff, really, and I must spend all my time and energy on the pressing matters of to-day, doing tedious business in service to my House. However, it happens that one of the names Lord Paarfi was digging out of the dusty past had been a scoundrel back then, and turned out to now—to-day, mind you— be embarking on a second career, increasing his villainy by trading in the forger's tools for those of the plagiarist!

Imperial law may not have much to say on that crime, but obviously a university must *scorn* it *absolutely*. And this is an important distinction, because who indeed was this resurfaced reprobate but Lord Paarfi's recent university rival!

You may think this could not be so, the coincidence too great, and I said as much to Lord Paarfi, but he assured me it was so and that he was in possession of certain irrefutable proofs. This was what caused his terrible dilemma, because to allow this to continue would be a certain evil, but how could such a gentle soul as he set out to cause ruin and loss of stature to his beloved university? For the truth of the matter would cause such a fuss and scandal among the scholarly set, as they aren't very *worldly* in tendency, and attach a great deal of meaning to words like stature and reputation, even though those things are merely, as the term is, "creations of common agreement." Moreover, the whole affair was certain to be seen as *vengeful* on Lord Paarfi's part, although if you had seen him that evening, you would know in your hearts as I do that such was not the case.

The poor man was dreadfully out of sorts. I couldn't bear to see such intelligence, such wit as I have always known him for, be dimmed by sorrow. The only course of action with any merit in it was clear to me, and you will not, I hope, think me speaking over-well of myself when I relate it. I spoke firmly to Lord Paarfi, convincing him that *living well is the best revenge*, and that he would be wise to finish his research away from the university, write it all out truthfully, and let matters fall out as they would, without working either for or against the downfall of the academic miscreant.

He couldn't help but be swayed by me and subscribed to my plan whole-heartedly, so I took him off to a country manor *at once*, giving up on my own much-needed rest, so that the perfumed air, good food and wine, and general lack of noise and bustle could bolster his spirits and allow him to work unceasingly. I only troubled him but rarely to entertain me with moments of conversation, and kept parties of visitors from Adrilankha to a *bare minimum* so as not to distract him. In only a few years, I am happy to say, he had finished setting his notes toward the manuscript in order.

With that important milestone passed, I permitted Lord Paarfi to return to the university, and I returned to Mermaid Cove, as I had been away from my lands and business perhaps a bit longer than intended, and had begun to worry about the state of things after being in my husband's *well-intentioned* hands for so long. It was not so many years after that when my constant entreaties bore fruit, and he sent me a very preliminary copy of his work in the hopes that I would find it either instructive or interesting (scholars don't believe in an intersection of the two descriptors). My husband, sister, and friend have all read it, and they declare it is *quite good* and have told me it contains pirates, revenge, swordfights, and other such adventures.

As I said above, it is only due to our *great friendship* that I am forwarding it now to you. As my position in the world is very far from that of publishers (and here of course I only mean different, not loftier), I would never pretend to know how your business is conducted or why you, in your wisdom, should choose to publish this or that thing over another, as it seems to me there are a great many worthy scribblers about in the world! However, it would please me exceedingly if you would allow all matters of the past to remain in the past—matters such as missed deadlines or tiny little duels with critics or distributing unflattering pamphlets about the publishing industry—and read this work of Lord Paarfi's with a fresh eye.

Your avowed friend,
Genphala of Mermaid Cove etc. etc.